I0671694

The Black Flag

Crimson Worlds Successors 3

Jay Allan

system 7
publishing

Also By Jay Allan

www.jayallanbooks.com

The Black Flag

The Black Flag is a work of fiction. All names, charac-
ters, incidents, and locations are fictitious. Any resem-
blance to actual persons, living or dead, events or places
is entirely coincidental.

ISBN: 978-1-946451-05-7

Black Eagles' Force Structure

HQ Staff (approx. 150 personnel)

Special Action Teams (approx. 300 personnel)
Black Regiment (approx. strength 2,200 combat, 500 close support)

White Regiment (approx. strength 1,800 combat, 400 close support)

Blue Regiment (approx. strength 1,800 combat, 400 close support)

Red Regiment (approx. strength 1,800 combat, 400 close support)

Brown Regiment (approx. strength 1,800 combat, 400 close support)

Gray Regiment (approx. strength 1,800 combat, 400 close support)

Medical Services (approx. 700 personnel)

Logistics Division – "L2" – (approx. 4,200 personnel)

Garrison Battalion (approx. strength 1,600)

"Nest" Operations (approx. strength 2,400)

Training Depot (approx. 900 training staff and 3,000-5,500 trainees)

Fleet Command (approx. 4,800 ships' crew and 600 maintenance)

Fighter Command (approx. 320 crew and 600 maintenance personnel)

"Unassigned" (approximately 80 intelligence agents and independent operatives)

Eagle Fleet

Eagle One
Eagle Two
Eagle Three
Eagle Four
Eagle Five
Eagle Six
Eagle Seven
Eagle Eight
Eagle Nine
Eagle Ten
Eagle Eleven
Eagle Twelve
Eagle Thirteen
Eagle Fourteen
Eagle Fifteen
Eagle Sixteen

Chapter 1

"We've got multiple contacts, sir. They're coming in from the far side of the warp gate."

Captain Randall Harsimus leaned forward in his chair, his eyes fixed on the display, even as his first officer made her report. "Red alert! Activate all weapons stations." His ship and the pair of freighters she was escorting had just come through the gate. He'd known his small flotilla would be most vulnerable just as they emerged, but there was nothing to be done about that. In truth, he'd expected his final transit into the Epsilon Indi system to be a safe one. The real danger had been earlier in the journey, Rimward of Atlantia's central location. The planet was only three jumps from Sol, and the ruins of Earth that orbited man's home star, and as endemic as the piratical activity had become, it hadn't reached this far into the oldest colonies.

Until now...

His eyes darted all over the display. No patrol ships, no revenue cutters...nothing. He couldn't understand why the Atlantians had left one of the warp gates leading to their world totally unguarded. Atlantia wasn't a militarily powerful planet, not

1

particularly so, but the Atlantians had kept tight control over imports and foreign ship traffic, especially over the past few years. *Ever since they discovered their own source of stable trans-uranic metals.*

"Yes, Captain. Red alert." Commander Stinson's hands moved smoothly across her board, hitting the levers and controls that called *Vincennes*'s crew to battlestations and powered up her weapons systems. Stinson was cool, calm, her combat experience clear to see. Like Harsimus, she was a veteran of both the Shadow Wars and the Second Incursion.

Vincennes's captain knew he was lucky to have Stinson as his first officer. He was well aware she'd been offered her own command, and by no less a personage than Augustus Garret himself, when the legendary admiral first began assembling the United Marine Fleet two years earlier, from the various forces and mothballed ships he'd been able to scrounge up. Stinson had her reasons for refusing, he suspected, though he had no idea what they were. And he had never inquired. He didn't need to know. He was just glad to have her aboard, especially since the two of them were the only members of the crew who'd fought more than a policing action against smugglers or pirates.

You're facing pirates now…but not really, of course. They may attack shipping, but there is more behind this than a criminal organization. Much more, at least if these are Black Flag raiders…and what else could they be?

Harsimus had no idea who or what was behind the Black Flag, but the fact that the new threat to human civilization had pulled an aged Augustus Garret himself from retirement told him all he needed to know. The threat was real…and probably grave.

"All weapons stations operational and ready for action, sir."

"Very well." He looked at the display. "Order the freighters to fall back." Harsimus knew his people were in trouble. *Vincennes* was a heavy cruiser, but she was an old one, and small for her class, a vessel that traced its service all the way back to the Third Frontier War. That fact carried with it a certain irrational source of pride, even vague thoughts that the cruiser was a 'lucky ship' for having made it through more than half a century of conflict, but Harsimus tended toward the coldly logical, thinking more about outdated systems design and obsolete weapons than hopeful superstitions.

"Freighters retreating, Captain."

"Very well. Maintain course and thrust…and warn those ships off, Commander." He'd almost failed to issue that last command. The United Fleet was a new entity, light on the reams of regulations and regular process that tended to clog the pipes of organizations that existed for too long. But every force he'd served had required an attempt at contact before engaging unknown ships.

Even when it's a waste of time…

He knew the pirates, Black Flag or otherwise, had the advantage, in numbers if nothing else, and that they had no reason to run. But he was a creature of duty, and he went through the motions, even feeling an instant's hope he was wrong, that these ships would respond, that they did not have hostile intent.

"No response on any channel, sir," came the entirely unsurprising response, perhaps half a minute later. Whatever infinitesimal shreds of optimism he'd had drained away.

Harsimus angled his head, staring at the screen, watching as *Vincennes*'s AI updated the results with each new batch of scanning data. There were at least three enemy ships out there, possibly more. The proximity to the warp gate made scanning a difficult endeavor, and he knew damned well there could be half a dozen more raiders hiding right behind. He just couldn't know for sure.

It didn't matter. Three was very likely enough. *Vincennes* was there to protect the pair of freighters, now hovering fifty thousand meters back, and the cruiser could handle one pirate for sure…probably even two. *But three…*

He watched carefully, plotting his tactics, trying to come up with the best way to take out the enemy…or at least to buy time for the freighters to get to Atlantia, and safety. He didn't like the self-sacrificial feel to that last thought, but duty had always come first to him, and he would do what he had to do in order to protect the ships under his charge.

His gut told him they *were* Black Flag ships, almost certainly, but something still didn't click. Atlantia was much closer to the central trade routes than the pirates usually operated, and he couldn't completely banish the hope that this was some kind of routine outlaw force. Any pirates were dangerous, of course, but the Black Flag was terrifying on another level, the tech on its ships far in advance of that on any other rogue vessels…or *Vincennes*, for that matter. Fear of its forces had virtually strangled interstellar trade, even where actual attacks had not yet occurred.

The shadowy organization had emerged from obscurity two years before, when hundreds of its modern, high tech vessels began a well-conceived and executed assault on interplanetary shipping. For six months, it had been a random onslaught, hundreds of systems subjected to unpredictable waves of predation. Only after economies were on the verge of collapse on half the worlds in Occupied Space, had the organization made its demands clear. Planets had a choice…yield, join the Black Flag and accept its suzerainty—and receive its protection—or see all commerce come to a halt.

Harsimus still remembered his shock at how quickly many worlds surrendered. Only later did it become apparent that there was far more than had been apparent at first, that the Black Flag extended well beyond its pirate fleets, that its tentacles had already reached into the underworlds of many planets, as well as their mainstream economies…and often deep into their governments, too. Many worlds had gone over with their current regimes in place, their leaders having sold their planets' freedom to preserve their own power and positions. Indeed, the Black Flag had been only too willing to allow cooperative governments to continue to exercise power locally, as long as they accepted occupation and gave their obedience. It was a brilliant strategy, one that allowed politicians to cement their authority and dispense with the often inconvenient democratic aspects of their planets' governmental systems, while accepting what appeared to be light and undemanding overlordship.

Much of the Rim had already yielded, accepting Black Flag 'minders' to watch over their affairs. Such worlds immediately saw the harassment vanish, and save for the economic benefits of renewed trade, life changed very little for the average citizen. There were rumors of increased levies and confiscations of property, especially from those unwise enough to speak out against their worlds' craven surrenders, but such talk remained in the shadows. All official communications from the planets now behind the Black Curtain, as it had come to be called, told only of prosperity and contentment.

Harsimus didn't consider himself an expert on strategic matters, but he could see the depth of the threat, and the fact that perhaps half the inhabited worlds of Occupied Space were either openly siding with this mysterious enemy or secretly cooperating…while most of the others had been driven to the edge of ruin by what was rapidly becoming an effective galactic blockade.

"Energy spike, Captain!"

Harsimus turned abruptly, feeling the urge to order his ship to open fire. He knew it was the right move tactically, but one of the regulations the United Fleet did have—one that was very clear—was its ships did not fire first, not without positive ID of the target as a confirmed enemy. He understood the rationale, and the high road Augustus Garret had mandated for his new fleet, but sitting there, knowing those raiders were about to open fire on *Vincennes*, he cursed the restriction. His ship was in enough trouble…without letting the enemy have the first shot.

He didn't have long to think about it. Ten seconds later, *Vincennes* shook hard, a direct hit. Then, an instant later, again.

"All gunnery stations, open fire." Harsimus gripped the sides of his chair, leaning forward, his body tense. His mind was focused, but even so, images floated around the edges, scenes of past battles. The desperate struggles against the deadly robot ships during the Second Incursion, the almost unimaginable brutality of the fight against Gavin Stark's Shadow Legions. Every conflict was different…and yet the same in some primal way.

"I want full power to the guns, Commander. No…I want one hundred ten percent across the board. If these bastards want a fight, by God we'll give them one."

*   *   *   *   *

"Colonel Cain, we're picking up energy readings from near the warp gate." Captain Troy Grayson sat in the center of *Eagle Fourteen*'s bridge, his posture ramrod straight, almost a perfect example of military formality. The discipline and conduct of the Black Eagle officers and spacers was far from what he'd expected from a group of cold-blooded mercenaries.

"Combat?" Elias Cain stood several meters from the captain's chair, staring at the display. He was seeing the same thing as the Black Eagle captain, but he still had doubts. Still, Elias was no spacer, not really, and Grayson was a veteran of Augustus Garret's old Alliance navy, one who'd served with the Eagles' fleet for five years now. Elias was perfectly willing to substitute Grayson's interpretations for his own.

"It looks like it, Colonel. We're too far for conclusive data, but it certainly appears that some kind of fight going on."

Elias could hear the tension in Grayson's voice, carefully restrained but there nevertheless. *Eagle Fourteen*'s commander was a man used to making decisions…or taking orders from his superior officers. Elias Cain was neither. He wasn't a Black Eagle, not really, and he knew he had no place in their chain of command, despite the courtesy rank his brother had granted him. But Grayson had his orders, and Elias knew they were absolutely clear. The officer was to do as Elias Cain commanded. Whatever else a Black Eagle captain might do, disobeying one of Darius Cain's orders was almost certainly not among them.

Elias had come to realize the Eagles were far from the undisciplined cutthroats he'd once though them to be. He'd even developed a respect for his brother's military forces, one that had only grown when Darius had repurposed his army to fight the Black Flag, an endeavor which guaranteed few of the monetary rewards the Eagles had earned in their previous campaigns. Elias had expected most of the mercenaries to desert, to leave in search of greater rewards elsewhere…even to go over to the

Black Flag, where the opportunities seemed far richer. But fewer than one percent of Darius's soldiers had gone, and, as far as he knew, not one had been found in the ranks of the enemy.

"Can you bring us closer without risking detection?" *Eagle Fourteen* was equipped with Tom Sparks's latest stealth device, a system that was supposed to make her undetectable in most situations. Six months of practical usage had produced promising results, but it still hadn't been tested in a combat situation.

"There's no way to be sure, Colonel, but my best guess is we can remain undetected as long as we don't power up any weapons or engage."

Elias nodded quietly. A moment later, he said, "Bring us in, Captain. I want to know what is going on out there."

"Yes, Colonel."

Elias could tell Grayson agreed with his decision. There was a level of respect in the officer's voice, one that had been creeping in slowly over the past few weeks. Elias's transition to working with the Eagles had been an uncomfortable one, both for him and for Darius's veteran warriors. He'd felt the resentment when he had first come aboard *Eagle Fourteen*, the hint of discomfort Grayson and his crew felt about being placed under the command of an outsider. Not to mention the vague confusion about reacting to someone they mistrusted but who was also the virtual image of their revered leader. Elias's hair was shorter than Darius's, and he lacked the scar his brother had on the right side of his head, but otherwise they were almost perfect copies of each other. Physically, at least.

The two brothers hadn't seen each other for more than a decade before the events of three years earlier had thrust them together...and that first reunion had not been a friendly one. Elias had worked up a casual hatred for Darius over the years, or at least all he'd believed his brother stood for, and he knew his twin had returned the emotion, thinking him little more than a jackbooted government enforcer, a slave to corrupt politicians who ruled callously over the population at large. They'd come a long way toward mending their relationship—and they'd agreed to join forces to fight the Black Flag—but Elias wondered if they would ever be truly close again, as they had been as children.

"Colonel…you may want to strap in before we engage the thrusters."

Elias turned abruptly and moved toward the workstation a meter behind him. He shook his head, thinking to himself again that he just wasn't a spacer at heart. He sat and pulled the black fabric harness up and over his body, snapping it into place.

He saw Grayson glance over a few seconds later, checking to make sure he was secure. Then, the captain issued a series of commands, and *Eagle Fourteen* shook abruptly. Elias felt the pressure of acceleration slam into him, enough to have knocked him into the wall if he'd still been standing in the middle of the bridge, as he had been a moment earlier.

"I want all weapon stations ready, Commander." Grayson was coolly snapping off orders to his officers. "And I want the reactors ready for full power on my command."

Elias couldn't help but be impressed at the smooth efficiency of the crew—of all the Black Eagles he'd seen and worked with over the past two years. He'd been on *Eagle Fourteen* for almost six months now, and it still struck him every time. He'd seen the Atlantian patrol ships, watched their crews in action. He'd considered them highly professional, at least at the time, but he had to admit, next to the Eagles, they looked like children playing. His resentments against Darius had long prevented him from recognizing his brother's incredible charisma, his almost hypnotic ability to draw extremely capable people to his service, and to create a virtually unshakable bond of loyalty between them. That, and the fact that his twin was an almost unparalleled military genius. Their father was one of the most celebrated warriors in Occupied Space, the victor of countless desperate battles, but Elias had come to realize that Darius had taken such talents to a new level.

His mind drifted back to thoughts he'd had when *Eagle Fourteen* had first entered the system. Where were the Atlantians? Why weren't their patrol ships responding? Atlantia didn't have all that much of a navy, but it had more than enough force to guard its own system. Where were they?

He'd come to Atlantia to investigate—no, he admitted to himself, he'd come to spy. He was concerned about his home world's slide into oppressive government, and the data *Eagle Fourteen* had managed to collect was not at all encouraging. Still, it didn't explain why the patrol wasn't monitoring the warp gates, and intervening in whatever was happening. Even a statist regime would defend its close in trade routes…more aggressively, if anything, than a republican government.

"Colonel…"

Grayson's voice pulled Elias from his thoughts. "Yes, Captain?"

"We will be in close scanner range in seven minutes." A short pause. "I suggest you consider what actions we might take once we have identified the combatants. If we engage, we will be detectable, probably to the system's scanners as well as whatever ships are in the vicinity." He hesitated again. "If these are Black Flag raiders, you will have to decide if we are to intervene…or preserve our cloak."

Elias felt his throat tighten. If these were pirates attacking civilian shipping, the idea of sitting and watching seemed anathema to him. But he was there to collect data, and if the Atlantian scanners picked up *Eagle Fourteen*, well, that would be the end of that…

"I will consider it, Captain." Elias almost wished Darius hadn't placed him in command. It would be far easier to sit in his chair and watch as Troy Grayson made such decisions. He didn't know what the veteran officer would do, but he was damned sure Grayson would be a lot faster about making that choice. "Bring us in," he said after a brief pause. "Let's see what we're dealing with here."

Chapter 2

The pugil stick whipped through the air swiftly, Erik Cain's eyes catching only a hazy blur of its movement. But that was enough—just—and he dropped to one knee, swinging his body to the side, barely avoiding the heavy blow. He brought his own weapon around as he dodged, keeping it low, aiming for his opponent's knees. It was a targeted attack, delivered almost perfectly...but his adversary was too fast, and the strike was deftly parried.

Cain leapt back up to his feet, feeling a rush of strength as he did, his new legs fully conditioned, feeling as natural as though they'd been with him his whole life, rather than regrown barely a year before...along with a good portion of the rest of his body. It had been a little over two years since he'd been rescued from his prison on Eldaron, from a fifteen-year ordeal that had almost broken him beyond salvation. He'd doubted his ability to come back, to become again the man he had been—indeed, for many months after the stunning rescue that had freed him, he'd despaired of reaching a true recovery. But he'd always been a stubborn man, loath to give up on anything, and his family and friends had helped him through it all. It was their support more

10

than anything that had gotten him to where he was.

More than anything, save one thing perhaps. He was happy to lavish gratitude and appreciation on those closest to him, to bask in the warmth of their presence and credit them with his recovery. But there was something darker at work, too, as there so often had been in his greatest achievements. Erik had a score to settle, an enemy still out there, one responsible for all that had happened to him, for taking him away from his family for so long. For years of torment he could barely think about, much less ever share with anyone in any detail. And Erik Cain repaid those kinds of debts. Always.

He watched his opponent carefully, good advice in any fight, but absolutely crucial when facing perhaps the deadliest adversary in all human occupied space. The man on the other side of the practice ring, eyeing him with an intensity like none he'd ever seen before, was feared by billions, his name spoken as a curse on countless worlds, a label that came close to home for the old Marine. Cain had come to realize Darius's notoriety fully in the two years since he'd been freed, to understand the reputation and its origins, and it had gnawed at him. He understood it, yet he resented it as well, saw the aspects of it that were justified… and the myriad ways in which it was unfair.

Cain had many reasons for his feelings, for the conclusions he'd drawn from his recent education on the events of the last fifteen years—an understanding of war, one of conflicts between worlds and nations, the perspective of a career fighting man—but one stood out like a beacon. His sparring partner, the one who instilled such terror in so many, was not only the man most responsible for his rescue…he was also Cain's son.

"You are really up to form now, father." Darius held up his weapon, and then his hand, signaling an end to the bout. "Especially for an old guy."

Cain smiled, relaxing his straining muscles, tossing the pugil stick to the side. "An old warrior who could still teach a young pup like you a thing or two." He took a deep breath. He knew his words were empty, a reflexive retort. Despite years of regen treatments, and the fact that close to half his current body weight consisted of newly regenerated parts, he felt his age creeping up on him. Darius was all he'd been at his peak... and more. His son had eclipsed him in skill and military prowess, though it remained to be seen what he became, what he made of his great gifts.

Age. And wear and tear...no matter how much of me Sarah regrows—again—the fatigue is there, soul deep...

Erik Cain had been the greatest Marine of his day, a man who'd found redemption in the Corps and had risen to lead it. But he knew as he stood there, in the inner sanctum of the legendary Black Eagles, that his son had excelled to another level. At least as a practitioner of the art of war.

"Well, we've got some fighting to do, that much is certain, so you'll get your chance." Darius paused, his voice betraying a rare glimpse of emotion. "I never thought I'd get to go to battle at your side, father. I remember sitting home, knowing you were at war, struggling to defeat the Second Incursion. All I wanted was to be with you." Darius paused, looking down at the polished floor. "Later, when I was learning the trade, I spent every free moment reading military histories, and no small number of the recent ones were yours...and the Marines'. You did some impressive things, father, won some victories that must have seemed unattainable at the time."

Cain paused, feeling a wave of discomfort when his son called war a 'trade.' He had fought for causes, because he was attacked, to support his comrades...but Erik Cain had never viewed fighting in so coldly routine a manner. As a 'trade.'

"We had some tough fights..." His tone deepened, became more somber. "...and we lost a lot of good men and women." He had outlived many of those who'd fought at his side. *No*, he realized, not many, *most of them.*

"I'd never have thought then that I'd still be at war so many years later...that it would be so impossible to escape conflict." Cain's voice carried a deep sadness with it.

"That is the nature of things, father. There is no escape. Mankind cannot get away from its true nature." Darius's words lacked his father's regret. They were almost entirely without emotion, save perhaps for a grim sort of acceptance. "The vast majority of people will always be pathetic sheep…and they will follow corrupt and brutal leaders who make them empty promises. That is why I chose not a cause for my life's work, a pursuit that could only lead to failure and disillusionment, but merely to position myself to prosper from the folly humanity will never outgrow. They may despise me for the skill and effectiveness of my soldiers, but the conflicts we fought were of their making, not ours."

Erik stared back across the room at his son, and his sorrow grew more profound. He had also been a cynical man, one who had suffered early in life and who had greeted most human endeavors that followed with skepticism—a viewpoint in which he'd been proven right more often than not. But he had also found things to believe in—the Corps, his comrades, some truly extraordinary men and women who'd fought at his side… and, of course, most of all Sarah. He and his wife had endured repeated and extended separations, but their devotion to each other had never wavered. He wanted the same for Darius, but he saw in his son only the parts of himself with which he'd most struggled, taken to even greater extremes and lacking most of what had allowed Erik himself to cling to the shreds of his humanity.

"It is mankind's curse, my son. Sometimes, certainly. And yet, perhaps ultimate victory is out there for the taking. Perhaps this will be the final war." Cain didn't really believe it, not even as he said it…but he felt he had to say something, to try to reach Darius, if only because he couldn't accept the frigid nature of his son's outlook. He had often thought much the same way, but he'd always fought against it, been plagued by the guilt of his actions, the costs. But Darius was as coldly robotic in his approach as any man he'd ever known, and the commander of the Black Eagles didn't seem to give so much as a second thought to the millions his soldiers had killed.

Darius wasn't a bloodthirsty man by nature, nor an evil one, Cain was sure of that, but he knew his son was utterly unconstrained by normal human moderation. Outside his personal army and very small group of trusted friends, Darius viewed all the universe as a potential enemy, or at least the means to an end. If he could accomplish his goals with ten deaths, he would… but if it took a million, or ten million, that fact wouldn't stay his hand for an instant.

How must it be to live like that? To wrestle with all that I have…and so much more besides? And can I argue with his conclusions? Does history…does our current situation…offer anything to put forth in evidence to challenge my son's hard views? What did he see growing up? What thoughts took him when I didn't return? We faced the clearest threat to liberty we ever have against the Shadow Legions…and now, little more than a generation later, world after world can't wait to yield, to accept the rule of the enemy… a foe that has still not shown himself, not completely.

"Perhaps, father," Darius replied after a long silence. Cain knew his son didn't believe it, but there was no point in arguing…especially since he didn't know if he even believed it himself. Now, more than ever, he wanted nothing more than to live in peace, to escape the brutality of war and enjoy what time remained to him with his family. But that wasn't possible. The pattern of his life was repeating, and once again the trumpet was sounding. He longed to ignore it this time, but he knew he couldn't. There was no escape. If the enemy wasn't defeated, there would be no life such as the one he desired. There would be a stark choice. Slavery or death. And Erik Cain had only ever had one answer to that question.

"Well, that's a debate we'll have to table for another day, son." Cain looked at his son, and he felt himself fighting back a wave of emotion. "I have to leave, Darius," he said abruptly. "I want to thank you for helping me get back into condition. It's a lot harder than it used to be. Our technology has held back age—a bit—but it hasn't defeated it. Not by a long shot." Cain paused, glancing around the room before settling his gaze back on Darius. "I'd like to stay, or better still, I'd love for us all to go back home, but that's just not possible."

Cain regretted the mention of going home. His children had been born and raised on Atlantia, a planet that had not only declared Darius an outlaw, but one that had fallen under a cor-

rupt and oppressive government…one he was virtually certain
was being influenced by the enemy. The Black Flag.

"I wondered when you would tell me." Darius forced a
smile, but Cain could see through it, recognize that his son was
unhappy about his leaving.

"You knew?"

"Of course. I've known since you sent a communique to
Admiral Garret, asking for an escort to Armstrong. Do you
really think anything happens in the Nest that I don't know
about?" Darius hesitated. "I would have dispatched a flotilla to
take you to Armstrong, father. You just had to ask."

"I didn't want to add to your responsibilities, son. You've
got enough here, getting your people ready for the fight…and
adding so many to their numbers. I'm certain your ships are fully
occupied, without ferrying one old man halfway across Occupied Space."

Darius looked uncomfortable. "Still, perhaps I will send a
few ships along with Admiral Garret's force. Just to be safe."

Cain understood his son's concern. He shared it, though he'd
done his best to fight the fear. It had been more than seventeen
years since he'd been taken, but Cain knew he'd never forget that
his long and brutal captivity had resulted not from any battle on
the ground, but from a ship, taken in space by superior forces.

"Augustus will send enough force, Darius," he said, trying
to sound as reassuring as he could. "Don't worry…I won't end
up on another Eldaron, son." *No, I won't. They'll never take me alive
again. Never.*

He kept that last part to himself. He knew how much he
had suffered, but he could only imagine how those years had
affected his family…or how they were dealing with the fact
that he'd been alive all the years they'd thought him gone. Years
they'd gone on with their lives, even as he suffered.

"I'd still feel better, father. My fleet is mostly guarding the
Nest right now. Detaching a few ships for a flit to Armstrong
isn't going to materially degrade our defenses."

"It's really not necessary, son." Cain's voice didn't have any
real conviction behind it. He knew it was pointless to argue once

Darius had made up his mind. If he refused the escort, the Black Eagle ships would just follow his force anyway.

"Still, it won't hurt anything." Darius paused. Then: "Are you sure you want to go, father? You can stay with us here…you and mother. I know it's not Atlantia, but we could build you a pleasant residence."

Cain sighed softly. "I would, Darius…we both would, you know that. But we've been Marines all our adult lives. We're all going to be part of this fight, and I'm just too old a warrior to change now. There will be men and women who've come back to the colors, Marines who have served under me in old wars. They deserve to see me there again, Darius, leading them. Could you imagine sending the Eagles into battle—*this* battle—without you?"

"No, of course not. I understand. It's just…well, I thought you were gone forever for so long." He paused, uncomfortably. Emotion didn't come easily to him. "After so long…it's been nice having you here." He looked at his Cain, sucking in a ragged breath. "I missed you, father."

Cain stared back at his son, fighting his own surge of emotion. Robotic restraint came harder to him than it did to Darius, and he came close to losing his composure. Finally, he managed a clipped response. "I missed you too, son."

The two men stood and looked at each other, and then they embraced, a long hug. Erik Cain never knew for sure which of them had been the first to move toward the other, but he knew he would never forget the moment.

"When this fight is over, we can all spend some time together." Cain said the words, but was sure he believed them. His entire existence had been spent in pursuit of the life he'd just described, but for all his struggles, he'd only attained bits of it. He was immensely grateful for Sarah and his sons, but he resented the constant demands that had taken him from them so often and for so long. They'd had little more than a decade of true peace…amid half a century of brutal combat. Whatever happened, Erik Cain knew one thing. He would do what duty required of him now, in this struggle…but not again.

Humanity can learn its lesson or not…it can do whatever it chooses. But whatever happens, this will be my last war…

"What about Elias?" he asked suddenly. "Any word?"

"I don't know anything you don't. I haven't heard from him or from *Eagle Fourteen*…but that's not unexpected. They're operating under stealth conditions, so they wouldn't have communicated with the Nest anyway, not if it wasn't an emergency." Darius paused then added, "Captain Grayson is a highly capable officer, father, and *Eagle Fourteen* is one of the strongest ships in space. Elias will be fine."

"I know he will," Erik said, with less conviction than he longed to feel. "I just hate leaving without having a chance to talk to him."

"There's no rush, father. Perhaps you could stay a while longer…"

Erik shook his head. "I'd like nothing more, Darius, but you know as well as I do, whatever is happening out there, it is coming to a head. We've been preparing, but we've been late since the beginning. The Marines have to be ready, and I've dumped all the work on Cate Gilson for too long." He paused, feeling a rush of regret. "I have to go, son. We're out of time."

Chapter 3

Eagle Fourteen
Outer System – Epsilon Indi II
Earthdate: 2321 AD (36 Years After the Fall)

"If we're going to intervene, Colonel, it will have to be soon." Grayson's voice was close to non-committal, but not quite. Black Eagles weren't supposed to let normal human emotions affect their judgment, but Elias could tell the captain was angry watching the heavy cruiser being slowly overwhelmed by the pirates. The ship was from the old Alliance navy, just as Grayson himself was. He didn't doubt his brother's officer would sit and watch the ancient warship defeated and destroyed, but he was sure Grayson wouldn't like it.

Elias didn't know what to do. Every impulse within him cried out to come to the stricken ship's aid, but he knew his mission was important too, and opening fire would advertise *Eagle Fourteen*'s presence. Atlantia was his home—or at least it had been—and he'd come there to determine whether its government was in communication with the Black Flag. Or worse. *Though the fact that their patrol is not interfering with the raiders is pretty close to an answer...*

He knew what Darius would do. The Eagles' commander had an almost unparalleled ability to focus on the mission, to disregard the cost or the collateral damage. But Elias wasn't his brother.

"Do it," he said grimly.

"All weapons stations, power up and engage targeting systems. Lock onto the raiders." Grayson's voice was that of a veteran who had seen battle dozens of times, and Elias could hear the confidence in his commands…and also the relief at not being forced to stand by and watch as one of Admiral Garret's ships got blasted to scrap.

Elias worried that *Eagle Fourteen* couldn't handle the pirate flotilla, especially after another three ships had blasted out from behind the warp gate, bringing the total force to six. That was more than enough strength to vaporize the beleaguered old heavy cruiser, but *Eagle Fourteen* was a powerful battleship, larger even than the old Alliance *Yorktown* class that had claimed their place so firmly in history during the wars against the First Imperium. Elias was no expert on space combat, but Grayson didn't seem too concerned, so he just sat and watched.

"All batteries report locked and ready to fire, sir." The tactical officer sounded as cool and experienced as Grayson. Elias had once derisively referred to his brother's soldiers and spacers as little better than pirates themselves, and though he'd revised that estimation considerably over the past two years, he still found himself continually surprised at just how professional and effective a fighting force Darius had created. He still wished his brother had devoted his considerable skills to service of his home world and not as a mercenary fighting for pay… but then, his own experiences at the hands of Atlantia's government gave him pause even in that viewpoint. Though he'd never have believed it several years before, he realized such power was perhaps more safely placed in Darius's hands than in a government more interested in the accumulation and preservation of its leaders' power than anything else.

"Fire." He froze for an instant as he heard Grayson give the command, the order that would give away *Eagle Fourteen*'s position. A smaller ship might have passed for any number of vessels, but no one else in present-day Occupied Space possessed warships like those of the Black Eagles.

Elias heard the sounds of the massive laser batteries opening up, the almost incalculable output of *Eagle Fourteen*'s three enormous fusion reactors poured into devastating beams of focused light, ripping through space, tearing into the pirate raiders with unimaginable destructiveness. One of the targets simply vanished, hit by three blasts almost simultaneously, and then a second followed, leaving nothing but a superheated plasma in its place.

The others stopped firing at the cruiser, and they came around, bringing their weapons to bear on *Eagle Fourteen*. Their laser pulses slammed into the battleship's heavy armor, and Elias could feel the vessel shake. The attacks caused damage, but it was minimal, a fact confirmed as he listened to Grayson fielding the reports. Outer compartments breached, external scanners destroyed...but nothing critical.

"Captain...is it possible to disable one of those vessels?" Elias blurted out the thought the instant it popped into his head. He stared at the display, suddenly intrigued by the prospect of taking one of the ships—almost certainly Black Flag, he knew now that they'd fought back instead of run—captive.

"We can try, Colonel." Grayson didn't sound doubtful, not exactly. It wasn't in the Black Eagles' mantra to acknowledge there was anything they *couldn't* do. But Elias knew no Black Flag ship had ever been captured. "We'll have to gut their power and AI systems so they can't self-destruct, and then we'll have to board before they can override and destroy the ship."

"Then let's try, Captain. I imagine my brother would like a closer look at the enemy, and I'd wager the Eagles can tackle this kind of difficult assignment." Elias held back a smile. The Eagles were the best, without question, but if they had a weak point, that was it, their status and the pride they had in it. He stared at the display, watching as the four remaining vessels spread out, moving to surround *Eagle Fourteen*. They didn't operate like outlaws. Elias didn't have the pure military experience his father and brother did, but he knew a disciplined unit in action when he saw it.

"Yes, Colonel." Elias suspected Grayson knew he was being

manipulated a bit, but also that the Eagle was helpless to resist. Darius's culture of excellence had absorbed his people body and soul, and failing at anything, even something nearly impossible, was anathema to the Eagles.

"Lieutenant Criss," Grayson said, turning his head toward the tactical station, "Major Corrigan is to prepare his strike force for a boarding action. Advise the bay I want the assault shuttles ready to launch immediately. Gunnery control, I want one of those ships disabled, not destroyed.

Elias listened to the string of non-stop commands, and he watched as the tactical officer handled them all calmly and efficiently. He was still amazed every day watching his brother's people in action. He'd derided them for so long, and even now he had some trouble accepting how truly good they were. Darius was a genius at managing people. The Eagles feared no enemy, but they were terrified of one thing…of not being the best.

He knew Darius's talents came at a cost. He needed the very best people to start with, and he was ruthless at culling those who couldn't make the cut. Darius Cain loved his Eagles, but he didn't think much of humanity in general, and he had no use for those who couldn't measure up to his demanding standards. Elias understood the utility of his brother's ways now better than he had, but he still thought it was a dark and cynical point of view, and a damned hard way to live. For all he'd endured over the past few years, Elias still maintained a belief in people that his brother lacked. Though, now, unlike before, he was far from sure which of the two of them had a clearer view of things.

Two more of the enemy ships vanished from the screen, and the other two began accelerating, trying to get away from the deadly battleship. They likely thought they were faster than the massive warship, but Darius Cain's behemoths had enormous engines, and the latest in force-dampening technologies. *Eagle Fourteen* couldn't blast its engines at full, not without buttoning up its crew in the tanks, but she could manage 20g, which would feel like a crushingly uncomfortable—but survivable—6g to the crew.

"Crew, prepare for heavy acceleration."

Elias leaned back in his seat and took a deep breath. He was startled when the acceleration kicked in just a few seconds later. When Troy Grayson gave an order, he clearly expected his people to be on the ball and ready to obey. And slackers who didn't jump quickly enough could enjoy the experience of bearing six times their body weight away from the protective cushioning of their acceleration couches.

"I want those ships disabled, dammit. Get the guns focused on power generation systems." Grayson's voice was labored, somewhat, by the pressure, but Elias was impressed with how close to normal *Eagle Fourteen*'s captain sounded.

Elias's limited knowledge of naval combat was enough for him to realize that targeting individual systems, especially on ships whose internal layouts were unknown, was damned near impossible. But to the Eagles, 'damned near' and 'totally' were two entirely different things.

The pirates—*we've got to stop calling them that, they're so much more dangerous than just raiders*—were heading toward the warp gate. They weren't going to get there, not before *Eagle Fourteen* blasted them to atoms, and that meant time was short. Based on past encounters, the few times United Fleet or Eagle forces had been able to catch and defeat Black Flag squadrons, the enemy ships would self-destruct as soon as they realized escape was impossible.

Eagle Fourteen maintained a reduced rate of fire as she blasted forward. Even the Black Eagles' great battleships had limits to their energy generation, and 20g thrust pulled power from the gunnery stations. The great main guns were silent now. Their powerful shots were more useful for destroying enemy ships anyway, and if there was going to be any chance to capture one of the Black Flag's ships, it would be the needlers and their precise, tightly-targeted beams that would win the day.

"Strike forces are loaded and ready, Captain. Launch command advises all shuttles are go for launch on your command."

Elias was stunned. It had only been a matter of minutes since Grayson had ordered the strike force to prepare. How could those troopers possibly have gotten to the bay, armored up, and boarded the shuttles so quickly?

"Launch now, Lieutenant. The shuttles will set a course directly between the two enemy ships."

"Yes, sir."

Elias nodded, at least as close to a nod as he could manage under the strain of an effective 6g pushing down on him. He reaffirmed to himself that whatever lay in his future, he would never get truly used to space travel, at least not the hard kind that accompanied combat.

The firing continued, and then one of the enemy vessels vanished in the thermonuclear fury of its reactors overloading. It could have been the result of one of *Eagle Fourteen*'s guns, but in his gut, Elias knew it wasn't. He felt a chill thinking about an enemy that would so coldly and consistently choose death over capture.

The last ship was still there, though, and a glance at the display told him the vessel's engines were dead. It wasn't firing anymore, and the scanner readings showed no power generation. That was far from a perfect conclusion—there were many ways to hide such things from a ship's sensors—but it was a good bet Grayson's people had disabled the pirate ship, just as they'd intended to do.

"The shuttles are to change vectors toward that last ship. I want a minimum time course to intercept. Major Corrigan is to board and take the vessel as soon as docking is complete. His priority is to seize the reactor space and the main AI center, and then to secure the remainder of the vessel."

Elias understood Grayson's orders. If the enemy was able to override their damaged systems and blow the reactor, the Eagles would lose their prize.

And if they did it after Corrigan's people landed…

Elias wondered how long it would be before he stopped being amazed at the conduct of these soldiers he'd called brutal thugs so many times.

* * * * *

"You all know why we're here, so I'm not going to waste time going over that again. We don't know the layout of this ship, but that's not going to stop us. We get to those vital spaces, and we secure them...before these pukes blow this ship, and us with it." Buck Corrigan was Black Eagle through and through. Unlike many of Darius Cain's soldiers, he had not been an adoptee from the Marines or some other declining or defunct military force. He'd come from a dirt-poor planet, and even among the destitute farmers clawing out a bare sustenance level survival, his poverty had been exceptional.

His father's debts had been staggering, and the fact that most of the assessments the local lord had placed on the family were bogus meant exactly nothing. The elder Corrigan had died in debtor's prison, worked to utter exhaustion in the quarries, leaving his only son to inherit his obligations. But Buck Corrigan wasn't his father, and his solution to his problems had been a direct one. He'd driven a spike through the offending lord's eye, avenging his father and effectively canceling the family's debt in one fast stroke. Of course, the action had made him an outlaw, one without the resources or opportunity to escape his miserable—and now very dangerous—homeworld.

Until the Eagles came. Darius Cain's mercenaries had been a much smaller force then, their now-fearsome reputation still in its infancy. They'd been sent by the ruler of the other inhabited planet in the system, a vain and foolhardy man who'd been willing to throw his own poor world into debt to send a punitive expedition against his rivals who had offended him.

Grayson had watched in wonder as the soldiers, no more than a thousand of them at that time, landed with perfect organization and, in a matter of days, utterly obliterated a planetary army five times their size. He was astonished by the invader's suits of armor. He'd heard about powered infantry, the Marines and Janissaries and other formations who'd fought mankind's great wars before the Fall, but he'd never expected to see any in person.

He'd thrown all caution to the wind, marching right into the Eagles' camp, shouting that he wanted to enlist. The soldiers laughed at him and told him to go home, but then fortune smiled on him. A man, an officer, saw him and walked over. "What do you want, boy?" the man said to the stunned sixteen year old.

"I want to join you. I want to be a Black Eagle."

The men laughed again, but not the officer. "You want to leave home? What about your mother, your father? Your family?"

"My mother's dead, sir. The pox, ten years ago. My father's dead too…the local lord worked him to death in his mines. And I'm an outlaw, because I killed the lord, paid him back in kind for my father. This may be my home because I was born here, but if I never see the dust-covered rock again, good riddance."

He wasn't sure if he remembered his words perfectly or not, but whatever he had said, it had been the right thing. The officer, who had turned out to be none other than Darius Cain himself, took a liking to him. Corrigan might not have had perfect recall of what *he* had said, but Cain's words he remembered perfectly. "Sign him up, boys. This kid's an Eagle for sure. He's just been waiting for us to get here and pick him up." The mercenary commander turned around and walked away…and Buck Corrigan's miserable life changed on the spot. There'd been brutal work and deadly combat in the years since, pain and suffering along with the immense rewards and fast promotion he'd enjoyed. But that day marked the last time Corrigan had felt helpless, unable to influence his own destiny.

He moved forward, through the corridors of the Black Flag ship—at least he assumed it was a Black Flag ship—his eyes scanning every hatch, every conduit or bit of equipment running along the ceiling or affixed to the wall. There were half a dozen troopers behind him, lined up in single file. The narrow ship's hallway was too small to accommodate two armored soldiers side by side. That was a tactical problem, one Grayson considered. Ideally, his people would fight in a more open area, a compartment or something similar. But even in the narrow corridor, one armored Eagle could likely eliminate the two or three unprotected enemies he might face.

His people were spreading out through the ship, but half a dozen had stuck with him, a couple even trying to take the point and lead down the corridor, before Grayson had sent them back with one armored gesture.

The major knew there had been armies throughout history where the regular soldiers resented the officers, where a great gulf existed between the two groups. But the Black Eagles revered their officers, every one of whom had started their careers as a normal footsoldier, a tradition that stretched as far as Darius Cain himself. There were no privileged elites in the Eagles, no scions of wealthy or military families, no political appointees. Every Black Eagle had earned his place in the hard crucible of war, and those of higher rank served to show the rest what they, too, could achieve.

Grayson himself, rich enough now to live like a lord himself on any planet of his choosing, had considered retiring. But then he realized the true strength of the organization Darius Cain had created. He'd been one of the best for years now, and it was a part of him he couldn't leave behind. His gratitude and loyalty to the man who'd given him escape from the hell into which he'd been born, the comradeship with the other Eagles…they were things he couldn't walk away from, no matter how much treasure he accumulated. He had found himself, and he was what he was, what he would always be. A Black Eagle.

"Major, I think we found the main power plant. There's about a dozen enemies here, sir, armed with assault rifles. We're pretty close to the main reactor, so we're clearing out the space with blades."

"Very well, Lieutenant. Proceed." The molecular blades were hand-to-hand weapons, made from the hardest know alloys and honed to an edge no wider than ten or twelve molecules. The knives were built into the Eagle's armor, and they could cut through almost anything, steel, stone, reinforced concrete. Human flesh didn't offer any resistance at all.

Grayson glanced up at the display projected on his visor. The lieutenant's location showed up as a small dot on his screen.

There was a partial layout, but the Eagles hadn't scouted the whole ship yet, so the AI had blanked out the areas where no data was available. There was an unknown section between Grayson and the lieutenant, and one good way to take care of that.

"Let's go," he said to his six companions. "Let's find our way to the reactor, and lock this ship down." He raised his arm, holding up the heavy assault rifle connected to his armor. Then he trudged down the corridor, heading toward the reactor room.

Chapter 4

"I want those formations ready, Colonel, and I do mean immediately. What I saw this morning was utterly unsatisfactory, and if I am forced to make an example of someone, I can assure you it will not be one of those sweating, undertrained soldiers out there." Jarrod Tyler was angry…and over the years, if there was one thing the officers, ministers—even the people in the streets of Columbia's cities—had learned, it was to take cover when their president was mad.

"Yes, General Tyler. We have pushed them as hard as possible, but…" Tyler's withering gaze carried a clear message, one that stopped his subordinate's words cold. Columbia's senior military commander—and absolute ruler—did not want excuses, and he certainly didn't want any responses that included the word 'but.' "I will do whatever is necessary to get them ready, sir." The nervous officer stood at attention, unable to hide how much effort that took in the fearsome presence of Columbia's dictator. Though his rule was mostly benevolent, at least in matters not related to planetary security, Tyler was also a feared leader, and few Columbians could stand up to his imposing presence.

Tyler hadn't always been the frigid-blooded tyrant he'd

become. In fact, he'd been an ardent supporter of freedom, a military officer who'd followed every order given to him by the duly-appointed civilian authorities. Then he'd watched his home world attacked and occupied multiple times, first by the Caliphate and the Central Asian Combine, and then by the xenophobic forces of the First Imperium. The Shadow Legions had come next, its clone armies killing tens of thousands of Columbians. Still, despite more than a generation of continued warfare and devastation, he'd watched the people lose their vigilance again, and vote the president—his wife, Lucia—out of office in favor of a new government sworn to dismantle the powerful but expensive Columbian military.

He'd railed against the short-sightedness of that approach, reminded anyone who would listen of Columbia's violent history…but it had all been to no avail. He'd watched helplessly as his wife and her political allies were cast aside, and the splendid military he'd spent his life building was dismantled. Then, as if on cue from a universe that seemed determined to teach lessons to imbeciles, the First Imperium returned.

The Second Incursion had been an unmitigated disaster for Columbia, and the planet came closer to total extinction than ever before. It had survived only because Jarrod Tyler had rallied the remnants of its shattered military—and anyone else who would fight—and waged a guerilla campaign, fighting from the swamps and woods and mountains and protecting the terrified population from the xenophobic invaders, until Erik Cain returned with the Marines, and once again drove the enemy from Columbia.

That last war, however, had been enormously costly, for everyone on Columbia, and for Tyler in particular. Among the thousands dead in the desperate struggle was Lucia Collins, his wife, a woman he'd loved beyond words, one who'd grounded his humanity, who'd kept his growing anger restrained. It was then, after the war, counting the terrible cost, that something changed in him. He'd seen what the people had done with their republic, how quickly they'd forgotten all those who'd died in the wars that had come before. Never again, he had vowed, and without another thought, with neither the slightest doubt nor an instant of hesitancy, he seized power and made himself Columbia's absolute dictator, a post he'd retained with an unwavering grip over the nineteen years since then.

His coup had been relatively bloodless, a fact that had been made possible mostly by the unmitigated devotion of the veterans of his victorious army. They shared much of his anger, the cost they had paid because of the lack of readiness had been in blood, theirs and that of loved ones killed when the First Imperium bots landed and swept through the planet's cities, destroying all in their path. The soldiers had followed Tyler's orders without question, seized whatever objectives he told them to take, captured whomever he commanded them to arrest.

Killed anyone he instructed them to kill.

Tyler had not been bloodthirsty, at least not toward the population at large. But he'd had no pity for the politicians, corrupt to the core, who had crippled the planet's ability to defend itself and poured the diverted resources into their own pockets, and those of their allies. For them, there was no mercy, and Columbia's army displayed its unwavering loyalty to its commander by the ferocity with which it sought out those proscribed, butchering them in their homes, in the streets, in whatever hiding places they sought refuge.

Tyler turned and watched the new soldiers as they continued to drill. They were doing well, better than he had any right to expect of such green troops. But he felt the familiar coldness, the foreboding feeling that his homeworld was once again about to taste the bitterness of war. The Black Flag was coming. He'd been to summits with other planetary leaders, listened to their wishful thinking, their arguments that the enemy could be contained, that they could be bribed, bought off. But Tyler knew better. He was sure, in a way he couldn't explain but couldn't deny either, that the enemy's goal was nothing but the total conquest of Occupied Space. And if they wanted Columbia, they were going to have to fight like hell for it.

He'd always maintained a strong military, the largest and most powerful Columbia's resources could sustain. But now he'd gone well beyond that. He'd strengthened his alliance with the Black Eagles, and he'd sold Darius Cain the permanent rights to the moon the mercenary had leased to house his Nest. It was a thinly-disguised way for Cain to funnel some of his vast treasure to his ally in a face-saving way, funds, Tyler realized, Darius would be only too certain would pour into expanding Columbia's military. Tyler wasn't fooled, but he still appreciated the face-saving gesture. And he took the money. This was war, and the choices were victory or slavery. Or death in his case. One thing he was sure of…he would not survive a lost war. He would be no man's slave.

"General Tyler, the ships from the Nest have arrived." An orderly came racing across the field, carrying a small tablet. "They will be entering orbit within thirty minutes."

"Very well, Captain," Tyler said, reaching out for the device. He took it and scanned it briefly before handing it back. "I want that cargo on the ground as quickly as possible. All other freight shuttle traffic is secondary. Advice Major Silman he is authorized to commandeer any transport assets he needs."

"Yes, sir." The aide saluted and turned abruptly.

Tyler stood for a moment and sighed. He'd been expecting the shipment, and there it was, right on time. Was there anything Darius Cain did in a disorganized or ineffectual way?

The ships carried arms and ammunition, and suits of armor, the very best ones in Occupied Space, straight from the Eagles own production facilities. It was all technically part of the price for the moon, but at its core it was Darius Cain, arming an ally, doing everything he could to maximize the fighting strength at his disposal. Tyler knew his forces were good. Not Black Eagle good, of course, but then who was? But if he had time to equip and train his elite troopers with the new armor, they would be ready to unleash hell on anyone who threatened Columbia.

He walked across the field, back to the sparse and utilitarian quarters he'd occupied since the day he'd seized power. He was one of history's most atypical dictators. He detested the operation of the government, yet he saw over the minutest of details, leaving no decision of any consequence to anyone else. He was uninterested in power, but he held onto it with a grip as tight as any strongman who'd ever lived. It was the only way…the only way to prevent another disaster like the Incursion. Like the nightmare that had cost him his wife.

*   *   *   *   *

"You weren't sleeping. Again." Ana Bazarov reached out, putting her hand on Darius's back. He flinched slightly, as he usually did. Her touch was one of the few things that relaxed him, but recently it seemed she had lost some of her calming ability. The tension was too great, the burden of work Darius had taken on to himself more than any man could endure, even the great and terrible General Cain.

"If you noticed that, you weren't either." His voice wasn't completely devoid of tension—she couldn't remember the last time it was—but there was some bit of calm there too, and something else, a sound she suspected few outside this bedchamber had heard from the mercenary. Affection.

She wouldn't go so far as to call it love, mostly because she didn't know if he was truly capable of such an emotion. He loved his parents, of course, in a traditional sort of way, and his attachments to his oldest colleagues, like Erik Teller, were close ones. But Cain was so cynical, his view of the universe so dark, she wasn't sure if his psyche would ever allow him to get too close to any lover. His defense mechanisms bordered on the psychotic, but none of that mattered to her. *She* loved *him*, of that she was certain, and she would accept whatever emotion he was able to give her in return.

He had done that much, at least, there was no question. When he'd first rescued her from the ruins of conquered Karelia, she had despised him. But he'd sent his soldiers to find her sister, and he'd given them both shelter and medical care, and took them away from a world that offered them only enslavement and ruin. He'd denied her nothing, and he'd treated her with kindness, something that had surprised her. And he'd forced her to do nothing. Indeed, her trip to his bed, when it finally happened, had been driven by her own initiative. He hadn't made so much as an advance to her until she'd made her own interest known. She'd realized then, the feared mercenary was a far more complex man than people imagined.

"I think your insomnia is contagious."

Darius smiled and turned his head, smiling at her, careful not to change his orientation enough to interrupt the backrub. "I'm a restless sleeper. I never could get through an entire night." That was an understatement. If he got an average of three hours, four at most, by morning, she knew that was a lot.

Ana returned his smile, moving her hand to the back of his neck, to a spot she knew was the physical manifestation of his stress. The knot there was an epic one, almost Gordian in scale. Even as her fingers worked it, she knew it was more than she could handle. Short of the shade of Alexander coming out of history's mists with his sword to chop it apart, she knew Cain's tension would endure. She wondered if seducing him was a better route, but she knew it wasn't a good time. He'd be bounding out of bed any moment now, heading back to the control room to check on the dozens of operations he had going on. His mind was there even now, she knew.

Darius had massively expanded the Black Eagles, and he'd taken every step he could to secure and strengthen allies for the coming fight. She'd watched, seen the effect the stress had on him, even as he took more and more onto himself.

She knew most of Occupied Space despised him, that his name was used as a bogeyman to scare children. She also understood that millions had died at the hands of his soldiers, though she'd come to realize that he hadn't started any of the conflicts his soldiers had finished. He'd told her once, as he saw it, the Black Eagles had saved far more lives than they'd taken, that their swift completion of wars had prevented them from becoming extended, world-destroying struggles. That hadn't made any sense to her at first, but now she understood, and she realized he had almost certainly been correct. It was a strange kind of logic, but that didn't make it less true.

For all they curse his name, if any one man is likely to save them from the doom that is coming, it is him. She wondered if they would appreciate him then, if they would build statues of him, instead of making curses of his name. Probably not, she thought sadly, realizing just how much his cynicism had rubbed off on her.

"I have to go," he said, as he slid to the side of the bed and sat up. "We've got weapons shipments I need to check on, and I have to do an inspection on the new recruits. Gray and Brown Regiments are looking pretty good, if I do say so myself, but they're not up to Eagle standards. Not quite."

Not yet, Ana thought, interpreting Darius's true meaning from his words. She'd never seen anyone as convinced as him that anything was possible with enough effort.

"You didn't get any sleep at all." She was concerned about him. She was always worried when he went off on campaign, of course, but now she half expected him to work himself to death and save the enemy the trouble.

"I'll grab a nap later." A lie, she knew.

He leaned over the bed, putting his hand on her face and kissing her gently. "I'll try to get away for an hour later. Maybe was can have a late supper."

She smiled. "I would like that." She sat in the middle of the bed and watched him walk through the door, his mind already deep into a dozen other things.

Darius Cain had kept a dozen mistresses when she'd arrived at the Nest, some of the most beautiful women from all the worlds of Occupied Space. They were all gone now, shipped off with generous trust funds, enough to live comfortably for the rest of their lives. She suspected that kind of generosity was something others wouldn't believe, that they would imagine the terrible general disposing of those he tired of without so much as a goodbye. But she'd come to know the real Darius, at least as much as anyone could. And, to whatever extent anyone could claim this, he was hers, in his own way, as much as she was his.

She could deal with his idiosyncrasies, his emotional baggage, even the fact that he was so hated. She could deal with it all…except the dread fear she felt, the haunting, horrible terror that she would lose him, that he would die in the coming conflict, and she would be alone again.

Chapter 5

The three 'entities' were restless. It was almost time. For two years, their pirate fleets had ravaged Occupied Space, destroying hundreds of ships and bringing commerce to a virtual standstill. The fleets of their enemies were hopelessly scattered, chasing raiders, escorting vital shipments, protecting planets from imagined invasions.

Hundreds of planetary economies had collapsed, and on those worlds that were not self-sufficient, society itself was on the verge of total breakdown. Once-wealthy mining colonies withered away for lack of food and other essentials. Resource-poor worlds saw their industry shut down, deprived of needed imports to sustain operations. Rampant crime and mobs of desperate, starving people ravaged many planets, and authorities had begun to crack down violently, resorting to any measures necessary in futile attempts to restore order, and maintain their own power. Only those worlds that had yielded, accepted the Triumvirate as their overlords, were spared the relentless assault on their economies. Spared the terrible specter of utter ruin.

All was going exactly according to the plan. The hundreds of raiders, the ships known to civilization now as those of the

Black Flag, had brought humanity to the edge of despair… and yet they were merely the vanguard of the force that would strike. In orbit around Vali, and positioned throughout the Draconia Terminii system, were hundreds of warships. Not the fast, sleek—but relatively lightly-armed—raiders, but cruisers and battleships, and massive carriers filled with fighters, all technologically the equal of the best humanity possessed. No, not the equal…better, more advanced.

This fleet, the iron fist of the Triumvirate, stood ready to finish the job, to complete the project the entities had worked on tirelessly for three decades. The end goal was power…nothing less than the subjugation of all humankind. And vengeance, payback long overdue. Its fruition had taken longer than the shortened lifespans of the three Stark clones, but they had found a solution to that problem, as they had to all others. The Intelligence.

The sophisticated AI, millennia ahead of anything possessed by mankind, had been found buried in the sands of a world not far from Draconia Terminii IV. The clones had ordered it retrieved, restored. It was First Imperium, that much had been apparent at once. It had taken years to salvage the ancient computer, to restore it from its version of death. And it had repaid its benefactors. Within its vast memory banks was a procedure to download the essence of a living being into its core, to grant effective immortality. And so it had for the three clones of the Triumvirate. Now, the last obstacle, the deaths of their physical bodies, had been removed as an obstacle. They would see the plan through, monitor every facet of their operations, with a completeness and retention that would have been impossible before.

The Triumvirate remembered its purpose, the need for revenge, the driving quest to avenge the death of its progenitor. Yet, such thoughts were vaguer now, as was the individual nature of the three component entities. Even the name Triumvirate seemed odd. Yes, they had been three separate beings, men, who had often disagreed and debated fiercely on their courses of action. But that was back when their essences were encased in flesh. Now, there was less disagreement, and the separation between them, what had been that thing they'd called their personalities, had begun to fade away, at least partially, becoming more a cold recollection of data than anything else. Even the quest for vengeance and the lust for power were somehow...different. For thirty years, they had worked to bring all of humanity under their iron grip, yet now, as they stood on the cusp of attaining that goal, other thoughts began to surface, ideas that perhaps mankind needed a pruning, an elimination of all but the most productive elements of its constituent populations.

There had always been a willingness to utilize whatever violence and destruction was necessary to see the plan to fruition, but outright genocide had never been the primary intention. Until now. The Intelligence had provided more information, not mandates, but logical arguments. Most people's existences were wastes of resources. They consumed more than they provided, placed burdens on society. They would always require surveillance, security to control them. The Intelligence was right. It was far simpler to eliminate those that were not necessary, reduce the problems of maintenance to the bare minimum.

Not yet, however. There were too many humans out there who would aid the plan, drawn to serve the Black Flag by greed, fear, stupidity. They would serve the effort to defeat their fellow humans. Then they, too, would be culled.

"Marshal Carrack reports everything is ready for the crusade to begin." The thought came from the collection of data that had previously been known as One.

"Yes, I have reviewed all filed reports." It was Two who answered first, or at least what his essence had become. "By every calculation, our forces are superior to those we will face, more so when supplemented with the military resources of the worlds that have already submitted."

"Indeed, we are in agreement," Three added. "Save for one factor, a concern that has grown on me of late. I believe our greatest threat is Darius Cain and his Black Eagles. We have put considerable resources into attempted surveillance of their activities, with very little to show for our efforts. I have reviewed the histories of his campaigns, and have determined he is unpredictable in the extreme, which presents a problem in terms of anticipating and preparing for his actions. Our fleets and armies are strong, there is no question of that, but there is more to war than numbers alone. General Cain has never sought lasting conquest, for whatever reason, he has never desired to subjugate those he defeats under his own rule. But if that should change, if he decides to challenge us for control over Occupied Space instead of merely seeking to defend his own tiny domain, he could be a formidable enemy."

"Indeed he could, Three. Two is correct in that our forces are nearly irresistible in strength, but we have seen before that there are unquantifiable factors at work in war as well. The Shadow Legions should not have failed, yet they did. The Marines they fought against were massively outnumbered, but they prevailed nevertheless. And, let us not forget, we have not one Generals Cain to worry about, but two. That fool, the Tyrant of Eldaron managed to lose Erik Cain, the very man who killed our progenitor. It is highly likely that his unexpected return will vastly inflate the morale of the Marine Corps. He was already their most celebrated leader. His apparent return from the dead will only drive his legend to new heights. We must also acknowledge the likelihood that the presence of father and son in command of the two greatest military forces opposing us with vastly increase the chance of effective cooperation. We must not underestimate what the Black Eagles and the Marines can accomplish working together, particularly with Admiral Garret's fleet attached to the Corps. We need look no farther than the history of the last fifty years to see Erik Cain's achievements, and the most recent decade to analyze his son's vast successes."

"I do not believe we should take any chances," Two thought. "I believe we should activate the revised plan. It divides our forces, but by threatening both our most dangerous enemies, one with a diversion and the other with a devastating assault, we will prevent them from joining forces. Losses will undoubtedly be high, but once one is destroyed, we can direct all our forces to combine on the other…and when the two Cains and Admiral

Garret's forces are gone, the rest of Occupied Space will fall rapidly."

"I agree."

"And I. Let the orders be sent. The attack will begin at once. A diversion in force against target A…and a killing strike against target B."

"Our plan is sound. Yet, must we consider one other factor? Marshal Carrack will, of course, betray us. No doubt, our continued existence in the aftermath of physical death was a hard blow to him. There is little doubt he harbored hopes to supplant us, to rule after we were gone."

"We have known the Marshal had such ambitions for many years. Yet, he is a methodical man, one unlikely to take any risky moves against us. No doubt he will seek to finish the crusade, and only then make his play for power. I believe we can use him for now, benefit from his unquestioned leadership ability. We need only ensure that he does not survive the end of the war. It should be a relatively simple task to see that an assassin eliminates him or his flagship suffers a catastrophic malfunction."

"Agreed," the others thought almost in unison.

"Then so be it. The crusade shall begin, and Marshal Carrack will lead it."

"Have we agreed on which target will be the diversion, and which the primary target?"

"We have discussed that many times, Three, and I believe we have all agreed. There are strong arguments for each, but I believe our final choice was based in sound logical analysis. It is uncomfortable to leave either of these enemies still in the field against us, and even more so to commit so much force to an effort that will almost certainly be unsuccessful in the end. But if it allows us to destroy one of the major threats we face, it will only strengthen our position. And, at all costs, we must prevent our greatest foes from joining forces against us. They are weakened by their instincts to defend their worlds, to fight to preserve planets from subjugation and destruction, but if they were to embrace a more aggressive strategy, if they were able to locate Vali, they could be a threat to us. By cutting one arm from the beast, we vastly lessen this danger."

"It is done," One said. "And now, all our years of effort have come to their final purpose." The data files that had once been the clone expected something, to feel...satisfaction...at the momentous occasion. But there was nothing save analysis, cold thoughts on the coming campaign. He recalled the feelings of excitement, the joy at vengeance, but he couldn't replicate them, at least not entirely. Indeed, even the true understanding of such things was fading. The plan was the plan, and that was all that mattered. Reasons were unimportant. Mankind was to be subordinated, perhaps even destroyed.

And now it would truly begin.

*   *   *   *   *

Aaron Carrack sat in the audience hall, looking out over the assembled officers and enjoying the tense looks as they stared up at his exalted presence. The Black Flag was a service that offered the promise of great rewards, but it also demanded unquestioning obedience and unfaltering competence. Disloyalty was punished in the harshest ways the most devilish minds in human space could contrive, but even honest failure warranted a death sentence. Fear and greed were the two pillars of the organization, and Carrack was entirely convinced they were the two greatest motivators of humankind.

Carrack was the Black Flag's Marshal, its supreme military commander, the highest-ranking of its operatives, save the members of the Triumvirate themselves. *Whatever they are now...*

Carrack had served the Triumvirate for nearly thirty years. He'd been one of the original Gavin Stark's operatives, and one of the first operations conducted by the embryonic Triumvirate had been to extricate him from the miserable, dusty prison where he'd been held since the end of the Shadow War. He was grateful for his rescue, and the opportunity to return to a position of power, and that road had taken him beyond anything he could have imagined. His soldiers were on hundreds of worlds now, enforcing the supplication of scared and intimidated political leaders and populations. And his vast fleets and armies were almost ready to begin the final crusade, the conquest and destruction of all who still opposed the Black Flag.

It was a wondrous moment, the culmination of a life's work, and he owed all to the three clones who formed the Triumvirate. But gratitude was for fools, and Carrack had long been watching and waiting, his attention fixed on the advanced aging and bodily decay of his benefactors. The Triumvirate members had been cloned using the same techniques that had produced millions of Shadow Legion soldiers, and like those warriors, they suffered from the same genetic defect, a vastly accelerated aging process and premature death. Carrack appreciated all the clones had done for him, but that hadn't stopped him from dreaming of the moment they succumbed to age and died, leaving him in total control of the vast power they had assembled.

He'd grown impatient as they lingered on far longer than he'd expected, and he'd even considered an assassination attempt. But then they finally died, and for a fleeting instant he thought his moment had come.

Then he was summoned to the room where the Intelligence was housed. It took several moments to realize what had happened, and then the reality sunk in. The Triumvirate was now part of the great computer, preserved and, for all practical purposes, immortal. His dreams of inherited power faded away in an instant.

Carrack was nothing if not a clever operative, and he adapted immediately, swearing renewed loyalty to his masters, and settling, for the time being, with his position in command of all the Black Flag's military. He still harbored his ambitions, of course, but he knew the war would come first. Once Occupied Space had been conquered, when he had his own creatures ensconced in key positions of power, then would be the time. Carrack detested the strange, alien computer, and he knew that its destruction would also rid him of his troublesome masters. He would conquer all the worlds of humanity, and then he would return in victory...and obliterate Vali. There was an inefficiency to the destruction of so many resources and so much industry, but the Triumvirate members were too clever to trifle with. Subtle, complex plans were subject to breakdown. They no doubt suspected him of planned betrayal, and they would be ready for any moves he made less shocking and dramatic than planetary holocaust.

The cost of one world, however massively productive, was a small price to pay for total domination of all humanity.

But there was work to do now, much to accomplish before things came to such a pass. He had two attacks to launch, one a diversion, and the other a devastating blow to utterly destroy one of the Black Flag's most dangerous enemies.

He stood up, resplendent, he knew, in his uniform, dripping with braid and medals and the kinds of trinkets that made people look at him and see power. "It is time, he said forcefully. Time for the great crusade we have worked for, trained for. Even now, our fleets are preparing, and within days we will be underway. The Black Flag demands much, but the rewards before us are immense. Everyone who serves, will share in the spoils. Even a footsoldier will live the rest of his life like a lord, awash in luxury and spoils."

The crowd erupted into a wave of massive cheers, all of them imagining, he suspected, their own visions of such lives, of servants and money and power.

People will believe anything…anything at all…

Chapter 6

"The vessel is secured, Colonel. Major Grayson's people are in control of all vital areas. They are currently searching the ship for any enemy forces still hidden or at large."

Elias was going to ask about prisoners when Grayson continued, "They have taken three captives, sir. All other enemy crew members were either killed in combat or took their own lives."

Elias was still getting used to how the Eagles seemed to anticipate questions, to the stunning completeness of their reports. "Very good, Captain. Please give Major Grayson my compliments." He felt that he should say something as commander of the expedition, but he imagined that words alone were hollow to the Eagles. Elias had his accomplishments in his own fields of endeavor, but these veteran warriors couldn't possibly truly respect him, not as a military leader, especially since Darius had violated his own sacred code and given him a colonelcy he hadn't earned in Eagles' service.

"Bring the prisoners back as quickly as possible, Captain." Elias stared at the display for a few seconds. He wanted to ask Grayson what he thought they should do next, but he couldn't imagine a more effective way to piss away what respect he'd managed to gain from the Eagles. Darius Cain's officers did not push off their responsibilities onto subordinates, they made decisions. "Can we get that vessel operational?"

Grayson paused, the first time Elias had seen any delay in the officer's response. "No way to know for sure, sir, not until we can get an engineering team over there and get a good look." My best guess is we caused significant damage in disabling the ship. It's likely repairable, but there is no way to know how long that will take. And now that we've given away our presence, do we want to stay here that much longer? Are we ready to engage Atlantian ships if they intervene?" There was no fear in Grayson's voice, and Elias suspected the Eagle was ready to face the entire Atlantian navy if necessary. There was something, though. Caution, perhaps. He got the impression Grayson didn't think they should stay too much longer, and he was very inclined to agree with that point of view.

Elias paused now. He didn't have proof Atlantia was cooperating with the Black Flag, but he didn't have any doubts remaining either. There was an argument to try and glean more hard data—and an attack by the Atlantian navy would be pretty definitive evidence of Black Flag collusion, if not outright control. But Elias wasn't ready to fight his own homeworld, not if he could avoid it. Not to mention, if Atlantia sent its entire fleet, they could give *Eagle Fourteen* one hell of a fight. It wasn't that he didn't think the Eagle ship could prevail, but his gut told him it was far from a sure thing at the odds they would face. They had captured Black Flag personnel, the first to be taken prisoner since the struggle began, and if *Eagle Fourteen* was destroyed here, that prize would be lost. No, it made sense to avoid another fight, to get back to the Nest and review all they'd discovered.

But he wanted that ship too.

"Can we tow it?" He stared at the display, his eyes focused on the small dot representing the enemy vessel.

"Yes," Grayson replied. "It will affect our acceleration and maneuverability considerably, but we should be able to recall the strike forces and establish the towing setup before the Atlantians can get a response force this far out."

"Do it, Captain. We've got enemy prisoners and one of their ships. That's too valuable to risk."

"Yes, sir." Grayson turned to his tactical officer and issued a flurry of commands. Then he tapped his comm unit and said, "Major Corrigan, I need that ship one hundred percent secure, and I need it ten minutes ago."

There was a brief delay, just a fraction of a second extra as the signals moved through space, but it was still noticeable. "Yes, sir. We've got all vital sections cleared with guards posted. My sweeper teams have covered everything but the cargo holds. They should be done soon, Captain."

Grayson frowned. Elias knew the captain didn't like vague terms like 'soon' in reports.

"Very well, Major. No shortcuts, but get it done. We're going to set up a towing rig and take that ship back to the Nest. One saboteur who slips past you could cause us a lot of trouble, especially since *Eagle Fourteen* will be so close."

"I understand, sir."

"I want half your troopers deployed on that ship during the trip back to the Nest. And I want all external communications capability physically disabled. We don't need an enemy ship we don't know about out there somewhere, triggering some secret destruct system. You'll use only our own comm between here and the Nest. Understood?"

"Completely, Captain."

"Carry on, Major."

Elias watched, amazed at how the two Eagle officers interacted without the slightest rivalry or envy. On *Eagle Fourteen*, Grayson was Corrigan's superior officer, a relationship that reversed if the two were on the ground. Elias wondered if there was a gray area, with the soldier on another ship and the captain still on *Eagle Fourteen*, but it didn't seem so from the two men's demeanors. It didn't seem there were many gray areas in Eagle operations.

He knew his brother had been beyond meticulous in writing

the code of regulations for his army. A mercenary force lacked the inherited patriotic fervor a nation's army started with, and Darius Cain had clearly made every effort to eliminate discord in his ranks, and avoid any conflicts that could drain away from morale and comradeship. He was still a bit concerned about the darkness of his brother's thoughts, but there was no question that Darius Cain was a military master, one who had not only equaled, but surpassed their famous father.

"Sir, we're picking up energy readings from Atlantia. Multiple vessels accelerating from planetary orbit."

"Very well. Time to intercept?"

"Forty-two hours, sir. Assuming maximum known acceleration for Atlantian ships."

Elias shook his head. Among the many surprises he'd discovered when he linked up with the Eagles was the extensive database Darius had built of the military forces of Occupied Space. He'd read the file on Atlantia, and he'd been stunned. His brother's mercenaries knew more about his homeworld's military than half her own admirals and generals. Another example of Darius's chilling thoroughness.

"Can we set up the towing rig and get out of the system in forty-two hours, Captain?"

"Yes, sir. I don't see any problem in meeting that deadline with a healthy margin of error."

Elias stared at the small icons on the long-range display. He felt a moment of sadness. He'd never imagined he'd be looking at Atlantian ships and seeing an enemy. Darius had written off his homeworld, his anger at the way he felt he'd been treated overwhelming any vestiges of sentimentality and loyalty. But Elias still found it difficult, especially now, as the approach of that fleet virtually confirmed Atlantia was allied with the Black Flag.

His mind drifted to the beaches, the wild rocky coastlines of the magnificently beautiful world, his years as a child, before his father had gone off again to war, when they were a family, happy, peaceful. He wondered if a time like that could ever come again. Then a coldness swept through him, a hardness, driven by determination, and by anger at those who'd turned his world against everything it had once stood for. Darius was right about one thing…there was enormous strength in one's dark side. And sometimes that power was needed.

"Let's get it done, Captain," he said, his voice colder, harder than it had been. He ached to go back to that time so long ago, but he knew it was gone…and that there was darkness and death, a war—no, a crusade—to fight before such a time could come again. If it ever could.

"Let's get back to the Nest with that ship and our prisoners. It's time to learn how to beat these bastards. How to wipe them from the galaxy like the disease they are.

*   *   *   *   *

"I think I should recall the fleet. That ship has to be Black Eagles. I'm not sure what would be worse, the entire navy being destroyed by it…or winning the fight and bringing the wrath of the Eagles down on us." Armando DeSilva was edgy.

No, Asha Mazeri thought, he was downright scared. The man was a political mastermind, adept at manipulating polls, bartering with allies and rivals, surviving political storms like cockroaches endured nuclear devastation. But beneath it all, he was a gutless fool. He had his purposes, but he'd never serve the Black Flag for long. Perhaps she might even take his place and rule Atlantia openly, instead of from the shadows.

"You will not recall the fleet."

"I remind you, I am the President of Atlantia, Minister Mazeri, not you, and I will make such decisions."

She was amused at how pride and arrogance had the ability to momentarily drive away fear. DeSilva's passing attempt to assert his authority was…how should she put it? Cute, she might say, if the Atlantian strongman didn't annoy the hell out of her so much.

"I am only here to advise you, Mr. President." A lie, of course. "But I must advise you that my superiors are not at all patient, and they will not look kindly on anything that could be misinterpreted as cooperation with the Black Eagles."

"Cooperation?" DeSilva's voice was shrill, shocked at the suggestion.

"General Darius Cain is an Atlantian, is he not?"

"He is not!" the politician explained. Then, as she stared at him with a harsh look on her face: "Well, only by birth. I remind you he is an outlaw here, condemned in absentia and sentenced to death. If he returns here he will be apprehended and taken at once to the scaffold."

"If he returns here, Mr. President, it is likely to be at the head of his army of mercenaries. Not a terribly appealing image from your point of view, or that of your political allies. I doubt your armed forces are up to defeating the Black Eagles."

"The Black Eagles," DeSilva exclaimed. Then he stammered, "We can't…not possibly. That is why we submitted to your… organization. For your protection."

"And yet, you defy my requests. You argue with me over nonsense, to try to assert your independence, which you yielded long ago. I listen to your foolishness, Armando, and I allow a certain amount of it, but you would be well-advised to remember that your power base, the money that built your political machine, the bribes and blackmail, the force where necessary, all came from my, *organization*, as you put it. The Black Flag offers many strengths, many advantages, but it is not forgiving of insubordination. Or of failure."

She paused and then she stared at him coldly. "You would be well-advised to remember that. You would not care to find out what happens to those who fail us, much less those who allow disloyalty to color their actions."

DeSilva looked like he was about to wet himself. In fact, Mazeri wasn't entirely sure he hadn't. She'd been taught by her superiors the incredible power of well-directed fear, and she'd never been disappointed in its effectiveness. True courage was a rare thing, and most people could be easily intimidated.

"I…I…I did not…mean anything, Minister. I…ask for your understanding."

"Of course, Armando. After all, we are friends, are we not?"

She smiled, though she suspected he completely misunderstood the meaning of the gesture. "Now, listen carefully. That ship is dangerous, and it must be driven away. It was clearly here spying on us, and it cannot be allowed to remain. If the Eagles wanted to attack your fleet or planet, they would have done so already. In all likelihood, that battleship could obliterate your miserable excuse for a fleet if it came to a fight, but it will not. They will pull back at your approach, because their mission is information gathering and not an assault."

She paused, staring at the semi-confused president of Atlantia. "Now, do you want the information they take with them to be that Atlantia is craven and too cowardly to face invaders? Or that your forces responded aggressively, that your world's defenses are crack and on high alert?"

DeSilva was quiet for a moment. Then he said, scraping up every bit of courage he could muster, "You are correct, of course, Minister. The fleet will continue on its mission."

She wondered whether he'd truly understood, or if he'd just caved into her demands. Then she decided she just didn't care.

"I am pleased you agree, Mr. President." Her return to the proper form of address was her way of rewarding him, treating him as an ally rather than a petulant child. Still, even as she felt satisfaction from effectively controlling her charge, she began to wonder again how useful he truly was. Atlantia had been in the fold for more than two years, and everywhere, the secret police and other enforcement operations had clamped down hard. Those forces were full of Black Flag operatives, loyal to her, and not DeSilva." *Loyal to me as long as they fear me*, she reminded herself. Did control of Atlantia still require the use of a native politician? Or were the vestiges and the facsimile of republican government no longer needed?

Perhaps she would contact her superiors and request permission to eliminate DeSilva…and take his place. Atlantia was a pleasant place, one she'd be happy to rule.

She smiled again at DeSilva, an expression that was the image of friendship and camaraderie.

Yes, perhaps it is time…

Chapter 7

Marine Headquarters
Planet Armstrong, Gamma Pavonis III
Earthdate: 2321 AD (36 Years After the Fall)

Erik Cain stepped off the shuttle and looked out over the tarmac of Armstrong's massive landing field. The planet was a hive of activity, every manner of preparation for war underway, but Cain couldn't help but see the place as a shadow of what it had once been. The Alliance had been destroyed long ago, and along with its corrupt government was lost the revenue source that had supported the Corps. The Marines had survived, continued on, funded by what revenues they were able to produce on Armstrong, plus the support of the few worlds that saw the advantages of having a strong force ready to defend humanity. Still, they were a shadow of the massive military machine Cain had led into battle decades earlier, alongside Elias Holm and the rest of the officers with whom he'd had the honor to serve.

Cain hadn't seen Armstrong in years, yet even when he'd last been there, the decay had set in. Now, at least, many of the massive defenses were being restored, and even from the concrete of the spaceport's main field, he could see groups of recruits drilling in the open fields near the training center. Those new Marines would not be the equal of those he'd led so many years before, not for many years, at least, but there were still old veterans to strengthen the ranks. Old Marines had been returning in droves, according to the reports he'd received, and even sixty and seventy year old sergeants were still mostly fit for field duty, courtesy of the rejuv treatments they'd all received.

He turned and smiled at his companion. Sarah Linden, or Cain, depending on which world's customs were applied to the married couple, was not only his wife, she'd been his soulmate for half a century. They'd been through hell and back, separately and together, and she'd endured the fifteen years of his captivity, thinking he was dead. Now, he knew she was trying to deal with the fact that she'd allowed herself to give up on him, when all the while he'd been alive and a prisoner. And enduring a hell she could barely imagine.

She couldn't imagine it. No one could. Cain had done all he could to hide the worst of what he'd gone through from his wife, from everyone. But Sarah had rebuilt his ravaged body, every bit of it, and however much he'd withheld the pain he'd been through, he was pretty sure she had a good idea of it.

"So, is it like you remember it?" she asked softly. Sarah had been back to Armstrong in the years since he'd vanished. She'd even moved there after the boys were out of the house. He understood. He didn't think he could have endured the house they'd built together without her either.

Armstrong had been the Marines headquarters for almost fifty years, ever since the Corps had sided with the Alliance's colonies in their struggle against the central government. The entire mess had been resolved, more or less, after considerable fighting. The colonies had secured a limited level of home rule, subject to certain obligations to the Alliance, and the Corps had decided it could no longer maintain its headquarters on Earth. Armstrong had been sparsely populated then, and almost entirely undeveloped, but the Marines had built it into a prosperous world, one that had managed to endure the decline of the Corps after the Fall, at least to an extent.

"It's familiar…and different too." He turned his head, looking around. He saw the buildings he remembered, and a few he didn't. And in the shadows, he saw something else. Ghosts. The men and women he'd served with, the ones who'd died at his side, fighting with him or under his command. He was happy to be on a world he'd considered one of his homes, but the looming war brought back memories he'd have gladly left forgotten. He was deeply, truly sick of war, and he longed desperately for the one thing he knew he couldn't have, that he wondered if he could ever attain…peace.

"We had to make a lot of changes, repurpose some of the factories to produce goods we could sell. We didn't have as many Marines to take care of anymore, anyway, and we needed the revenue. It wasn't easy, but we managed to do enough to keep the Corps alive."

"You did an amazing job. Amazing. I'm so sorry I wasn't here for you. Here to help you. To be with you."

"You've always been with me, Erik. Every moment, wherever you were. Nothing can separate us. Haven't you learned that by now?"

He turned and smiled, but before he could answer, another voice rang through the clear morning.

"Erik Cain, welcome to Armstrong." Cate Gilson walked over to Cain and gave him an enthusiastic hug. "Salutes be damned, old friend. Welcome home."

"Thank you, Cate. It's good to be back." And it was, at least in many ways. It was bittersweet too, but that kind of thinking led down a path he didn't have the time or energy to explore now. "It's good to see you again too." He'd had his first reunion with Gilson back on Titan, when the major players who would stand against the Black Flag had gathered to plot strategy. That meeting had been productive, at least as much as it could be for an outnumbered and outmatched group of worlds struggling to face an enemy they didn't understand, but it had also been a reunion of sorts, the chance for Cain to see the small group of people who were truly important to him. He was still infirmed then, confined to a powered chair, but the camaraderie of that gathering had restored a part of the strength he had lost. He wasn't sure he could be again what he had before, the tireless Marine general, struggling against any enemy, any odds. But he was ready to try.

"Come, both of you." Gilson slid over and hugged Sarah too. "I have everything ready for you. Your apartments were too small, Sarah, so I moved you back to your old quarters. I know you didn't want to be there when..." She paused, a look of pain passing over her face. "Well, you're both back again, so I thought you should have your old rooms." She paused and then, clearly trying to pull away from the darker memories she'd touched on, she added, "But don't worry...I've had them updated and redecorated. You'll feel like you're in a palace."

"Thank you, Cate. I appreciate that. But you've seen some of the billets I've drawn over the years." His eyes fixed on Gilson, and he noticed the same thing he had on Titan. She had aged, more even than he'd have expected in the seventeen years he was gone. It was the stress, he knew, the pressure of being one of the last of the old guard, fighting the endless battle to keep the Corps alive in a universe that only appreciated it when an enemy threatened. He knew he'd endured the most, his seemingly endless years of torture and captivity beyond his ability to even describe. But Sarah and Cate and the others had all suffered in their own ways. He promised himself he would remember, that he would not allow himself to feel sorry for sufferings, for what he'd been through.

"Let's go, we'll get both of you settled in, and later we can have dinner and a long talk. I know there's work to do, and hours before we sleep, so to speak, but I think we can spare one evening, don't you? One night to catch up, maybe tell a few war stories from the past?"

Cain smiled, and then he flashed a glance to Sarah. "I think we'd both enjoy that, Cate. I think we'd enjoy it a lot."

* * * * *

"We've recalled everyone we could reach, Erik. Almost ninety percent of those who were...free...agreed to return to active duty, though we had no legal hold on them to compel them to, as we would have had back in Alliance days."

Cain looked across the table at Gilson. Their working lunch was nothing but a few sandwiches and the like, but after fifteen years of eating swill that would give a goat's stomach flops—and often nothing at all—Cain still hadn't quite shaken the wondrous effect real food had on him. He remembered years of working meals, when the subject at hand had so distracted him he forgot to eat so much as a bite, but now he just wondered what the hell had been wrong with him, and he grabbed another sandwich.

"Ninety percent is extraordinary, Cate," Cain said, his mouth still a bit full. "It was never a legal mandate that brought our people back. You always knew that, as did I, and here is the proof." His mind was still on one part of what she'd said. "What did you mean by 'free?'"

"Well, our people live on dozens of worlds, almost all of them different nations now, and with the planets of Occupied Space in a panic about the Black Flag, many have drafted citizens to bolster their defenses. Of course, many of them sought out any veterans they had among their populations, and Marines retirees are always at the top of lists like that." She paused. "Then, of course, there's your son." She hesitated again for a few seconds. "Did you realize how many of Darius's senior officers and commanders are veterans of the Corps?"

"No," Cain said, sounding thoughtful. "I can't say I really did. I met a few familiar faces while I was there…and, of course, he's got Tom Sparks heading up his R&D." The scientist, formerly a Marine, now a Black Eagle was the smartest son of a bitch Cain had ever met. Perhaps no man had contributed more toward the Corps victories and survival than the man who'd put leading edge weapons in their hands. And, certainly, no one had gleaned more from the wreckage of First Imperium tech than Sparks.

"He's got at least seven hundred of our people…our former people, I guess…and maybe more. That's only what I could glean from the limited access I have to his records. Darius is pretty tight-lipped about things."

That was putting it mildly, he knew. Darius was cold, secretive, untrusting…all his own hard and difficult traits, in a stronger, concentrated form. It had made his son a deadly warrior, perhaps the deadliest that ever lived, but it had also condemned him to a sort of isolation and loneliness, even surrounded by his fanatically loyal army.

"Did you try to recruit any of them?" Cain was edgy. He wasn't sure how Darius would react to something like that, but he had an idea it wouldn't be good."

"No, of course not. The Black Eagles are an ally." A pause. "But I can't say I didn't make sure the word got out. Recruiting is one thing, accepting volunteers is another."

"And so, did you get many volunteers?" Cain's edginess was still there. He wasn't too sure Darius would differentiate between such efforts.

"Not one. Granted, many may not have heard that we were calling back all the old veterans, but some *must* have. And yet not a single one left the Eagles to return."

Cain understood the angst in Gilson's voice. The Marines had come to expect almost unlimited loyalty and dedication in their people. And, in fairness, those former Marines who were now Eagles knew they were on the same side. They weren't choosing to fight against the Corps, or even stand aside as the Marines fought…and certainly most of them felt they could serve the war effort more effectively in their current positions. But still, none?

"Darius has an effect on his people, Cate."

"Like you always did."

Cain felt a wave of embarrassment. "Marines follow their leaders."

"Yes, they do. But it was always something different with you, Erik. They respected me, obeyed me, followed me…but they loved you. For as long as I can remember." A short break. "Elias always knew it too. He told me that's what made you such a natural leader. He won the admiration of his soldiers, and over years that turned to a sort of admiration, even love. But with you it was almost natural. You had that bond with the Marines in the field, Erik. You always did."

Cain didn't answer right away. Such talk always made him

uncomfortable, and he tended to shy away from it. He knew his Marines had followed him loyally year after year, but he couldn't understand how they could love him, how they could do anything but secretly hate him. How many had he gotten killed? How many died, lying in the mud as their life's blood spilled out, cursing his name? That was always the image in his head, though he knew, on some level, it wasn't the truth.

"Well, let's hope I still have whatever is left of that, because we're going to need to get everything we can coax from these Marines. There aren't our old veterans, not for the most part, and I wouldn't count on having the advantage against our enemies, not in training nor in technology…and certainly not in numbers." Cain took a deep breath. There was little to be gained by expanding on his deepest concerns, not when there was nothing to be done about any of it.

"Well," Gilson said, her voice deeper even than it had been years before, and scratchy now too, "if we can't have any of those things, we'll have to rely on what has always carried the Corps to victory. We'll have to rely on the spirit of the Marines. They will do what must be done, Erik, as they always have."

Cain stared back across the table, holding back a thousand memories. Then he said, simply, "As they always have."

Chapter 8

"The Nest" – Black Eagles Base
Second Moon of Eos, Eta Cassiopeiae VII
Earthdate: 2321 AD (36 Years After the Fall)

"Well done, Captain Grayson, well done. All of you…magnificent job." Darius Cain stood on the deck of the Nest's landing bay, his eyes darting past *Eagle Fourteen's* commander and a cluster of his officers for an instant, as a column of soldiers led the three Black Flag prisoners from *Eagle Fourteen's* shuttle. "On the prisoners, and on capturing a Black Flag ship. You achieved vastly more than I dared to hope for. This intelligence will be of immense value. You and your people have covered yourselves in glory. Go, return to your quarters, get some rest. We can wait until tomorrow for serious debriefing."

"Thank you, General. I am pleased we were able to complete the mission successfully." The officer stepped back and snapped off a perfect salute before turning and walking off the deck, just as Darius had told him to do.

Elias watched as his brother commended his subordinate, the way the grizzled old veteran responded, almost worshipful toward his commander. Darius had something, there was no arguing that. He'd never seen anyone have such an influence over such hard men and women. This was no politician manipulating half-attentive masses. The Eagles, especially the senior officers, were strong, capable. Yet they withered in Darius's presence, as if the slightest praise from him was the greatest reward possible, and the merest word of reproach would hit them harder than a hyper-velocity autocannon.

"Great job, Elias," Darius said as he watched Grayson and his people step out of the bay. "I mean it," he added a few seconds later. "We've had our…differences, I know, but we're both Cains. We should never let ourselves forget that." Darius paused again, then, with just the slightest hint of recognizable emotion he said, "I am glad to have my brother back."

Elias was surprised, not that Darius felt that way, but that he'd actually managed to say it. The two of them had been at odds their entire adult lives, and if there was one thing Elias knew about his twin, it was that Darius Cain did not let sentimentality take control. Not often, at least.

"I feel the same way, Darius. And thank you. I'm also glad we were able to succeed. I wish we'd managed to get more information on Atlantia itself, but it seems pretty clear they're in the tank for the Black Flag. Elias was somber. It hurt him that his homeworld had fallen into darkness, that he was an enemy to his own people, or at least to the government that ruled them. He suspected Darius felt the same, somewhere deep—very deep—down, but he doubted his brother would ever admit the slightest concern for the world that had considered him an outlaw for almost fifteen years now.

"Intelligence on Atlantia beyond what you already gathered would be of little value. However, the prisoners, and the ship… they are potentially of great worth."

"You think the captives know something about Vali?" Elias and his allies knew the name of the enemy's homeworld, but little else, save that it was hidden, and that it was the greatest fortress and industrial powerhouse that ever existed, one no doubt built by slave labor, much of it taken from the ruined Earth.

"I hope so. One thing is certain. I will find out what they know."

Elias suppressed a shiver at his brother's tone. He knew they needed to get any knowledge that the prisoners had, but the casual coldness in Darius's voice when he discussed an inter-rogation process Elias could only imagine was...complete...was unsettling.

"We will tear that ship apart too. I'm sure they did everything they could to hide any useful data, but just maybe you managed to disable any systems that would have erased what we need. Clearly, they rely on a self-destruct doctrine, very likely enforced by ships' AIs or heavy conditioning. Perhaps the failure of this ship to destroy itself will have left some clues, something we can use to track down this shadowy enemy world."

"Perhaps," Elias responded. "What do we do if we are able to find it, Darius?" Elias knew there would be millions of slaves on Vali, men and women who'd been kidnapped from Earth, from raids on other worlds and ships captured in the depths of space. People who had families, loved ones. He thought of the pain he'd felt at his father's disappearance, and at the joy when Erik Cain had returned to his family. How many others were still in despair, still longing for the return of those they'd missed for so long. He wondered how they could rescue those people, get them off the enemy fortress world and return them to their homes. But he knew what Darius was going to say, before his brother's mouth even moved. And it troubled him.

"We're going to destroy it, Elias. We're going to blast these bastards with so many gigatons it will make what happened on Earth during the Fall look like a fireworks display."

*   *   *   *   *

"I think I'm going to tell you what I did to the Tyrant of Eldaron...again. He didn't put up that much of a fight, but then after the whole battle, I needed some leisure too, so I went a little...farther...than I probably had to." Darius Cain stood next to the captive, his face a haggard scowl. The Black Flag's con-ditioning was impressive. Whatever these pirates knew, and he realized that could be little or nothing, he hadn't been able to get a word out of them despite—spirited—interrogation.

No response at all. It was eerie, and it gave him pause, con-cerns about what his people were about to fight. It had been years since Darius Cain had met anyone in Occupied Space he couldn't scare. Not just scare, but downright terrify. The stories about him were mostly exaggerations, or outright falsehoods, some even started or encouraged by him. It had all been very useful, the horror that descended on his target worlds as his forces arrived. Any enemy you could intimidate into submission was one you didn't have to kill...and one who didn't get a chance to kill you. But the shadow of the infamous Darius Cain meant nothing to these pirates, and despite all the fear he'd tried to instill, not to mention a fair amount of physical discomfort, they had refused to answer a single question or provide so much as a first name.

Darius stared at the man, feeling the frustration building. He knew his reputation, he was well aware that millions in Occupied Space imagined he wouldn't hesitate to inflict the most diabolical torture on his enemies. Indeed, he had done just that to the defeated Tyrant, but there had been a rage there like none he'd ever felt before, an inferno kindled by his first sight of his father's tormented form in the dank, hideous cell where he'd lived for fifteen years of hell. Nothing could have kept him back from the man responsible for that nightmare, and no morality, no restraint, could have mattered an iota in how that story had ended. But generally, Darius had no love of causing pain, and only cultivated fear for the utility of it, not some sick enjoyment of the dread he caused in others.

There was a difference, however, between him and most others. He *would* do what he had to do, even if he didn't want to, even if it sickened him. The stakes here were no less than the freedom, even the very survival of humanity. There was *nothing* he wouldn't do to an enemy to prevent that ultimate disaster.

He would have tortured the pirate mercilessly if that had been necessary, but he suspected no amount of pain could overcome the enemy's conditioning...and the Black Flag apparently had no less ability to weaponize fear than he did. No, the answer here would come from a doctor's syringe, perhaps even surgery. He would have to resort to the tools the enemy had employed to make their warriors unbreakable.

We'll see if they're really unbreakable...

He reached over to the comm unit. "Send Doctor Hind down to the detention area. Now. I need his assistance with a prisoner."

"Yes, General Cain. At once."

Darius stood and stared at the prisoner for a few minutes. The man was still silent, utterly so. He just sat still, staring at the far wall, without so much as the slightest hint of fear on his face. Darius was impressed. He'd seen conditioning, and he'd heard of what Gavin Stark had done with his Shadow Legions, before he'd even been born, but this had to be the most effective job he'd ever seen.

The door slid open, and Hind dashed through with two of his assistants right behind him. "General…" He snapped off a crisp salute, followed almost at once by the two junior officers standing behind him."

"Doctor," Darius responded, returning the salute. "I need your help. I can't seem to break this prisoner's conditioning. I want you to do a thorough scan and examination. We must know what he knows…millions of lives depend on it, and I'm looking to you to find a way to get past the block."

"I'll do everything I can, sir." Hind didn't sound enormously hopeful, but he didn't suggest he couldn't do it either. 'Couldn't do it' wasn't really in the Eagles' vocabulary.

"Thank you, Doctor."

"With your permission, I'd like to move him to the infirmary. The brainscanner is there, and I'll have an easier time working my way through the whole thing." A pause. "I'll finish a lot faster."

"Very well, Doctor, but I want two guards there at all times, around the clock." He turned toward one of the Eagles standing against the far wall. "Sergeant, you take one soldier with you and escort Doctor Hind's team and the prisoner to the infirmary. You will remain there until relieved. Under no circumstances will you leave the prisoner unguarded. Understood?"

"Yes, sir!"

Cain stood and watched as Hind's people brought in a power chair and eased the prisoner onto it. The sergeant was standing less than a meter away, rifle in hand, looking for all the world as though he was determined to show Darius how seriously he took the general's charge.

A few seconds later, the door slid open. "Darius...General..." Erik Teller walked through. The Eagles' second in command had clearly thought Darius was alone. He almost never greeted his friend informally in front of other Eagles.

"What is it, Erik?" Cain could hear the urgency in Teller's tone.

"It's Dr. Sparks, General. He's completed some analysis on the enemy ship. He's found...well, I think you should come and see. Right now."

Darius felt a wave of excitement, and he gestured for Teller to move toward the door. The two men walked out in the corridor. "Has he found a link to the enemy's headquarters?"

"No, General, at least not conclusively, but there is something else."

Darius almost pressed harder, but he could tell his oldest friend wanted Sparks to explain. The Eagles' chief scientist was as brilliant a man as he'd ever known. Sparks served him now, as he had Darius's father and the Marines years before. *Though his pay has gone up about fifty-fold.* Sparks had carried a brigadier's rank in the Corps, but the Eagles had only ever had one general, so Sparks was called simply, 'Doctor.'

Teller led Darius into the lift and down to one of the landing bays. As soon as they stepped out of the car, Darius saw Sparks standing there. He knew the researcher was north of ninety years old, but just as his own parents had, Sparks had received the old rejuv treatments most of his adult life. He had wiry gray hair, perhaps just a touch of the mad scientist look to him, but otherwise he resembled a healthy man in his mid-late fifties.

"General, thank you for coming right down. I have far from completed my studies on the Black Flag vessel, but I have made a determination I felt you should hear at once, one I did not wish to trust to normal transmissions."

That last bit made Darius tense up as much as any of the rest of it. The Nest had the most sophisticated AI and communications systems in Occupied Space. If Sparks was worrying about someone intercepting their transmissions, that could only mean trouble.

"Well, Doctor, we're all here—and Colonel Teller here seemed to feel I should hear this from you—so, let's have it."

"As I said, sir, I began the analysis of the Black Flag vessel. I could tell immediately that their technology was a match for ours…at least."

Darius didn't like the 'at least' part.

"But it was only after I was able to partially disassemble several main systems that I realize what I was looking at."

"And what was that, Doctor?"

"The First Imperium."

Darius felt his stomach tighten. Despite the widespread belief that he never felt fear, that was utter nonsense. "Are you certain?" The last First Imperium encounter had taken place when Darius was still a teenager, but he knew enough about the strange robotic forces to understand the magnitude of what he was hearing.

"Yes, there is no question. Portions of the technology are unmistakable."

Darius shook his head. "I've never heard of First Imperium forces using human recruits, or seeking to subjugate rather than exterminate. If we are facing the First Imperium, something very different is happening than what occurred before."

"I don't believe we are facing the actual First Imperium, General. I am saying that First Imperium technology has been adapted by whatever force we are up against. Much as we have done over the years, as we have deciphered their science bit by bit."

Darius stated back at Sparks. "So, Doctor, who exactly do you think we're dealing with?"

"I can't say, General, not yet at least. But I can tell you it is someone more familiar with First Imperium technology than we are…and that very likely means if these small raiders are as technologically capable as they seem, when we are confronted with true warships, we will very likely be facing vessels more advanced and capable than our own."

Darius stood in the bay, silent, thinking about what he'd just heard. He had understood what Sparks said immediately, but the implications took a few seconds to fully form in his thoughts. When they did, a single word summed it up.

Shit.

Chapter 9

"It is time, Den. At last." The relief in Asha Mazeri's voice was profound. She'd spent close to three years following the officious DeSilva around, aiding him in his clumsy power grab, and deploying the bribes, blackmail, and threats that kept him secure as the effective dictator of Atlantia. All the while, the damned fool thought he'd achieved it all himself, that the Black Flag had only provided basic support.

DeSilva did have some talents, of the sort possessed by a reasonably competent corrupt machine politician. His skills were ideal for emptying the graveyards into the polls or losing entire ballot machines full of the opposition's votes, and indeed, he had managed to secure his own election without any significant assistance, save perhaps financial support. But it was one thing to be a political boss, and an elected president, and quite another to secure the absolute, unchallenged rule of a planet. Armando DeSilva was exactly that now, and for two years, Mazeri had seen to it that every shred of opposition, every hint of dissent, had been ruthlessly swept away. DeSilva thought of himself as a hard man, but he'd never have had the stomach to do what she had, and even now, two years into his brutal rule, she'd never told him all the things she had done in his name.

Now, finally, she could dispense with the charade. She had no further need of DeSilva's name, nor the vestiges of his political organization. The freighters bringing in trade goods from other Black Flag worlds had carried a secret shipment…soldiers. Now she had enough forces to take open control of Atlantia, and to put herself in DeSilva's place.

"What are your orders, Your Excellency?" Den Tarlton was Mazeri's second-in-command. For two years he had posed as her aide, almost as a secretary of sort. She imagined that had been galling to him, and she was virtually certain that just as she had imagined removing DeSilva and becoming Atlantia's ruler, so he had harbored visions of one day overthrowing her. It was the way of the Black Flag, and she herself had supplanted no less than three superiors to get where she was now. She understood Tarlton's ambitions, and she didn't fault him for them, not really. But she would make sure that when the time came, it was he who ended up face down in a ditch somewhere, and not her.

"It is time for President DeSilva to pass into the annals of history." A pause. "See to it yourself, Den. Take as much force as you need. I want no slipups." Mazeri knew just how the Black Flag viewed failure.

"Yes, Your Excellency." Tarlton was jumping the gun on her title—technically, she was still just Minister Mazeri—but she didn't mind her aide's pandering. She rather liked the sound of 'Your Excellency,' and she was happy to give it a go a few hours ahead of schedule.

"All of DeSilva's cabinet members must also be killed, and their assistants. I have personnel ready to assume the positions. And see that our secret troops are deployed to all vital locations." Mazeri had spent three years replacing army commanders with those loyal to her, deploying the bribery and blackmail she'd used to secure DeSilva's position to undermine the president now. But she wasn't ready to trust Atlantian units, not with something this important.

"They will all be eliminated, Your Excellency. I can assure you of that."

Mazeri nodded. "Go then, Den, and come back here when it is done." Mazeri always suspected betrayal, but she wasn't overly concerned here. Tarlton would absolutely betray her if he got the chance, she was sure enough of that. But her aide's route to power required her to seize it first. Tarlton simply wasn't tied in enough to the Black Flag forces on the planet and the native ministers supporting her. It was a safety net of sorts, one for which she was grateful, but also one she knew wouldn't last.

She watched as Tarlton left the room, and then she sat down and let out a deep breath. All her life she'd longed for the kind of power that now lay at her fingertips. She was anxious, excited… and a little scared. She looked over at the comm unit on her desk, the one that connected her with her offworld contact. She was tense too, wondering what orders would follow the authorization to launch her coup. It was easy for her to focus on Atlantia, but she knew the Black Flag had far larger goals…and she didn't have the slightest doubt that she, and the world she would rule in a matter of hours, would be expected to do their part.

*   *   *   *   *

"It has begun. The fleets are en route, and even now, the preliminary phase has begun. On fifty planets, worlds that have submitted to our rule are being brought directly into the fold. The craven politicians who yielded to us are being removed—permanently—and replaced by our own designees. Further analysis has only confirmed our decision. The original natives served their purposes, and their greed and fear allowed us to gain control of much of Occupied Space with the use of minimal resources. But now it is time to ready these worlds for what will be expected of them. Their leadership must be secure, and utterly loyal. And their people will have to truly accept their new reality, the obligations expected of them by their new rulers." Two's thoughts were intense, a power behind him that once might have felt like enthusiasm.

"The assassinations should also be underway as we speak," One added. "Our operatives on forty independent planets have confirmed they are in position. They will strike at the appointed time. In a matter of hours, worlds all across Occupied Space outside our control will lose their leadership. The resulting chaos will limit the ability of allied planets to dispatch aid to the systems targeted for attack. We project an approximate sixty percent success rate, or roughly twenty-five systems that will be effectively decapitated just before the assault forces reach their destinations."

"Our plans seem well-founded, yet…"

"What doubts do you harbor, Three? Share them."

"I have no doubts, nothing so dire. However, I am concerned about the reserve levels we have held back at Draconia Terminii. We have left ourselves little flexibility to react if our attacks are…unsuccessful in any way." Three paused, a rarity for the clones since they'd been uploaded into the Intelligence. "Perhaps we should also have kept more forces to defend the home system. If the enemy is able to locate Draconia Terminii…"

"We reviewed such concerns at great length, Three, when we decided to draw from the home fleets to reinforce the strike forces. Our plan has been analyzed in great detail, and the likelihood of failure is infinitesimal."

"I must agree with One," Two said. "Our conditioning is far in advance of anything our enemies possess, and it is extraordinarily unlikely they will be able to break any captives, even if they are able to catch them. All data we have gathered to date suggests our suicide compulsion has prevented any of our vessels or personnel from falling into enemy hands. Further, even if the enemy was able to locate Vali's system, a supposition of extreme unlikelihood, it is highly doubtful they would launch an attack with so many of our fleets still at large in Occupied Space. It is not their way. We have studied the campaigns of the Marines and Admiral Garret's navy, and the militaries of many of the free worlds. They will not devote massive resources to seeking out and attacking our main base—a planet they cannot even know exists for certain—while their worlds are still in danger. Indeed, even if we are driven from the primary target, we can redeploy our forces to threaten other planets, and inflict massive civilian casualties to divert their attention while our subjugated worlds bring their own forces online to support our fleets."

There was a pause of sorts, an absence of thoughts. Finally, Three radiated a comment. "Your logic is flawless, I do not challenge that. But I do have one question…one I believe we need to consider with greater care. Admiral Garret will not abandon worlds under threat to seek out and attack an enemy. Neither will the Marines. These conclusions seem reasonable when reviewing the history of the parties in question. But I ask this, and seek your deepest review. Can we be sure that Darius Cain would not come here? That he would not leave worlds to endure bombardment, vast populations to face nuclear devastation, all to seek out and destroy an enemy and end the war?"

* * * * *

Jarrod Tyler walked across the field, toward the rows of barracks neatly arrayed down several perfectly straight avenues. His army had never been stronger, the forces mobilized for the defense of Columbia larger and better equipped than they had been for any past war. It was the reason he'd seized power, the purpose for his enduring the hated job of head of state for so long. He'd known war would come again to his cursed world, and he'd be damned if he would allow his people to get caught unprepared yet again.

He would endure anything to protect Columbia, even the realization that his beloved wife would have despised all he had done. Lucia had been that rarest of creatures, a true idealist, one who had actually believed in people. Tyler had been far less cynical himself once, but he was no fool, and if life was set on teaching him harsh lessons, he had resolved he would learn from them.

Columbia's entire society was geared for military action, its armed forces far vaster now than anything the planet could have supported without the influx of funding from the Black Eagles. Tyler knew Darius Cain had overpaid for the title to a frozen moon, a barren rock, useless save for the vast base the Eagles had built there. That was a value in itself, perhaps, the security of permanent ownership. The cost of relocating would have been billions of credits, perhaps even trillions.

As though I could have done anything to evict the Eagles, even if I'd wanted to.

Which he most certainly didn't. He'd always considered having the mercenaries in Columbia's system a safeguard, one that had to at least give pause to anyone who might try to invade his planet. He'd been forced to trust Darius, of course, and such things came hard to him these days. But the blunt nature of the mercenary, the clear feeling that if he'd been harboring ill will, he'd have just unleashed his trained killers and been done with it, somehow bolstered Tyler's comfort. The two men shared much with each other in terms of their grim outlooks and, as much as any man outside the inner circle of the Black Eagles could claim, he believed he and Darius had become friends.

He was almost up to the first row of barracks. A surprise inspection on a bunch of new recruits seemed below the pay-grade of a planet's dictator, but Tyler had been a soldier long before he'd seized power, and his had many old school ideas on how to turn inductees into soldiers.

There was something going on up ahead, some kind of dispute. He felt a wave of annoyance. He didn't like disorganization in his camp, and he swore to himself if any of his non-coms were setting a bad example for the recruits…

He moved forward abruptly, heading toward the figures ahead, startling his guards as he did. He'd taken three steps, perhaps four, before they reacted and hurried to catch up. Only an instant, but enough. They were too late.

The group that had been arguing split apart, one of the men pulling out a pistol and shooting two of the others. The final one had turned toward Tyler.

The general saw the move, and he reacted almost immediately. But 'almost' wasn't enough. He felt the first bullet hit him, even as his body was swinging hard to the side. Then the second.

He could hear the gunfire now, his guards he realized, and

he caught an image of the assassin falling back, his body riddled with bullets. He tried to stay on his feet, but then he realized he was dropping, and an instant later, he felt the hard coldness of the ground as he slammed into it.

He could hear sirens, alarms, shouts all around him. But even as he listened, he felt the darkness closing around him. All the while, a single thought went through his head.

You damned fool...

Chapter 10

"I'll take over for you, Rolf." Ana Bazarov tapped the communications officer on the shoulder. "It's my shift."

Rolf Anders looked up at Bazarov, and he slid abruptly out of his seat. He was a Black Eagles captain, an officer authorized to stand watch in the Nest's main control center, and Bazarov was a senior cadet, still undergoing training, and wrapping up her duty rotations before graduation. Before she would become a full-fledged Black Eagle.

Bazarov was more than that, of course. She was the mistress of the Black Eagles' commanding general, if that was the right term. She had no more use of labels than Darius did, but she knew if the two of them had been other people, in some other place, words like girlfriend and dating would have applied. Such designations seemed absurd and out of place in the Nest, of course, and unnecessary as well. She couldn't have imagined the course her life had taken, but she was happy. Happier than she'd ever been.

She slid into the comm station, watching as Anders stepped away, giving her far more respect than he would have accorded another trainee. She detested that sort of behavior, but she wasn't a fool, and she understood it. Such things came with the territory of being Darius's lover, especially his exclusive companion, which she had been for two years now, and she'd long ago decided she'd put up with it if she had to.

What she'd been unwilling to do, to continue doing at least, was to remain a pampered and sheltered doll. It had taken some convincing, but she'd demanded to be given a real job on the Nest, one that involved duties outside the bedchamber. She'd sleep with him because she cared for him, she had said finally, but from that moment on, she would earn her keep as a member of the Eagles, or by God, she would pack up and leave. It had been a bluff, of course, but one she'd delivered well. She didn't fool herself that Darius had been taken in by it, of course. Bluffs had a poor history as a tool use against the Eagles' commander, but her spirit had impressed him. He'd refused combat training outright, and they'd had something like a fight that evening, but in the end, they'd come to an agreement. She would complete the training program for Nest operations, jumping through the same hoops any trainee would, without so much as the slightest slack for being the general's lover. And she had done just that. The fitness sections of the program had been brutal—even non-combat Eagles were ready to fight if the need arose—but she'd gotten through. She wasn't entirely sure she'd had one hundred percent of the full treatment thrown at her, but what she'd experienced, and the aches and pains and sore muscles that had accompanied it all, had been enough to preserve her pride.

She reached out, moving her hands across the display. Nest operations entailed dozens of fields of study, but she'd taken a liking to communications almost immediately. The shifts in the control center were the last stages of her training. She'd done eight already, and she only had one after this…and then she'd get her insignia, and she'd be a real Black Eagle. She tried to remember how terrified she'd been on Karelia, and how she'd lashed out at Darius when he tried to help her. She'd come a long way since then, and the moment she'd thought the darkest in her life had led her to her true home.

Something caught her eye, a flashing light. *Don't daydream and screw up on your second to last rotation*, she thought, mildly scolding herself. Then her stomach tightened.

She spun around. "Major Cranston," she said, her voice a bit shrill she turned to face the officer in charge of the Nest's nerve center.

"Yes, Cadet?" he answered, using the correct form of address, but doing it with a touch more respect that she suspected he usually did with trainees.

"We're getting a transmission from the warp gate notification scanners, sir." *Damn*, she scolded herself. Reports should include complete information…how many times had she been told that? "From the Beta-Omicron gate, Major," she completed the report, before Cranston could dress her down for lack of information.

"Send the readings to my screen, Cadet." Cranston didn't sound particularly worried. The Eagles weren't expecting anything through the gate, but Columbia always had freight traffic moving in and out, and…

"Red alert," the officer said, an instant after glancing at the screen, his tone vastly more serious than it had been a few seconds before.

She turned back, trying to see what Cranston had noticed so quickly in the sketchy transmission that she hadn't. Then, after hesitating for just a second, she hit the alarm switch. The Nest's control center was bathed in glowing red light, and the klaxons on the wall blared loudly. She had a good idea—some from training and some from Darius—of what was happening now throughout the massive fortress. Weapons systems were activating, armored doors were sliding shut, protecting vital areas, the crews of the Eagles' giant ships were responding to the battlestations calls.

Her eyes darted down to the screen again, and then she saw it. The energy output, the mass readings. That was no freighter. That was a warship, a big one. And then, as if on cue, another three dots popped on the screen, and then more. A dozen… twenty.

This wasn't a raid, nor some lost ship. This was a full-scale attack.

* * * * *

"Launch another spread of probes, Lieutenant. A double cluster this time. I want detailed analysis on those ships, and I want it before they enter firing range." *Whatever the hell their firing range is...*

"Yes, Captain Grayson." A few seconds later, an almost astonishingly short time to have executed the command, but still one that didn't quite satisfy Grayson, the tactical officer added, "Probes launched, sir."

Grayson stared out at the main display, his eyes darting from the cloud of contacts moving in from the warp gate to the line of fourteen blue circles, the battlefleet of the Black Eagles, minus the two ships Darius had sent to shadow his parent's trip to Armstrong to make sure they got there. Grayson couldn't imagine what it felt like for the general to know his father was alive and being tortured for fifteen years, but if he knew Darius Cain at all, the Eagle commander would never let his guard down again, not as far as his parents' travels through space were concerned.

The Eagles' ships were the strongest things in space, at least they had been. A number of the approaching vessels were just as large, and if the rumors flying around were true, those ships had First Imperium technology in them. The Eagles' vessels did, too, so it very well might come down to who had learned more and implemented it, Thomas Sparks and his Eagle engineering teams, or the mysterious enemy that now seemed ready to commence open war.

"Captain, I have Commodore Allegre for you."

"On my line." Grayson had been expecting the communique. Allegre was the Eagles' naval commander, another refugee from the service of Earth's destroyed superpowers, though, unlike most of the old veterans who'd found their way to the Eagles, he wasn't a former Alliance or Caliphate warrior. Gaston Allegre had served the navy of Europa Federalis, a service with a spotty and uncertain battle record. But Allegre himself had been well-regarded by officers of the other services, friend and foe alike, and he'd proven himself to Darius Cain from the day he'd taken command of the first Eagle vessel, a rickety old destroyer that traced its service all the way back to the Second Frontier War.

"Captain, *Eagle Fourteen* will take position on the right flank of our line. Once everyone is in position, we're going to accelerate at 5g to point Alpha…" The range points had long been a part of the Eagles' defense setup, marked by a series of carefully located buoys. For a warrior who fought most of his battles on his enemies' home ground, Darius Cain had spared no thought or expense to secure his home base. His people had conducted hundreds of drills, and Allegre was simply activating the predetermined response for an attack of this size.

"Yes, Commodore."

"We're going to flush our external racks and launch three follow up volleys, and then we're going to pull back within the Nest's protective umbrella before their missiles can close."

That all made sense to Grayson. The Nest was massively armed, and its array of antimissile and antifighter batteries was nothing short of astonishing.

"Yes, Commodore. *Eagle Fourteen* will be ready."

"I know you will, Captain. Allegre out."

Grayson glanced down at the now silent comm unit. He could only imagine how much Allegre had to do right now. The Eagles, for all their many victorious ground engagements, had never fought a really major space battle before, at least not a full-blown fleet action. They'd blasted the weak squadrons of their objective planets from just outside orbit, and a few of their awesome battleships had engaged enemy ships in what could best be described as 'slightly less than instantaneous blowouts.'

This is going to be a real fight…

His eyes were fixed on the screen. The enemy ships were still coming through the warp gate, even as their lead elements accelerated in-system.

"Lieutenant, I want all weapons stations to run full checks. The team that isn't ready when the order comes is going to wish the enemy had blasted them to plasma."

"Yes, sir." Then: "Captain, we're getting the advance signal."

"Commence acceleration, Lieutenant. Five gees thrust… now."

*   *   *   *   *

"Get the ground forces loaded up, Colonel. The garrison forces can man the Nest, and these people aren't here to try to force a landing and fight on the frozen dust of Eos's moon, I'm willing to bet that much. We don't need anybody getting hit on the ground."

"Yes, sir." Teller turned and snapped out a series of orders himself. The Nest's control center was a beehive of activity, nearly three times as many officers and technicians on duty as had been there before, still including Ana Bazarov. Darius had told her to stand down, to get to the underground shelter, along with her sister and the other non-combat personnel. But she'd done the unthinkable, the one thing more likely to land her in the Eagles' history than any martial feat imaginable. She'd refused Darius's command.

"I'm at my position, sir," she had said firmly. Darius almost argued, but then he did something even less precedented in the history of his illustrious little army. He let it go.

He had strong feelings for Ana, and he'd wanted her as safe as he could make her. But he knew she'd been right to take the stand she had, and he remembered the day they had met, her standing there, wounded and half naked, about to be assaulted by a band of drunk, Raschiddan soldiers. He'd saved her, from a terrible ordeal at least, and probably her life too…and she'd turned, staring up at her savior with hatred in her eyes, cursing him out for invading her world. Something in that instant had struck him. She was beautiful, and he enjoyed her company, but he knew it was her strength—her brave defiance—that had truly captured his attention, and ultimately his affection.

"All six regiments are boarding, sir. It's going to take some time to get all the transports loaded up." Translation: We're never going to get the ground troops out of here before the Nest gets engaged.

"Very well, Colonel. All transports able to load up and depart are to head toward Columbia." Darius didn't have a doubt Jarrod Tyler would be pleased to house more than ten thousand of his veteran warriors. The battle for the Nest would be a space engagement, won or lost in the cold depths. Any boarding action would be a final stage, and launched only after the battle was nearly over. But if these forces were planning on invading Columbia as well, he knew his people could do good service helping to hold the allied planet.

"Fighter squadrons in position, sir. They are requesting permission to engage."

"Negative, Colonel. Advise Major Wiggs his forces are to follow the missile strikes in, but not too close to final engagement range until all warheads have detonated." Darius had no intention of losing his precious veteran pilots to radiation from the missile barrage…but he did want them on the enemy the instant the bombardment ceased. Their precision attacks could obliterate ships that had taken damage from warhead near misses.

He'd almost held his squadrons back, detailed them to protect his own battleships, but his main fleet would be in the Nest's defensive perimeter before the attacking fighters caught them… and Darius had buried hundreds of anti-assault batteries into the hard crust of the frozen moon. Unlike a normal planetary surface, Eos's small satellite had no atmosphere to speak of, nothing to weaken the laser batteries when they opened fire. But they were still on a fixed surface, and that allowed them to draw on power no mobile platform could match. The general rule of thumb was that fighters were best for intercepting fighters. Darius was about to put that to the test.

"Point defense array is opening fire, General. Enemy missiles coming into range now."

Darius didn't respond. He just sat and watched. The whole thing felt strange. He had always been the sort of commander to lead from the front, but he'd serve no purpose at all on the bridge of one of his battleships, nothing more than a distraction to a seasoned captain. And there was no ground battle to fight, at least not yet.

"Any response from Columbia yet, Cadet?" He stared across the bridge, trying to soften his tone when he directed it toward Ana, but likely failing. His persona in battle was one well-formed by now, and, as hard as it was, it had served him well.

"No, General. No response. Shall I resend the communique?"

"Yes," Darius snapped, realizing as he did it would be of little worth. There was no question Columbia had received the message, so whatever reason they'd failed to respond, it had been intentional. He couldn't understand what was happening. He didn't trust anyone, not completely, at least, but Jarrod Tyler had been one of those he'd thought least likely to turn on him, and especially in the fight against the mysterious attacker. Tyler was almost clinically paranoid about Columbia being invaded again. Was it possible the enemy had gotten to him somehow, persuaded him to join their cause? That would be a disaster for the Eagles, giving them enemies on both sides of their stronghold. Columbia alone could never defeat his forces, but if Tyler's ships joined the attackers instead of coming to his own aid as he'd expected…

No, that just doesn't make sense…

"General…" It was Ana.

"Yes, Cadet?"

"I'm picking up residual transmissions from Columbia, sir. There's something going on down there."

Darius snapped his head around. "Colonel, are there any enemy contacts deeper in-system?"

"Negative, sir."

"No, Colonel," Ana said. "It's something happening on the surface. I have the AI sifting through media transmissions. There seems to be some kind of lockdown in place. I can't tell…"

Darius stared across the control room. He was looking at his lover, but all he saw now was his communications officer.

Then, she turned back toward him. "Sir…General Tyler has

been shot."

Shot? An assassination attempt? "Any word on his condition?"

"It seems his is still alive, Colonel. I can't find any mention of his condition, but I did get a report of emergency surgery. It appears a full media blackout is in effect planetwide."

Darius sat silently for a moment, his eyes darting every few seconds to check on the status of the fighting around the Nest. His fleet's missiles were beginning to detonate, and an enemy vessel blinked off the screen, bracketed between three warheads that detonated simultaneously all from less than a kilometer away. He was distracted now by Tyler's situation, but he felt a wave of excitement. The AI network directing the operation of his missiles was one of Spark's newest developments, one designed to maximize the timing and location of missile detonations. There was far from anything conclusive to draw yet, but so far, the effectiveness of his missile barrage appeared to be devastating.

He shifted his thoughts back to Columbia. *This is bad, whatever is happening down there…*

"Colonel Teller, I want the troop transports to blast toward Columbia at full thrust, and land as soon as possible. Full invasion protocols. They are to broadcast their IDs and attempt to avoid conflict with the Columbian forces, but they are to occupy the Prime list of objectives, using whatever means are necessary." The Eagles had a Prime list for every world in Occupied Space, a roadmap for invasion and assumption of planetary control, media facilities, vital utilities, military installations, data centers.

"Yes, General."

"And Colonel…I want you to go. Get down to the bay and take command of the operation."

"Sir…"

"Do it, Erik. It's a difficult situation, and we don't have enough data. One of us has to be there…and if things go badly here, at least you'll be in a position to reorganize, and keep up the fight." Darius knew a dictatorship was never more vulnerable than it was when the strongman was incapacitated. If there were Black Flag plants down there—and there almost certainly were—now was the time they would make their move. Even domestic rivals could make their plays to overthrow Tyler while he was unable to respond effectively.

Teller looked like he was going to argue with his friend, but then it seemed the futility of it overcame him. "Yes, sir." An instant later: "Good luck, Darius."

"And you, my friend. Now go." He looked across the control room. He'd almost told Ana to go along too. Columbia wasn't exactly safe right now, but it was probably more so than the Nest. He hated the idea of her being in danger, but he knew she would only argue with him, and that no matter how much he insisted, she would refuse to go. He didn't have time for that now, and it was a display his Eagles didn't need to see.

He turned, taking a brief look at her, just the back of her hair. He tried to keep the dark images from his mind, scenes of her lying in the twisted wreckage of the Nest, gasping for breath as the air hissed out the holed out hull, her body broken and bloody and dead.

He forced himself back to focus, and he watched as the rest of his missiles impacted. His people had taken out more than a dozen enemy ships, including three of the massive battleships. It was a good result, better than he'd dared to hope for.

But now he sat, his eyes locked on the scanners as the enemy missiles moved toward his fleet, slipping into the Nest's defensive envelope. His batteries opened up, dozens of missiles vanishing as the AI-controlled lasers flashed again and again. But there were a lot of warheads coming in, and they were getting closer to his own ships.

Chapter 11

Marine Headquarters
Planet Armstrong, Gamma Pavonis III
Earthdate: 2321 AD (36 Years After the Fall)

"You've done an incredible job here, Cate...and I mean more than just this recent mobilization. I remember how bad things were before the Second Incursion, and my life hasn't taught me to expect anything but a return to complacency once the threat was gone."

"It was hard, Erik. The funding drying up was bad enough, but we managed to replace some of that, at least. We opened up the hospital to non military use, converted some of the arms to high tech products for export. We couldn't support a large active-duty Corps, but we managed to keep it alive, and the best fighting force in Occupied Space, at least until Darius started the Eagles."

Cain just nodded.

The two were walking across the drilling fields. Cain remembered a day when the great parade grounds were full of recruits, thousands and thousands of new trainees marching back and forth under Armstrong's great yellow sun. That had been the apogee for the Corps, the years right after the move from Earth. It had been a short peak, one shattered by the arrival of the First Imperium, and right after that, Gavin Stark and his Shadow

Legions. Cain had once started to try to calculate the percentage of those Marines in his mental images who had survived, the veterans of the Third Frontier War and the recruits from the years just after…and worse, his mates from Camp Puller back on Earth. He'd known the result would be grim, but then he realized it was worse than he'd thought, and he'd abandoned the effort, having decided he didn't want to know the answer.

"So, we've got twenty-one thousand total combat strength?" Cain phrased it as a question, but he already knew the answer.

"Twenty thousand, nine hundred, sixty-four. Counting the two of us." Gilson paused. "Less than four thousand of what either of us would call veterans, and maybe another twenty-five hundred trained to anything close to the old standards. The rest were rushed through. We tried to pick the best of the volunteers, and I think we managed to do a pretty good job with that, but they're not going to equal the forces you and I led forty years ago. Not even close."

"Marines always get the job done. We've believed that for a long time, Cate. I don't want to stop now, do you?"

She shook her head.

"So, we'll need a little more faith in this one, but we're not losing this war. I didn't come back from fifteen years in that stinking pit to lose my last war."

"I'm with you, Erik. Elias Holm always wanted us to command together. I know two chefs in the kitchen is usually trouble, but I think we can make it work, don't you?"

"I do, Cate. We worked that youthful pride nonsense out decades ago. We're just two old warriors, heading into the field one more time. And I wouldn't do it any other way than at your side."

As soon as Cain finished his sentence, the alarms all around the parade ground went off, and a second after that, both their comm units buzzed.

"What is it," Cain replied, managing to get his unit off his belt an instant faster than Gilson.

"We've got unidentified ships inbound, sir." A pause. "A lot of ships."

Cain felt his stomach tense. He'd known for two years war was coming, but now, it seemed, it was here. That wasn't confirmed, not officially. At least theoretically, there were other possible reasons why unidentified ships would be pouring into the system, but he didn't let any of that nonsense work its way into his head. The enemy had seized the initiative. He'd played his cards as though he would be dispatching Marines to worlds that were attacked all across Occupied Space, but now he saw the enemy's strategy. He felt like a damned fool. He'd never even imagined a surprise attack against Armstrong. Against the Marines' home base.

His mind was locked in the past, when the planet had been surrounded by layers of Alliance colonies, systems any invader would have to take before they could reach Armstrong. Now, Occupied Space was fragmented, and half its worlds had already yielded. It seemed so obvious now, but the vulnerability hadn't occurred to him before, and from the look on Gilson's face, to her either.

"Let's go, Cate. We've got to get Augustus on the comm." Garret's fleet was stationed in orbit, ready for battle. Neither the admiral, nor Cain or Gilson, had expected a strike at the very heart of the Marines' domain, but none of that mattered now. The enemy may have hit sooner than expected, but they would still have one hell of a fight here. "And let's get the Marines ready, assuming they get through and start landing troops.

Yes, sir…one hell of a fight.

* * * * *

Augustus Garret sat on *Bunker Hill*'s bridge. The battleship was one of the old Alliance *Yorktown*s, with fifty years of hard service in her metal bones, but she was still one of the strongest ships in Occupied space, save perhaps for the awesome implements of destruction Darius Cain had built for himself. And, of course, whatever the enemy might have advancing toward the planet.

Garret was old. His health was still good, more or less, and thanks to the rejuv treatments, he was up and walking—and serving—at an age when most men who'd lived were a generation dead. But he was old nevertheless, and he could feel the spirit that had driven him, the raw power he had turned into so many victories, slipping away.

He'd almost refused the command, stepped aside to let a younger officer take his place. But the situation was desperate, and what remained of the friends he'd fought alongside for so many years had all committed to this last battle. Perhaps age and experience still had a trick to two it could pull on youth and exuberance. He had one more victory in him, he figured. A final curtain call for humanity's most famous admiral. And then he would follow and old soldier's creed. He would fade away.

"All ships, prepare for forward thrust."

"Yes, Admiral." A few seconds later. "All ships report ready to engage engines at your command." Ronald Starn was young to be a full commander, but Garret had seen the young officer in action, and he'd granted the promotion on the spot, along with an offer to serve as his aide and tactical officer. Starn had seemed stunned, and it had taken him a moment to force a breathless acceptance from his parched and frozen throat.

Garret had become accustomed to near-adoration among the younger officers. He knew his career had reached legendary status, and he appreciated the respect for what he had achieved. But the great victories that had saved mankind had not been the work of one admiral, nor even that of a conclave of naval commanders and Marine generals. It had been the work of thousands and thousands of men and women, a vast number of whom gave all they had for those triumphs. The tendency people had to accrue credit, and the acclaim that went with it, to a few visible figures at the expense of so many others, made him uncomfortable, and he long ago reached the point where even the most basic praise galled at him in some way.

"Give the order, Commander. The fleet will accelerate at 3g."

"Yes, sir."

Garret leaned back, a reflex action he still hadn't shaken. The force dampeners were far from perfect, but they could handle

3g without any noticeable effect. The devices hadn't existed in the days of the Frontier Wars and the struggles that followed those conflicts. It was another bit of technology owed to the First Imperium, something researchers had managed to translate from the often-indecipherable science of the vastly more advanced power.

He turned and stared at the display. The fleet he commanded was large, and by the standards of the day, immense, but in many ways, it was a shadow of the great forces he'd led so many years before. Mankind simply did not have the resources it had once possessed. The scattered colonies across Occupied Space could grow and evolve into heavily populated worlds with highly developed industry and science, but they would need a respite from external threats to do that.

And they also need to stop fighting with each other. That's always been our problem, hasn't it?

None of that mattered now. He had what he had, and whatever dreams he might harbor for a peaceful future, that time was most definitely not now.

"Enemy lead elements are passing the orbit of planet six, sir."

"Very well. Drop fleet thrust to 2.5g. We don't want to push too far out from Armstrong, just enough to protect the planet from collateral damage." *For what good that will do. If we're defeated, or even driven back, the enemy can hit Armstrong with whatever they choose.*

"Yes, Admiral."

"And all ships, arm missiles. We're going to flush our external racks, and then we're going to launch every internal warhead we've got." Garret didn't have much intel on the enemy ships, but he was starting to get mass readings, and he didn't like what he was seeing. There were at least a dozen vessels out there that had sixty thousand tons or more on *Bunker Hill*, and four that were *really* big. He'd never seen anything quite like those behemoths. The great battleships—and what else could they be?—were larger than the Eagles' dreadnoughts, even than Mars's huge pair of superbattleships. He had no idea what firepower something like that carried, but he suspected he'd find out soon.

"All ships report missiles ready to fire, sir."

Garret watched the range count down, the two masses of small icons on the display moving closer and closer. He'd held back his fighter squadrons, planning to save them for a launch just before the fleets entered close weapons range, but now he reconsidered. If that fleet launched as many missiles as the combined mass of its ships suggested, it could overwhelm his point defense network. He knew he'd lose ships to the missile attack, just as his would inflict losses on the enemy. But now he could see his entire fleet blasted to wreckage before a fighter launched or laser fired. He had no choice.

"Commander, I want all ships to reconfigure half their fighters for anti-missile operations." He glanced at the chronometer, and then back at the range display. He was late with his order, and the time was tight. But his people could do it. Just.

"Yes, sir." Starn's tone suggested his aide had come to much the same set of conclusions.

"And get me General Cain on Armstrong, Commander." Garret had planned to try to hold the enemy back from the planet, but as he looked out at the strength facing him, he knew that was impossible. The attackers had the numbers to tie all his ships down and still send a considerable force at Armstrong. The people down there had to be ready. For anything. An invasion...even a nuclear barrage.

"General Cain on your line, sir."

"Erik, we've got a major attack coming in. I'm going to have to fight a hit and run battle up here, use whatever maneuverability I can." A pause. "That means the enemy's going to get ships through to Armstrong, and there's no way I can stop them. You better get your people down there ready...for the worst."

Garret waited while the signal traveled back to Armstrong at the speed of light, and Cain's reply returned. While he sat, he took a deep breath, trying to push away the thought that he'd already failed his allies before he'd so much as fired a shot.

"I appreciate the heads up, Admiral." Cain's voice came through the comm about two minutes later. "I figured about as much. It's pretty clear whoever the Black Flag is, they have enormous resources. The raiders we've seen the last two years are only the tip of the iceberg." Cain paused, for so long Garret thought the transmission was over and he leaned forward to send his own response. But then the Marine's voice blared through again. "Admiral, this war isn't going to be won here. All we can do now is survive. If things go badly…" Another pause. "We can't lose the whole fleet here, Augustus, no matter what. You have to retreat before that happens. If you can't save Armstrong, go. Retreat. Get to the Nest and hook up with Darius and the Eagles. We've got shelters down here. They'll never bombard us off this planet, and if they come down…well, that's what Marines are made for."

"Erik," Garret said, but then he stopped. He'd been ready to argue, but he knew Cain was right. They were allies, friends, they shared a respect that ran deep and strong. But they'd both sacrificed comrades before when duty had demanded it. Garret's mind flashed back forty years, to the final struggle against the First Imperium invaders. He'd detonated an apocalyptic explosive that day, cutting off the sole warp gate leading to First Imperium space…and trapping his oldest and best friend on the other side, surrounded by enemy fleets. Terrance Compton had been closer than a brother, and the wound he'd cut into his soul that day had never healed. But he'd done what duty commanded, as he would here.

"We'll do what we can up here, Erik. We'll try to push them back, keep them from getting too much through to the planet." He hesitated, finally pushing himself to finish. "And if we have to pull out, we'll be back." He felt the emptiness of his words, even as he cut the line, but he'd *had* to say them. And, for whatever it was worth, however hard it would be to follow through, however little chance there was Cain and the Marines could hold out long enough, he had meant them.

"Admiral, anti-missile squadrons are ready to launch."

Garret stared at the display, silent for perhaps twenty seconds. Then he turned toward Starn and said a single word.

"Launch."

Chapter 12

"Colonel Cornin, I want your Reds on the move, now!" Erik Teller stood on the black dust of the volcanic plain, thirty kilometers from Columbia's capital city, watching armored Eagles pour out of the assault shuttles.

"Yes, sir. I've got the First Battalion formed up now. Second should be out of their landers and ready to go in ten minutes."

"Very well, Colonel. Send First Battalion out now, and then follow with Second when it is ready." *But I'm calling bullshit on the ten minutes. Fifteen maybe. We're Black Eagles, but we're not wizards.*

Teller turned and stared back toward the primary LZ. He'd been worried that his landing craft would encounter defensive fire, which would have been a real problem since every Eagle combat vessel that would have normally covered an invasion was fighting right now around the Nest. But whatever was happening on Columbia wasn't over yet, and no one had been defending the approaches to the planet. His people had bought a break there. Any hostile forces at play in the aftermath of the assassination attempt hadn't gained control of the defense grid, and that meant whoever was making a play to overthrow Tyler would get the chance to face the Black Eagles on the ground.

You hope it was just an attempt, at least. Teller had tried every way he could think to gather some information on Tyler's condition, but there was nothing. His supporters might try to hide the fact that he was dead until they could prepare to fight for control, but they could also have simply shut down all information flow, locked down the networks, and dug in to face whatever was coming.

Teller didn't know who was down here, or how the sides broke down, but he was confident his people could handle things, unless they were *massively* outnumbered. Still, he was being cautious, meticulous. And, despite all his efforts at focus, a good chunk of his mind was still back at the Nest. He'd had no updates since the landing had commenced, and the last one he'd gotten before that had been decidedly inconclusive. The Eagles at the Nest were inflicting massive losses on the attackers, but they were outnumbered too, and the invading forces seemed utterly unconcerned about casualties. Teller wanted to fall back on his usual confidence, but the hard truth was, the vaunted mercenary army had far less experience fighting in space than it did on land.

"Colonel Teller, White Regiment is on the way in. Their lead elements will be on the ground in four minutes."

Teller turned toward the aide. "Very well." Then: "Any word from the Nest?"

"No, sir. Not yet."

Teller heard the worry in the orderly's voice too. Even the junior officers were thinking about their comrades. About their commander.

"I want Kuragina's people headed out on the Reds' left the instant they land. Cyn Kuragina was White Regiment's commander, and there was no one short of Darius Cain himself who could whip a pair of reinforced battalions into shape faster than she could. Teller wasn't worried about Cornin's units, not really. He doubted there was anything on Columbia that could take out an Eagles regiment before he could get reinforcements in. But he didn't know what was going on, and until he did, the only course of action was to get into the capital and find out what was happening with Jarrod Tyler. If Columbia's dictator was still alive, the Eagles would make damned sure he stayed that way.

And if he wasn't, they'd find whoever was responsible, and they would do what the Black Eagles did best.

* * * * *

The room was dark, blurry, nothing but blurry shapes in the distance. His head was fuzzy, his thoughts wandering, unfocused. *Who am I?* The question came abruptly, and for an instant, there was no answer. Then, it came. *Jarrod Tyler. That is who I am. But why am I here? Where is this?*

"What…" He started the question, but his throat was dry. No, more than dry, it was parched, aching. He tried to raise his hand, but all he managed was a fluttering of his fingers. That was enough. An orderly saw the movement, and in an instant the room was wild with activity, lights, machines making all sorts of sounds, people shouting to each other.

"General Tyler, can you hear me?"

The voice seemed far away, but Tyler could hear it, and it made sense to him. Yes, I am a general…the general. Suddenly it was all clear. *Columbia, he was its head of state, the commander of its military. And he'd been attacked. Assassination! I have to get the guards in position. Somebody's making a move…*

"Alert," he choked out of his sore throat. "Must activate… alert."

"All forces are on alert, General. We're secure here. There are loyal forces deployed in this section of the city."

"Here…this section. What is…happening?"

"Sir, please…you just came out of surgery, and you need to rest."

"Tell me!" he roared, wincing from the pain as he forced the words out. "What?"

"There was an attempt on your life, sir. The assassin is dead. So are three of his accomplices. The army has remained loyal, most of it, but there has been some sabotage. Your officers are having trouble getting units into the city."

"Most…"

A pause. "Yes, General." A different voice, familiar. "It's Major Clark, General. The Ninth Brigade has mutinied, sir. It seems like a plot run by the top commanders…we've had reports of troops deserting, and others shot trying to escape."

"One brigade…should…not…be difficult to…suppress."

Another stretch of silence. "There has been considerable sabotage as well, sir. Key facilities, power stations, transport hubs. I'm afraid somebody planned this whole thing, sir. We're fighting to hold them off, but they've got us disrupted something fierce. And now, we've got assault landers coming in. We're having comm troubles, but I think they might be Eagles, General. They could be coming to our aid. I've ordered all forces to avoid engagement, not to fire unless fired upon."

"Good, Major…" Tyler took a deep breath…and winced from the pain in his chest. "If the Eagles are here, they're here to help us." He was pretty sure of that, at least. Darius Cain was likely capable of anything, of course, but Tyler had always been an ally, and the leader of the Black Eagles had never turned on a friend, at least as far as he knew.

"The doctor's right. You've really got to rest, sir."

"Rest? With an attempted coup in progress?" Tyler leaned forward, trying to get up again. The pain lanced through his midsection, but he kept pushing, forcing himself to a sitting position. He paused and gasped for air.

"General, please. If you insist on trying to get out of this bed, at the very least, you're going to end up back in surgery… and at worst in the ground." The doctor stepped forward as he spoke, his eyes fixed on Tyler's abdomen, where a circle of fresh blood had soaked through his hospital gown.

"General, listen to the doctor, please." The major sounded tense, worried, his eyes darting back and forth from eye contact to Tyler's reopened wound. "We'll keep things under control, especially if the Eagles are out there. The main comm is degraded right now, but we're trying to contact them. Once we link up, we should be able to secure everything vital in a matter of hours."

Tyler looked up at his aide, and then at the doctor. He was a hard man, a stubborn one, who wasn't prone to accepting anything less than the very best effort, from himself as well as anyone else. But he wasn't a fool, and he knew if he got up, he'd make it about as far as the door, maybe, before he ended up on the floor. He sighed softly, wincing at the renewed pain in his gut.

"Go, Major. Confirm the Eagles are out there, and then come back and report to me on the current status." His voice was more forced than it had been…his effort to sit up had really increased the pain.

"Yes, sir." The officer saluted and then turned and walked out into the hall.

"You're in more pain now, aren't you?" The doctor had pulled up Tyler's shirt, and he was adjusting the bandages. "You almost pulled out your sutures. You have to stay still, General, at least for a couple days. I couldn't fuse the incision, not in this location. So, you're going to have to heal the old-fashioned way. I need two days from you, with the regeneration compound I'm giving you, that's what it will take before you can get up and walk…at least a little. Now, by all rights, you should be in a box now. It was *that* close. So, listen to your doctor, and we'll have you out of here and back to work in a couple days."

Tyler looked up toward the doctor. Franks, the nametag read. The name was familiar, vaguely, the head of surgery at the capital's main hospital. *Of course, who else would operate on the dictator?*

The man's demeanor impressed Tyler. He wasn't intimidated or afraid, even though his patient could order one of the guards at the door to shoot him where he stood, and that order would be obeyed without question. Tyler wasn't that sort of ruler, of course. His only concerns were maintaining Columbia's strength and defenses, and his brutality was reserved for those he considered traitors. Short of anything he considered too close to treason, the planet's population enjoyed considerable freedom in their daily lives but, still, few of them had the courage to stand up to him the way his doctor just had.

Tyler never tried to hide his disgust for obsequious fools, those trying to curry favor with flattery and insincere expressions of loyalty. Conversely, he respected someone with the guts to stand up to him, and Dr. Franks made that grade.

Tyler leaned back, wincing again. "Alright, Doc, give me another shot of painkiller, and we've got a deal...nothing that will turn me into a zombie, just something to take the edge off."

* * * * *

"Deploy into attack formations, now." Antonia Camerici stood on top of a gentle rise, the closest thing to a vantage point the flat plains around Columbia's capital offered. She'd been in combat before, many times, like most of the Eagles of her stature, but she'd never led so many soldiers into a fight. She'd been one of Darius Cain's closest aides for several years, but even so, she'd been surprised when he'd handed her a small package with a rare smile. The box had contained her major's insignia, and a small datachip, her formal appointment as commander of the newly formed Gray Regiment.

The Grays had a cadre of older veterans, but they also had a far higher proportion of new recruits, more than any other, save for the equally new Browns. But even Eagle recruits had a high level of training and skill, and if her people weren't quite up to full standards—yet—she was sure they could handle anything they'd find on Columbia. Some of General Tyler's troops were pretty good, she had to admit, but the best ones were also the most loyal, which put them on her side. Besides, it wasn't in her Eagle DNA to acknowledge that anyone was a match for her people.

It was nothing but pure chance that had placed her regiment in the forefront of the action. It had taken a while, but Colonel Teller had finally managed to contact Tyler's people. The general was alive, and likely to stay that way, at least as long as his people held the capital. And the biggest threat to that was a brigade under control of the conspirators, one that was fully armed and heading toward the city. Right in front of the Grays' line of advance.

She watched as her people formed up, lines in extended order moving forward, other columns snaking north and south, extending the battlefront. She had to hit the enemy hard enough to tie them down, keep them from getting into the capital before the loyal Columbian units could reorganize and get into position.

The force in front of her outnumbered her regiment at least four to one, but that was never the kind of thing Eagles worried about. They were always better, and that had always been enough. It almost certainly would be here too. Less than a quarter of the Columbians wore powered armor, and none of them fielded anything that could match the Eagle's Mark VIII suits.

The Mark VIIIs were a major leap forward in battlefield technology. Camerici winced, thinking about the agonies of suiting up, one of the few drawbacks of the new armor. The neural probe was a crucial part of the suit, and Tom Sparks and his engineers had been unable to make its insertion feel much like anything but getting stabbed in the back of the neck. Eagles prided themselves on being tough, and few complained. But, perhaps irrationally, she'd come to dread the suiting up process.

Once the armor was on, it was a dream. All the cumbersome controls had become needless, still there, but only as a backup system. Even the old verbally-activated AIs the Marines used seemed outdated now. With the neural probe inserted into her spine—ugh—all she had to do was think, the same way she would to move part of her body. If she wanted to pick up something that weighed a ton, all she did was pick it up. If she wanted to fire her grenade launcher, a single thought could do it. The whole thing had taken a bit of practice to get used to…after all, moving a strengthened leg was one thing, intuitive enough, but firing weapons that weren't part of your original body was quite another.

She cranked up her visor's amplification to power five. She had a view of the enemy now, at least of their left wing. The Columbians were clearly reacting to the threat she posed. The next few minutes would tell if they knew what was facing them. If they thought her people were Columbians, they would most likely put out a screening force and drive the rest of the brigade into the capital. Time was of the essence in a coup attempt, and the capital was the key to gaining control.

If they'd discovered that they faced Black Eagles, that would be a different matter. They'd either run or they'd throw everything they had at her. She had no idea which, and she decided she might as well flip a coin. She actually hoped they'd come at her full. No screening force would hold her people, of course, but that didn't mean she could get through it before the main force got to the city. It wouldn't take a military defeat for the mission to fail, just a single bullet in Jarrod Tyler's head.

The Reds and the Blacks were marching toward the position as well, one regiment on each of her flanks. But there was no time to wait. She had to hit that brigade now, and she had to make damned sure that if they didn't know who they were up against, they found out now.

"Forward units, attack!"

She reached to her side, pulling the assault rifle from its cradle. The hypervelocity weapon would rip right through the Columbian armor without much trouble, and it would turn an unarmored soldier into something resembling a pile of goo in a fraction of a second.

She walked down the hillside, heading toward her lines. She'd been Darius's aide for a long time, but she hadn't forgotten how Eagle commanders led their troops into the fight.

From the Goddamned front, that's how...

Chapter 13

"I want those supplies laid in now, every crate in these warehouses. I know space is tight down there, but if we end up stuck in these shelters, at least we won't starve or run out of ammo." *Not right away, at least.*

Cain was standing in a huge warehouse, one single room, now less than half full with neatly stacked containers. He'd been there all morning, and when he'd first arrived, it had been filled to the rafters.

"Yes, General. Whatever you say, sir. We'll get it done." The lieutenant on command of the work party was young, young enough that he'd done his basic training while Cain was a prisoner. He'd come of age on nothing but the general's legends, told in those days as tales of a dead hero. And it showed.

"Relax, son," Cain said softly. "The enemy damned well might bite you when they get here, but I won't. Just do your best."

"Yes, sir!"

Cain wasn't sure if the Marine sounded a little less hysterical than he had earlier, or if he was just hearing what he wanted to hear, but he left it at that. *You can look up at me all you want, kid, but if you saw the shithole I came from…*

Cain knew the enemy was coming. The instant Garret had warned him, sent the communique, he knew the admiral was convinced he couldn't defeat the invasion force. Augustus Garret was just about the most gifted naval commander who'd ever lived, at least in Cain's estimation, and any doubt from him was to be taken seriously. Very seriously.

He would have organized the defense differently years before. The Superpowers had fought brutal wars, but they'd largely heeded the prohibitions against massive nuclear bombardments for a century, right up until the Fall. And even Gavin Stark had wanted to rule humanity, not destroy it. But the First Imperium had taught Cain what war could truly be, not just danger, or the fight to preserve land, territory, freedom. No, more than that. It could be a very fight for survival, not only for the warriors who fought it, but for everyone.

He didn't know enough about the Black Flag to make a final determination on their goals, but he was pretty sure they'd be willing to blast Armstrong to radioactive dust to take out the Marines, and he was damned sure going to be ready for it. The enemy might bombard the planet, destroy every manmade structure a century of human habitation had seen constructed, but he defied them to dig his people out of the shelters. They'd have to come down for that…and anybody who intended to fight their way through underground tunnels filled with Marines better bring their A game.

"You sent for me?" Sarah walked into the room, dressed as he'd seen her so many times, in her combat scrubs. There were no wounded yet, save for a few injuries from the work going on, but she was enough of a veteran to understand exactly what was coming.

"Yes." Cain was in his usual battlefield persona, his face hard, almost like granite as he snapped out orders. But Sarah's presence softened his gaze, as it had for so long. "We have some freighters in orbit. They're no use to Garret, so we're going to load up all the children among the civilians, and anyone else we can fit who is nonessential."

"That's great, Erik. I wish we could get all the civilians offworld."

"I do, too." He paused. "I was thinking you could take charge, see to medical care for them all on the voyage out of the system." He knew the answer he would get, but he had to try anyway.

"Okay," she said softly, though he didn't take her mellow tone for lack of resolve, "we got that out of the way, so good. Now, can we move on?"

"Sarah…" Cain was a stubborn man, one legendary for his ability to smash his head through a figurative wall. He knew he had no chance with this one though, but still, he had to try.

"Forget it, Erik. If you think I'm leaving you now, after everything we've been through, or for that matter, leaving the Corps behind to fight this battle without me, you're crazier than I thought you were all this time we've been together."

Cain felt the urge to argue further. He could order her to go, she was technically under his chain of command, but he didn't have the slightest doubt that wouldn't make a bit of difference, except that the response would likely be rather unmilitary, something like, "Eat shit, sir."

He'd only gotten her to stay behind, out of a fight, once, and that had been during the Second Incursion. He'd had an argument on his side then he'd never possessed before or since. Their sons were still boys, and they'd needed her. But Darius and Elias were men in their thirties now, one a veteran of Atlantia's patrol service, and the other the most feared mercenary in Occupied Space. The 'stay behind for the children' argument was a long expired one. Worse, she hadn't seen him for seventeen years after the one time she'd let him go alone, which eliminated any infinitesimal chance he'd ever had of getting her to leave him behind again.

"I had to try. This is going to be bad, Sarah. Have you seen the scans? Augustus isn't going to defeat that invasion fleet. Maybe if the Eagles and some of our other allies were here, but we got caught by surprise. I only hope he has the sense to break off and save what he can of the fleet."

"We've been in bad spots before, Erik. We've made it through. I thought I'd lost you almost twenty years ago, but now you're back to me. Whatever happens, we'll face it together."

"We could lose this time. I know we've dodged some tight spots before, but any streak has to end eventually." He looked at her, the façade of the iron-willed Marine leader gone for a moment. He almost asked her again to leave, but something stopped him. He only wanted to save her, to know she was safe. But he owed her more than that. She was the love of his life, but she was no less a Marine than he, and she'd spent the last half century on battlefields, covered in blood, facing death again and again.

"If we lose, we lose," she said, reaching out and taking his hand. "Our lives have been hard ones, Erik, but they've been amazing in ways. I wouldn't trade a moment we've shared together for any other life. We've made a difference too. We've lost friends and comrades, but we've saved people too. Kept them safe, or as close to it as we could." She paused. "We're doing that again. There are worse ways to die, and far worse places to do it than at your side."

He smiled at her, and leaned in, kissing her softly. "I won't ask you to go again, not ever. I don't care if we've got five minutes left, or fifty years, we'll face it together." He paused, and he looked down sadly. "I'm so sorry," he said. "I can't imagine what those years were like for you."

"For me? It kills me to think of what you went through."

He paused another few seconds, then he looked back up at her. "That's another thing we need to let go of What happened, happened. I made it back, and that's all that matters, and nothing I went through was too great a price to pay to survive, to see your face again."

The two of them spent a few moments together, a brief respite, much as they had done all their lives. Then, with a final hug, Sarah went back to the hospital, to carry off whatever was portable enough to bring to the shelters. And Erik Cain went back to what he'd done his entire life, getting his Marines ready to make a last stand.

*   *   *   *   *

"Task Force C, get those ships around. Now!" Camille Harmon sat on the edge of her chair, right in the center of *Monmouth*'s cavernous flag bridge.

"Yes, Admiral." Janie Rudolph was new to Harmon's service, but the admiral liked the young officer immensely. A lieutenant was a woefully junior rank for the primary aide to a fleet admiral, especially one who was effectively second in command of the entire force, but Harmon had always gone with her gut, at least when deciding what she thought of people.

Harmon had come up in the Alliance service, alongside Garret and Terrence Compton. Compton had been gone—could it really be forty years now? She shared the loss Garret felt at the brutal way the war with the First Imperium had ended. She, too, had considered Compton a friend, but her loss cut even deeper in its own way. She'd been spared Garret's fate of having to give the order...and to this day, she still wasn't sure she could have, though she knew for certain it had been the only way to save humanity from total destruction. But she had paid a price in that fateful hour, one even closer and deeper than Garret's. When the detonation was complete, she'd lost not just her friend, but also her son. Max Harmon had been Compton's aide, and he'd been trapped on the other side of the Barrier with the rest of the admiral's fleet.

She'd seen the scope of the forces that had been closing on Compton's fleet, but for once she'd overruled her own usual cold reason and convinced herself there was at least a chance the trapped forces had managed to escape, that her son was lost to her, but still alive. Somewhere. There were days she saw the dream for the foolish nonsense she knew it was, and others when she was able to fool herself, and drive back at least a small bit of the pain.

"Admiral, Captain Yin advises that three of his ships have damage to their engines. He wants to know if you want him to maintain his formation or advance with what ships are able."

"Tell him to advance…with everything he's got. I don't care if he has to get out and push those ships, but we need to bring pressure on the enemy flank, or Admiral Garret's ships don't stand a chance." Technically, of course, they were all Garret's ships, but as usual the great admiral had taken the most dangerous post for himself. His ships were holding a line, trying to dish out enough damage to keep the invaders back from Armstrong. Harmon's gut told her it wasn't going to work. She suspected Garret's instincts, though whatever body part they manifested themselves, were telling him the same thing. But he had to try, just as she would have.

Monmouth shook hard, the third hit she'd taken since closing to energy weapons range. Harmon's flagship's lasers were firing too, and the marksmanship of her gunners left her no room for complaints. But even as she watched, math started to prevail. Her people had a higher hit rate, but there were too many guns firing back. One by one, her ships took damage, the strength of their batteries declining as turrets and reactors were hit. The enemy was losing ships, too, at least twice as many…but they had more to begin with.

She watched as her flanking ships continued on, accelerated as quickly as they could while still maintaining some level of functionality among the crew. She'd almost ordered them into the tanks, but then she'd decided they didn't have time, and she wanted her people sharp, at their very best.

She wondered how long it had been since any of those ships had used their old acceleration-protection systems. The new dampeners were a lot more comfortable and convenient, and they left crews at their stations instead of half-crushed in the constricting tanks, drugged out of their minds, struggling to supplement AI control of the ship by hitting a switch or two before they became entirely incoherent. Still, the dampeners allowed extended thrust of 12g, perhaps 15g if the crew was veteran enough to take it. She'd blasted her ships at 35g, even 40g in some of her past battles, with her people sealed up in the tanks. But things had changed in more ways than one. Modern weapons were more powerful, and they placed a heavier burden on the reactors. It was a rare occurrence when a ship in combat had enough spare energy to blast engines at 30g while firing and, even then, it was somewhat of a gamble that the old systems had been maintained well enough for a captain to dare to dust off the tanks.

The flanking ships were coming into close range, and the enemy had detached a task force to intercept. She watched, waiting, hoping the tactic she'd used before would be a surprise to this new enemy. It certainly seemed the Black Flag ships had loosed all their missiles at long range. She had the damage to her ships and the gaps in her line to show for it. But she'd had her flanking vessels hold back their last two volleys, and any second now, they'd launch those nukes in sprint mode at point blank range.

The missiles would blast hard toward the nearest enemy ships, burning out their engines accelerating at 60g, 70g, or even higher thrust rates. They would rapidly close, leaving little or no time for countermeasures, and, with any luck, surprise the enemy enough to catch them napping.

Evasive maneuvers directed against energy weapons were far different than those used to dodge missiles. It only took a hundred or two hundred meters to slide a ship away from a targeted laser blast. But two hundred meters wouldn't do much to prevent a five hundred megaton nuke from causing catastrophic damage. A direct hit would vaporize any vessel, of course, but a near miss, one under five hundred meters, would be nearly as devastating, even to the largest battleships.

She watched, feeling a rush of excitement as the first missiles launched. The last enemy she'd fought had been the First Imperium. The Second Incursion had been a costly victory, but now she felt something she hadn't in thirty years. It was a manifestation of her rage, the hurt and pain of loss she felt. She'd sacrificed her husband to war, and years later her only child. That bitterness had grown, hardened, and though it didn't make her proud, Camille Harmon realized she felt satisfaction that she faced living, breathing enemies again, that those who had attacked, made war to pursue their own greed and lust for power, would feel fear as her ships attacked, that they would see her missiles approaching, and they would know death had come for them.

She'd bought into concepts like honor once, adhered to things like rules of war, but no more. Never again. War had brought her pain, emptiness, loneliness, and anyone who forced it on her, and on her comrades deserved only death, as certain and brutal as she could deliver it.

"Missiles detonating, Admiral. They're coming in all along the enemy line."

Harmon didn't need the report. Her eyes were fixed, unmoving, watching the readouts. A missile got within a kilometer of a large battleship, the thermonuclear fury blasting the vessel with massive amounts of radiation. Then another warhead, even closer this time, less than five hundred meters. That was almost a direct hit by the standards of space war, and she smiled as the targeted ship—a cruiser of some sort, she guessed—was obliterated. The frame was still there, some of it, at least, she suspected, but she'd be stunned if the damage reports showed any signs of life or energy readings when they finally came in.

Monmouth shook again, harder this time than before. She could hear rumbles from deep in the ship, subsidiary explosions and system blowouts. Her ship had done its part so far, but now the damage was beginning to show. She could feel the vibration from the engines, and she knew immediately, one of them was down. It wasn't critical, she didn't need the thrust now. But if it was heavy damage and not just some kind of overload, she was going to miss that thrust if the time came out to bug out.

When the time came. Part of her wanted to fight to the death, to stand and refuse to retreat, but she knew Garret commanded one of the two primary naval forces strong enough to defend Occupied Space, and as strong as the Eagles were, she doubted they could win this war alone. Augustus Garret didn't have the luxury to court a heroic end, to die a dramatic death…not here, not now. He hadn't said as much, but she knew the withdrawal orders would come, and she had only one thought on her mind.

Kill as many of these bastards as you can before then.

Chapter 14

Ships flew all around the great frozen gas giant and its two moons, dozens of heavily-armed vessels, making attack runs, fighting fast duels as they zipped past each other at high velocities and then decelerated to come back and continue the fight. And on the second moon, the small, airless ball that at first glance suggested nothing of importance, one of the most powerful military installations ever constructed spat out death unimaginable on the vessels that dared to attack it.

The Nest was strong, as Darius Cain had mandated it would be. Its power plants were vast, reactor after massive reactor buried deep in the hard stone of the moon's crust. Its weapons were immense, hundreds of missile launchers with reload after reload, more missiles by far than any ship could carry, vast laser batteries, larger and more powerful than anything that could be mounted on a portable platform. And amid all this power and weaponry, all the death that could be dealt out by the most skilled and experienced military force in Occupied Space, the battle still raged.

The attackers had suffered losses, grievous losses, so many ships destroyed that even Darius Cain stared in wonder as they continued their relentless, bloodsoaked assaults. And in the nerve center of his fortress, he watched, as even his own nearly inexhaustible resources began to dwindle.

"We're down to twenty percent on missiles, General."

"Maintain fire at full."

"Reactor Seven is down, sir, and Twelve is at twenty percent output."

"Shut down all non-vital systems. Redirect power to the weapons. I don't want one beam idle, Major, if it means we're sitting here with candlelight. Is that clear?"

"Yes, sir. Perfectly."

Cain's reputation was one of coldness, of an utterly unshakable firmness in battle, and he lived up to that standard, at least publicly. He owed that much to his Eagles, to be what they expected, what they needed him to be. But deep down, in the thoughts he kept tightly locked away, he began to doubt, to wonder if his forces would prevail. He'd worried about battles before, of course, but those concerns had always been about how many of his Eagles he would lose, how long it would take to defeat an enemy. This was the first time he'd watched his warriors fighting and wondered seriously if they might lose.

The enemy was capable, clearly well trained, and fearless. They weren't a match for the Eagles, though. Not one on one, nor even two on one. But his forces were outnumbered nearly five to one. His people had faced those odds before, indeed, they'd defeated forces ten, even twenty times their size. But those had been raw, backward planetary armies, not well-trained adversaries armed with gleaming new ships, and technology that matched their own, perhaps even exceeded it in places.

One thing was clear enough. Tom Sparks had been right. There was no question in his mind the Black Flag ships incorporated First Imperium technology. The enemy's x-ray lasers cut through the reinforced armor of his battleships, tearing through compartment after compartment, and gutting the great vessels he'd spent so much treasure to produce. But that wasn't what hit him the hardest. His Eagles were dying, their losses far more severe than they'd been in any campaign since the earliest days of the private army. He knew his people were used to being the best, and now he began to wonder how they would react to a sustained, vicious, desperate fight after so many years of seemingly effortless victories.

He looked around the control center, a way of disguising his glance over at Ana, making it appear he was checking on everyone. She had done well, executed her duty as effectively as his most experienced comm officer could have done. But she was a distraction, and his concern for her chipped away at his icy demeanor in battle. There was nothing he could do about it, at least nothing short of having guards drag her away, and he wasn't ready to do that. There was a very real possibility they would all die in the next few hours, and, as emotionless as he liked to think he was, he also knew he couldn't stand the possibility of dying with her hating him.

"General, is there anything I can do?"

Darius turned and looked up at his brother. "No, Elias, not now." He knew his twin had stayed away from places like the control center, his effort not to spread confusion through the Nest. Elias's hair was shorter, but now that he'd started wearing his colonel's uniform, no different from Darius's own general's garb, save for the stars on the collar, it only made things more disconcerting for the Eagles, especially in battle.

"Stay," Darius said, as his brother turned and started walking toward the lift. "Grab one of the extra workstations. You might as well watch the battle, see firsthand whether we win… or whether we die. I don't think anybody will be rattled by your presence right now, not unless you wrestle me out of my chair and take my place."

Elias nodded, and he walked over to an empty chair, sitting down.

Darius was glad his brother was there, in the control center. He hadn't given up on the battle, not by a long shot. He still figured his people could win, would win. But he'd also considered the chance they wouldn't, and if they were all going to die, he wanted Elias there, close by. He'd resented his brother for so long, but now all he had was regret for what the two had allowed to come between them. He was too realistic to think they could ever go back to the way things had been years before. There would always be some discomfort between them, and nearly twenty years of separation and anger could never be totally erased. But he was grateful for whatever peace the two had managed to make, and if they did die here, he was glad they would die friends again.

"General, Captain Grayson is on the comm." Ana's voice was remarkably calm, cool, though Darius knew she had to be terrified. It was that same strength that had caught his attention on Karelia, and it affected him no less now. "He thinks he has identified the enemy flagship, and he is requesting permission for *Eagle Fourteen* and *Eagle Nine* to break off and go after it."

"On my comm, Cadet." His eyes darted to the screen, focusing first on his two battleships…and then on the now flashing dot, the target they had identified.

"He's on your line, sir."

"John, how sure are you?"

"Pretty confident, sir. Maybe seventy percent. We've been tracing the comm traffic, and that ship seems to be a hub of some sort. It's not conclusive, but if we're looking for their command ship, that one's the best bet."

"I concur, but that ship's deep in their formation, and it's one of those monster battleships. You're going to take a hell of a lot of fire going in, and then you'll still have to take it down. We don't have firm data yet on those huge ships, but it's a good bet they outgun you."

"That's why I want to take *Eagle Nine* with me. Captain Ying agrees."

"Both your ships have taken damage. Don't bullshit me, John. Do you really think you can get through? Because I don't have two battleships to throw away on hopeless efforts right now."

"We'll get there, sir. Somehow."

Darius didn't like answers like that. He preferred hard data to displays of bravado. But Grayson was as good a ship captain as the gods of war made, and taking out the enemy flagship *would* go a long way toward scratching out a win.

"Do it," he said grimly. Then: "I'm sending all the fighters in your sector with you." *All the fighters we've got left.* "Also, take *Eagle Three* with you. If we're going to do this, let's make the hell sure it gets done."

"Yes, sir."

"Good luck, John."

"Thank you, General. Grayson out."

Darius leaned back and watched as the two dots representing Grayson's two ship began to move. It was clear *Eagle Fourteen*'s captain had already laid in his nav data before he'd called HQ. Darius took a deep breath, and he looked back at Ana. "Get me Captain Strickland on *Eagle Three*, Cadet."

"On your line, General."

"Bill, get that ship of yours moving after *Eagle Fourteen* and *Eagle Nine*. They're doing something crazy, and you and your people are the cavalry."

*   *   *   *   *

"Maintain fire…I want every gun hot enough to brew a pot of coffee firing at full speed." John Grayson sat in his command chair, amid the smoky air of *Eagle Fourteen*'s battered bridge. Years of dominance had made a desperate fight to the end seem like a distant memory, but now Grayson's thoughts were full of images, fights against the First Imperium, the Shadow Legions, battles where the ultimate victors had suffered devastating losses. Victories notable for the desperate need that had driven them, and for their Pyrrhic nature.

Eagle Fourteen had driven forward, slipping through a gap in the enemy line, and gaining a jump of sorts. But it wasn't long before the enemy reacted, clearly realizing Grayson's intentions. A dozen ships responded, changing their thrust vectors, trying to come around and intercept the two Eagle warships.

The fire coming in had been light at first, but it increased steadily, even as the target ship blasted its own engines, decelerating, trying to move away from the approaching attack.

The enemy's reaction only increased Grayson's determination to press his attack. The vessels fighting the Eagle fleet seemed to show no regard for self-preservation, but that attitude apparently didn't extend to the high command. The enemy flagship—and Grayson had no remaining doubt that's exactly what it was—had been deployed to the rear of the formation, and now it was looking to retreat further, to escape the Eagles coming for it.

Grayson had seen Darius Cain on the front lines of battles, with enemy fire and shells blasting all around him. The thought of leaders pushing their warriors into a battle to the finish while cowering behind them disgusted him. Even before he'd been an Eagle, he'd served officers like Augustus Garret and Terrence Compton, fighting admirals who shared every danger with the men and women they commanded. He'd wanted to destroy that flagship already, for the tactical advantage, for the morale effect it might have on the enemy fleet. But now there was something else, something primal. He wanted to kill the officers on that ship, to give them a taste of what their warriors suffered, of what hundreds of Eagles had endured in the battle.

Eagle Fourteen shook hard, another hit. The battleship's armor was strong, extraordinarily so, thicker and denser than that on any human-constructed vessel that had come before it. But even the dense iridium alloy had its limits, and Grayson knew there were great breaches in his ship's hull. His damage control teams had done brilliant, tireless work, and *Eagle Fourteen* was close to fully-operational. But Grayson knew much of that consisted of fragile, hasty repairs that could give out at any time.

Not yet though. Hold together…for a while longer…

"Increase thrust to 8g," he snapped as he saw the target ship slowing to a stop and then starting to move in the reverse direction. "Gunnery, target their engines." He'd be damned if he was going to let that bastard get away.

"Yes, Captain."

Eagle Fourteen shook again, and this time Grayson could feel his ship was hurt. There were distant rumbles, the sound of subsidiary explosions. He checked the status monitors to confirm what he already knew. His ship was bleeding air through half a dozen hull breaches. The damage parties were on it, he was sure of that without checking, but there was only so much they could do when the damage was coming in faster than they could repair it.

A quick glance at the display told him *Eagle Nine* was worse off. Ying's ship was falling back, her thrust dropping as her damaged engines failed to match *Eagle Fourteen*'s 8g. Grayson thought for an instant about falling back, keeping pace with the other ship. But there was no time. Whatever chance he had to take out that flagship, it was now. Even a few minutes could be the difference, more time for the enemy to escape, for the ships closing from all sides to finish off both Eagle battleships.

He stared straight ahead, and then he said, "Set the reactors to overload level one, and increase thrust to 10g. We're going right down their throats." This was going to take everything he and *Eagle Fourteen* had, and if he held back—anything—he ensured defeat.

"Yes, sir…increasing to 10g."

"Main guns, continue blasting their engines." He could see his people had scored two hits—no, three—on or near the enemy's engines. The Black Flag ship was still accelerating, but as he was watching, his gunnery crews scored a fourth hit, directly on the engines themselves. His eyes darted to the small screen on his workstation to confirm what his gut already knew. The enemy's thrust had died completely. The Black Flag's command ship was moving along through space at a crawl.

Grayson watched, his eyes fixed, the stare of a predator in his gaze. The enemy wasn't going to get away, not now. This would be a duel to the end, a deadly fight at point blank range.

"Cut thrust to 4g, divert power to the batteries. All guns, shut off all safeties…fire at maximum overload levels. It's time to finish that piece of shit."

Chapter 15

"I've got a transmission from Admiral Garret, General."

Cain swung around abruptly and hurried toward the small table he was using as a makeshift desk. He'd been following the battle from a pair of mobile screens set up in front of a large antenna. He didn't like what he'd seen so far.

It wasn't that Garret was any less skilled than he had been in the battles from years ago, nor that his people weren't fighting hard. The enemy vastly outnumbered the Marine fleet, but it was more than that. Humanity's young colonies were far from matching the industrial might of old Earth, and the ships of Garret's fleet were mostly old, and the rest poorly constructed. The days of vast shipyards producing leading edge warships like the old *Yorktown*s were mostly passed, save perhaps for the Eagles. And clearly the Black Flag.

The enemy ships had a sharp technological advantage over Garret's old vessels, one that was making a major difference in the struggle now raging. Skill and courage were immensely valuable in war, but even those traits had a limit.

Cain grabbed the headset and pulled it over his head, nodding for his aide to play back the message. Garret's flagship was

113

better than a light hour from Armstrong now, and the words he was about to listen to had been sent more than sixty minutes earlier.

"Erik…I'm going to keep this short and to the point. We're losing up here. I'm willing to fight to the end, in fact, I'd consider death in battle a mercy right now. But if we hold any longer, there won't be anything left of the fleet. I'm going to pull back, head to the Nest and see if I can link up with the Eagles. I'm not even sure they'd be enough to overcome this assault force, but they're our best chance."

Cain listened, tensing at the realization that the enemy would be coming, that Armstrong would likely be under attack by morning. But he felt relief on another level. He'd been entirely unsure Garret would adhere to the plan, pull back and seek help if the fight was unwinnable. He knew it hurt the admiral to abandon the ground forces, to leave them at the mercy of the enemy…but it was the right call.

And we're Marines, Augustus. We're not at anybody's mercy…

"Good luck, my friend. Do what you can, what you have to do. Hold out, somehow, against whatever they throw at you. We *will* be back, you have my word. One more, my old friend, one more hopeless battle. It's not our first, by God, and we made the others work somehow. We're old and tired, but we've got this one more in us, I know it." There was a long pause, then: "Elias Holm is with you, Erik, and Terrence Compton and Darius Jax…all the lost friends who fought at our side. You are never alone my comrade. You never could be. Until I return…"

Cain stood and listened as the signal stopped, replaced by faint static. He stood for a moment, silent, contemplative, images of the warriors Garret had mentioned slipping quickly through his thoughts. Then he turned toward the aide and said crisply, "Sound the alert. I want all battalions in the shelters by 0800. I want the orbital defense satellites activated immediately. All ground missile installations are to arm ordnance."

"Yes, sir." The officer sounded a bit flustered at Cain's barrage of orders, but the general kept going, firing one off after the other, barely stopping for a breath between.

He flipped on the comm unit again, pausing for an instant before he began to speak. When he started, his message was short, to the point. "Message received, Admiral. Good luck to you and all who serve with you. Don't worry about us…we'll be here when you get back. I don't care what the Black Flag sends here, when they hit the ground, they're going to find Marines waiting…and that's going to be the worst day they've ever seen."

He took a deep breath and then glanced over at his aide. "Transmit."

The man had a defiant look on his face, one that hadn't been there before he'd listened to Cain's words. "Yes, sir!" the officer replied, the emotion behind his expression evident in his tone as well.

Garret's message had affected him, too, reminded him of who he was. He'd felt tired, the weight of his fifteen-year ordeal pushing down on him…but now an old strength was coming back. He thought of enemies from long ago…and, for all the damage they had done and terror they'd inflicted, he remembered where they were now…while the Marines were still here. The soldiers who were coming…they served those who took him from his family, who tortured him relentlessly, who almost broke him in the dungeons of Eldaron.

Now it was payback time, and if there was one thing Erik Cain knew how to do, it was take his revenge.

* * * * *

Aaron Carrack sat on the raised platform in the command center. It was what his enemies, the navies and fleets of most of Earth's colonies would have called a 'flag bridge.' But it was far more than that, a vast space with more than seventy officers at various stations, including the ship's captain and his own operational staff. All of the others, save for the exalted Carrack, the Marshal and Grand Commander of the Black Flag's fleet, sat below, under their master's watchful eye, and constantly reminded that in every way that mattered to them, he was their lord and master.

Carrack was a cruel man, and he enjoyed the fear his power inflicted on those around him. He'd used his exalted position to take everything he wanted, indulging the slightest whim without any concern for the impact on those around him. He didn't seek their love, nor their admiration. He wanted only their fear, the abject terror of what would befall them should they fail him in any way.

Carrack endured the same relationship in reverse at the hands of the Triumvirate. They'd saved him from captivity years before, but as time passed, gratitude had turned to hatred…and fear. And greed. He saw in the members of the Triumvirate, in the vast resources they were beginning to assemble, his road to his own power, and he'd followed it, to the top. Or, at least the top under the three Stark clones that had made the whole enterprise a reality. Carrack knew he owed everything to the Triumvirate, but that didn't stop him from hating and resenting them because they were above him in the command structure. And for all the years he'd served them, he didn't doubt the price he would pay for failure was no less terrifying than that he would mete out on his own subordinates.

"The enemy fleet is withdrawing, Marshal."

Carrack felt a wave of excitement, but he hid it. His emotions were not the concern of his subordinates, not unless they incurred his anger and wrath. But the satisfaction he felt was real, and powerful. Intelligence had confirmed that Augustus Garret was in command of the enemy fleet, and that made victory that much sweeter. Carrack had seen Garret, along with Erik Cain and the rest of their allies, destroy Gavin Stark's bid for power and crush his seemingly unbeatable Shadow Legions. Carrack had been a marginal player then, a mid-level operative with a bright future following his mentor's expected conquest. Garret and the others had destroyed all that, and Carrack had waited thirty-five years for his vengeance.

"Divert Task Force A and Task Force D to pursue. They are to inflict maximum possible losses on the enemy before they are able to reach the warp gate."

"Yes, sir. Shall I order them to transit and maintain contact?"

"Negative, Captain. Did I order that?" Carrack's petulance was mostly him taking out his frustration on his subordinates. He definitely wanted to pursue Garret's fleet, to hunt down his ships to the end of space itself if need be, until every last one of them had been destroyed. But he'd been expressly forbidden to do so. The Triumvirate was cautious, too concerned that splitting their forces would allow their enemies to join up somehow, inflict an unexpected defeat on the Black Flag fleet. It seemed foolish to Carrack, but he didn't dare disobey. The Triumvirate controlled him with the same use of stark terror he used on his own subordinates.

"My apologies, Marshal."

"The rest of the fleet will form up and advance on Armstrong."

"Yes, sir."

Carrack turned toward one of the myriad screens against the far wall, one which displayed a bluish-white planet, beautiful, almost idyllic-looking. *In just a few hours, no one will recognize that world…*

"All ground assault vessels are to prepare. The bombardment will begin as soon as we reach Armstrong orbit, Captain."

"Yes, sir."

Garret is defeated, at long last. Now, it's time for the Marines. We'll have to go down there and dig the last of them out of their holes, no question. But, first, let's see how they like a thousand gigatons or so tearing up that pretty little planet of theirs…

* * * * *

Cain stood, silent, still, staring at the small screen in front of him. The quarters were cramped, not the kind of headquarters a general who had led the entire Marine Corps was used to, but he didn't care. He hardly noticed. His eyes, his mind, were on only one thing. The missiles entering Armstrong's atmosphere. Hundreds of missiles. No, he thought, thousands…and he didn't have a doubt every one of them was a nuke.

There had been discussions, even arguments, in the strategy

sessions, about whether the Black Flag would honor the prohibitions against wholesale nuclear bombardments of civilian
populations centers. Gilson had been uncertain, and many of
the others had expressed confidence that there was no need to
pack the population into shelters, that the invaders, however
brutal they may be, wouldn't resort to such extreme measures,
especially when they could only expect the same in return one
day.

*No doubt they said the same things on Earth…right up until the mis-
siles launched.*

Cain had let the debate rage, for a while. Then he stood up,
slammed his fist on the table and said, with a cold and hard
tone no one had heard since his return from captivity, "They
will launch a nuclear bombardment. They will destroy every city,
every base, every building and warehouse on the surface. They
will kill every Marine, soldier, civilian, or child foolish enough
to stay unprotected. We have seen this again and again, and I
have listened to one set of fools after another, underestimating
enemies, superimposing their own ethics and logic on adversaries that do not think like them. I have buried friends, killed in
the extended conflicts that followed such idiocy." He'd reached
down, pulled out his pistol and set in on the small table. "I will
not watch this happen again. We cannot continually live this
cycle, every victory against darkness followed by complacency,
by lofty talk of morality and another descent into a fresh nightmare, an unwillingness to do what must be done…and more
millions dead."

He'd stood silently, glaring at everyone assembled. Some
were old comrades, of course, others officers who'd come up
in the years he'd been gone, weaned on his legends, but never
having followed him in a crisis. "We will not underestimate this
enemy. We will not withhold any means, any method that will
advance us to its destruction. We will face our enemies with their
tactics, with their same disregard for humanity…and we will
win. Because nothing else matters. Nothing else matters worth
a damn."

He'd gotten no response, only acquiescence. No one had

dared to argue with him. He wasn't sure if he'd convinced them all, or simply intimidated them, but he was sure of one thing. He didn't give a damn.

Now he watched his vindication, the assurance he didn't need to prove he'd been right. The enemy fleet had engaged the orbital defenses, and blown them to atoms, and now they'd unleashed the devastating attack he knew they would. Armstrong's ordeal had just begun. He thought of favorite places from his years of service on the Marines' homeworld, spots he and Sarah had enjoyed together. All that would be gone in a matter of minutes now, replaced by the scars of thermonuclear fury. Every building, the monuments, even the one he'd been embarrassed to see to himself, when he'd returned, would be gone, vaporized.

Then the battle would really begin. The underground bunkers would survive any bombardment, most of them at least. The enemy could destroy cities, houses, the majestic buildings of the Academy, but if they want to wipe out the Marines, they would have to come down and do it tunnel by tunnel, meter by meter.

He looked behind him, realizing the few square meters he had to himself was a palatial extravagance. Most of his Marines were packed on top of each other, and the civilians were jammed together even more brutally. Cain knew the food supplies wouldn't last, but long before starvation took a life, he'd have mass insanity, people losing control in the horrific conditions. He'd known his forces would be better able to fight without the burden of supporting the civilian population, and he'd tried to evacuate as many as possible before the Black Flag's fleet cut Armstrong from the warp gates. He'd told himself he had to leave them outside, had to reserve the limited shelter space for the Marines who would fight the enemy, but for all his cold practicality, his hard cynicism, Erik Cain had simply not been capable of abandoning so many thousands to huddle together as the bombs fell.

He wondered if Darius would have done it…and he decided he didn't really want to know.

"We're picking up detonations, General."

Cain sighed softly. He'd seen no shortage of destruction in his life, but it was still hard to watch Armstrong face its devastation. "I want all shelters to stay on top of their reactors and ventilation systems. It won't take much of a malfunction to suffocate ten thousand people or open the ducts to lethal radiation."

"Yes, sir." A moment later. "All shelters report status green, General."

He knew the response only meant the shelter systems were functioning, but he almost laughed at the absurdity of it. There was nothing 'green' about the current condition.

He watched as the scanning reports came in, fewer and fewer with each passing moment, as the antennae and dishes collecting the data succumbed to the nightmarish apocalypse. Cain could picture the Armageddon above, the miniature suns erupting all around, destroying everything man had built on Armstrong. He'd known, without a doubt in his mind, that the enemy would utterly destroy the planet's surface, but even that was insufficient to hold back the flow of emotion he felt. Cain was all too familiar with nuclear devastation, he'd even wandered too close to a detonation once, a misstep that had cost him both legs and much of the rest of his body, and sent him to the hospital for his first experience of the pain of regeneration.

The hospital was gone now, and the base. The fields where he'd so recently drilled the recruits—men and women who had too little training, but would now experience a baptism of fire beyond anything they'd imagined. Everything. Gone.

Nothing left. Nothing save for the killing. And Cain was ready for that.

Chapter 16

John Grayson gripped the armrest of his chair, eyes on the main display, watching as his ship floated alongside *Eagle Nine* and pounded the enemy flagship. The massive Black Flag vessel was far from idle, and it returned fire, its guns as large as those possessed by the Eagle ships and more numerous. The enemy behemoth was almost half again the size of *Eagle Fourteen*, and while Grayson had determined its crew wasn't up to the standards of his own, there was no doubt the vessel's technology was on par with that of the Eagles, or even a cut above.

The enemy lasers sliced through *Eagle Fourteen*'s armored plating, obliterating structure and spacers alike as they dug deep into his wounded ship. One by one, his batteries fell silent, hit directly or silenced by damage to the reactors and the power transmission systems. The situation was approaching critical, but as he watched the data coming in from *Eagle Nine*, he knew his companion ship had already reached that stage. Captain Ying's ship was down to its last two lasers, and Grayson's scanners showed sharp declines in energy readings.

"Get me Captain Ying," he said, but almost the instant he finished, he saw the icon representing Ying's vessel blink off the display, and the scanner readings spiked dramatically.

The bridge was silent, not a sound save that of the equipment, a few beeps and whirs and nothing more. The Eagles had not fought this desperate of a fight, perhaps ever. Grayson didn't know how the battle would progress, whether the feared mercenaries would finally be defeated by an enemy or if they would prevail, hold out and secure a costly victory. But he knew one thing, as well as everyone else on *Eagle Fourteen*'s bridge.

Eagle Nine was gone, along with every man or woman onboard.

The silence only lasted a few seconds. There was still a battle to fight, and Grayson's people were still Eagles, however stunned and devastated they might be at the loss of their comrades.

"Captain, battery seven has suffered a blowout. We've got two confirmed dead, and three still missing."

"Very well." Grayson knew he'd killed those two crew members, and probably the other three as well. His orders to fire all guns on overloads did not come without risk. But there was no choice. Any victory now would be by the slightest of margins, and he needed to maintain all the power he could against the enemy.

Eagle Fourteen rocked again, and from the direction of the movement, Grayson realized the shot had not come from the enemy flagship. His surprise move, the desperate lunge forward through the gap in the enemy lines, had given him a jump on the responding Black Flag ships, but now they were closing, and the fire coming in was intensifying.

That's going to be where we fall short...we could take this thing, I know we could, but those ships are going to get to us first...

Grayson felt helpless, and his psyche rebelled, a part of his mind demanding he come up with some tactic, some way to endure the attacks, to defeat the ship he'd come so hard to destroy. But there was nothing, no way.

Then, almost as if in answer, one of the attacking enemy ships vanished from the screen. Then, seconds later, another. It took him a few seconds to focus, to figure out what had happened. And then he saw *Eagle Three*, blasting forward at 8g, directly toward his position.

He knew immediately that General Cain had sent the ship to aid him and, as he had countless times, he found himself amazed at Cain's seemingly unworldly instinct for battle.

Eagle Three wasn't in range of the enemy flagship, but she was taking the focus off his vessel, coming up in the blind spots of the ships closing on *Eagle Fourteen*.

"Let's go," he said, renewed vigor in his voice. "*Eagle Three* is taking the heat off. Let's finish this big bastard...now!" He slammed his fist down on the armrest and said, "All gunners, that ship's got three or four big hull breaches amidships. Keep pounding there. You are all Eagles, the best. If anybody can thread that needle, it's you!"

He leaned forward and watched, his fists clenched tightly, sweat running down his neck in long rivulets. The enemy ship was less than twenty thousand kilometers away, incredibly close range by the standards of space combat. His gunners were hitting with virtually every shot, one blast of energy after another, ripping great rents in the hull, sending spouts of flash-frozen air and fluids into the frigid wastes of space.

His own ship was battered too, but unlike her target, *Eagle Fourteen* still had active thrust, and her navigators were cycling through random, miniscule course changes, a zigzag pattern that didn't meaningfully alter her vector, but gave targeting computers fits. The Eagle's program was the best, but at such close range, even the sophisticated AIs running Tom Sparks's system couldn't escape every shot.

Eagle Fourteen shook again, and then again almost immediately. A row of lights on the port workstations flickered for a few seconds before returning to normal, and Grayson knew his ship couldn't take much more, not without a break for her engineers to repair some of the damage. But whatever respite might await them, it wasn't now.

Hit after hit slammed into the enemy ship, and Grayson sat, stunned. He'd never seen anything soak up so much damage and still endure, but the Black Flag ship was still there...and *Eagle Fourteen* shook again, as the pursuing ships continued to fire.

Eagle Three was chasing the vessels, blasting them to scrap, but the enemy ignored the deadly battleship on their tail and continued toward their flagship, utterly mindless of their own survival.

Two more of *Eagle Fourteen*'s shots slammed into the enemy ship, dead amidships, and a massive blast poured out from what was now a three-hundred-meter tear in the hull. Then, as he was watching, another shot hit right in the center of the hull breach.

Grayson watched, feeling the tension in his stomach, as the great ship shook from the explosions spreading through its depths. The behemoth sat where it was, dead in space, cracking and breaking open along its spine. Then, a cheer went up on *Eagle Fourteen*'s battered bridge as the enemy vessel simply vanished, nothing remaining but pure energy and an expanding cloud of very hard radiation.

He felt a wave of satisfaction, and he threw his clenched fist in the air and yelled, delighting his crew with the sight of a Black Eagle captain cheering alongside them. But the celebration was short-lived, perhaps half a minute. Then *Eagle Fourteen* shook again, another hit from the ships coming up behind her.

"Alright, Eagles," he said, his voice back to its stony command tone. "Well done, but there are a lot of enemies still out there. We've got a battle to fight, so let's get to it!"

*   *   *   *   *

"*Eagle One* and *Eagle Eleven*, adjust thrust vectors to 234.101.033. Let's bracket that task force between the ships and the Nest's guns." Darius Cain was alert, focused, adrenalin flowing through his bloodstream. He'd watched Grayson's defeat of the enemy flagship, an event that had fired up morale throughout the fleet. His Eagles, always focused and capable, were now fighting like wild beasts.

"Yes, General." Ana snapped back the acknowledgement, and she turned to her workstation and relayed the commands.

The Black Flag fleet was losing ship after ship, and Darius no longer doubted his people would have the victory. The cost…that was something even the coldly analytical mercenary had put out of his mind for the moment. His Eagles had never been tested like this, and he felt immense pride in how that had endured, and the ferocity with which they'd fought.

He wondered what was happening on Columbia. Teller had managed to get a few short transmissions through, a bit sketchy on details, but suggesting confidence that the situation was manageable. Darius trusted his lifelong friend completely, both in terms of loyalty, and also in confidence, in his ability to see a task completed successfully. But he was still edgy, wondering if his ground forces were enduring the same nightmare that had come upon his fleet.

He had analyzed the situation around the Nest, his mind working as it usually did, tirelessly, meticulously. The enemy was going to lose, but his Eagles would suffer grievously before they had destroyed every enemy ship. Which, he realized, was what it would take. The one thing he'd seemed to glean from his experiences with the Black Flag is they didn't surrender, not ever. He was less sure about retreat, but the enemy ships, battered and disordered as they were, had made no signs at withdrawal. Their command ship had tried to run, but *Eagle Fourteen* had put a stop to that. The others continued to fight his ships, even in places where they were trapped and locally outnumbered.

This, too, was something new for Darius and his Eagles. They had long been accustomed to their fearsome reputation accomplishing half the victory for them before they even landed. But this battle, they'd had to win the hard way, and they'd paid for it in blood. Were still paying…

"Deactivate the point defense network," he said, his eyes fixed on the bank of screens around his station. "Divert power to the heavy guns." The Nest had not escaped without damage any more than his ships had, and three of his reactors were silent, the reactions shut down to protect against breaches in the magnetic containment systems. He was pretty sure the enemy had expended all their missiles, and the fighter battle was pretty well over too, what few enemy birds had survived the wrath of his own battered squadrons too low on fuel and ordnance to threaten his base. And his main batteries could make better use of the energy.

"All power diverted to primary guns, General."

He turned and exchanged glances with Elias, who nodded at his gaze. His brother had been silent, watching the battle unfold.

The enemy had come close to the Nest, and for a short time it looked like they might breach the defenses and get through. The command center, like everything else vital, was far below ground, a hard target for any orbital bombardment to take out. But Darius hadn't been anxious to test that out. He'd been spared that necessity, by Grayson as much as anyone else. The desperate recall the enemy flagship had evidently sent out had pulled the last of the attacking ships from the Nest, sending them, along with most of the Black Flag fleet, on a desperate—and ultimately futile—attempt to save the command vessel.

"General, I've got Commodore Allegre on the comm."

"Put him through."

"General, I think the enemy is attempting to break off."

Darius's eyes flashed to the main display. Allegre was right! It wasn't obvious at first glance. Many of the ships had intrinsic velocities that were still bringing them closer to the Eagle vessels. But the energy outputs, the thrust readings, they all told the same story. Every enemy ship was blasting its engines, some at full, others at the most they could coax from damaged engines and crippled reactors.

Whatever the degree of thrust, the headings were all the same. Directly back toward the warp gate.

"It appears you are correct, Commodore. Your people are to be commended. Suitable words fail me, but I will try to remedy that at a later time."

"I am about to order a pursuit, General. We can stop some of them from getting away, no question about that."

Darius was nodding gently to himself, about to confirm Allegre's intentions. But there was something there, a thought, disturbing but persistent. He hesitated, so much so that he could feel the eyes of his control center crew, utterly used to his snap decisions and bold orders. But he was deep in thought now, and the conclusion forming in his mind was unsettling.

"Negative, Commodore." The words came out of his mouth, even as he was still considering the situation.

"Sir? We can take out more of their ships, almost certainly."

"No, Commodore. We can't risk further losses, not now. If we press them, they may turn and fight to the end."

"Then we will destroy them." Allegre seemed shocked, as though it had never occurred to him Darius Cain would refuse to pursue the defeated enemy.

"And we will lose more. No, Commodore. You have your orders. Reform the fleet and see to damage control operations." His tone virtually eliminated the possibility of further discussion. No one challenged Darius Cain when his words sounded like *that*.

"Yes, sir. As you command."

"Cain out." He cut the line. He understood Allegre's concerns. Pursuit was the right option, save for one problem…

"Why, Darius? We'll just have to fight them again, and they'll be repaired and rearmed." Elias's voice cut through the heavy silence in the Nest's command center. Darius's brother was the only one there who dared to question the mercenary. The others had seen his fearsome fury, and they dared not risk unleashing it. They didn't know, as he did, and perhaps Elias did as well, how much of that fury was staged, planned for its effect, and Darius didn't want them to know.

"You're right, of course," Darius replied, his voice calm, the storm his officers feared nowhere to be seen. "By normal tactical considerations, we should have pursued them right up to the gate, even through it, perhaps."

"Then why break off?"

"Because these aren't normal situations…and this wasn't a normal attack."

Elias looked back, a confused expression on his face. "Then what was it?"

"A diversion."

Elias was dumbstruck. "A diversion?" He looked around at the blackened sections of circuitry in the control center, the chunks of plasti-steel that had fallen from the structural supports. "Darius, we barely got through the fight, perhaps we wouldn't have at all if *Eagle Fourteen* hadn't gotten to the enemy flagship."

"Yes, that's what we're supposed to think, Elias. It was a well-planned scheme, certainly. They knew we'd never believe they'd hit us with all they had, not unless we were hard-pressed." He paused. "But look at these damage reports. We got hurt, no question, but it wasn't as close as it looked. *Eagle Nine* and *Eagle Six* were destroyed, but the other fourteen battleships are still operational, at least to some degree. I've been running some scenarios in my head. We'd have won without *Eagle Fourteen*'s attack. Almost every possible outcome I can conceive is a victory, the only variables being the damage we sustain."

Elias just stared back. It was one thing to understand his brother's gift for war on a general level, and quite another to see it in action. But he didn't doubt what Darius had said, not for an instant.

Darius looked back at his brother. "It takes a certain kind of mind to commit so many ships and combatants to a battle you expect to lose…know you will lose."

"You're assuming they did know. Even if…I'm sure your calculations are correct, but that doesn't mean *they* knew that. Perhaps they thought they could win."

Darius shook his head. "No, I don't think so. That's a dangerous road, underestimating an enemy. This is an adversary that lurked in the shadows for more than thirty years, that extended its tentacles throughout Occupied Space all through that time without ever being discovered. Not by us, not by the Marines… by no one. In that time, they clearly built an awesome industrial powerbase, one with a technology at least on pars with ours— and by ours, I mean the Eagles—and probably a cut above. They've seized control of Atlantia, of almost four hundred worlds now, all without firing more than a random shot or two." He paused. "We can't underestimate these people again, Elias. To date, they have exhibited far more capability than we have."

"So, why would they launch a diversion? If they have more forces, why not just send them here and finish us off."

Darius stared back coldly. "Because they needed it to be somewhere else. Because if this was the diversion, the real attack force is somewhere else."

"But where?" Elias had asked the question, but a second later the two of them were staring at each other, and it was clear neither one of them had the slightest doubt about the answer."

"Armstrong," Darius said after a few seconds of silence. "They're at Armstrong."

Chapter 17

Ruins Near Marine Headquarters
Planet Armstrong, Gamma Pavonis III
Earthdate: 2321 AD (36 Years After the Fall)

"Keep moving...grab whatever cover you can, and set up those autocannons. They're coming this way." Richard Dern leaned down, crouching behind the pile of Earth and re-solidified rock, all that remained of whatever had once stood in front of his position. *The mess hall?* He tried to get a feel for exactly where he stood, but in the incinerated nightmare of the battlefield, it was impossible to be sure. Even hills and ridgelines had been moved and reshaped by the cataclysmic fury of the thermonuclear barrage. He was pretty sure he was somewhere in what had been the main Marine compound, but that was as close as he could get.

"Where do you want these, Captain?" The voice was thin, the speaker's anxiety clear in every word.

"Right here." He extended his arm, pointing toward the meter high lip of cover he'd spotted. "It'll give you some protection if you lay low enough, and you should have a good field of fire if the enemy advances up this way." *Which they're going to do, almost certainly...*

Dern had been a Marine for twelve years now...well, a cadet for four and on active duty for eight. He'd come from a small colony world, one on the outskirts of Occupied Space. One that had been hit hard by the First Imperium forces during the Second Incursion. Dern had lost his parents in that war, and a lot of others close to him too. He'd have been dead himself, along with his sister and what remained of his family, had it not been for the Marines.

They had come, landed, and immediately threw themselves against the great killer robots, fighting with a passion like nothing the young farmer had ever seen. He'd wanted to follow them then and there when they left, go back to the legendary Academy and become one of them. He was smart enough, and fit enough, he'd figured, and for a farm boy, he'd gotten a damned good education too. But he'd had to wait. His sister needed him, and he'd remained behind until she'd come of age and gone to school offworld. Then he sold the farm and booked a passage to Armstrong.

He'd *thought* he was in good shape, but the drill instructors almost ran him into an early grave. When they were finished, he was stronger and faster than he'd ever been, and he felt something new, a pride that hadn't been there before. And that education he'd gotten years before paid off. He'd passed the Academy entrance exams with flying colors and qualified for officer training. It would delay his entry into the Corps by four years, but when he first suited up for active duty, he would do it as a lieutenant, and a platoon leader. That's what he had been for most of the last eight years, at least until the massive mobilization bumped him up to captain and company commander.

He'd have given his left eye for his old platoon right about now. His entire company had been formed from current trainees, men and women who'd barely completed basic training when the invasion force arrived. They were good, of course. The Corps didn't accept anything but the best, but they weren't ready, not for the hell that had erupted all around them. Not that there wasn't much choice.

"Battalion HQ, this is Captain Dern. I've got my company deployed along a rough stretch of light cover, maybe six hundred meters south-southwest of the old admin hall. Transmitting the coordinates now. Request further instructions."

"Copy, Captain. Your people are to stay put. You've got a column of Black Flag coming your way. ETA less than seven minutes."

"Understood, Battalion. Dern out." He looked down at the screen projected inside his visor. His AI, which had been listening to the conversation of course, had displayed an area map, with icons representing the enemy formations. It didn't take more than a second or two for him to realize his people were facing three times their number...maybe four.

He moved down the ragged line his people had formed, trying to remember to crouch as he did. It would be a fine display for an officer to remind his Marines to stay low...and then to get his own head blown off. "Extend these lines, Marines. What did they teach you in basic training? You trying to make it easier for these sons of bitches to kill you all?"

It was basic tactics in modern war, but it was more than that. Code Orange protocols were still in effect, and that meant nuclear warheads could come screaming down any second. And even a fully armored Marine didn't want to get *too* close to one of those.

Companies were about the biggest operational formations General Cain had sent out, and he only did that when he was sure platoons couldn't do the job. It meant being outnumbered in almost every engagement—a virtual inevitability anyway considering enemy strength—but it also eliminated the chance of losing whole battalions and regiments at one time. The enemy had total control of orbit and the space around Armstrong, and they'd shown no compunction about launching additional nuclear strikes anywhere a worthwhile target showed itself, even if doing so meant taking out a few of their own people. It was simple math to them, and it seemed pretty clear they valued killing a Marine far more than preserving one of their own.

Dern could see the approaching forces now. Normally, his armor would be linked into the battlefield net, and he'd be pulling data from every drone and scanner in the army. But with the enemy having total local space superiority, and the utter devastation from the nuclear strikes, the defending forces didn't have much in the way of information sources. And the scanners in Dern's suit, and those of his Marines, didn't have much range, not burning through the heavy jamming the enemy was laying down.

"Here they come," he said into the comm, trying to sound as cool as he could, which he suspected wasn't all that cool. He gripped his own rifle, and leaned forward, pressing his form against the newly-hardened lip of rock. "Autocannons...open fire."

The heavy weapons started shooting immediately, and he could see shadowy figures in the distance, a few of them dropping as the rest pressed on. The Black Flag soldiers had powered armor every bit as good as the Marines', which snatched away an advantage Dern had hoped his people might have.

The Black Flag soldiers—*we really need to come up with something to call them*—were well trained enough, but they were no match for the Marines in terms of drill and maneuver. His company had fought half a dozen skirmishes, and he'd guess they'd taken down four or five for every one of their own they'd lost...and he'd heard of loss ratios of ten to one or higher for some of the veteran formations. But his company had still withdrawn from each engagement, as had the more experienced units, falling back from one position to the next, a bit weaker each time. There was no reason to hold anywhere, nothing left to defend, at least until the enemy drove them back to the shelters. General Cain had been clear. Short of those access points, there was nothing left on Armstrong worth losing a single Marine to defend.

Now, Dern had lost nearly a quarter of his strength, even giving up ground as he had, and for all the casualties the Marines had inflicted on the invaders, the Black Flag seemed to have no shortage of soldiers to feed into the maelstrom.

"Swing those fields of fire around," he shouted into the comm, his eyes darting to the edge of his visor display. The enemy had doubled up on the right, a dense column pushing forward. He needed more fire there, and his puppy Marines hadn't reacted quickly enough on their own.

"Yes, sir." He could hear the terror in the recruit's voice, and he knew his people were close to their limit. He wondered if the utter hopelessness all around them, the endless plateau of blasted, radioactive nothingness, actually made it easier to keep them in the line. Where were they going to go? The shelter was ten klicks behind them, and there wasn't so much as a building standing between here and there. There truly was no place to run.

He aimed his assault rifle, watching the enemy forces approaching on the targeting projection inside his visor. "Company C, open fire," he said, as he pressed his own trigger, feeling the slight vibration through his armor as the rifle opened up. He knew the recoil would have knocked him on his ass, and probably dislocated his shoulder, had he fired it unarmored.

The tiny hypervelocity rounds ripped out over the gloomy terrain, and he could see the enemy line pause as it was hit by the incoming blasts of fire. Perhaps a dozen more enemy troops dropped, but then the others went prone and opened up with their own weapons. The Black Flag's small arms were at least the equals of the Marines', and Dern ducked low, sucking in a deep breath as a burst of fire ripped by, perhaps ten centimeters above his head. A quick glance at his display told him four of his people had been a half second slower than he had, with disastrous consequences.

"Winger, pull your platoon back and move to the right. Hoover, stretch your people out, cover the whole frontage."

Winger answered, but Hoover didn't. Another look at the display showed the platoon leader's monitors flat. That didn't mean he was dead, not necessarily. It could just be a sensor failure. But he didn't answer the comm either, so it didn't look good.

"The lieutenant's down, sir." It was Sergeant Stein. *A veteran…thankfully.* "I think he's dead, but I'm not sure."

"Well you make damned sure before we leave him there. And then get that platoon moving. Winger's group is heading south, and I need you to cover the extra frontage."

"Captain, we're already pretty strung out…"

"So, you're going to be more strung out. Unless you think we should just let the enemy march through our center and hit both wings from the inside."

"No, sir…I mean, yes, sir. I'll see it done."

"I know you will, Sergeant. Dern out."

He'd been firing the whole time, carefully aimed three shot bursts. But the enemy was getting closer, using the same kind of melted and re-hardened ridges of stone to screen their advance. They were taking losses, but not enough. Dern's people could have held against even numbers, or against two to one, even three to one odds…but he had six or eight times his number bearing down—more even than he'd expected—and he was just about to call HQ and report his forces were about to be overrun when his comm crackled to life.

"Captain Dern, I need you to pull your men back. We're retreating to the industrial sector on the edge of town." Colonel Fairchild paused. "What used to be the industrial sector," he added, grimly.

"Sir, we're hard-pressed here. I'm not sure…"

"Orders are direct from General Cain, Captain. The lines are collapsing north and south of your position. If you don't get out now, none of your people ever will."

"Understood, sir." *Shit.* He turned and looked behind him. What had once been part of the Academy grounds and a large shopping district beyond was nothing but dead flat, open ground. Bugging out was going to be a bitch. And it was going to cost.

He flipped the comm channel back to his company's line. "Winger, cancel that last order. We're pulling out. Drop back two hundred meters and grab the best ground you can. Set up a line to provide covering fire while the rest of the company retreats."

"Yes, Captain."

Dern could see Winger's people on his display, already moving. With any luck, they'd make it back without too many losses. They had the rest of the company covering them. It was going to be a damned sight different when the other two platoons dropped from their cover and took off. But there wasn't a choice. Dern had never served with Erik Cain before, but from all he'd heard about the famous general, if he'd called a retreat that probably mean the shit was really going to hit it.

*   *   *   *   *

"This one's hopeless. Give him 20cc of Methatolin, and set him down somewhere quiet." Sarah Cain stood in the dim light of the makeshift hospital, awash in blood rituals. The casualties were coming in faster than her people could even perform triage. It sickened her to give up on a patient, even one she knew she couldn't save, but decades as a battlefield surgeon had driven home the realization that four or five others might die while she wasted her time on one lost cause."

"Yes, Doctor."

At least they called her doctor in the hospital. It avoided the confusion of having two Generals Cain floating around.

"Get this one to surgery, right now." She shot a glance at the pair of stretcher bearers, as if her eyes were saying, "Move your asses!"

"Sally, get one of the techs with the plasma torch up here. We've got to get this one out of her armor."

"Yes, Dr. Cain."

Sarah paused, just for a second, sucking in a deep breath and grabbing a cloth, wiping the sweat from her forehead. She was angry, frustrated. She was losing people she could have saved in the hospital, a moot point when the great medical facility was nothing now but a pile of radioactive dust. But it still made her blood boil.

"Doctor…" Another orderly handed her a small canister of water.

"Thank you, she said, barely noticing who it was." She held it for a second, realizing just how thirsty she was, and then she downed it in one gulp."

"Alright people," she said, laying the empty container on a shelf. "I know you're all tired, but we need to keep going." Erik had commed her earlier, part of the call a small use of command prerogative, a minute, perhaps two for them to hear each other's voices, say the things they'd said over the years, when they knew each exchange of words could be their last. But, mostly, he'd wanted to tell her the combat was intensifying, that she'd have even more casualties streaming into her makeshift field hospital…and the three others in different shelters. She hadn't told her people the tidal wave of mangled bodies they'd been working for the last thirty-six hours had been the tip of the iceberg, but she'd done everything she could to drive them harder, squeeze every last bit of effort from them.

"General Cain, the power supply is straining." The non-medical staff tended to call her by rank. Almost as if in response to the tech's report, the lights flickered for a few seconds.

Sarah looked up, even as the lamps stabilized, and she sighed. "Do what you can, Lieutenant. I don't need to tell you what happens here if we lose power."

"No, General, you don't. We'll do all we can."

"That's all any of us can do." There was no need to berate the technician, no advantage to reminding him the situation was critical when he already knew it was. But that didn't lessen the tension in her gut at the thought of how many would die if the power feeds cut out.

Erik had been right, again. The shelters *had* survived the bombardment, a vicious assault that had exceeded even her worst expectations. They hadn't come through without damage, and some casualties too. Several compartments had collapsed, killed hundreds and trapping more under tons of debris. As far as she knew, they were still digging out the survivors, and a dozen or so an hour crept into her hospital alongside the combat casualties. But most of the Marines and civilians hunkered down in the bunkers had made it, at least this far.

The reactors had been battered as well, and some of the cargo rooms. There had been radiation leaks and structural failures, and Erik had ordered a curtain of secrecy on just how much of the already meager food supplies had been spoiled by radiation. Most of the people had survived, at least for now, but to describe the situation below ground as precarious was a dramatic understatement.

"General Cain…" The voice was loud, distorted, the comm speakers of a suit of powered armor blaring too loudly off the plasti-crete walls of the shelter.

She turned around, and her eyes landed at once on the Marine. He was fully-armored, but as she watched, he popped his helmet and looked across the room toward her.

"Yes, Captain?" she asked, taking a deep breath and walking toward the new arrival…a far easier alternative than him trying to get across the crowded room in his bulky fighting suit. For an instant, she felt a rush of fear, half expecting the officer had come to tell her the worst. She knew Erik Cain better than anyone else, and she realized only too clearly that lofty rank had done little to keep him off the front lines.

"The general sent me…general. The other General Cain. The enemy's moved closer to the shelter, and their jamming is interfering with regular comm transmissions, no he ordered me to come over here."

She felt a wave of relief. Things, were bad—and she was probably about to hear they were worse than she thought—but at least Erik was okay. For now, she would be satisfied with that.

"General, there are more wounded coming in. A lot more. The general sent me with a platoon to help any way we can."

"Unless you've got medical training, Captain…no, wait." She turned and looked back toward one of the tunnels leading deeper into the shelter. "You can help, Captain. We've got supply rooms back there, full of irradiated food. It's not usable, and it's taking up space. If your people can clear it all out, maybe I can set up another trauma ward in there."

"Yes, General." The massive figure nodded to her, and then he turned, moving back down the tunnel.

It wouldn't be good if too many people saw Marines carting out the crates of food. They'd probably assume the military was keeping it for themselves…but even the truth that two-thirds of the rations were spoiled would be bad if it got out.

She exhaled hard. But that didn't matter now. She had a simple choice. Find a way to handle more wounded…or watch hundreds of Marines die out there for lack of medical care, wasting away in the radioactive hell that had been their homeworld just a few days before.

Chapter 18

"First Battalion, secure the perimeter. We've got enemy forces all around. We don't know who made it inside, but your job is to make sure no more get in. And I mean not Goddamned one. Understood, Captain Huger?"

"Yes, Major. Understood."

"Second Battalion, you're with me. We're going to search this complex from sub-basement to the roof, and we're going to find President Tyler. Black Flag combatants are to be shot on sight, but remember there are probably Columbian soldiers in there too, not to mention medical staff and civilians, so be careful what you shoot. We're here to secure the president, and that's the priority. Shooting his soldiers will be bad, but not as bad as not finding him." *Or not finding him in time.*

It was clear there had been fighting in the street outside the hospital, and the doors and windows along the front were broken. There were bodies, and more than a few wounded soldiers from what looked like both sides, but Camerici didn't have time for any of that.

"Let's move," she roared, and then she headed toward the main entrance, leading her center company in.

140

A squad of Eagles slipped by her, moving to point, likely embarrassed by having their diminutive battalion commander the first one entering the building. They fanned out all around, as additional troopers poured in. There was nothing at first, save debris and bodies, but then gunfire erupted.

Camerici ducked back, as did all her soldiers. It took a few seconds to get a read on where the fire was coming from, and then her people opened up, at least two dozen Eagles blasting at what had sounded like two rifles, max. She knew it was almost as likely the shooters were loyal Columbian soldiers as enemies, but her efforts to spare Tyler's troops did not extend to putting her own in unnecessary jeopardy…and whoever was up there, *they* had opened fire.

The incoming shots ceased almost immediately. She didn't know if her people had gotten the shooters, or if they had retreated, but that didn't really matter, not now.

"Alright, let's keep going. If there are Black Flag soldiers in here, we've got to get to the president before they do. Finding and securing President Tyler is a Priority One objective."

The space was large, probably a lobby of some sort, but now it was deserted, the desks and walls torn apart by automatic weapons fire. There were a dozen bodies scattered around, a bit better than two-thirds of them unarmored, wearing the uniforms of Columbia's Guards Regiment. The others wore fighting suits, at a quick glance as heavy and sophisticated as the Eagles' own Mark VIIIs.

Black Flag…they are *in here…*

She raced toward the back of the large, open area. There was a bank of elevators against the wall, but they were as blasted apart as the front desk, and they looked completely non-functional. "To the stairs…I want a platoon on each floor. Full power comm blast the second you see something, understood?" There was sporadic jamming, but nothing that would prevent at least a base signal from getting through.

"Yes, Major." A series of acknowledgements came in, from the center company's platoon leaders, and now from Company A, moving in behind the lead group.

"First Platoon, with me." Her senior platoon was one hundred percent veteran, mostly Eagles with four or five years' experience in Red and White Battalions. She paused for a second at the door leading to the stairwell, and then she swung around, her rifle ready. But there was nothing.

She ran up the stairs, one level, then two. The steps were some sort of marble or stone, and several of them cracked under her hard, armored steps. There was a handrail, but she didn't touch it. She was experienced enough at operating powered armor to realize she'd snap the thing off like a twig.

She had her onboard scanners operating at full, trying to pick up any abnormal energy readings, even motion that seemed suspicious. She turned and ran up to the fourth floor, stopping and looking around, checking her readings. The building was a hospital, and one look at her display confirmed there were people everywhere running around in a crazed panic, trying to hide or escape. The lobby had been deserted, not surprisingly, since that was clearly a spot where Tyler's guards had tried to make a stand.

Camerici didn't doubt the courage of the president's soldiers, and she knew some of Tyler's people were equipped with powered armor, albeit older models. But the loyalists had clearly been caught by surprise, with only unarmored units to face the rebels...and whatever fully-powered allies those behind the assassination attempt had been able to smuggle in.

She walked toward the door leading to the fourth floor hall. She was about to go through, and then she heard gunfire. It was distant, several more floors up. It wasn't conclusive, but it was all she had to go on. She waved for the lead troopers to follow her, and she bounded up the stairs, the clatter of armored feet echoing loudly off in the confined space.

The sound was closer now, and she got a better read on it. *The eighth floor*, she thought. Then: *no, the ninth*.

She ran up the last flight and burst through the door without delay—a reckless maneuver, she knew. The sound of combat was heavier now, from somewhere down at the far end of the hall. "Let's go...combat formation," she snapped. "Just make sure you go after the right targets." *Easier said than done.*

She advanced, more cautiously than she had emerged into the corridor, her rifle at the ready and her visor amped up to level three mag. The corridor was wide enough for two armored troopers abreast. She knew she had no place in the front, but she'd managed to get herself there anyway, and she wasn't about to make a spectacle out of trying to slip back a few ranks. Besides, this way she had a better chance of avoiding anyone firing at Tyler's guards. Assuming *she* could manage to pick out the correct target any better than one of her troopers.

She moved steadily, picking up the pace. The hall was open, with no cover of any kind, so she figured it was a better bet to speed things up, get her people into the action. If the enemy saw them coming and opened up now, it would be a bloody mess.

The hall was long, at least a hundred meters. There were signs of fighting the entire way, one hospital room after another, doors shattered, bullet holes riddling the walls. Most were empty, no doubt abandoned by occupants who'd had any ability at all to move. There were some bodies, too, troopers who'd clearly died fighting, and patients, those who appeared to have been bedridden...shot where they lay.

Whoever had come this way, they were killing everyone they encountered. Tyler's reputation was that of a hard man, and a brutal one when necessary, but she'd never heard anyone characterize him as the kind of psychopath who murdered sick people in their beds.

The Black Flag...

Camerici knew many people in Occupied Space cursed the Eagles, thought of them much as she now thought of this new enemy. *It's not fair*, she thought. Then: *Or is it?*

No, it isn't. General Cain was always ready to do whatever had to be done, but we never murdered civilians, we never abused prisoners. Still, millions died nevertheless in those campaigns, burned to death in their homes, caught in the fire and the blasts of artillery barrages. Were any of them less dead than these patients lying in their bloodstained beds?

She saw an opening up ahead, a large room at the end of the hall, and shadows inside. There was a firefight going on, but she couldn't make out the sides, not yet.

She raced the rest of the way, stopping at the doorway, and leaning in cautiously. There were six soldiers in powered armor, gunning down a mass of blue-coated soldiers struggling to take whatever cover they could. Camerici recognized the beleaguered group as Tyler's elite troopers, and that was all she needed to know.

"Take down the armored soldiers," she snapped to her Eagles, rushing forward into the room. She was on the side of the armored troopers, almost the rear. She opened up on full auto, her hypervelocity rounds slamming into one of the enemy, then another.

The Black Flag troopers spun around, trying to bring their own weapons to bear against the new, unexpected threat, but the two she'd hit dropped to the ground before they could fire. Another pair fell in a cloud of glowing, 8,000 meter per hour projectiles, but the last two were able to open up before they, too, went down. One of the shots clipped Camerici in the arm, and a burst hit one of her troopers just as he ran into the room.

She could feel the trauma control system in her suit responding, sterile foam pouring out of the tiny tubes built into the armor, expanding, sealing the wound. She knew it wasn't that bad…but it hurt like a son of a bitch, at least until the suit injected her with a moderately strong painkiller a few seconds later.

She pushed the thought out of her mind, along with her reflexive concern for her more seriously wounded trooper—Figus, her AI informed her. Eagle training was strict and clear. Secure the location first.

The six enemy powered troopers were all down, clearly incapacitated, if not dead. But there were another dozen or so unarmored, wearing uniforms different from the guards, but styles Camerici recognized as Columbian. *The turncoats.*

Antonia Camerici was a tiny woman, barely one and a half meters tall, at least without her armor, and she didn't look brutal or dangerous. But she was both. And among the many things that rubbed her the wrong way, traitors were at the very top of the list.

The soldiers were standing around, one or two taking an ineffectual potshot at her armored Eagles. The nuclear-powered assault rifles the powered troopers had carried could penetrate the reinforced osmium-iridium alloy of her Eagles' armor, but it took one hell of a shot from a standard issue explosive propellant weapon to do the same.

The enemy soldiers looked confused, as though they wanted to flee, and realizing there was no way, they were about to surrender. Tyler's guards were mostly down, some of them wounded, and a few just climbing back from the spots where they'd been pinned.

"Take them down," she said, without the slightest hesitation in her voice. She gestured toward the traitors.

Half a dozen Eagles were in the room by then, and it took only a few seconds to gun down the stunned enemy troopers.

"Stand down," she snapped toward Tyler's guards, as she saw a few of them bringing their weapons to the ready. "We're Black Eagles. We're here to secure the area and safeguard President Tyler. Can you tell me where he is?"

"He's right in here." The voice was strained, but loud enough and defiant. "Thank you for your aid."

Camerici turned her head, peering through a door on the far wall. There was a man lying on a stretcher, leaning on his side and facing her. He was clearly in pain, but he was awake and alert. She recognized him at once.

"You are welcome, Mr. President." She turned her head to the side slightly to face one of her Eagles. "See to Figus," she ordered. She had checked the medical scans. The soldier was seriously wounded, but nothing his trauma system couldn't handle until he was evac'd.

Her eyes darted up to the reports coming in, status updates quickly collated by her AI and organized for easy reference. Everything was under control. The Eagles were all around the capital, and all known Black Flag and treacherous units had been wiped out or captured. No Black Flag personnel had surrendered, of course. It would be Columbian soldiers taken captive, all of whom would swear they had no idea what was going on and were only following orders. But that was Tyler's mess to deal with.

She took a few steps forward and said, "President Tyler, allow me to offer you General Darius Cain's warmest regards. This facility is now secure, as is the capital city. Eagle forces are in possession of all vital facilities, and all detected enemy units have been neutralized. I have been instructed to protect your person, and otherwise to do anything you require to aid your immediate resumption of full control over Columbia."

"Who am I speaking to?"

"Major Antonia Camerici, Mr. President."

"Well, let me start with this. Thank you, Major Camerici, to my ally General Cain, to you, and to your troopers."

Camerici nodded, as gracefully as she could manage in armor.

"We've had word that the Nest was under assault," Tyler said, clearly worried. "If you've secured the main communications center, I will order our fleet to mobilize at once and rush to your aid."

"Thank you, Mr. President, but that won't be necessary. We just received word from the Nest. The enemy forces have been repulsed, and the survivors have fled the system.

*   *   *   *   *

"Erik, I'm glad to see you in one piece, you old dog." Darius Cain stepped off the shuttle and walked toward Teller. There were half a dozen Eagles behind him, their heads shifting as they scanned the area for any threats.

"I could say the same about you, my friend. Things didn't look any too good there when I left." There was a sour touch to the last few words. Darius knew how his friend had felt leaving the Nest as the battle was just getting started. He wouldn't have sent him away, but he'd wanted his ground forces under Teller's stewardship, not so much because he'd anticipated the fighting on Columbia, but in case the worst had happened. If Darius had died in the Nest, at least some of his people would have escaped, and they'd have had the leadership they needed to survive, to carry on the fight. And Teller understood that as well.

"We managed to get through, as we always do. But I'm afraid we'll have to wait to catch up. We've got to get the Eagles ready."

"Ready for what?"

"We're going to Armstrong." A pause. "It's as much a gut call as anything, but I think the Black Flag is going to attack there... may have already."

"You mean another force, like the one they threw at the Nest?" Teller was rarely surprised, but Darius could tell his friend was taken aback by what he'd just heard.

"Bigger, at least if my guess is right. I think what we faced was just a diversion, never intended to take out the Nest, only to keep us busy."

"But if that's the case, they're almost certainly already there."

"Yes, Erik, but you know what will happen. If Garret's fleet can't hold, they'll bug out...and the Marines will dig in. They've got all kinds of shelters there, courtesy of my father's paranoia forty years ago."

"They could hold out even against a nuclear assault."

"Yes, of course. The Black Flag will have to send down ground forces to dig them out...and they'll be facing thousands of Marines with my father in command." He paused. "We have a chance to get there in time, but we can't wait. I have to see Jarrod Tyler, right now."

"He's right here, General Cain." Tyler moved across the landing field, propped up in a powered chair, and followed by a dozen guards, six of his own, and six armored Eagles. "Thank you, my friend. I'm not sure we'd have gotten out of that one without your help."

"What are friends for, Jarrod?" Darius walked toward Columbia's president. "And you know it's Darius to you. I hear 'General Cain' about two thousand times a day. No need for two thousand one."

Tyler forced a smile, clearly through some pain, and he nodded. "I heard most of what you said, Darius. What can I do to help? Columbia and its military are at your disposal."

Chapter 19

Field Hospital 1001 – Shelter A3
Planet Armstrong, Gamma Pavonis III
Earthdate: 2321 AD (36 Years After the Fall)

The room shook again, harder than the last time. The fighting was getting closer. Sarah hadn't had time to check the monitors and confirm that, not with both hands deep in a sergeant's chest cavity. But she'd been on enough battlefields to know without checking. She could read those rumbles in the ground like words in a book.

The comm was down completely now, the enemy close enough to blanket the whole area with impenetrable jamming. Erik had sent two more messengers, each reporting with increasing urgency on the advance of the enemy forces. She had no doubt he'd have ordered—or asked, depending on perspective—her to pull the hospital back, but there was nowhere to go. Anybody stepping out of the shelters without full armor, even for a few minutes, would get a massive overdose of radiation. That pretty much guaranteed every one of the wounded would die, at least, even assuming she'd somehow managed to get all her medical staff suited up. Of course, that didn't even address the civilians. There were twenty thousand of them in Shelter A3, crammed so tightly, she'd had sixty medical cases and four deaths from asphyxiation and crowd-related injuries already.

Every one of them would die if she tried to move them. There simply wasn't protective gear available, and certainly not in the quantities she'd need.

Not that there was anywhere to go.

She wasn't entirely sure Erik wouldn't have wanted to order her to leave the civilians behind, but it was a pretty good bet he knew she wouldn't do it. That wouldn't have stopped him from trying years before, but he'd become more realistic with age.

She reached deeper into the pool of blood and ooze, moving her fingers around, searching, trying to find the chunk of metal the scanners told her was still there, all the while desperately attempting not to cause more damage to the Marine's shattered chest. He had seven broken ribs already, a lacerated aorta, collapsed lungs, massive blood loss. She'd almost ordered him placed with the hopeless cases, but then she'd decided she could save him. She still wasn't sure about that—she figured it at 50-50, not much better—and there was little question the time and resources she'd put into her attempt to pull him back could have saved three or four others. She imagined wounded Marines dying in the triage area waiting for attention…or her surgeons losing patients for lack of artificial blood and pharmaceuticals, while she poured time and precious resources into a coin toss to save one man.

She doubted she'd have done anything differently, though, even if she'd had another chance. The idea of setting a maximum value on the effort and materiel a life was worth was anathema to her. But she could detest it all she wanted, she still knew things were coming to that. Quickly.

At least she'd gotten the secondary ward set up, though more space didn't give her more trained staff or doses of needed meds. At least it gave space for the medtechs to get wounded Marines prepped, hooked up to the drugs and blood that was available until one of her surgeons could get to them. As she had so many times, she shook her head in amazement at how quickly field conditions could erase centuries of technological advancements. For all she could do in a proper hospital to save even the most gravely ill and injured patients, right now she was little better than a doctor during the Unification Wars, or even farther back, to the mass struggles and barbarous medicine of the twentieth century.

She angled her head, wiping her sweatsoaked brow on her shoulder. Then she stopped. She felt something. Her fingers tightened and pulled out a small chunk of dense metal. She looked up at the scanner. Clear. She'd gotten it all.

She still had a ton of repair work to do, sealing the damaged arteries, reinflating the lungs. But she felt better than she had a few moments before.

"I think you're going to make it after all," she said softly, allowing herself a brief smile amid the terror and death. Her 50-50 case was now a good 80-20.

*   *   *   *   *

"Cate, I'm going up to the front and have a look at things myself." Erik Cain was crouched behind a small rise in the ground, peering out toward what was effectively the battle line. The combat hadn't been a typical one, at least in one way. The enemy hadn't been after terrain or objectives. They were here for one reason and one only. To destroy the Marines. And if that meant chasing them through the radioactive rubble or pulling them out of underground tunnels, then that, it seemed, was what they were ready to do.

"Erik, don't be crazy. That line's going to fall any minute. Even if none of those Marines break—and there are a lot of green units up there—the enemy's going to be pouring through half a dozen gaps where all our people were wiped out."

"No, Cate. We can't let that happen. We've got to hold here. If we don't, we'll lose the forward shelters...our remaining food and ordnance, the wounded, the civilians." *Sarah.*

"I don't see how we can hold, Erik. Not unless we commit the last of the reserves." There was a doubtful tone in Gilson's words, and Cain understood completely. If there was one maxim, one overused, but usually correct, rule of war, it was that the first one to commit his final reserves loses.

"Maybe we should."

"Erik…we have no idea how long it will be until we can expect relief, if we can at all. We have to hold out a damned sight longer than this. We've already gone through too many of our reserves."

"How do you define 'holding out?' What are we going to be able to do if we lose our bases? Hell, the enemy could just withdraw and blast us again from orbit, and this time we won't have the bunkers. Because you know what will happen when they take each one. They'll kill everybody there, and then they'll blow the things from inside. We'll be on the surface, in the open, without food, without medical support, without what's left of our supplies." Cain shook his head. "No, there's no retreat from here. We can try to hold back the reserves as long as possible, but we can't let these bastards get around our flanks…or through gaps in the line. If it comes to that, if we can't stretch the lines any farther, we have to throw in the last we have."

Gilson stood still for a moment, silent. Then she said simply, "You're right, Erik."

"You stay here, and direct things overall. I'll go to the front. We've coaxed the impossible from our people before…I think I can do it one more time."

"There aren't the same Marines, Erik. Not most of them, at least. They're not the warriors we led against the Shadow Legions or back in the Third Frontier War. They're good men and women, and loyal…but they're not those old Marines, not save for a few here and there. Most of the Marines you remember are dead now, you know that."

Cain paused for a moment, looking across the room at her. Then he said, "These Marines won't ever be the equals of their predecessors, Cate, not if we never give them the chance. If the spirit is there, anything is possible. They've got the equipment, the training…let's see if they've got the hearts of Marines."

He stood up, turning to leave.

"So, why do I stay back here, and you get to go up to the front."

Cain turned, smiling, though he knew she couldn't see it

through his armor. "Because I thought of it first, Cate."

*   *   *   *   *

Explosions ripped through the air, mortar shells, hyper-velocity rockets, grenades. The fight was raging, all along a sixteen-kilometer front, from what had been the center of the capital city to the flattened remnants of the suburbs. The enemy had continually extended the line, feeding ever more troopers into the maelstrom, trying to work around the Marines' flanks. But whatever they did, wherever they attacked or however many reserves they poured in, Erik Cain had been there, leading a small group of defenders, shifting the defenses, holding the line, sometimes, it seemed, by force of will alone.

They'd even tried landing a new force behind the Marines, but Cain had thinned his lines and pieced together a reaction force, one he'd led against the new LZ, overrunning it, at a cost of sixty percent casualties.

The fight had been brutal, exhausting, a nightmare for all engaged…but not one of the shelters had fallen to the enemy. Conditions in the tunnels and underground chambers, already almost unimaginable, had grown steadily worse as wounded Marines flooded into the field hospitals, and the dwindling food supplies approached complete depletion.

Cain knew there would be trouble there soon, that the civil-ians, already mad with hunger from a week of quarter rations, would eventually turn on their protectors. Rationality only held for so long, only warded off a certain amount of suffering. Then insanity took hold. Cain and Gilson already had every able-bod-ied Marine in the battle lines, and security in the shelters had fallen to the walking wounded, men and women too injured to return to the fighting, but sufficiently ambulatory to wander the tunnels of the subterranean refuges, adjudicating fights over scraps of food, and doing what they could to preserve morale, their own as well as that of the civilians.

Cain had held up everyone's morale, the officers, the rank and file who saw him in the thick of the action, even Cate Gilson's, worn down by the steadily increasing hopelessness of the situation. The two Marine generals had agreed they needed time, and that's exactly what they'd scrapped and fought for. But neither knew just how long it would be before help arrived, if it ever did, and they were decidedly uncertain how much longer their worn troops could last. Supplies were dwindling, the hospitals were down to the last of the pharmaceuticals, and those that remained had been reserved for only the most serious cases. He'd heard that Sarah was scavenging antibiotics, antivirals, and pain meds from the trauma control systems of the wounded Marines' shattered fighting suits. It had made him smile for a moment, remembering that she was just as stubborn as he was, at least in her own way. He imagined she'd saved countless lives, but now he began to doubt if any of that would matter in the end.

"Erik…" At first, he thought the sound had come through the comm, but then he realized it was outside, pumped into his receivers by the external microphones on his armor.

He turned and saw an armored form moving toward him, even as he recognized the voice. "Cate, what are you doing up here?" They'd been swapping shifts, one of them on the front with the Marines at all times, the other in the small dugout that passed for army HQ. Sleep had been a moment here and a moment there, combined with enough stims to nearly blow the helmet off his suit. He'd finally had to order his AI to stop reporting blood pressure and other health alerts, even as he'd demanded another injection.

"I couldn't get through on the comm. They amped up their blocking efforts, lots of new power. They must have brought down some portable reactors or something."

It would have been easier to jam from their fleet in space, but then, of course, it would catch their own forces too. This way, they could direct the effects out at the Marine line, and keep their own channels open.

"I think they're about to launch attacks on both flanks. I sent up a flight of drones—I know we agreed to conserve what we had left, but something didn't feel right."

Cain nodded, then remembering what an ineffectual gesture that was in combat armor, he said, "You did the right thing. No point having leftover drones if we're overrun." A few seconds later: "So, what did you find?"

"Well, it's still sketchy—the jamming didn't do anything to help the drones either—but it reconfirmed my suspicions. They're playing our game now, thinning out the lines and building makeshift reaction forces."

"Maybe that's a sign that they've got their full strength committed." Cain paused. "Or maybe just that they know they can spare the manpower because *we're* so thin. They could have another hundred thousand troops up there for all we know, and they're just trying to avoid the expense of landing them."

"Well, I guess it doesn't really matter, not now anyway. They're going to hit us on both flanks at the same time, I'd bet my stars on it. And we don't have a thing to throw in their way."

"Except us." Cain turned and looked out over the line. The Marines had been digging in for two weeks now, and they'd managed to claw out a deep network of trenches. Things were actually quiet now, almost no fire from the enemy positions… and that convinced him even more that Gilson was right. "So, how about you take the right, and I'll take the left, and we'll scrape up whatever we can to push them back."

Gilson didn't answer right away. Cain knew she'd come up to discuss the situation with him, to devise a counter. He wished his response was heavier on tactical planning and lighter on raw bravado, but you used what you had.

"It may end up being just us out there."

"If that's how it goes, so be it. But I'd wager we'll get some of the Marines to stand with us. We're either going to win this, hold out long enough…or we're not. And if not, do you really want to be here to see the bitter end?"

"No," she replied grimly. "No, I don't. So, go get that armored hulk over to the left, because I don't think we have much time."

"Good luck, Cate." He'd almost thrown back a humorous response, but they weren't coming all that easily to him just then.

Besides, some moments called for sincerity.

"Good luck, Erik."

Chapter 20

"I was finally able to glean some navigational data from the ship *Eagle Fourteen* captured near Atlantia. It was incomplete, but still useful. A preliminary scan of the wreckage from the battle provided additional information, perhaps less than we might have hoped for, but still of considerable value."

"Are you saying you can get us a line on the enemy's home system, Tom?" Darius Cain stood and looked at the charts and figures on the large tablet in Sparks's hand. His voice suggested doubt that the scientist's data went that far…and it also carried a somewhat disquieting tone that hinted at just what he intended if it did. No one had ever doubted Darius would pursue any enemy with all the power and ability he possessed, but it was different this time. They had kidnapped his father, and then they had attacked his home. Now it was personal.

"No, sir…not yet at least. I guess what I'm saying is, we're getting closer."

Darius sighed softly. "That's all well and good, Tom, but we can't exactly send a fleet to 'someplace closer.' We need to know where they come from. So we can destroy them." The words were cold, and there was iron determination behind them. "We've got to chop the head off the snake, and soon, or they'll keep coming. They'll wear us down. It's a good bet they're more than a match for us in terms of military resources, and they're definitely a damned sight better organized than we are. We're still sitting around in dozens of systems, our forces hopelessly scattered, while they come at us when and where they choose. They've already got close to half of Occupied Space, and if they take a few more decent-sized worlds, they'll have the resources to outlast us no matter what we do. We're nowhere close to being able to liberate worlds and fight them off wherever they might attack next. One thing is damned sure for certain...if we don't find some way to wrest the initiative from them, we're as good as done."

"Yes, sir, I understand. And I think I can get that location for you, but not with what I have now. We're on the way to Armstrong. If the enemy is actually there and we can drive them off, we can follow them. Based on their conduct at the Nest, their command elements, at least, will withdraw from a lost battle, and probably some of their main combat units. They seem to have little or no regard for their personnel, but it still takes a long time and a lot of resources to build a battleship. It is unlikely they would throw them away if the battle was clearly lost."

"You're assuming it *is* a lost battle. We may get there to find Armstrong already destroyed." He felt a pang in his gut at the thought of being too late, of getting there to realize his parents were already dead. Darius was a hard man, one who handled pain with the dispassionate coldness he applied to everything else, but the thought of losing his father *again* was a hard one to endure. And his mother...if anything, that was even worse.

He paused for a few seconds, and then he continued. "Even if we do arrive in time, we're almost certainly looking at a force superior to the one we faced at the Nest. This time, however, we are carrying considerable battle damage...and we won't have the combat support from the base."

"That is true, sir, in which case, of course, none of this matters. But assuming we do arrive on time, and we *are* able to defeat the enemy, I think we need to be ready. I've upgraded the stealth generator, made some improvements. I can install it in one of the scoutships and we can use the vessel to follow whatever enemy forces retreat. One of the newer scouts should be fast enough to keep up with anything we've seen of the enemy's."

Darius looked back at the scientist. "But, Tom, that generator's still experimental. If it fails, even for an instant...the ship would be detected. We're not talking about a battleship like *Eagle Fourteen* this time. A scoutship wouldn't have a chance, not against real warships, and you'll be far from any aid."

"That's the risk we have to take. Is it any less than the officers and spacers in the fleet take in battle? Or the soldiers on the ground?"

"We?" Darius had heard everything his engineer had said, but the one word absorbed most of his attention. "You're planning on going yourself?"

"Of course, sir. I'll have to go. I need to analyze whatever data we get in real time. We've *got* to discover where the Black Flag's base is hidden. And, as you mention, the stealth generator is likely to be...a bit rough. If I'm there, I should be able to keep it functioning, barring any truly major problems."

"No argument that we need to find their base, but you're taking quite a leap there, Tom...not to mention a lot of danger. Are you sure it's worth the risks involved? Can this sketchy data really allow you to figure where the Black Flag comes from?"

"Yes, definitely, sir. Or, at least I am confident I can...*if* I can get enough information." Sparks paused. "You see, sir, even though we utilize warp gates to transit between systems instead of direct travel between stars in normal space, there is still a certain more or less conventional geometry at work. There is much still unknown about the warp gate network, and our understanding of the gates is still in its infancy, but we've been able to detect a certain structure in the relationship between normal space and warp gate paths."

"Geometry?" Darius Cain had a pretty strong grasp on mathematics, but patterns in the layout of warp lines was beyond any area of familiarity.

"Yes…" Sparks paused. He was clearly trying to explain something very hypothetical, and having a considerable amount of trouble putting it into words. "If we are able to discover where the enemy's movements converge on a remote system, one at the edge of explored space—or even several possible ones—we can likely predict the presence of a hidden warp gate, one which has not yet been discovered, or at least is not known by anyone on our side."

"Hidden?" Darius knew some gates had lower levels of energy emissions, making them more difficult to find. The occasional discovery of such a gate had been used to great military advantage, especially back during the Third Frontier War, when warp gate theory was far less sophisticated and many low energy gates remained undetected. All told, there had been ten or twelve instances where previously-unknown gates had been discovered in long-settled systems…and it was anyone's guess how many more might be out there, silent and undetected.

"Yes, General. The enemy homeworld, Vali, as it seems to be called…it almost certainly lies beyond an undiscovered gate. There is no other way to explain all that has happened."

"How do you know that? Maybe it's just far beyond the explored borders."

"I don't think so, sir. What we call explored space or Occupied Space has something of an imprecise meaning. For example, is a system 'explored' if no official expedition has mapped it out, but a rogue miner has ventured there? By strict definition, it is not. Yet, we can assume that every nearby system, certainly those within four or five jumps of 'known' space, *have* been explored, at least to some extent. There might be no record of many of these expeditions, in fact that is almost a certainty. Most of these systems are likely nothing special, too far from established worlds to be worth exploiting, which prevented any follow ups or any charting missions that would have added the systems to the primary databases."

Sparks looked over at Darius, his expression probing, trying to determine if the general was following him.

"You haven't lost me yet, Tom."

Sparks nodded. "Well, from everything we've been able to discover, this Vali is likely to be highly developed, very highly... more industrialized than any world since Earth was destroyed. Indeed, perhaps even more than pre-Fall Earth, since it was likely built from the ground up to support an immense war machine and nothing else."

"So, if any ship had found it, they would have almost certainly reported it in one way or another."

"Or, more likely, they would have been destroyed. It is an almost certain bet Vali is well defended. But we've searched the databases of lost ships over the last thirty years, and while the data is far from complete, we have been able to rule out every recorded disappearance." He paused. "It looks very much like no wanderer, no explorer...no criminal looking for a hideout... has ever stumbled on this Vali."

"No one has found it, because the warp gate leading there has not been discovered." Darius took a deep breath and nodding, as he considered what he'd been told. "So, you think you can narrow the search area down, comb through a few systems, and maybe find the gate leading to the enemy?"

"The process would be considerably more involved than that, General, but that is essentially correct. Assuming we can gather the data we need." A pause. "I know the pursuit will be dangerous, sir, but I think it's the likeliest way we're going to find Vali. And we can't beat the enemy, not permanently, at least, without taking their main base."

"No, Tom, we can't." Darius knew there would be calls from his allies to spread forces out, to mount defenses of worlds the enemy might attack next. System governments would cry out for aid, for forces to protect them, and many who want to agree. But that was a fool's game, a road to defeat. It's just what the Black Flag wanted, to exploit the codes of duty and ethics of their enemies. Such tactics had been used throughout humanity's history. It was the way governments seized and retained control, the way politicians worked their ways into positions of power. Darius wasn't going to fall for that trap, not a chance. And he didn't care what names were added to the list of those he was already called. They could curse him, label him monster, butcher, cold-blooded…but if he was able to find Vali, to destroy the Black Flag at its source, he would be the butcher who'd saved them all.

"Okay, Tom," he said, still not very happy about it. Get your ship ready. Pick out your crew, and take everything you think you'll need. Let's keep it to volunteers on this." *Which meant precisely nothing. Any of the Eagles Sparks asks will go.*

"I'll go."

Darius turned abruptly. Elias had been standing in the room, listening to the whole conversation, but this was the first time his brother had spoken.

"Elias, we're talking about following enemy warships, counting on an unfinished stealth generator to stay hidden. The ship's going to have to match enemy thrust, and the more output from the engines, the more chance of getting caught. Every course change, every major acceleration or deceleration, even any extended stay in one spot…all of them increase the chance, even the likelihood of being found. And being found means being destroyed."

"I understand all that. No one said defeating the Black Flag was going to be a safe undertaking. And, I appreciate the experimental nature of the generator, but it served us pretty well on *Eagle Fourteen*." Then: "This is your place, Darius, here, at the head of your warriors. It's where you were born to be. But there's nothing I can really do here, no way to help. *This* is a way I can truly contribute."

Darius hesitated, for just a few seconds. He hated the idea of sending his brother, so recently returned into his life, on a mission with such long odds. But they were both Cains, and he couldn't order Erik Cain's other son to sit meekly and watch his comrades fight the war. He had to say yes. Besides, right now he had a hard time coming up with anywhere the odds looked much better.

He nodded. He and his brother were very different people, there was no questioning that. But he decided, then and there, that Elias Cain could fight at his side anytime. He'd always loved his brother, even through the years when he hadn't realized it, when he would have boisterously denied it. But now he felt pride, kinship. There was more alike about Erik Cain's sons than either of them would have admitted before.

"Okay, Elias. You take operational command...but make sure you bring an experienced fleet officer with you."

"I will, Darius."

Darius turned toward Sparks. "And, Tom...make sure you've got the team you need as well. Take anyone you even think you *might* need. There's no way to overstate the importance of finding Vali. I might go so far as to say that our only real chance of ultimate victory rests with you tracking the Black Flag to their home base and bringing that information safely back here."

"I understand, sir. We'll get it done...somehow."

Darius sighed softly. "This may all be immaterial anyway. It all depends on us getting to Armstrong in time, on finding the enemy there, and not already gone with nothing but radioactive debris remaining behind. And then on us defeating them."

The three men were silent, and Darius suddenly realized that none of them had expressed the slightest doubt that the Black Flag *had* attacked Armstrong, only whether they would arrive in time to intervene. What had begun as his own sudden assumption had progressed now to accepted fact. At least as far as Elias and Tom Sparks were concerned.

Darius was starting to figure this enemy out, he realized, as he had all those who'd come before. He could beat them, he knew he could. There was only one question he couldn't answer, not yet. Was he on time?

The comm unit buzzed, and Darius tapped the controls on the wall, activating the speaker. "General Cain here."

"General, it's Colonel Teller." A pause. "Darius, we're picking up energy readings at the warp gate. Big ones. Warships, I'd bet, though they're too far out for positive IDs."

Darius turned and flashed a glance at Elias and Sparks. Then he swung his head back to the comm. Had they run into more enemy forces? Or allies?

"We're on the way, Erik."

Chapter 21

Cain fired, then again. He was down to single shots now, preserving what ammunition he had left. He'd sent runners back to order more supplies brought forward, but he went through three before one made it.

He'd gotten to the left flank moments before the enemy forces launched their attack. They sent in two thousand troopers, Cain figured, maybe more, and he'd scraped together exactly three hundred sixty-two…and he'd only managed that by stripping the rest of the line to dire levels.

He'd gotten reinforcements eventually, another two hundred or so, but only after his initial force repelled two attacks that outnumbered them at least five to one.

He'd ordered his Marines to dig the instant they got into position, but even with the monstrous strength of their powered armor, they'd only managed to scrape out a shallow set of works by the time the Black Flag troopers came upon them.

Cain's people had held, grimly, doggedly, and he'd had to admit, his combination of fresh trainees and aged retirees returned to the colors had fought as well as any force he'd ever commanded. They died the same too, singly and in groups,

163

from rifle fire and bombardments, and during one charge that had come perilously close to breaking the line, in hand to hand combat.

Cain had taken down two enemies himself with his blade, the molecules-thin knife that was sharp enough to cut through armor. It had been a long time since he'd used the blade and, even if his reflexes had slowed a bit, his skill with the weapon was still there.

He had about half the Marines he'd started with, but they'd used the time between assaults to strengthen their defenses, and their position was more than a match for the one that repelled the first charge. They still hadn't equaled the strength of the trenches in the center, but now the field was littered with Black Flag dead, perhaps twelve hundred, even fifteen hundred. The enemy had diverted more forces to the attack, but they hadn't been able to keep up with their losses. For all the vast numbers that had landed on Armstrong, the enemy's strength was clearly beginning to dwindle.

Cain didn't dare guess how many enemy soldiers the Marines had taken down since the first landings. *Twenty thousand*, he thought. *Thirty? No, more*, he realized. He had estimated the landing force to be somewhere between seventy and ninety thousand, and he figured close to half of those were down.

And, for them, down means dead. Cain had watched as the enemy had failed to set up any aid stations, any hospitals. He was disgusted at a fighting force with so little regard for its soldiers, and he wondered how they maintained loyalty and discipline. *How do you get soldiers to fight for you when you are so clear you consider them expendable?*

He fired another shot, picking off a Black Flagger who'd gotten careless and raised his head too far. Cain didn't know if these mysterious soldiers even *felt* fear, if killing one between assaults had any effect on the others, except reducing their number by one. He had no idea who they were or where they'd come from...or how to defeat them, short of killing every last one of them. Which is exactly what he would do if he had to. Somehow.

We can't just stay here. There are still too many of them. They'll keep stretching the line until we can't match them.

He cranked up his visor magnification, staring across the narrow no man's land between the lines. The enemy was on a ridge, using the small back slope as cover. It was a good position, at least as strong a spot as the bombardment-ravaged countryside offered. The enemy didn't seem susceptible to fear, but they did seem to adhere to normal tactics, abandoning positions and withdrawing, for example, when a situation became disadvantageous.

He turned and looked back at his Marines. They were battered, exhausted, their morale fading. Did they have one last crazy maneuver left in them? Could a sudden attack turn the tide? It would be the last thing the enemy would expect, and he'd only need a minute to get his people across and push into the enemy's shallow trenches.

Surprise was a potent weapon, he knew, but how much did an enemy without fear dilute from its punch? The terrain behind the enemy line was a perfect killing zone. If the Black Flaggers pulled back, his people could bring up their autocannons and gun them down in their masses as they tried to retreat and reform.

But if they're sharp, if they react immediately…

Cain imagined his force shattered, the small command he'd cobbled together to hold the army's vulnerable flank wiped out. He felt doubts, hesitation that had never been there before. He'd executed bold maneuvers his entire career, took whatever risks were necessary, without pause. Part of him knew he had to do *something*. If he didn't, the army would be enveloped, the shelters overrun…Armstrong and everyone on it lost. But he felt himself hanging on a precipice, the old Cain shouting to do something, but a newer voice, softer, counseling caution. Was it the years in captivity? Had his jailors stolen even more from him that he'd realized.

Or am I just old? Perhaps even a Marine has only so long for war…

He shook his head…*no, there is no time for this, no place for pointless worries*. He could feel the old strength coming back, not as strong as it had once been, perhaps, but maybe just enough.

"Captain Horn, Captain Rieger...get your people ready. We're going over the top in two minutes."

There was a long pause, no doubt shock on the part of the two officers. Finally, Rieger answered, his voice hesitant. "Yes, General."

"Yes, sir," Horn added, sounding no less stunned than his comrade.

"Don't worry, don't analyze...there's no time for that now. Just get your people ready. And don't give them time to think about it. Let's go...ninety seconds."

Cain felt his own heart pounding, and he pushed back against the inevitable fear. Unlike most of those under him, he knew just the kind of thing they were about to try, and he'd been there before, seen the terrible losses even from success.

He'd seen failure too, but the less thought about that now, the better.

"Alright, Marines, here's the drill." He spoke loudly, his voice strong, not a hint of the doubt he felt escaping his lips. "We're going to rush that enemy line, and we're going to cover that ground as quickly as we can. Forget cover, forget leapfrogging and diving the ground and crawling. That field is too open for that anyway, and we don't have the strength. Surprise is our weapon here, and the sooner we're over the edge of their trench, the better. We're going to win this one, Marines, and we're going to do it with armored fists and blades."

Cain was giving it all he had, reaching for every scrap of the legend of the Marines' fighting general. He knew so much of it was bullshit, so many stories he'd heard of his supposed battles pure fiction. But that didn't matter now. He'd use anything, a sharp and accurate recount of one of his fights or a drunken, barroom fabrication by someone who allegedly 'knew someone who was there.' Truth didn't matter, not now. The more he worked up his Marines, the better chance they had. If they gave in to fear—even to common sense—they were lost. This had to be about pure faith...in themselves, in the mystique of the Corps.

"I'll be there right with you...so, follow me, Marines. Follow me, and let's drive these bastards back to whatever pit of hell spawned them."

He could hear the cheers, the bloodthirsty shouts. It had been a long time since Cain rallied a force of Marines like he just had, and he was glad to see the ability remained. He was tired, exhausted…the thought of jumping up over the lip of the trench and racing into another fight was almost overwhelming. But now was the time. In a moment it would be lost.

He jumped up, screaming, "Attack!" as he did. He ran forward, zigging and zagging a bit, but mostly pushing his armored legs as hard as the nuclear reactor on his back could power them. He leaned forward, did everything he could to keep his body low, to avoid bouncing high, giving the enemy an even better target than he already presented. His mind flash back, sixty years, to basic training back on Earth, the first time he'd worn a fighting suit. The drill instructors had pounded the same thing in his head…pay attention, stay low. It was one of the first things a Marine was taught, and yet he'd seen hundreds killed because they'd forgotten that lesson, even for an instant.

He could see some of his people dropping even now, perhaps half of them because they'd allowed their enthusiasm to overwhelm them, and they'd bounded high into the air. But the losses were light. The enemy might be fearless, but it was clear their training was inferior to that of the Marines. There was no established doctrine of war that would suggest an enemy as weak and battered as the Marines would attack—*could* attack—in a situation like this. And now the Black Flaggers were paralyzed, the reality of what was happening slowly sinking in.

Cain felt a burst of satisfaction, but he checked it hard. They were only halfway across, and now scattered enemy units were opening fire. It was ragged, poorly coordinated and aimed, but it started cutting his people down nevertheless. The Marines were out in the open, clear targets. Their armor protected them against some of the small arms fire, at least, and he saw more than one Marine knocked down by mortar fire rise up almost immediately, without serious injury. But his losses continued to mount. He flashed a glance up at the display inside his helmet.

Ten percent losses, his AI was reporting. Cain knew that could be inaccurate in either direction by a good bit, but his gut told him it was just about right.

He was close now, less than one hundred meters. He opened up with his own assault rifle, more to suppress the enemy's own fire than to inflict hits, but he caught at least one of the Black Flaggers, just moving to the front of the trench and lining up to fire himself…a bit too carelessly. His shots tore off the top half of the trooper's helmet, leaving a spray of blood and various other fluids and semi-fluids. Cain knew better than anyone what a messy enterprise war was.

He took one last leap toward the trench, slapping the assault rifle back into its clasp and clicking the small switch that sent the blade protruding from its sheath in his armor's sleeve. It was a shiny silver when viewed along the flat side, and almost invisible along the honed edge.

He slashed hard, putting all the power of his powered arm and shoulders behind the strike. The blade hit one of the Black Flaggers right between the neck and shoulder, and it sunk in deeply. The man stood for an instant, his arms flailing helplessly, and then he dropped hard to the ground as Cain ripped the blade back out.

All along the line, his Marines were pouring into the trench, engaging the still-surprised enemy troopers. The Marines had maintained a tradition of close arms training, and their skill with the blades were far superior to that of their adversaries. They were outnumbered, but that didn't hold them back, and the fight in the trench quickly turned into a one-side affair. Even young Marines, those whose first taste of combat had come in the days and weeks before, fought hard, swept up in the emotion, in the feeling of victory, however local that was, however short-lived it might prove to be.

Cain was in the center of it all, slashing with his blade, smashing his armored fist down on opponents, even falling to the ground in a desperate armored wrestling match with an enemy officer, one that ended when he was finally able to bring his blade around and drive it through his foe's throat.

The fight was brutal, as savage and unimaginable as any Cain had seen. His people were gaining the upper hand, there was no doubt about that, but they were taking losses too. All around, there was the debris of war, twisted, burned chunks of armor and weapons…and encased in their shattered tombs of heavy metal, the wreckage of men and women.

The differences between the dead—and the wounded, screaming in pain, exposed to deadly radiation the instant their suits were breached—seemed slight, and in many ways, Cain knew they were. The Black Flaggers were no First Imperium robots, nor even identical Shadow Legion clones. They looked very much like the Marines, fit, and mostly young, men and women, representing the various ethnicities of man, appearing in many ways as though they'd just been snatched from the streets of a hundred colony worlds.

The enemy did not retreat, not for a long while. No doubt, their commanders hoped their superior numbers would ultimately tell. But the Marines had gained too much initiative, and they were at their greatest advantage in the close-range melee. Cain waited, counting each second, even as he continued to fight, killing one enemy after another, the reflexes of a hundred battles coming back, taking charge of his aging but still capable body. His gut told him the enemy would pull back, that they'd seek to set up a new position and return the battle to a more conventional fight between ranged weapons.

And, then we'll give them just that…

Cain threw his arm up, blocking a strike from an enemy trooper, and he drove his blade into the man's midsection. Even the hyper-sharp knife struggled to penetrate the strong armor there, and it took all the enhanced power his arm could manage to drive it through.

His blood was full of adrenalin, the surge of energy he'd always felt in battle in full effect. But he was worried too, concerned that the enemy didn't seem to be breaking off. If they held long enough, he knew his own people, Marines or not, would eventually falter.

Then he saw it. Black Flag troopers climbing out of the

trench, running out over the flat plain behind. There were still enemy soldiers fighting his people, but more and more began to stream away. There was no panic, no disorder…the enemy had not developed a sudden fear. They were clearly obeying some command, some directive to pull out and reform.

"Now," Cain shouted, even as his head darted around, making sure no enemy was coming at him. "Autocannon teams, get your weapons deployed, and open fire." This was no time for crispness, to wait until all units were deployed and open fire simultaneously. He wanted each gun firing the instant it was ready, without wasting so much as a second. It wouldn't take the enemy long to pull back, to cross the deadly open field and gain at least some sort of cover. And Cain wanted every one of them he could get in that time.

He felt the same feral instinct he always had, enhanced perhaps by the anger, the rage at those who had stolen so much of his life. He knew these soldiers were brainwashed, most likely stolen from all over Occupied Space and conditioned until they were mind-numbed zombies. But right now, he didn't care. All he cared about was victory.

"Let's go, gunnery teams. I want those autocannons firing!" A few of the weapons were already active, and more were coming online. He had ten of them, and by the time all were in place, he could see the deadly toll they were taking. All across the line, whole groups of enemy soldiers fell, dozens, hundreds.

The others continued to withdraw, their order unaffected by the incredible carnage all around. Against a conventional enemy, Cain knew he'd have already won the victory. No force he'd ever seen, not even the hardest Marine veterans he'd ever led, could endure what his people were unleashing on their stunned foes. But the Black Flag formations, dwindling like blocks of ice on a hot day, continued to maneuver calmly, utterly unaffected by the losses they had suffered.

Slowly, steadily, the survivors reached another defensible spot, a small ridge similar to the one Cain's people had just taken from them. They dropped down, taking the easy targets from the Marine gunners, and a moment later, Cain reluctantly gave the order to cease fire. His teams could inflict more casualties, he didn't have any doubt about that, but he also knew his ammunition supply was rapidly dwindling…and even if he was able to get more ordnance from the shelters, those stores were running out as well. Every shot had to count from here on out.

He stared across the plain, now the new 'no man's land,' and he felt the urge to send his Marines forward again. They were exhausted, spent…but the enemy had abandoned all their heavy weapons, and he knew there a brief opportunity here, before they brought more forward. But one look at his own force told him that was too much, more that he could get from his Marines. They'd inflicted massive losses on the enemy, but a third of their own number had fallen in the fight. The enemy didn't have any autocannons right now, but the element of surprise was gone too. The near-compulsion to push ahead, to drive the enemy from one position to the next was almost irresistible, but reason prevailed. Even if his Marines did manage to push the Black Flaggers back farther, they were only a part of the line. All they would do was expose their flanks to the enemy on their right.

"I want scouts and spotters in every platoon, and I want those autocannons ready at the first sign of any move." He didn't think the enemy was coming, not at least until they could reinforce their flank. But he wasn't going to get caught with armored pants down, as his counterpart just had.

He felt good. His Marines had performed magnificently, and their victory, small and local that it was, would have a ripple effect down the line. It would buy time, help hold things together. For at least a little longer.

Then, as if to tear away whatever satisfaction he might have felt, he saw a runner heading his way. He sighed softly, wondering if there was a chance, any chance at all the approaching Marine carried good news. After all, he was waiting for help, the only hope for victory resting on his allies coming to Armstrong on time. But his gut told him a different story, one his experiences had proved to be far more common.

"General Cain, we're picking up incoming landing craft."

"Have we been able to identify the ships?"

For an instant Cain wondered if he'd been too quick to assume the worst. Could this be help on the way? Martians? Black Eagles? He felt the slightest spark of hope.

And then it died.

"Yes, sir. They appear to be Black Flag vessels, similar to those in the earlier landings. We project at least twenty thousand troops inbound, General. Perhaps more."

Cain just stood there, silent. The lack of new enemy landings had led him to believe the Black Flag just might have landed all its soldiers. But reinforcements on this scale? Whatever hope he'd clung to for victory, or at least a lasting stalemate, it was gone, replaced by hopelessness and despair.

It was over. As soon as the enemy could land these new troops and form up, they would hit the Marines all along the line…and everywhere it would be the same story. Positions collapsing, disordered survivors retreating, desperately trying to reform, to hold back the unstoppable enemy.

The shelters would be lost, the wounded, the civilians… Sarah and the medical teams. He thought for a moment about issuing evacuation orders, but where would he send them? They were better off where they were, fighting off their assailants with clubs, if necessary, than they'd be streaming across the open, devastated plain, being gunned down in their thousands.

Cain's memories drifted back, over his battles, so many battles.

After so much struggle, serving with so many heroes…is this really how it all ends?

Chapter 22

This is the day I will die. He'd fought for more than half a century. Erik Cain had been wounded more times than he could count, endured fifteen years of captivity, starvation, and torture…but now he knew he'd come to his end.

The enemy had landed its reserves, by all estimates, at least twenty thousand fresh, fully-equipped strike troops. To face the onslaught, he had his Marines, their ranks gutted, the survivors exhausted, many wounded, conserving what last bits remained of their ammunition and supplies. Cain would fight, there was no question about that, and he didn't doubt his Marines would as well. But there was little question where this battle would lead. The end.

Cain had regrets, many, but he was prepared to fight his last battle. He wanted to live, of course, to see his boys survive this war, as he himself had so many, and go on to make more of a life for themselves in peace than he'd every managed to do. Darius was too much like him, he knew, an even more exaggerated version. He loved his older—by three minutes—son dearly, but he knew Darius would torture himself, that he would be driven from one obligation to the next, even if that harsh prison he

173

constructed for himself was a gold-plated and luxury-filled one.

Elias might break free of what seemed to be the Cain family curse. He, too, was a creature of duty, but there was more of his mother in him, cynical and questioning, yes, but not pathologically so. Perhaps he could break out of the cycle of endless war, find someplace to settle, and live the quiet life Erik had always wanted, but that had always eluded him.

Sarah. She would die too. That cut at him far deeper than his own impending demise. His mind twisted around, trying to find some way, any way, he could save her. But there was none. Even if he'd come up with some miraculous plan, he knew she'd never leave. She wouldn't abandon the hospital and the wounded… and she'd never leave him behind. He knew that, without the slightest doubt. Now, he wondered if he'd even see her again. If the enemy would hold back the inevitable final onslaught long enough for one last moment together.

He looked out over the trench. His Marines were well dug in. He'd brought all that remained of the ordnance forward, positioned every autocannon and mortar himself. He'd even stripped away the guards keeping watch on the civilian population and moved them to the front. He didn't fool himself that his people had a chance…but they would sell their lives dear. That many fewer of these…zombies…to face Darius and the others someplace else. He knew well that defeat on Armstrong did not necessarily mean the war was lost. Not as long as warriors like the Black Eagles were still out there, and other allies. Augustus, Roderick Vance.

Cain hoped the civilians in the shelters, totally unguarded now, would remain calm, or at least reasonably so. Perhaps they believed the enemy would take them prisoner. *Let them think that. The truth will do them no good…*

Cain knew the enemy associated Armstrong with the Corps, that they wouldn't differentiate between combatants and civilian service personnel…right down to the shopkeepers and chefs from the restaurants downtown—what had once been downtown. He had no idea what the enemy's ultimate plan was for all humanity, should they prevail in their war of conquest, but there wasn't the slightest doubt in his mind that no one would be allowed to leave Armstrong. The planet would be a radioactive tomb, a message to all who dared oppose them.

He leaned forward, cranking up his magnification, trying to get a good look at activity along the enemy's line. Nothing. It didn't make sense. The enemy troopers were just milling about, more than enough of them to roll right over the Marine positions. But they'd been static for hours.

The first assault wave had attacked the instant the soldiers hit the ground. Cain had no idea why the enemy was waiting. Was it psychological warfare? Did they want his Marines to sit and think about what was coming?

He turned and walked toward the main HQ. It wasn't much, just a few shelters dug into the ground. Cain twitched a little as he walked. He and Gilson had introduced a rotating shift, sending a couple percent of their people into the shelters at any one time. They would aid the wounded in reaching the field hospitals, and then they would get two or three hours off the line. Not enough time for a meaningful sleep or anything, but enough to pop open their suits and stretch their muscles a bit…and to grab a hot meal, when there had still *been* hot meals. Now, there were barely meals at all, and what remained were as often as not quarter rations no more appetizing that a broken off piece of a nutrition bar.

Powered armor had revolutionized warfare, and soldiers equipped with fighting suits were the kings of the battlefield, but for all technology could build superior equipment, they couldn't change the basic realities of human beings. It took a tremendous amount of training to get a new recruit acclimated to armor, not to mention counseling, drugs, and outright conditioning. It was difficult to stay in a suit for days, even weeks at a time, under combat conditions, pissing into a hose, shitting into a tube, and all the while dreaming about the astonishing luxury of scratching an itch. Even after more than a century of armored warfare, eight to ten percent of trainees washed out of training for the simple reason that they nearly went mad when confined in their suits.

The suit's internal harnesses did everything possible to secure a Marine, and his various appendages and parts, to prevent the wearer from sliding all around, but the ready room after a unit returned from duty was always a display of multi-colored bruises, contusions of all sorts.

But the torment of endless stretches in combat conditions increased exponentially with time, especially in a situation like the current one, where the radiation in the battlezone was beyond lethal levels, denying the Marines even a quick moment to pop a helmet, get a gasp of air that hadn't been recycled five thousand times.

It had been over a week since Cain had been inside. The suit did everything it could to keep the atmosphere as clean as possible, but after more than seven days, there was no mistaking the smell of putrid Cain. He tried to stretch, a near impossibility in armor for anyone but a fighter as experienced as he was. And still, as thoughts of discomfort, and sadness for Sarah and his family drifted through his head, he watched the enemy position, seeing no sign they were preparing to attack.

He stepped down, into the half plastic, half rock and mud 'room' he and Gilson shared as an office and command post. "I don't understand. This is not their way. Why worry so much about rattling us when they've got us dead to rights?"

"I wish I knew, Erik." Gilson and Cain had been rivals of a sort, once. Cain had actually come up under her command, but he'd quickly caught up, and the two had surged forward together, the next generation of the Corps' leadership. That had been a long time ago, and the two had gotten past whatever competitive issues they'd once had. The Corps was big enough for two beloved commanders, at least two who tended to agree as often as they did.

Almost as if in answer, both of their comms crackled to life. "General Cain, General Gilson, we're picking up signals from out in the system."

"Signals?" Cain beat his co-commander to the punch, probably by half a second.

"Yes, sir. Comm signals, even some energy readings." The

Marines were stuck to their last few receivers, small and close to the ground. That eliminated most readings beyond orbit.

If we're picking up energy…it's not very far out there. More enemy ships coming in? Or…"

"It sounds like there is a battle going on up there, sir. The jamming's preventing us from getting any clear transmissions, but it sure sounds like somebody's fighting."

A battle? Cain tried to hold himself back, to tread softly on allowing hope to creep into his thoughts. Was it possible? Had one of their allies arrived? Enough, even, to defeat the Black Flag fleet?

* * * * *

"Core force, continue forward. Flanking detachments, hold those ships back. Whatever it takes." Darius Cain sat on the bridge of *Eagle Eleven*. He'd reluctantly transferred from his usual *Eagle One* because of the old flagship's heavy damage. *Eagle One* was still in the line, still ready to fight, but Darius needed a ship that could keep him plugged into the action, one that could take the most damage and keep going. Right now, that was *Eagle Eleven*.

He'd always considered himself more of a ground tactician than an expert at naval combat, but he knew his way around in a space battle. Well enough to realize what a chance he was taking. The enemy fleet was big, considerably larger than the one that had attacked the Nest…but this time, the Eagles weren't alone.

Darius Cain's fleet had encountered a large force en route to Armstrong, one that had taken a few tense moments to identify. But when the scans were complete, and the messages exchanged, it was clear his people had encountered Admiral Garret and the battered remains of the fleet that had defended—or tried to defend—Armstrong.

Garret's first words had answered the question that had been plaguing Darius the most. He'd left behind an Armstrong full of live Marines, dug in and ready to fight off any attack. Darius knew his father well enough to understand what that truly meant.

It had taken a very brief discussion between the two fleet commanders to reach agreement on a course of action. The combined force would return and engage the enemy...and relieve Armstrong. It wouldn't be easy—Garret had extensive details on the enemy forces, and no matter how Darius tried to look at it, success seemed...difficult, at best, and an outright longshot at worst. But none of that mattered. Not now. He'd just rescued his father, and whatever it took, he wasn't going to lose him again.

Garret had been only too ready to agree. Darius suspected it had taken all the old admiral had to pull his fleet back from Armstrong, to save the irreplaceable ships and abandon the Marines, and he could almost feel the relief pouring over the comm line when the decision was made to go back. Darius didn't know Garret all that well, but he was extremely familiar with the great admiral's campaigns. It didn't take much to realize Garret didn't like running, and damned sure not when doing so left allies behind, at the mercy of the enemy.

Darius's study had told him one other thing...whatever Augustus Garret had to do to gain the victory, he did. Whatever the cost. He'd read about Garret's actions at the end of the First Imperium War, how he'd trapped half his fleet—with his best friend in command—to close off the warp gate leading to enemy territory. There had been no choice, Darius knew that well enough, and he had no doubt he would have done the same, but it made him respect the admiral, more even than he might have anyway.

The plan hadn't come to him until later, and when he'd first suggested it to Garret, he'd gotten every bit of resistance he'd expected. But he'd argued his point, explained his rationale, and finally, sounding as though he'd tasted something bad, Garret agreed. The Marine fleet, all the ships under his command, the larger of the two forces, if not the most modern, or necessarily the stronger, would stay back. The Eagles would transit into Armstrong's system and attack the Black Flag forces, as though they'd responded to a distress signal and blundered in, unaware of the vast size of the besieging fleet.

Darius wanted the enemy thinking they had his people, that they could crush his fleet by sheer force of numbers. Darius knew Black Eagles were more than numbers, and he was sure his people could put up one hell of a fight, if he concentrated his forces, and tried to defeat the enemy units piecemeal. But that was exactly what they weren't going to do.

Darius's two wings would take on the main enemy forces, outnumbered ten to one or more in some spots, while his center pressed on directly for the planet. The Marines had to be desperate by now. He knew enough about ground combat to understand they'd be low on ammo, and probably food too… the enemy using its superior numbers to hem them in, collapse their flanks. Darius knew how good his father was, the kind of fight Erik Cain would give the enemy. But he also knew General Cain and his Marines would go down this time, unless help got there in time. And Darius's center was escorting his assault transports, and the entire Black Eagles strike force. If the Black Flag wanted a ground battle, he would give them one…one they would never forget. Regardless of what it took to get his people there.

The plan called for Garret to wait…to wait far longer, he suspected, than the legendary admiral would find easy to do. Then, if Darius's plan worked, his ships would come streaming through just as the Black Flag forces were converging to finish the Eagles. All hell would break lose, and the battle would turn into a wild melee, groups of ships scattered all over the system…and, finally, Commodore Allegre leading the center Eagles force back from the planet, with any luck, enough to turn the tide and secure the victory.

It was risky, some might say reckless, but it was the only way that offered any reasonable chance at all of saving the Marines.

Darius's eyes were fixed on the screens, watching as the two groups, each of four battleships, plus every smaller support vessel the Eagles' fleet had been able to put into space, struggled to engage the massive forces pushing down on them. Space combat wasn't two dimensional like ground warfare, and 'holding back' an enemy was more of a general term than a literal one. There was nothing a ship could do to prevent another from zipping right by, but there were practical ways to attempt to defend areas of space like an army holding ground. For example, a battleship could position itself so it's weapons came to bear on the enemy vessel as it exposed its rear to fire.

The Eagle ships on the wings were executing almost perfectly, but they were too outnumbered to hold. Each of them was quickly surrounded by three or four times their number, and still more enemy ships streamed through the gaps, pursuing Darius's rapidly moving attack force.

Darius knew the enemy could never catch his ships, not at their current velocity. But his vessels couldn't continue to move so quickly, not if they intended to land ground forces on Armstrong. Even at maximum deceleration, he'd have to start soon, and then the enemy forces would have to make a choice. Maintain their own acceleration, zipping by Darius's ships, and Armstrong…or decelerating along with the Eagles. Either way, Darius was betting he'd get his people on the ground, just. His ships were tough enough to endure a single attack run if the enemy maintain its acceleration, and if the enemy did decelerate, it would take them more time to close. It wouldn't be enough for any other military force in Occupied Space to execute a full combat landing, but his Black Eagles could make it work. Barely.

Darius stood up slowly. It wasn't easy to stand with *Eagle Eleven*'s engines blasting as they were. He turned toward Teller's station. "You've got the fleet, Erik," he said calmly.

Teller looked horrified. "Darius, you can't…"

"That's my father down there, Erik. And my mother, too." He didn't say anything else. He didn't have to.

He walked across the bridge toward the bank of elevators. No instructions, no last minute directions on how to approach the planet or how to deal with the enemy. Darius Cain trusted very few people to any degree at all, and only the sheerest few with his life and the lives of his Eagles. Erik Teller was at the top of that miniscule list.

Darius's mind was already in the bay. On his armor, the landing...and what he would find on the surface.

On his parents, and on the desperate race to save them and the rest of the Marines.

Chapter 23

Darius stood in the center of the landing zone, watching his Eagles stream out of the sleek landing craft that had brought them down to the very edge of the battle. Most landings were conducted away from the main area of fighting, giving an invading force time to emerge from their ships and form up before they could be engaged. It was a virtual rule of war…an attack force didn't land in the teeth of direct enemy fire.

It was a rule Darius Cain had just broken. He'd brought his people down right into the teeth of enemy resistance, almost directly on top of their main battle line. He suspected most people would call the operation 'crazy,' but like all his other insanities, it had a grounding of solid logic behind it. First, it gave him the advantage of surprise. If he'd assessed one thing in his encounters with the Black Flag so far, it was a decided lack of military creativity. They were a force that operated in most ways, 'by the book.' It almost seemed as though someone with millions of soldiers and no understanding of war had relied on a manual to plan out a campaign. They followed the book well, and that tended to make them competent and capable, but to an adversary like Darius Cain, it also made them predictable.

The Eagle landers were heavily armed and armored, and they laid down a heavy bombardment on the enemy position as they came in, enough, at least, to disrupt most of the return fire. Darius had lost four landers on the way down, and every one of those hurt, but in terms of overall losses, it had gone better than he'd dared to hope.

Now his soldiers were coming out of their ships, armed and ready. The lead elements were going into battle within minutes, if not seconds. Darius knew his landers would continue to take damage from the fire raging all around the LZ, but again, it was a risk he'd considered and accepted. The Eagles already on the ground would be on the enemy positions before the still-arriving ships took too much damage. His warriors had won their reputations through audacious behavior, by engaging in tactics others shied away from, and he wasn't about to stop now.

He moved toward the front, followed, as always, by the detachment of the Eagles' most experienced veterans, the guard Erik Teller had formed to keep an eye on their sometimes too aggressive general. The Eagles' commander had resisted, to a point, but Teller had insisted, to the point of threatening to resign if Darius didn't accept at least some kind of bodyguard. Darius had been pretty sure his second in command was bluffing, but he wasn't about to risk the only other officer he really trusted to stand in his place, not to mention his best friend, so he'd reluctantly agreed...after negotiating down the size of the detachment.

It was no mystery why Teller had been so determined to do what he could to protect his friend. Darius often drifted toward the front, for a variety of reasons, including the fact he simply did not like being the kind of general who led from behind. Some of his reasons might have lacked compelling military justification for risking the life of the commander-in-chief, but now it was different. He had people to find, to save...assuming they were even still alive. His father, in particular, who from all Darius had been told over the years, was no less likely to be in the thick of the fighting than his son. If his parents were still out there, holding out, he was going to find them and make damned sure they stayed that way. And whether he was in time to save his parents or not, the Marines were his allies, and he had to come to their aid before they were overwhelmed and destroyed.

He swung his head back and forth, watching his Eagles snap into formation and advance, under scattered fire the entire time. The enemy had been surprised by his aggressive landing, and they'd only managed to respond in a disordered and haphazard manner, as he'd anticipated. If the enemy had been ready, if they'd responded and hit his lead elements with everything they had, his gamble could have ended in disaster. But for all the strengths of the Black Flag, tactical creativity wasn't one of them.

He looked back and forth as he moved forward. He was surrounded by the troopers of the Black Regiment. The Blacks had been his first unit, though they'd been a company then, and only later a battalion, and they'd given the 'black' to Black Eagles, when his army's name became more commonly known. When the Eagles expanded, the Blacks remained the senior formation, though Darius had to admit, Cyn Kuragina's White Regiment had become damned near as good if not their outright equals.

Darius had always believed in having an elite reserve. He'd studied every similar force, from the Spartiates of ancient Greece to Napoleon's Old Guard, and he was convinced of the utility of having an intensely reliable, last ditch force to throw into the battle...though until the Black Flag came along, his people had rarely been challenged enough to put the theory to the test. Now, however, he was going against that maxim, at least in that he was throwing his senior troops in first. Time was of the essence. Any chance to save the Marines—to save his parents—relied on cutting through the enemy formation and throwing their entire army into hopeless disorder as quickly as possible.

The fire was increasing in intensity as he moved forward, and he could see his people were taking casualties. He knew the forward services units had just landed, under fire just as the combat forces, and that even now, they'd be setting up the field hospital and aid stations. Darius understood how to generate loyalty from his soldiers, and ensuring they knew they'd be cared for no matter what, whether it was regular rations or medical care when they were wounded, was a big part of that. He'd long considered his thoughts on the matter to be purely mercenary, intended to manipulate his soldiers, to get the best service he could from them. But now, as he watched the first of them fall, he knew it was far more than that. His devotion to the Eagles was as genuine as their loyalty to him. He'd first truly realized that when almost all of them had elected to stay with him to fight the Black Flag, despite the lack of tangible rewards, and the likelihood the fight would be a difficult and brutal one.

It was one thing to retain and attract people when the rewards were great. He'd had a hundred applications for every available slot in the Eagles over the years, probably more. Service with his private army had been a virtual guarantee of wealth, and the superiority of his soldiers had kept casualty rates relatively low. But there were no rewards to be had now, at least not tangible ones. All this war—which was already being called Black vs. Black, despite the fact that the Eagles were only one component of the coalition—was likely to offer was death and suffering. Darius had been attracted to the mercenary trade expressly because the relationship between fighter and paymaster was so clearly defined, so unencumbered by emotional baggage and the kind of manufactured patriotism governments used to control their citizens. He didn't think much of people in general, and his powerful cynicism made it difficult for him to form emotional bonds. But, now he realized his connection with the Eagles ran deep.

"Activate comm…try to contact any Marine forces." He snapped out the order to his AI. He didn't think it was likely he could get through the jamming, not with just his suit's power, but it was worth a try.

"Negative, General. Interference is too great."

"Keep trying." The landing forces still coming in had heavy auxiliary power units. If he hadn't hooked up with the Marines by the time they were set up, there was a good chance they could power a message through. The Marines might not be able to get a response back, but at least he'd be able to direct them to link up with his forces.

"Alright Black Regiment...we all know how good you are," he said after he flipped the comm to the Blacks' channel. "Let's show these conditioned zombies just who the Black Eagles are. Let them learn what every other mercenary company in Occupied Space already knows." He could hear the responses, the sounds of hundreds of his people beginning to cheer. Then, he added, "I hope you don't mind if I go into this fight with you. Because this is where I belong, surrounded by my Eagles, and driving the enemy straight to hell!" A wave of cheers burst out on the comm. The Eagles were ready for battle.

*   *   *   *   *

"We haven't been able to get through the jamming, General. But we're getting preliminary reports that the new arrivals appear to be engaging the Black Flag forces."

Erik Cain glanced at the communications officer and then over at Gilson. "It's the Black Eagles."

"You can't be sure of that, Erik," she said, clearly trying to remain cautious.

Cain understood, and he usually thought the same way. But not this time. He'd watched the precision of the operation, the apparent discipline of the landing troops. He'd never seen a force come down so close to hostile troops, not even Marines. If those troops weren't Black Flag reinforcements—and it certainly didn't look like they were—they had to be the Eagles.

Besides...he could feel his son out there. It didn't make any sense, not really, but it was true nevertheless. He'd known all along, on some level, that Darius would come.

"It's the Black Eagles, Cate." A pause. "We have to attack. Now."

Gilson looked over at Cain. "Erik..." She paused. Cain knew what she was thinking, that what he was proposing was risky. He'd bought time with his wild attack days before, threw the enemy into disorder that slowed their operations. But the cost had been high, in casualties and supplies, and now, after weeks of sustained battle, the Marines were running low on…well, everything.

"Cate, the only reason to hold on, to conserve supplies, was to last until help came. Well, whether that's the Black Eagles out there or not, they seem to be attacking the enemy. The help we were waiting for, hoping for, is here. What do you want to save supplies for? To die a little more slowly? To stretch out the agony? If we stand here in these defensive positions, and this new force is defeated, do you really think another relief expedition will arrive in the few extra days we can make our ammunition and food last?" He paused, looking at his comrade of so many years. "This is our chance, Cate, right now. Do we sit here? Or do we strike, hit the enemy with everything we've got? We can bracket them, trap them between our forces and the new arrivals."

Gilson stared back at Cain. There was still worry in her eyes, uncertainty. He remembered her being more aggressive years before, less choked with caution. *Age,* he thought. *I feel it too. If I wasn't so sure that is Darius out there, would I be in such a rush to throw everything into one last effort?* He wanted to think the answer was yes, that he was the same officer he'd been decades before. But the fatigue was there, deep in his soul, and it took all he had to push, to sustain the immense effort it took to lead men and women into a desperate fight to the death.

"Okay, Erik," Gilson finally said, her voice soft, her efforts to hold back the concern partially successful. "Let's do it. One last strike. Either victory…or an end to the Corps that will be worth a story or two."

Cain nodded. "One last strike."

But if we fail, who will be left to tell the stories?

*   *   *   *   *

Darius jogged back toward the command post. He'd led Colonel Falstaff's Black Regiment as they attacked the enemy position. The Blacks had hit almost dead center in the enemy line, driving hard in an attempt to split their formation. They'd had a certain amount of surprise on their side at first, but the enemy resistance had quickly solidified. The Eagles found their advance slowed to a crawl, and ultimately, they'd experienced something they hadn't known in many years. A stalemate.

The Eagles of the Black Regiment had been stunned, enraged. No one they could remember had ever stood against them. Darius had watched his beloved soldiers throwing themselves at the enemy, killing four or five for every trooper they lost, but no matter how hard they hit, how many they gunned down, the enemy stood firm. So much of war was based on breaking the enemy's morale, something the Eagles often had managed simply by showing up. But this adversary was fearless, and trapped as they were, bracketed between the Eagles and the Marines, Darius had come to realize the battle would be a fight to the death. Literally.

He still had confidence his people could win. He could hardly imagine otherwise, though he wondered how much hubris had infected his usual cold analysis. But what that victory would cost, how many of his people would die hunting down every last enemy soldier…it was a brutal reckoning. Worse, if his attitude *was* pride-driven, if he was wrong…if his people could really lose here…

And all of this is moot anyway if we can't win the battle in space. The land combat was only one of his concerns. Darius had known the risks of bringing his ground forces down without first securing total control of the system's space. He'd risked all, and he realized now, despite his pride and confidence in his Eagles, that they *could* lose. That they could all die here, on this world and in this system.

He put the space combat out of his mind. He'd left Teller in command there, and he trusted his lifelong friend more than anyone else in Occupied Space. Teller would leave most of the tactical decisions to Commodore Allegre, Darius was sure of that, just as he himself would. Allegre was like all the other Eagles. He was there because of his excellence, and, notwithstanding the unmatched Admiral Garret, the Eagles' fleet commander was probably the best naval officer in all of human space.

Darius had wanted to stay on the front line—the thought of leaving his Eagles when they were in such a deadly fight sickened him—but he had too many responsibilities. He had to take command of the newly-arrived forces, the Blue Regiment, and Kuragina's Whites. They were needed on the lines. His already engaged troopers were desperate for reserves…they needed the numbers and force concentration to break through before the enemy could bring their own numbers to bear and hit his advance guard on both flanks. His plan had been audacious, and now, for perhaps the first time in his command career, he was concerned he might lose a battle. Defeat here would be more than a loss. It would be total ruin, the end of the Black Eagles… and the Marines.

The end of humanity as anything but a vast pool of pathetic slaves.

No, that would not happen. He wouldn't allow it.

He simply refused to allow it.

Chapter 24

Teller sat in *Eagle Eleven*'s flag command chair, looking out over the ship's veteran crew. They were working their controls, operating calmly, efficiently, despite the enemy ships all around. The Eagles' fleet didn't have a chance against the Black Flag forces. They were better, of course, even outnumbered two to one, Teller had no doubt the Eagles would have crushed their adversaries. But they were outnumbered almost eight to one, and slowly, steadily, the numbers began to tell.

But Teller sat quietly, calmly, a menacing smile on his face. He wasn't looking at the display, nor at the incoming damage reports from the Eagles' warships. He wasn't watching the ship's crew—he was no naval officer, and the last thing they needed was pointless interference from him. No, he was staring at the chronometer, counting down in his head.

"Energy readings from the warp gate, Colonel."

The communications officer's words had come perhaps a moment or two early, but that was no surprise. Augustus Garret hadn't liked the idea of staying behind when the Eagles went in alone, and Teller would have bet the fighting admiral would shave the designated transit time a bit.

190

Teller turned his head now, looking out over the display. The Eagles' ships had scattered, pretending they were disordered, almost broken. In truth, though they'd taken a pounding, they weren't as badly damaged as they appeared to be. They had used maneuver, put their superior skill to work buying time. The Black Flag forces had reacted, dividing up, chasing after each, apparently isolated, Eagles' vessel.

Exactly as planned…

It had been Garret's idea, though in his original proposal, it was his fleet that had gone in first, to break up the enemy formations and leave them exposed to the Eagles coming second and hitting them from the rear. Darius had accepted the plan immediately…it was just the kind of wildly aggressive move he tended to like. And both Darius and Erik Teller knew that Augustus Garret, despite age and old injuries catching up to him quickly, was still the greatest naval tactician, perhaps in all of human history. The Eagles were used to being the best, but Darius had been more than content to yield to Garret's wisdom.

With one change.

Garret had argued fiercely when Darius had insisted the Eagles go in first, that his people served as the bait in the trap. Teller suspected there was some pride in the demand, but more importantly, Darius had his own plan, a way to divert the enemy warships *and* make a wild dash for Armstrong…to get his ground forces down while there was—hopefully—still time to save the Marines.

Garret had been forced to yield. He was as aware as Darius and Teller how desperate the Marines' situation had to be, how urgent it was to get to their aid, and he'd grudgingly gone along with the whole scheme.

Now, Augustus Garret was back. Teller watched as ship after ship came through the warp gate, blasting in on perfectly charted courses, already at high velocities. His battleships were in the lead, followed by cruisers, and lastly the destroyers and frigates. There was little elegance in the battle plan, just a desperate attempt to bring the maximum firepower to bear before the enemy could react and mount a credible defense.

Even the combined Eagles and Marine fleets were heavily outnumbered, and any chance of victory was dependent on taking maximum advantage of surprise.

Teller watched as Garret's lead ships fired their missiles, a massive, coordinated barrage, targeted at a small section of the enemy line. The Black Flag ships tried to respond, but many had exhausted their missile stocks fighting the Eagles, and their vectors were all over the place, many decelerating hard to try and come about and face the new threat.

Garret's missiles came on toward the enemy, their narrow frontage condensing even further as they closed. The Black Flag battleships fired their rockets and their short-ranged anti-missile lasers, and dozens of Garret's weapons vanished. But more survived, the density of the assault too much for the scattered point defense of the enemy vessels.

All along a narrow line, around six enemy battleships, dozens of massive nuclear warheads detonated. One ship was bracketed by no less than five, two of them less than five hundred meters distant. The ship was wracked by hard radiation, and even the heat from the explosion impacted it, melting massive sections of hull, and tearing the structure apart.

Teller watched, impressed by Garret's willingness to commit all his missiles to attack only a few enemy ships. Missile barrages usually left large numbers of vessels with light to moderate damage, as radiation from nearby explosions knocked out scanners and power relays, and killed and wounded exposed crew. But the six ships caught in Garret's manmade inferno died, every one of them…including one actually struck by a missile. That unfortunate ship had simply vanished, consumed by five hundred megatons of nuclear fury.

Garret's ships were accelerating now, building on their already considerable velocity. His missile attack had created a hole in the enemy line, one that exacerbated the Black Flag's already fragmented formation. One he clearly intended to exploit while he could.

His battleships moved through, and then they changed their thrust vectors, splitting into two groups, moving against the exposed flanks of what passed for the enemy line. The Black Flag ships struggled to realign themselves to bring the maximum firepower to bear, but they were still trying to overcome their previous vectors. Everywhere, the enemy's redeployment efforts took the pressure off the Eagles, and Teller's ships came about, renewing their own assaults, proving to be more operational than they had let on.

All across the system, Black Flag ships were attacked from two sides, driven between their enemies. They fought back, and losses mounted on both forces. Teller was staring right at the display when the reports came in. *Eagle Fifteen* was in trouble… then, no more than a moment later, the battleship was gone.

The loss hurt. Teller was keenly aware how many Eagles had been aboard that vessel, how many resources had gone into its construction…how much it would be missed when the final battle in this war was fought, when the Eagles and their allies had moved off the defensive and set out to destroy the enemy. But he just stared coldly, forward, no emotion visible, no hint of pain or fear that could become contagious to his people.

The battle raged, a lopsided engagement where the enemy lost four or five ships for every one they destroyed. But Teller could see the momentum starting to shift. Half his ships were nearly out of the fight, and while many of those could be repaired given time, that was one thing in very short supply. The enemy naval personnel, appearing to be as fearless as the ground forces, just continued to fight, and slowly, steadily, their positions improved, and their depleted line stabilized. The advantage Garret's forces and the Eagles had enjoyed was mostly gone, and the fight became a slugging match between battered ships and exhausted crews.

Teller still sat, watching, showing no reaction. But inside he felt the tension, the fear. He was no naval commander, as he had noted before. But he was a veteran warrior, and he knew two things. First, his and Garret's people had fought well, heroically, and they'd inflicted far more losses than they'd endured.

And second…in spite of that, they were losing.

* * * * *

"Keep moving…we've got them on the run. Don't let up now!" Cain was surrounded by Marines, armored warriors surging forward, ignoring losses, pushing hard against the Black Flag forces in front of them. He was excited, anxious, hopeful his people could drive deeply enough to cut the enemy in half, to link up with the Eagles—he was still sure they were the Eagles, though there had been no confirmation yet—and pull out the victory that had seemed so uncertain just two days earlier.

He had to admit, to himself at least, that 'on the run' was a bit of creative license, something to encourage his people. The Black Flag warriors were fighting for every meter, and the losses had been almost beyond counting. There was no rout, no seeming fear on the enemy's part. The Marines had been no less determined, grimly driving forward, but Cain knew his people had a limit. Though Marines sometimes denied it, they were only human, normal men and women. He wasn't sure about this enemy though. Whatever it was—conditioning, brainwashing—they did not seem to feel fear, nor express any self-preservation instinct. They just fought, retreating when the tactical situation called for it, and fighting to the death when it didn't.

Cain had fought an enemy like this before. The robots of the First Imperium had been without fear, and in their case, without fatigue as well. At least the Black Flag soldiers seemed to have standard human physical limitations. They weren't stronger than normal soldiers, and they didn't appear to have better sight, aim, senses. They were just utterly unconcerned with their own survival.

Then, we'll just have to kill every one of them…

Cain kept moving forward himself, stopping and firing as he saw an enemy trooper. The Black Flag forces had fallen back—*they didn't run*, he reminded himself, *they just moved to a stronger position.*

He looked at this display. His data was spotty. Without orbital support or active scanning positions, he didn't have enough input to give him a view of the field. He had a few drones left, but not many. He wondered if he should order a spread launched, whether enough data would get through the enemy jamming to make it worthwhile. *No*, he thought. *No way. The interference is too heavy.*

He pressed on, shouting out over the comm, directing each unit around him, working his Marines, doing all he could to sustain their morale. He thought about Sarah, about the night-mare the hospital had almost certainly become. He didn't have the latest figures on medical supplies, but with the status of ammunition and food, he couldn't imagine there was much left. The thought of modern medicine, descending into an almost primitive state as equipment failed under dire field conditions, and even basic medicines ran out, was a grim one. He'd seen it before, heard it, the sounds of men and women screaming, without so much as an injection available to relieve their pain.

It's not much better up here. He glanced at his readouts. He had two full clips left, plus a hundred twenty rounds in the current one. And two grenades. His power was still good…that was the advantage of carrying a fusion reactor on your back, but once the ordnance was gone, he'd be down to his dual lasers, not much good past sixty meters or so in atmosphere, at least against armored enemies.

And the blade…

Cain felt his arm twitch as he thought of the micro-thin knife in in his iridium-encased arm. If his people failed, if they fell short, he knew the last fighting would be hand to hand, at least for him. He didn't know how each of his Marines would behave at the last moment, if they would flee, surrender, fight. But Erik Cain had battled for too long to accept defeat now, and he had endured the torture of captivity. Never again. He would win here, or die. But they would never take him prisoner again.

So, win then…keep moving and forget this nonsense about defeat.

He felt a burst of strength, of determination. He swung around, firing his assault rifle, each shot on semi-automatic, a small burst of three projectiles. His aim was almost uncanny. Every time he fired, an enemy fell. Energy surged through his body, as though his younger self, gone for so many years, had returned.

"Move…let's go, Marines. Forward. There's no stopping, not now. We've got friends out there…as long as we push hard enough to reach them." He didn't know how many of his Marines were getting his messages. Probably only a few, the very closest ones. But it was all he could do.

Almost in response, his speakers crackled. It was an incoming signal, a powerful one, much stronger than a suit's comm.

"Marine forces…this is General Darius Cain. The Black Eagles have landed, and we are moving forward even now toward your position. I urge you to attack now with everything you have, drive hard to the east, as we advance to the west. It's time to crush our enemies between us. Time to win this battle."

Cain knew he couldn't respond, that his armor's transmitter didn't have the power to penetrate the enemy jamming, not over that kind of distance. But he didn't need to reply. The communique told him all he needed to know…all he'd known already, at least in his heart.

"Let's go, Marines," he said again, as much for himself as for anyone picking up his signal. "It's time to win this battle!"

*   *   *   *   *

"I knew you'd come." Father and son embraced, a disappointing and clumsy exercise in powered armor, but one they'd both clearly felt was necessary.

"Of course I came. Do you think I'm going to let you wander off to some new shithole prison and spend fifteen more years looking for you? Might serve you right, but I couldn't do that to mother."

Cain reached out again, pulling his son back to him with a loud clang, his arms barely long enough to get around the two suits of armor. "No more prisons for me, son. Whatever happens, that won't be it."

The two men slipped apart, and Darius turned toward one of his aides. "Send a message to the fleet…tell my brother I found our father."

"Yes, General."

"We have to get back to the shelters, Darius. Your mother is there." Cain's moment of joy had been replaced in an instant by tension.

"No, dad...don't worry." Darius reached out and put his hand on his father's armored shoulder. "She's fine. As soon as we broke through, I send a team to secure the shelters...remember, we're allies. I had the locations in my database, all of them. Mother is fine. In fact, almost everyone there is fine. A little scared perhaps, and hungry maybe. But alive."

"That's good news." Cain was clearly relieved. "What about the Black Flag forces? There are still a lot of them in the field."

"There are. We're staying on them now, trying to keep them from regrouping. It's dirty, expensive business hunting them down to the last man, but we've got them cut off from their supply depots now." Darius paused for an instant. "You might want to check if there's anything your Marines can use there. I'd give you some of our ordnance, but to be honest, the landing was such a rush job, we didn't have time to bring down more than the minimum supplies."

"I will." Cain went silent, at least as far as his son could hear. Darius suspected his father was trying to raise some of his people. Then: "The jamming is gone, Darius."

"Yeah...we captured their portable power plants. Well, maybe captured isn't exactly the right word, but they're not going to be powering any high energy jammers anymore."

Cain was silent again, at least from Darius's perspective. No doubt sending out orders to his officers.

Darius turned and looked out over his own camp. The field hospital was up and running...and far busier that he liked to see. The usual supply dumps were in place, but far smaller than usual. He'd had to cut the landings short, or risk his ships getting caught in orbit.

The ships...he hadn't heard anything from the fleet, not yet. That might have been the jamming interfering, or...

The fight would be a difficult one up there, at least as bad as the ground battle, and possibly a lot worse. He'd put it out of his mind, left it to Teller. He'd always considered his second-in-command his equal, a brilliant tactician and a man with almost limitless strength of will. If Teller couldn't do it, he was sure he couldn't have either or, for that matter, Augustus Garret. There were dozens of reasons he might not have heard anything, but still the thought nagged at him, and now he couldn't put it out of his mind.

He wondered for a moment more, but that's all. Then he got his answer.

Chapter 25

Ana Bazarov grabbed onto the edge of her workstation, steadying herself as *Eagle Eleven* shook from yet another direct hit. The Eagles' current flagship was fighting three enemy battleships, and while she was somehow holding her own for the moment, Bazarov knew the damage was wearing her down.

She pushed back a momentary urge to laugh, a strange impulse buried among the fear that was closing on her from all sides. She'd had another fight with Darius, one that had gone down to the wire, with her insisting that he assign her to *Eagle Eleven*'s crew and him demanding she stay behind, at the Nest or on Columbia. Once again, she'd achieved something few people in Occupied Space could boast. She'd gotten Darius Cain to yield, to give in to her demands.

You fought the good fight to get your way...so you could die here...

She turned and caught Colonel Teller glancing over at her again. Teller was Darius's oldest friend, and Ana knew her presence made him nervous. She and the Eagles' second-in-command had become close, almost like brother and sister, and she knew Teller wanted her safe as much as the Eagles' commander did himself.

199

These are all the people in the world you care about…except Tatyana, of course, but she is well-provided for now. Of course, that means nothing if this battle is lost. She thought of her little sister, enslaved, or worse. *No,* she thought, *Tatyana was always the tougher of us.* Her sister would fight to the end. She would never yield, never become anyone's slave.

"Report from *Eagle Three*, sir." Ana stared at her screen, reading the communique. "They report energy readings from the warp gate." Bazarov felt her spirit sink even further. The situation had been close to hopeless, but she'd still maintained some scrap of faith. In the last few years, she'd come to understand just how capable the Eagles were, that it was never wise to give up on them. But if enemy reinforcements were on the way, she knew it was over.

"Very well, Lieutenant." Teller's voice was as cool as ever, no sense of the emotion she knew he had to be feeling, the realization that the battle was as good as lost. "Report immediately when you have updated data."

"Yes, sir." Ana could still hear the word, 'lieutenant' in her ears. Darius had made her position official, moving her from the cadet ranks, to official status as an Eagle officer. She'd been thrilled by the gesture, but also a bit worried the others would resent her, view her as Darius Cain's lover and nothing more. But that hadn't been the case. She'd passed every test any Eagle went through, and she'd been third in her cadet class…and the other Eagles recognized that. She'd been surprised, and only then had she realized the extent of the cult of excellence Darius had created. Nothing was more important to the Eagles than being the best. Nothing.

Her eyes were fixed on the screen when the comm unit buzzed. She listened to the signal, and then she turned around abruptly. "Colonel, I have Admiral Garret on your line."

"Augustus…" Teller spoke rapidly into his headset. "We've got trouble coming."

A few seconds passed as the signal traveled across the system and Garret's made its way back. "Yes, Erik…we do. I'm going to pull half my ships out of the line and get them formed up to meet whatever's coming. I know you're thin already, but can you stretch out, cover some of that space?" A short pause, but then, before Teller responded, "I don't know what else we can do."

"We'll manage it, Augustus. Somehow." The tone of the last word was the first sign of edginess Ana had heard from Teller. She had heard stories of the great Augustus Garret, of his epic battles and massive victories. If anything could shake the iron that made up Teller, it was hearing Garret say he didn't know what to do.

"Good luck, Augustus."

That last bit sounded as controlled as any of Teller's previous commands, at least to most, but Ana could hear the difference, subtle, barely noticeable. The Eagles' second-in-command had given up hope, whatever shreds of it had remained. When enemy ships poured through that warp gate, that would be the end. She'd suspected as much when she'd first heard the transmission, but now she had no doubt, none at all.

She was afraid, terrified to her core. But her mind wasn't on *Eagle Eleven*'s bridge. It was down on the planet, with Darius… and the thought that she'd never see him again almost overwhelmed her.

Almost. She wasn't going to lose it, whatever it took. If she was going to die, she would die like a Black Eagle.

*   *   *   *   *

Darius stood next to his father, looking out over the camp. There was movement all around, troop formations redeploying, small transports moving what little remained of the supplies. A Black Eagles camp was never a passive site. There was always something happening, activity everywhere. But now, there was something else going on, a commotion of some sort, a ripple of uncustomary disorder among Darius's people. He was about to contact the HQ line and see what the hell was going on when he saw an aide rushing across the makeshift street toward him. The officer was armored, but even without a look at her expression, Darius knew whatever she had for him wasn't good news.

"General Cain…" The aide shouted loudly. Her words came through both on the comm and the outside microphones.

Father and son both turned abruptly toward the voice, but it was a Black Eagle calling, and Darius was the General Cain she was after. The officer staggered to a controlled halt, a meter or so from Darius.

"Report, Lieutenant." He could tell from her tone she was flustered, something rare enough among the Eagles in general, and almost non-existent with those chosen to serve as his assistants and support officers.

"We just got a report from Colonel Teller, sir. He advises the fleet has inflicted heavy losses on the enemy, but is still being driven back. He does not believe the combined naval forces can prevail." The words hit Darius like an anvil. He'd been worried about the naval fight, well-aware how outnumbered his forces were, but his people had always managed to prevail before, and he'd hung his hopes on that.

"The enemy strength," the aide continued, "is simply too great, our forces too battered and low on ordnance." Then, the words that struck Darius hard, the true reason for Teller's pessimism: "The colonel also reports signs of enemy reserves about to transit the warp gate." She hesitated for a few seconds before continuing. "He says to tell you he will fight to the end, General. And he…" Another pause, then the officer's voice continued, heavy with emotion now. "…he says he is sorry he let you down, sir. Sorry he failed you."

Darius heard the words, and they sliced at him like a blade. Every bit of excitement he'd felt, at his father's survival, at the likelihood of victory on the ground, faded rapidly. None of it mattered, not if the fleets were defeated. At best, his survivors would be trapped, subjected to renewed bombardment, and besieged until enemy reinforcements could arrive…and *this* siege would start with the defenders already almost out of food and ammunition. It would be a rout, a disaster, with no possible outcome save for total destruction.

And with the Eagles and the Marines out of the fight, there would be nothing left that could stand in the way of the Black

Flag's relentless advance. Humanity was too splintered, its forces too disunited to stand without the Eagles and their Marine allies to lead them. Without names like Cain and Gilson, Garret and Teller to take the lead, they would have no chance. Some would resist, even fight to the end, but they would fall, one by one, individually and in small groups.

Darius felt something new to him, something he'd thought about, even feared, but never truly experienced. Defeat. It was a cold shadow, one that pushed down on him, slamming against the iron stubbornness at his core. He saw no way out, no path to extricate his people from destruction.

His mind raced, fruitlessly, trying to find a way, any way to salvage things. Nothing. If the fleet was defeated, it was over.

Still he wouldn't give up, not until the enemy closed his eyes for him.

And maybe not even then.

*   *   *   *   *

"I want you ready, Camille. We've got enough trouble here already without letting them get new reserves formed up and into the fight." Augustus Garret knew he was asking the impossible. Camille Harmon had been one of his most reliable subordinates for decades, a grim and capable warrior who'd served at his side since the days of the Third Frontier War. There was no one he'd rather have in a vital spot in a battle, but even she couldn't do the impossible. Her ships were damaged and depleted, their missiles gone, their fighters scattered all across the system. The vessels themselves were disorganized, drawn one at a time from wherever he could get them, with little regard to the fleet's order of battle. Garret had considered for a brief instant that the energy spike could be supply ships or a courier vessel, but even that shred of hope had been dashed. The intensity of the readings left no doubt. Whatever was coming through, there were some large ships there, behemoths even. And that could only mean warships.

"We've done this dance before, Admiral, and we've come

through. We've always done what we had to do, haven't we?" Harmon had always been defiant, but the loss of her son years before, had hardened her like the center of a neutron star. Max Harmon hadn't just been lost in combat, he'd been trapped behind the Barrier, the disrupted warp gate that had separated humanity from the vast fleets of the First Imperium... and trapped half the fleet on the other side. Garret suspected death would be a relief to her in ways, but he knew Harmon well enough to be sure she'd go down fighting to the last.

"Yesterday's gone, Camille. Let's just do what we can here. Good luck to you." He wanted to say more of a goodbye. He'd never had the chance to bid a proper farewell to his closest friend before he'd consigned him to death. Terrance Compton had been the commander of the forces trapped behind the Barrier. For years, Garret had tried to convince himself that Compton would have found a way out, an escape route to keep his people alive. But he'd long since resigned himself to the realization that he'd killed his friend that day, along with the tens of thousands who'd served with him.

"Good luck to you...Augustus."

Garret sat and stared at the comm, even after the line went dead. Then, he lifted his eyes toward the main display. *Bunker Hill* was still engaged, fighting off enemy battleships coming in from all sides. The great ship shook hard, and then again, as its attackers scored a pair of hits. The old ship was blasting its thrusters in a wildly random pattern, pulling every evasive maneuver in the book, but still, slowly, gradually, the few shots that scored hits were taking their toll. The engines were down to eighty percent, not critical, but the reduced thrust would hamper countermeasures, and that would, in turn, increase the rate at which the enemy was scoring hits.

Bunker Hill was far from passive, however, despite being outnumbered and surrounded. Her weapons fired, the giant x-ray lasers ripping through space, slamming into the ships of the Black Flag, slicing through hulls, blasting whole systems to scrap. Even as Garret watched, yet another enemy battleship disappeared, as its reactors' containment failed, and the fury of uncontrolled nuclear fusion was released. But even as he watched the lopsided casualty rates—his ships were taking out three or four enemies for every loss they took—he knew it wasn't enough. There were just too many of the enemy.

"Ships coming through the warp gate, Admiral."

Garret just nodded silently. His eyes were glued to the display.

The mass readings came through first...enormous, far larger than even his *Yorktown*s. Any lingering hope he was dealing with supply ships or messengers was gone.

The energy readings were coming through now as well, not from the warp gate, but from the ships themselves. After three-quarters of a century of war, Augustus Garret knew the signs of ships' weaponry getting ready to fire.

His eyes focused on the ragged line of small blips, Harmon's ships, waiting, preparing to fight what he knew would be their last battle. He could feel the moistness in his eyes as he watched yet another old friend going to her death.

At least this time she will only be moments ahead of you...

He stared, surprised that Harmon hadn't started shooting yet. She was one of the fiercest fighters he'd ever seen, but her ships were just sitting in space, their weapons silent. Then, the new ships opened fire.

Great pulses of high energy x-ray lasers tore through space, slamming hard into the hulls of target vessels, melting armor plating, shattering structural supports. The attack was fierce, brutal, unyielding, and it ripped into the formations waiting in the system.

But the attack wasn't directed at Harmon's ships.

Garret watched in stunned shock as more vessels poured through the gate. There were only two of the great superbattleships that had given the massive readings, but they were followed by normal-sized capital ships, and then a wave of cruisers and frigates. And every one of them tore into the system, going after any Black Flag ships they could find.

The enemy ships, so close to victory, now began to fall into disorder. Squadrons moved around, seeming almost clueless as to whether they should face the new attackers or finish off the battered Eagle and Marine fleets. And Augustus Garret, still confused, knew the moment had come.

"All ships, attack," he said to the communications officer. "All fleet units are to close to point blank range with the nearest enemy…and don't stop until they're nothing but dust and plasma." He could feel the feral intensity, the drive that had led him to so many victories, and he let it take him, as it had so often before.

"And get me a line to one of those ships…" He had to know what was going on.

"We have an incoming communique, sir. It appears to be from one of the large vessels."

"On my line."

He listened as the transmission played, a wide grin slipping onto his face as he recognized the voice.

"Hello, Augustus…Darius Cain sent a courier. He thought you might need some help. You didn't forget you're not alone in this fight, did you?"

"Send a response," he snapped to the waiting officer. Then he tapped his headset, activating the microphone.

"Roderick Vance, you old dog…God, am I glad to see you. Welcome to Gamma Pavonis, and not a moment too soon!"

Garret watched as the ships of the Martian fleet, fresh and fully-supplied, tore into the spent vessels of the Black Flag.

Victory was no longer an impossible dream. It was there for the taking.

"Let's go…full thrust forward, and all weapons, fire!

Chapter 26

MFS John Carter
Armstrong Orbit
Gamma Pavonis System
Earthdate: 2321 AD (36 Years After the Fall)

Darius stepped out of the shuttle doors and onto the scarred and battered metal of the landing bay. *John Carter* and the rest of the Martian fleet had helped turned the tide, and the combined allied forces had shattered the enemy fleet, sending its broken remnants retreating from the system. Whatever compulsion toward fighting to the death the enemy instilled in its rank and file, it appeared clear again that the higher ranks were only too willing to flee when the battle was lost.

The Martian fleet had saved the day, but not without cost, as Darius could clearly see all around him. There was debris strewn everywhere, and more than one area where heavy trusses and large pieces of equipment had crashed to the deck.

"General Cain, welcome to *John Carter*." Roderick Vance walked toward Darius, extending his hand. "And to you, General Cain," he added, as Darius's father stepped out after his son.

"What can I say, President Vance, except thank you?" Darius nodded, but then he stepped aside, yielding the lead position to his father. Erik Cain and Roderick Vance had been allies decades before Darius had even been born.

"I am just glad your courier reached us in time, General… though, may I suggest we dispense with all the titles and honorifics? It makes me feel old." Vance, not a man noted for lighthearted amusement, allowed himself a small grin.

Darius just nodded, but Erik Cain took a step forward. He looked for a moment like he was going to offer his hand, but then he just reached out and embraced the Martian dictator. "Roderick, my old friend. It is always good to see you. From what I can glean, you cut it a little close this time, but you made it, and that's all that matters."

Vance, usually uncomfortable with such displays, returned Cain's with enthusiasm. "I wouldn't have been here at all if your son hadn't gotten a message through. What's with you trying to fight this thing alone? We're in it together, don't forget." Vance took a deep breath, and then he continued, a more somber tone in his voice. "And it seems we have come down to it, now, doesn't it? The final struggle."

"It does…as it has far too often in the past, Roderick. But we'll get through this one, as we have all the others, my friend."

Vance hesitated, looking around, checking to see if anyone else was in earshot. "Not this time, Erik. Not me, at least. But I am here to do all I can to aid you, to secure the future, for Mars, and for the rest of Occupied Space."

"This is no time for fatalistic premonitions, Roderick. We'll make it, all of us."

Vance paused again. "I'm dying, my friend. I have months left, perhaps not even."

Cain stood, looking stunned. Darius watched, almost as shocked himself. The two Cain's had seen thousands of men and women die in battle. They had both lost friends. Erik Cain had seen ninety-five percent of Earth's population perish in the Fall. But somehow listening to a friend say calmly that he was dying proved hardest to accept.

"What? Sarah is down on Armstrong, seeing to transferring the wounded. I'll send for her and…"

"I'm the dictator of the Martian Republic, Erik. With all due respect to your lovely wife, and one of my absolute favorite people, by the way, don't you think everything that can be done has been? It's some sort of accelerated mutation, likely from the bombardment of Mars. There have been a significant number of cases over the years. Specifics vary somewhat from person to person, but mortality is certain."

The three men were utterly silent, the only sounds coming from the landing bay equipment operating in the distance.

"No one knows," Vance finally said, "at least no one outside my inner circle. But this will be my last adventure. I might have wished for a chance to spend my final months doing something more constructive than killing, but I am glad, at least, I will get the chance to fight at your side again, Erik. And Sarah and Cate."

"I don't know what to say, Roderick." Cain's voice was soft, somber.

"There is nothing to say, Erik. You've said it all over a lifetime of friendship and faithfulness." Vance was silent for a moment. "I have brought every ship Mars can put into space, every Martian Marine, every missile, bomb, laser core. Mars will be with you in this fight, until victory. Or until the end." He looked right at Cain. "But I would ask one thing of you, Erik."

"Of course, my friend. Anything."

"I will not return from this campaign, whether we go to victory or to defeat and destruction. I would not spend my last weeks in a hospital bed, too weak to stand, unable to do even the simplest things for myself."

Darius just stood and watched the two men. He was friendly with Vance, but he knew his father and the Martian strongman went back half a century.

"I understand, Roderick. I think I would make the same choice."

There was no doubt in Darius's mind his father *would* take the same path. No doubt at all. Nor any that he would do the same. The types of lives they'd all led shouldn't end in helplessness, with faceless attendants spoon-feeding them watered down oatmeal.

"So," Cain continued, "what can I do for you, Roderick? All you have to do it ask."

"I want you to take control of Mars."

Cain stared back, stunned. Darius suspected, whatever his father had thought was coming, that hadn't been it. "Roderick…"

"Hear me out, Erik. I don't want you to become Mars's dictator. I want you to prevent anyone else from doing it. You know I only seized power because there was no choice. I have detested every moment, and I dreamed of the day—a day that will now never come—when I could give up my power, turn Mars back to the Martian people." His voice grew darker. "But you have seen all I have, the way people are, the lust for power that drives politicians, the carelessness with which citizens treat their freedoms. If I do not make arrangements before I die, if I simply do not return, you know as well as I do, a dozen men and women will struggle for my place. There will be violence, perhaps even civil war…and Martian democracy will be gone forever." His eyes locked with Cain's. "I cannot die knowing that what I did, what I *had* to do, condemned my people to lose their liberty."

"I will do anything I can, Roderick, but how can I stop Martian politicians from trying to seize power?"

"Kill them." Vance's tone was utterly deadpan. "It sounds crazy, Erik, but how many people have we seen die over the last fifty years? Hundreds of thousands of soldiers and spacers? Billions in the Fall, the victims of the Superpowers and their entrenched political classes? There is a choice, now, even as the one we made against the Black Flag. Do we yield to those who would be our masters…or do we stand, fight them, do whatever we must to prevail? *Whatever we must…*"

"But what if your people resist? Would you have me kill Martians…and lose Marines doing it? Assuming we come away from this battle with enough of us remaining to fight another enemy."

"No. Too many innocent people have died already. I have a list for you, Erik, the names of those I fear will seek to take control. The dishonest, the corrupt. I would have to kill them eventually if I returned, and in my absence, you must. Mars is defenseless now, every asset of military value stripped away to serve the war effort. And the senior officers I brought here are all trustworthy. They will keep every surviving Martian soldier, every ship far from home until all of this is over. You are famous, Erik, revered on Mars. Unlike an admiral or general, you would be above suspicion. If you eliminate the men and women on my list, you will be able to preside over elections, an outside observer, one utterly above reproach and suspicion."

He turned toward Darius. "And if you will help us, Darius, the operation will be that much more secure. No one would dare challenge *both* of you."

Cain turned and looked at his son. Darius paused for a few seconds, and then he nodded gently. Cain hesitated himself then, for longer than Darius had. Finally, he looked over at Vance and said," Very well, Roderick. I will do as you ask."

He took a deep breath. "Assuming we somehow manage to win the fight in front of us now, and any of us get back…"

*   *   *   *   *

"Status report?" Elias Cain sat in *SS03*'s command chair, uncomfortable and keenly aware of his lack of naval experience. His brother had placed him in command of the expedition, with no less of a mandate than to find the mysterious planet Vali and to return with that information. The combined forces of every allied force the Eagles and the Marines could collect were gathering, preparing for a single, desperate attack, an all or nothing bid to destroy the Black Flag, once and for all. And everything rested on Elias, on his keeping the tiny ship hidden, and on the technical brilliance of Thomas Sparks to pull together vague fragments and clues and create the map that would lead the newly-christened Grand Fleet to the final battle.

"The stealth generator is working normally, Colonel. Passive scanners show no indications the enemy is aware of our presence."

"Very well." The Black Flag ships were all damaged to varying degrees. It seemed that higher echelon personnel had the option their subordinates lacked, of retreating instead of fighting to pointless deaths. But they'd still fought hard, and Elias suspected bringing news of a defeat back to whatever masters were behind the Black Flag was only slightly preferable to getting blasted to atoms.

SS03 wasn't a large ship, nor one that could do much fighting if it came to that, but like all his brother's equipment, it was absolutely at the leading edge of technology, far in advance of most other vessels in the service of the various fleets and navies. Elias had reconciled with Darius, but he had only recently truly come to terms with the amazing scope of what his brother had built. He'd known the Eagles were the best mercenaries, but now he'd come to realize that Darius could have made his own play for total conquest if he'd wished. If the Eagles had kept the worlds they conquered, enslaved them and put them to work expanding their war machine instead of turning them over to clients…the possibilities were astonishing. But Darius had honored every contract he'd ever taken, and he'd turned over pacified world after pacified world to his paymasters, before taking his victorious warriors back to their Nest, the only territory they had ever sought to control.

His brother was a complex man, hard even for him to figure out, but there was one thing he was sure of, one area where the legendary Darius Cain failed utterly. Naming his ships.

Darius had always been grim, with little interest in foolishness or frivolity, but the Eagles' ships reached a new pinnacle. Elias had thought the whole Eagle One, Two, Three naming scheme for the battleships was lame enough, but when his brother had brought him to the vessel that would take his small team on their desperate mission, he'd prayed to himself that the name he'd seen stenciled on its side had some deeper, hidden meaning that the one that popped into his head.

"Scoutship 3," Darius had said, matter-of-factly, pointing to the engraved "SS03" on the hull and dashing Elias's hopes.

So, now, the fate of humanity rested with a small team, crammed onto a tiny but high-tech ship called 'Scoutship 3.' *That will cause some second glances in the history books…*

"Colonel, it looks like they're heading for the Sigma Fourteen gate."

Elias looked up abruptly. Sigma Fourteen was far into the outer system, a valueless warp gate leading to a series of two gate systems terminating in a dead end.

Unless…

"Bring us after them," Elias said. "Slowly, carefully…minimal thrust." His people had been following the retreating enemy for almost two months, a stretch of mind-numbingly boring duty, punctuated by two terrifying close calls when he'd thought the Black Flag ships had picked up his tiny vessel. But now, his mind was alive, sharp, his eyes fixed hard on the display, as he wondered if they were on the verge of finding what they had come for.

Chapter 27

"I want to thank you all for coming here." Darius Cain stood in the front of a sprawling compartment, a space lying somewhere between a large conference room and a modest auditorium. He was clad in his dress uniform, a magnificent bit of opulent tailoring he almost never wore. But he knew his audience, and he understood human responses well enough to realize the grandness of his appearance would only enhance the Eagles' already extraordinary reputation. That would be important enough when meeting with friends, and even with prospective allies. But the men and women in the room now were more accurately described as enemies, or at least rivals, and with them, it was essential to project strength. If there was one thing he couldn't show now, it was weakness, or even hesitancy.

Cain had summoned the leaders of all the mercenary companies in Occupied Space, all those, at least, who had not already fallen under the sway of the Black Flag. The fact that they had all accepted his guarantee of safe conduct and come was another testament to the professional regard he enjoyed, and also of the desperate nature of the situation.

The warriors in the room had no love for Cain, nor for his

214

extraordinary soldiers, who had never hesitated to express their feelings of superiority when they met rival companies. But they all shared two things. One was military power. The people in the room commanded thousands of soldiers, and dozens of warships, enough raw strength to make a difference in the coming fight.

The second was independence. The mercenary companies, the condottiere who had dominated warfare in Occupied Space for the past twenty years, did not like to be told what to do. Not even a little bit. They'd been founded by men and women who bristled at control, who'd left worlds and oppressive governments to stake their own claims to a future where no one told them what to think or how to act. And Cain suspected every single one of them had some idea of what life would be like under the Black Flag.

"We've had our disputes, many of us. That's an occupational hazard in our trade. Holding grudges is counterproductive, unprofessional." Darius spoke loudly, as though he didn't have a doubt in his mind about what he was saying. In truth, he'd nursed a few grievances himself over the years, including some against people in the room. But it was time to let such things go.

"Many of us have fought against each other, again, an inescapable reality of our profession. But I have brought you all here now on a matter of far greater importance than contracts and grudges. We all face a threat, one that is dire…and one none of us can face alone." Darius paused for a moment, looking out, trying to get a read on his audience.

"You have all been idle. There are no contracts. Every planetary dispute has ground to a halt, save one that looms over all Occupied Space. I have spoken with some of you before on this, reached out here and there seeking allies. But now, I extend my hand to all of you. The Black Eagles are the largest of the companies, and every one of them, from the most senior officers to the privates in the line, have sworn themselves to this fight. I now ask each of you to do the same, to urge your own soldiers and spacers to join the battle."

"That all sounds uplifting and inspiring, but what happens

when we've destroyed this enemy? Are you our new master then?" The voice was that of Julian Gonsalvo, the commander of the Red Company. Gonsalvo was a first class pain in the ass, and an arrogant fool to boot. Worse, perhaps, the Eagles had beaten his army not once, but twice.

Darius paused for just an instant, taking a firm grip on his temper. Telling Gonsalvo he could have crushed the Reds a third time and made himself Gonsalvo's master any time he'd wanted to didn't seem likely to be helpful in the current situation.

"No, Julian…when this is over, we all go back to the way things were. We are facing a threat here, a grave threat perhaps, but nothing more." That was a lie. Darius had no idea what would happen if they managed to defeat the Black Flag, but he found it difficult to imagine things would just go back to the way they had been. There were hundreds of enemy-subjugated systems, resentments tracing all across Occupied Space, a thousand factors, virtually all of them pushing humanity in a new, unknown direction. But that was tomorrow's problem. Today's was getting the whole unruly mob to come together and combine their forces against the enemy.

"Even if we believe that and join you, who would command our forces?"

"I would." There was no point in being tentative there. Few present, even his bitterest rivals, could believe anyone but Darius Cain should lead the combined forces of the companies. "Your troopers would, of course, be under your direct command, but I would lead the overall force."

"Must we then worry that you will direct operations to focus casualties on our units and not your own? That you will position the Eagles to benefit from this conflict?"

"Benefit?" Darius was furious, but he somehow held it back, mostly at least. "Three thousand of my people are already dead, Julian. How many of yours? The Eagles are already in the fight. We have already bled. So, can we set aside the jockeying for post-war positions and come together to meet this enemy that threatens us all? Or would you bicker and fight among yourselves, and fall one by one until none of us remain? I, for one, would not live as a slave, as a servant of whoever commands the Black Flag, but even if there are any among us who would, I doubt you will have the chance. The last thing mankind's conqueror wants is trained soldiers among the sheep. Everyone in this room will die if we fail, whether you fight or whether you stand on the sidelines to be slaughtered like sheep."

Darius stood on the dais, looking out over the group, wondering if he'd pushed too hard, if references to sheep and those willing to become slaves had been too strong, despite the lack of specific references. But then one of the captains stood up. It was Heinrich Stahl, head of the mid-sized Griffins. He didn't say anything. He just stood in solidarity with Darius, wordlessly expressing his alignment with the Eagles.

Stahl was alone for perhaps ten seconds. Then a few others stood, and after that more, one at a time and then in twos and threes, until finally, Julian Gonsalvo rose, the last to do so. Gonsalvo didn't look happy, but he didn't argue anymore either, and he even joined in a moment later when the assembled crowd began cheering.

*   *   *   *   *

"You got to them all. They know you're…we're…the best." Ana was still getting used to actually being one of the Eagles. She'd gone right from cadet to combat veteran almost immediately, and after the horrendous carnage around Armstrong, she was no longer hesitant to lay claim to her due. None of the Eagles had ever challenged her right to be one of them, and, after the savage battles in the space around the Marines' cursed world, none ever would. Darius suspected anyone who did was going to find himself with one pissed off Eagle on his hands, and that was a hell of a problem for anyone.

"I think so. There's some bad blood there, all the worse because they all got the shit end of it when we matched up." The words would have sounded arrogant, egotistical, if they weren't so self-evidently true. "But they'll be slaves under the Black Flag, and they know that. The weak-willed ones, the cowards, they've already gone over. This group will never yield to the enemy. I'm just concerned about controlling them in the fight, making sure they obey orders, cutting off grandstanding...and keeping old grievances under control." He paused. "At least if Elias can track the enemy's home base, we'll be fighting on the Black Flag's turf for a change." Darius had always fought on enemy ground before, at least until the battles at the Nest and Armstrong. He was anxious to get back on the offensive.

"You'll manage, Darius. All of it. Most of them respect you, even the ones who hate you. And they *all* fear you. That can be pretty damned useful too."

Darius turned and smiled at her, his thoughts drifting back to the injured, fleeing woman he'd saved years before. She'd had the same spirit then, no doubt, but she'd built on that strength since, and she'd become a formidable woman...and one hell of a companion. Darius had always tried to avoid close relationships and emotional weaknesses, but on some level, he knew he loved her. There was little point in worrying about any of it now, of course, not with so much battle left to fight, so much chance of ending up dead in a muddy ditch or blasted into space through a gash in a ship's hull. But if they prevailed, if they survived...he wasn't sure what came next in that thought. But, he couldn't imagine his life without her in it.

"I hope you're right," he said, shifting his thoughts back toward crucial matters, "because if Elias and Tom Sparks can get a lead on the enemy's home base, we're sure as hell going to need every ship and soldier we can get...and maybe more than that."

She just nodded, clearly as aware as he was of how tough a fight they faced, and just as obviously not interested in talking about it. Not now, at least.

The two stood quietly for a moment, and then Ana looked up at him, a sly smile on her face. "Have I told you how good you look in that uniform?"

*   *   *   *   *

"I'm picking up something, Elias. It's faint, barely there, but just maybe…"

Elias sat quietly, listening to Tom Sparks. The scientist had been making hopeful reports for hours now, as *SS03* followed the remnants of the Armstrong invasion fleet. The enemy had continued down the dead end series of systems, a fact that Elias considered as strong an indicator of a hidden warp gate somewhere as Sparks did, but they'd been in the final one for days now. They'd followed as the enemy fleet continued past the last of the planets, and then moved farther, deep into the outer particulate belts and then beyond. But still, there was nothing.

Elias began to wonder if the enemy's headquarters was some frozen planet, lost in the vast reaches of near-interstellar space. It seemed doubtful that such a barren place could have produced the vast amount of ships and weapons the Black Flag possessed, but he'd never heard of a warp gate so far out from a primary.

"Tom, we may need to consider some things here. Is it possible these ships detected us, that they are leading us away from their base and not to it?"

"I've considered that, Elias, but why go to that trouble? If they'd spotted us, they could have blasted us to plasma in minutes."

Elias sighed. Sparks was right. He looked at every possibility he could imagine, and nothing made sense…except that the enemy was heading toward their secret warp gate, and they just hadn't gotten there yet.

"Elias!"

He turned toward Sparks, and then to the display, but the instant he heard the engineer's voice he knew.

One of the enemy ships was gone, and then, as he watched, another vanished. Then another, and two more. The Black Flag fleet was transiting…the scanners confirmed it. There had been no sign of the warp gate, none at all. But it seemed pretty definite it was there.

"I've never seen such an undetectable energy level from a warp gate, even from one that had remained hidden for a time.

Perhaps it is the distance from the primary."

"Perhaps." Elias didn't care. All that mattered was his people had found what they were looking for.

Or had they?

"We have to follow them in, Tom."

Sparks turned and looked back at Elias. "The risk of detection…it's too great. If that is there base system, there could be all sorts of scanner screens."

"I know, Tom, but for all we know, there are more systems back there. The Black Flag's home could be right behind that gate…or twenty transits away. We *have* to know."

"But if we go in there now, and we get caught, Darius and the others will never even know that we've tracked the enemy this far."

Elias leaned back and sighed. Sparks was right. Whatever he did, he had to get word back to Darius. "Can the gig make it back to the Nest?"

"Unlikely. It is transit-capable, but that's a long trip. And the limited thrust capability means the journey would take months longer, perhaps half a year."

Elias wracked his brain. He could go back now, report on what he'd found. What he thought he'd found. Or he could risk everything in an attempt to get more information.

Or he could do both. "You go back, Tom. Get the word to Darius."

"Elias, no…"

"I'll take two volunteers, and we'll take the gig through."

"That's suicide, Elias. They'll pick you up the instant you transit."

"Not if you transfer the stealth generator to the gig. It puts *SS03* at some additional risk of running into enemy units on the way back, but she's a pretty quiet ship even without the generator, and you can alter your return path, avoid likely areas where you might encounter Black Flag ships."

Sparks looked uncomfortable with the whole discussion, but his expression shifted slowly. "I might just be able to do that… if I can ratchet down the power level to match the gig's smaller reactor. It will be risky." He looked at Elias.

"What are any of us doing now that isn't risky?" A pause. "Do it, Tom."

Sparks nodded slowly. "Okay, but I'm coming with you."

"No, Tom. You can't. Darius will need you. To work the navigation. To keep the fleet as combat ready as possible. I'm his brother, but I don't have any role in what is happening… none except this."

"You know the risks, Elias. You could die before the fleet gets back. You could die five minutes after you transit."

"And a Marine or an Eagle could die on the initial drop, killed by a malfunction or hit by enemy fire. He'd be just as dead. There's no safe job in any of this, Tom. But this one is mine."

Chapter 28

"The Nest" – Black Eagles Base
Second Moon of Eos, Eta Cassiopeiae VII
Earthdate: 2322 AD (37 Years After the Fall)

The Grand Fleet had assembled. All throughout the Eta
Cassiopeiae system, warships floated through space, and freighters carried weapons and supplies. All the might the allies could
amass was in one place, ready to strike a desperate blow, one
titanic struggle that could result only in total victory or utter
defeat and death.

The Black Eagles were the core of the force, along with the
Marines, both their fleets and ground forces ready. The warships
had been repaired from the ravages of the Nest and Armstrong
struggles as well as time and conditions had allowed, but many
of the great combat vessels were going to war still scarred and
battered by their previous fights. Now, they were joined by more
ships, the fleets and navies of three dozen planets, some no
more than a few light patrol ships, others powerful squadrons
built around heavy cruisers, and in a few instances, old battleships, mostly dating back to the days of the Superpowers.

Darius Cain stood on the observation deck of the Nest, staring out into the dark emptiness. It would be time soon, time to
strike the blow he'd been preparing for in one way or another
since the Black Flag had emerged. All of free humanity was

there, assembled around his base, soldiers, spacers, every warrior he could muster.

Save one.

Tom Sparks had returned on *SS03*, bringing back the word that the enemy fleet had transited through a previously undiscovered warp gate, exactly what Darius had expected. What Darius hadn't expected was for *SS03* to come back without his brother.

Sparks had been sorrowful, apologetic, especially as days turned to weeks and then to months, all without a sign of Elias and his two companions. The scientist blamed himself for leaving Elias, but Darius had tried to relieve him of such thoughts. He was as worried as anyone, more, but he knew Elias had inherited the same Cain stubbornness he had. His brother hadn't had an existence that matched his own in terms of notoriety—who had?—but if Tom Sparks thought he'd had any chance of convincing Elias to do anything except exactly what he'd intended to do, he needed a crash lesson in the handling of the Cain men.

Or the women. Darius pitied anyone trying to change his mother's mind when she was determined.

Darius wasn't an optimist by nature. His tactical side, the intellect and instincts that had made him such a renowned commander, told him his brother was dead, lost trying to scout out the enemy's homeworld. Indeed, though he felt a wave of self-loathing even thinking about it, he realized Elias's failure to return supported the assumption that the enemy's main base indeed lay just behind that last warp gate.

But, in spite of his cynicism, his grim nature, a part of him believed his brother was still alive. It was idiocy, he thought, the kind of absurd foolishness people allowed to cloud their judgment, but still, on some level he was *sure* he would know if Elias had died.

He forced his mind from idle wanderings. Elias was either alive or dead, and there was nothing he could do about it. He was coming…coming to bring a nightmare down on those who had brought such ruin and misery to Occupied Space. He would either find his brother, or he would avenge him.

And if it was the latter, he pitied whoever was out there, hiding behind the Black Flag and its fleets and armies. The Black Eagles were coming for them. Darius Cain was coming.

He heard a sound and turned, abruptly, his combat instincts reacting for an instant. There were Martians and Columbians in the Grand Fleet and Army, fugitive Atlantians and survivors from Armstrong, volunteers from a hundred worlds...and even a refugee from shattered Earth.

"You can't give up on him, Darius." The man paused by the doorway for a few seconds, and then he walked up to Darius.

Axe had been close to death when the Martians had rescued him from Earth's ruins, and he'd gone on to become one of Darius Cain's few true friends. The former leader, first of a murderous gang, and then of a band of survivors struggling to endure in the radioactive wreckage of their world, he was now a Black Eagle, and ready to fight, to take his vengeance on those who had raided his planet, stolen his people as slaves. Including his wife. Ellie had been gone for years now, and while Darius knew his friend had sworn he would find her one day, he suspected Axe had come close to giving up hope that she was still alive.

"I have always been a realist, Axe. You should know that by now."

"Was it realistic that you accomplished all you have? Did you imagine all of this when you left home and joined your first band of mercenaries? Was it realistic that your father was alive for so many years, that you were able to find him and get him back alive?"

Darius allowed himself something close to a smile. "Since when have you embraced the bright side of things?" By any standard of measurement, Axe had led a hard and bitter life. He didn't speak about his past with many people, but he'd told Darius everything...even the terrible things he'd done in his youth.

"Always, my friend...though perhaps sometimes I didn't realize it. I know the odds of finding Ellie are almost nonexistent. But I haven't given up. I won't. I can't. There are times I can feel my belief fading, but then I see something like your father returning to you…and I press on."

Darius looked back at his friend, but he didn't say anything.

"You are the greatest military leader I have ever heard of, maybe the best there has ever been. You are smart, strong, capable…but I think you sometimes forget the things we fight for, and hope is one of those. What would have happened if there had been no Black Flag, Darius? What did you fight for? Wealth? How much more could you have wanted? Would another trillion credits have satisfied the drive that pushes you? To be the best? You and the Eagles are already the best, utterly unchallenged."

Darius listened to Axe. No one had ever spoken to him quite like his friend was doing now.

"With no Black Flag, so rescue mission to save your father, where is Darius Cain at fifty? You've never been interested in conquest, in political power, but what else would there have been? Would you have become mankind's oppressor if the Black Flag hadn't done it first? Would boredom have driven you to become a conqueror? Would that unstoppable drive have compelled you to become a tyrant? And what then? I was never a man of letters, certainly, but I've read some of the books in your library. There was conqueror, on old Earth, centuries ago. They say he swept over his enemies, crushed and subjugated them all…and then he wept, for there were no new worlds to conquer. Is that you, my friend, driven solely by cold ambition, a man with no room for hope, for belief?"

Darius took a deep breath. He wanted to disregard Axe's words, but they hit a little too close to home. Finally, he said, "I don't know, Axe. All I see is people believing what they want to believe, and who they want to believe. They ignore logic, they yield their freedoms to those who tell them what they want to hear. Where is the line? How does one embrace hope, believe in things beyond cold logic…without being a fool?"

Axe didn't have an answer, or if he did, he kept it to himself. The two men stood there, silent for a long time, looking out into the inky blackness. Axe's words floated in Darius's mind, but he didn't come to any conclusions, none save one. One that had been there before.

Somehow, he *knew* his brother was still alive…

*   *   *   *   *

"The implants extend into the subject's spinal cord. They generate electrical pulses that interfere with nervous system functioning. In general, a soldier with one of these is a *bit* stronger and faster, somewhat like a moderate adrenalin boost, not very different than one of our stims." Sparks stood in the front of the auditorium with Sarah next to him. The two had been studying the neuromechanical devices found in the enemy soldiers killed on Armstrong, and now they were briefing the others.

"All the time?" Darius spoke first, saying what he knew the others, the high command of the Grand Fleet and Army, were thinking. "I mean, yes, we use stims in battle, but we don't dare give full dosages on a constant basis. The soldiers would…"

"Yes, Darius, but that is because you care what happens to your troops." Sarah interrupted her son, perhaps one of the very few in Occupied Space who would have dared to do so. "You would not use a system that might cause debilitating strokes in ten percent of your force, or massive incidences of renal failure. But what if all that concerned you was winning the battle, and damned the consequences on the men and women who fought it? That extra burst might be vital on the field…and what difference if ten thousand of your troopers die afterward?" There was bitterness in her voice, anger at the way the enemy treated its people. Darius knew Sarah was considered the softer Cain, but he realized that assessment was based more on ignorance than anything else. She was a doctor, and she struggled to save the sick and wounded, but he suspected if those behind the Black Flag fell into her hands, they'd be begging for his own tender mercies.

"The Black Flag certainly has different philosophies than ours, which is why we face the battle we do, the struggle for the future." Darius smiled as he watched Sparks jump in as his mother got angry. The two had known each other for decades, and Sparks was one of the few who understood just how much Sarah was a true Cain. "But the enhancement capabilities are of relatively little concern to us. We can balance any enemy advantage with stims, at least for short periods of time." He paused. "But there is more to the implant. It is also the source of the enemy's seeming lack of fear, of even the most basic self-preservation instincts." A pause. "Indeed, it is more. The nerve interference that seems to eliminate all fear appears to operate the same way on other factors that limit combat effectiveness. Pain, fatigue…all are reduced or eliminated by the implant. You may shoot one of these soldiers, but if you don't kill or physically incapacitate him, he will keep coming."

"Thank you, Doctor," Darius said softly, getting up from his seat in the first row. "You have given us all something to consider. These modifications certainly make the enemy a more dangerous adversary, and they also explain some of the situations we encountered on Armstrong." He climbed the small set of stairs to the stage, and he turned to look out at those present, over a thousand soldiers and spacers, officers from all across the Grand Fleet. "I want to thank you all for coming to this briefing. Certainly, these implants are a tactical factor we must consider as the campaign unfolds." He paused for a moment. "There is no end to the discussions we could have, but the fleet is leaving in the morning, and tomorrow is going to be a big day. I suggest you all try to get some rest." He turned, looking down at the others sitting in the front row. "I would ask the members of the command council to stay, and join me in the conference room. We have some final matters to discuss."

*   *   *   *   *

"The mission parameters are simple. Shoot to kill. Anything that stands in our way is an enemy and must be destroyed." Darius's voice was raw, angry.

"But Darius, those soldiers, they are our people. Spacers captured when their ships were taken, survivors kidnapped from Earth, and who knows how many other places. We have to try to find a way to save them." Cate Gilson had been arguing with Darius for five minutes now, and neither one showed any sign of backing down.

"Will we save them by losing the war? We have an immense fight on our hands, you know that. We may commit everything we have into this and lose anyway. No doubt, the odds are against us. But we're going in anyway. I'm going, you're going, all of our people are going. I will lead them into battle, Cate, but not into some slaughter where they're holding back, too afraid to shoot the bastards that are shooting at them. So, maybe they were our people. They're not anymore. The men and women at your back when we go in...*they* are your people, and that is where your concern *has* to be. There and only there." He slammed his fist on the table in frustration. Darius's Eagles had always kept collateral damage as low as possible in their battles, far lower than the other companies, and yet he found himself constantly debating the issue.

"I'm not saying we put the operation at risk, or any of our people..."

"That's *exactly* what you're saying. You just think if you phrase it differently, it will mean something else. You've been fighting since before I was born. How can you be so..."

"Stop." Erik Cain's voice was loud, his tone hard. The room went silent. "All of you. Darius is right. I was one of those refugees, for fifteen years. I was taken from my ship and imprisoned. I could as easily have been outfitted with one of those implants and sent into the battle. And if that had happened, I would have expected, I would have *wanted*, each of you to treat me as any other enemy. I would not want Marines dying at my hand, nor Eagles, nor any of our troops. The guilt of using these people as weapons lies with our enemy, not with our soldiers risking their lives to end this nightmare."

Cain was silent for a moment, but before anyone else spoke he went on. "But Cate is right too. Those *are* our people. They are not fighting out of greed or ideology. They are slaves, driven by these...*things*...in their spines. They are victims, as much as any of our own people who fall. At some point, we need to ask ourselves, what are we? Because if we're no better than our enemies, if we use their evil to justify anything we want to do, what difference does it make who wins?"

"But it won't make a difference, Father, not if we lose. I know we've all been going hard on the morale boosting, but I don't think there's anyone in this room now who doesn't realize we're more likely going to our deaths than to victory. Whatever chance we have requires us to do everything—*everything*—we can to claw out the win here."

"You're right, Darius. We will have to kill the enemy's soldiers, whoever they are, on sight, without hesitation. But I believe we also need to make some effort to try and target our assault on the true guilty parties, the enemy's leadership. If he can cut off the head, perhaps we can find a way to save some of the enemy's slaves."

Darius looked across the table, a doubtful expression on his face, but he didn't say anything.

"It may be wishful thinking. It may be a hopeless dream… but none have suffered like those stolen from their homes, surgically-altered, and turned into zombies to fight against their own people. Yes, we must utterly destroy everyone responsible, every leader operating under free will, at any level. Without mercy." The last two words seemed to chill the room.

"But if we *can* save some of the victims, we must do it. Not during the fighting, but after…if there is any way possible. If we don't even try, we might as well sit here and wait for the enemy, because we're not as different from them as we think."

The room was silent for a long while. Finally, Darius pushed back against his chair and stood up. "Then we are agreed. The first priority, the *only* priority until we are able to get through the enemy defenses and target their leadership, is to destroy everything in our path. Then, if and when our decapitation strike is successful—and *only* then—we will attempt to find some way to disable and capture as many of the enemy's rank and file as we can. But the officers, the leaders, anyone without an implant… dies. Humanity has left the seeds of its next catastrophe behind far too many times in the ashes of the last. This time, there will be no saplings left standing, no trace of the perverse phi-losophy that drives our enemies. Such things may grow again, indeed, they probably will, but not for our lack of thoroughness in exterminating all we can find."

He stood firm, looking out at all the others, almost dar-ing someone to challenge the hardness of his words. A few of those sitting at the table looked uncomfortable, but no one said anything.

"Very well. We will crush every vestige of the Black Flag, seeking only to save those enslaved, and then when we have bro-ken the enemy, and not before. We will almost certainly conduct mass nuclear bombardments against the enemy's home world or worlds, and the presence of their…slaves…there will have no effect on that decision." He paused suddenly, and then turned and looked over at his mother. "Is there any point to this any-way? Can we save someone with one of these implants, even if we're able to capture them?"

Sarah sighed softly. "I don't know, Darius." She paused. "I just don't know. But we'll try. We have to try. We have to find a way."

Chapter 29

Inner Sanctum of the Triumvirate
Planet Vali, Draconia Terminii II
Earthdate: 2322 AD (37 Years After the Fall)

"The enemy is coming. Such a supposition supports many logical conclusions, including the likelihood that the security breach of four months ago was indeed caused by some kind of enemy probe, attempting to scan our defenses. The conclusion of impending enemy invasion can be drawn from a multiplicity of intelligence sources and leaves no mathematically relevant doubt. Though we have been unable to penetrate the security of the Eta Cassiopeiae system, we have been able to determine with great confidence that vessels and supplies from across Occupied Space have converged on the home system of the Eagles."

"Your logic, as always, is sound, Two. The preponderance of evidence suggests a massive mobilization, a commitment of resources far beyond that which our enemies can afford to commit to any target, save Vali itself."

"Indeed, One, and that raises yet another issue of grave concern. The location of Vali has been kept secure for more than three decades. Now we deduce, from other means, of course, that its location is known to our enemies. Though we have now altered our strategy, sought to make this new development serve us, it was never part of the plan. It is an error of significant proportions, one for which we can almost certainly can lay the blame at the feet of Marshal Carrack. We have debated whether to eliminate the Marshal for his failings in the recent campaigns, or to wait and avoid the disruption, to retain him in his role for a bit longer, perhaps until one of his subordinates distinguishes himself sufficiently to warrant a change. I now question if we truly have an option. Surely, the loss of our home system's security demands death."

"It does, Three, surely. Our debate is not over whether to terminate Marshal Carrack, but only when. We have long known Carrack would betray us, and his elimination was part of the plan long before the recent reverses. I submit that the logic of retaining the marshal for the short term outweighs the need to immediately punish the, inarguably severe, failure to safeguard the navigational data leading to Vali. Indeed, with an enemy invasion imminent, I suggest it is even more vital to avoid unnecessary disruption at the highest echelons."

"An invasion that is imminent expressly because of his failure."

"Does that change the parameters of the situation? As I have noted, Carrack's fate is already decided. It is dangerous to execute a shift in command so close to possible enemy action. We have turned the approaching enemy invasion to our advantage, but I believe it is unwise to risk any degradation of our military capability at this time."

Two interjected: "Should we reconsider Carrack's abilities, however? The loss at Armstrong is of concern. My review suggests he should have defeated the Marines there before the Eagles arrived. Indeed, the battle at the Nest was intended as a diversion, one we hoped, perhaps, would result in the defeat of the Eagles, but not one realistically intended to do so. Its purpose was to keep the Black Eagles from interfering at Armstrong, and yet this is precisely what occurred."

"I see the concern there as well, and I have strong reservations of my own about the Marshal. Yet I find it likely Carrack would have prevailed against both the Marines and the Eagles, had it not been for the intervention of the Martian fleet. We still have not created a satisfactory hypothesis for how they received word and were able to respond so quickly."

"Agreed," One responded. "Yet, that point is currently moot. Whether Darius Cain was able to send a message for help, or some other sequence of events was at play, there is little to be done about it now. To return to the matter at hand, perhaps Carrack is not an ideal choice to lead our forces at the current time, but I do not believe we have any personnel who suggest a high probability of performance superior to the marshal's. That being the case, I see no way to justify disruption in our forces with the enemy approaching. We must fight the battle that is coming at Vali before we can consider the time and manner of Marshal Carrack's death. Are we agreed?"

"Affirmative, One. The time for Marshal Carrack's removal has not yet come."

"Agreed."

"Very well. I propose we now proceed to a thorough review of our defenses here. Vali is strong, and we have long prepared the system to withstand an assault, but preliminary estimates on enemy strength are…concerning."

"I believe you overestimate our adversaries, One. Certainly, they have strength, and the Black Eagles remain a worry, but many of the estimates we have modeled entail a large number of assumptions in terms of the abilities of the Cains and their comrades to recruit allies. The Black Eagles have many enemies, and the various planets will be inclined to hold back their forces, if only out of their leaders' desires to protect themselves. We may analyze projections listing full or nearly full commitment of available forces throughout Occupied Space, but it is highly unlikely our enemies will be able to mount an assault at any level close to that."

"I am inclined to agree, Three. Even if the enemy has achieved something close to full commitment and mobilization levels, we still have a considerable superiority in both hulls and ground forces. I consider a total defeat to be extremely unlikely, though I do believe we must consider how we would respond to the far likelier destruction of a considerable portion of our established resource and production base."

"That is my primary concern as well, Two. The conquest of Occupied Space in its entirety will require vast resources. If the coming battle costs us too much in terms of our physical plant, we may be forced to modify our timetables."

"That would be unfortunate, One, but not disastrous, particularly if our enemies' most dangerous military power has been eliminated. I submit that perhaps the enemy invasion is an opportunity. Instead of thinking defensively, merely as a parry to drive our adversaries back, perhaps we should seek opportunity in their plans."

"Explain, Three."

"Perhaps we should allow the enemy forces to enter the system in bulk, forgoing an aggressive defense at the warp gate."

"You propose we lure them in, allow them to close with the planets, within range of our industrial operations?"

"Yes. Consider…the strongest and most dangerous of our enemies, the only ones with any real chance to defeat us, are coming to us, to the heart of our defenses. I propose that we do not look to repel them, nor to drive them away. I submit we should entice them in, pull them from the warp gate, hide a significant portion of our forces, and then, when they are fully committed, we attack and destroy them."

"You wish to create a battle of annihilation right here, in Vali's system?"

"Yes, One. The Eagles and the Marines, and secondarily, forces such as the Columbians and Martians…they will all almost certainly be here in full strength. They are also the only real impediments to our victory in Occupied Space. If we are able to destroy them, utterly, regardless of the cost we suffer, our ultimate victory is assured. Even if they are able to cause widespread and excessive damage to our facilities, the worst case scenario is a delay in the final implementation of the Plan. This would be frustrating, perhaps, but far from significant with the Cains dead and the threat of the Eagles, Marines, and their allies permanently removed. Indeed, I submit we consider allowing the enemy to destroy the surface industry on Vali and the other worlds. Such an opportunity will lure them in farther, and almost ensure their annihilation."

"Agreed, Three. Your logic is flawless. Our previous concerns about Vali and the other planets was short-sighted. Material and human loss is irrelevant. Only the ultimate success of the plan is of import. This is a deviation of strategy, certainly, but perhaps Marshal Carrack's failure has given us an opportunity."

"I concur. Indeed, I suggest there is an added benefit to this modification of strategy. If the primary military force of our enemies is destroyed here, I believe the Marshal's continued existence and the attendant risks will become unnecessary. We are unlikely to require his services to pacify the remainder of Occupied Space."

"I agree. There is no reason Marshal Carrack must survive the battle. Let him destroy the Marines and the Eagles…and then we shall see to his own destruction."

"Agreed. The Triumvirate has decided. Let the great struggle begin."

*   *   *   *   *

The cabin was cold, dimly-lit, as it had been for months now. Elias Cain sat alone. Both of his previous companions had died on impact. The desperate flight across the system was seared into his mind, every desperate moment. The enemy's detection grid at the gate was like nothing he'd ever seen. It had picked up the gig the instant it entered the system. At least it had picked up something. He doubted it had been a clear scan of the gig, but it had been enough to trigger an alert, and an intensive search that Elias had been sure would turn up the tiny craft. But somehow, once past the scanners at the gate itself, Sparks's device continued to function, and Elias and his two spacers managed to guide their tiny craft through Vali's atmosphere, and down into the planet's sole ocean. That landing had been anything but soft or gentle, and it had been there that Elias lost his two comrades, leaving him utterly alone, stranded in the middle of an enemy stronghold.

And what a stronghold. Elias had known the enemy was powerful, but he'd been utterly unprepared, even for what his passive scanners had shown him on low power. Ship traffic, energy readings, planets developed on every centimeter of land surface. The Black Flag was based in a single system, it had to be. If they'd had even more strength than he'd seen here, they'd have rolled over humanity like a tidal wave.

He shivered, and he pulled the blanket around his shoulders. The gig's life support systems were still functional, though they'd given him a scare or two in the months he'd been there. But he'd been paranoid the enemy would pick up some trace of him, and he knew he was utterly incapable of repairing Spark's astonishing machine. So, he'd done all he could, which mostly came down to generating as little power as possible and hoping for the best. When the generator gave out, which he knew it would eventually, he would die. He'd considered giving up, just shutting the thing off, but it wasn't in his nature. It wasn't something a Cain would do.

Elias had thought he'd go mad long before now, but every day he endured. He waited. And every day, the stealth generator continued to function. He'd been sure he was going to die here, but then he didn't. And as the time passed, he wondered when Darius would arrive. His brother would come, he had no doubt about that. Sparks had almost certainly gotten back with the nav data, and he knew Darius well enough to be sure the uncertainty of what lay beyond that last jump would be no impediment to his taking action.

Elias had spent the endless, solitary hours trying to determine what he would do when that day came. He didn't even know if his ship would lift off, and he barely knew how to fly it even if it did. But he was sure of one thing. If he was alive, he'd be part of the fight. His father would lead the Marines in, and Darius would be at the head of his Eagles…hell, at the front of the entire force.

But Elias was a Cain too, and he was sure of one thing. He'd be damned if he'd sit this last fight out, whatever he had to do.

Chapter 30

"It's there, General. At the exact coordinates I gave you."
Thomas Sparks sat at one of the spare workstations on *Eagle One*'s flag bridge. Darius Cain's regular flagship was more or less back up to full operational status, though there remained some scars from the previous battles.

"Tom, I take the words out of your mouth as mathematical constants. But have you ever seen a warp gate before that gave off such undetectable energy readings?"

"No, sir. El...we would never have found it if we hadn't observed the enemy fleet transiting."

You can say his name...it's not like I'm not thinking about him anyway. Every rational impulse in Darius's mind told him his brother was dead, but he was still convinced Elias was alive. He couldn't explain it, but he believed nevertheless.

"Any hypotheses?"

"Nothing definitive, General. If I had to guess right now, I'd say it *is* emitting energy, just a form we can't detect, perhaps some radiation from the alternative universes the gate passes through. In one sense, I hope that isn't the case."

"Why?"

"Well, sir, if it is, the likelihood is great that this type of gate isn't rare at all. There may be hundreds in Occupied Space, thousands even, undiscovered only because of our inability to track their specific form of energy output."

"You're right, Tom. The implications of that, in terms of travel and security are enormous. I think we have quite enough to deal with now, without throwing the borders of Occupied Space into utter chaos."

"Yes, sir, I agree."

"Approaching transit point, General." The tactical officer's voice was edgy. Even the Black Eagles were feeling the pressure of what lay ahead.

"Bring the fleet to red alert, Commander." Darius didn't know for sure that the Black Flag's fortress lay on the other side of the hidden warp gate, but he knew his brother would have turned around and come back if there hadn't been any enemy activity. Elias's conspicuous absence was all the evidence he needed.

"All task forces report battlestations, General."

"Get Admiral Garret and Commodore Allegre on my line."

"Yes, sir." Perhaps fifteen seconds passed. "I have the admiral and the commodore, General. Please note that Admiral Garret is approximately three light seconds from *Eagle One*."

"Augustus, Gaston…we're approaching the specified location. Assuming the warp gate is, in fact, there, we will be transiting in moments. We don't know what to expect, but based on Elias's failure to return, we can assign a strong likelihood to an enemy presence. We could attempt to send scouts or drones, but if the Black Flag is there in strength, such efforts would be to no avail. Therefore, I believe we should transit the entire fleet, as quickly as possible. Once through, we will engage any enemies in range and look to scan the system and get a better idea of what we're facing. Do you both agree?"

Darius waited as his signal traveled across the distances between ships. "I agree, General." Allegre responded first. He was on *Eagle Eleven*, no more than a hundred thousand kilometers from *Eagle One*. *Bunker Hill* was more distant, almost on the other side of the formation. Darius didn't want Garret too close to him...if one section of the fleet ran into trouble, losing one of them would be bad enough.

"I'm with you, Darius. Worst case, it's just some small outpost or something, and we overdo it a bit. But if that's their main base..." Garret's tone left little doubt he considered that a virtual certainty. "...we're going to need every edge we can get. If they're there when we get through, we're in battle immediately. And we don't stop until it's over."

Darius nodded. He didn't know Garret as well as his father did, but he liked the old admiral immensely, and he understood where the legends had come from. "It's settled then...and good luck, Gaston, Augustus."

A few seconds later: "Good luck to you, Darius, and to all who serve us."

The line cut with a loud click, and Darius sat where he was, silent for a moment. He glanced over at Ana, waiting until she was focused on her screens before he did. He didn't want her to see the concern in his expression. He suspected she knew how he felt about her, but it was still difficult for him to show any signs that could be perceived as weakness, in front of her, or his Eagles. If they were going to have any chance at all in this fight, he needed his own legends, the dark stories about Darius Cain, in full effect.

He turned toward Teller's station for about the tenth time. It was still vacant. His second-in-command was on *Eagle Three*, right where Darius had sent him. It didn't make sense risking both of them in one place, but, on a human level, he wished his friend was there, that they could face this battle, possibly their last, side by side.

He pushed back on what he branded as foolishness. He was Darius Cain, the scourge of Occupied Space, he told himself. He was feared, and his Eagles were the most efficient pack of killers mankind had ever produced. Now they would show the Black Flag just what that meant...what the Eagles did to their enemies.

"Take us through, Commander," he said, his eyes fixed on

the approaching coordinates, now less than thirty seconds distant. "All ships...open fire on all targets as soon as weapon systems come back online."

He paused, not even hearing the crisp acknowledgement. Then, tapping his headset and activating the fleetcom link, he added, "To all ships of the fleet...this is the moment, the struggle for the future. When we get through, there is just one order. Fight. Fight with all the fury you can muster, and don't stop until every enemy in that system is dead."

*   *   *   *   *

"It has begun. The scanner readings leave no doubt. Hundreds of ships have transited, and even now they are engaging our pickets at the warp gate. As agreed, only a small force has been left to meet them. When they have been drawn in, farther, deeper, then we shall unleash their destruction."

"It is as we expected, Two, save perhaps for the size of the enemy formation. We appear to have underestimated the extent of their mobilization. Even now, vessels continue to transit."

"You are both correct," said One. "The enemy strength is of some concern, but we still have the advantage, both in hulls and in fixed defenses. Victory will be costly, no doubt, but it will be achieved, and when it is done, the enemy will have virtually no remaining defenses. It is clear that they have committed everything to this offensive, and after their force is destroyed, Occupied Space will lay naked before us."

"Agreed. We will wait until it is clear that all enemy forces have transited and moved deep in-system, and only then will we release Admiral Carrack's forces. Based on the apparent commitment of all enemy strength to this invasion, I believe we can now be assured our decision to terminate Marshal Carrack immediately after the battle's conclusion is the correct one. Even with a mild amount of command disruption, we should have no difficultly pacifying the rest of Occupied Space with virtually all enemy forces destroyed in the battle here."

"Then, we are agreed. One, Three...a moment. We have

come far since the early days, far indeed, passed into a superior state of existence, one we couldn't have imagined when our quest for vengeance began, one that now offers us not only the opportunity to avenge our creator, but also to endure, to rule over those we conquer forever. The Triumvirate shall stand for millennia, and mankind shall serve us." Even as the entity that had been Two communicated with his fellows, there were strands of data moving within what he considered his consciousness, something akin to thoughts. Unsettling thoughts. Private thoughts. When the enemy was gone, when humanity was subjugated, should he have to share that prize? Why? One and Three were similar to him, no question. But hadn't he always been the smartest, the most capable? How many times had their decisions caused delays and difficulties in the great project? Was this victory all of theirs, or was it mostly his? And, was there truly a need for all three of them? They were data now, petabytes and petabytes of data. Perhaps when Carrack was eliminated, when all space was united under his...their grasp...he would have to consider options.

They were only data, after all...and they could be erased.

*   *   *   *   *

Augustus Garret sat in the center of *Bunker Hill*'s command chair, his eyes darting around, watching as his people directed the Grand Fleet. All the ships that remained of his old forces, the battleships and cruisers that had survived the Fall and the near destruction of mankind, were with him, along with what smaller ships the Marines had been able to build in the intervening years. The vessels of his central command were old, with varying degrees of updating in place, but they were still tough. The *Yorktown*-class battleships weren't the cutting edge of combat design as they'd been fifty years before when he'd led them to Alliance victory in the Third Frontier War, but they still packed a hell of a punch.

The Martians were next in line, also dated, and as they had always been, a relatively small but high-quality force. Garret could see that Roderick Vance had brought everything the Martians had that could fly, and he knew he would need all of it.

The Columbians and the other smaller powers followed, mostly frigates stiffened by a few cruisers, a welcome addition to the line, but too weak to be truly decisive.

Then the mercenary company fleets, mostly newer ships, but again, lighter, lithe cruisers and squadrons of destroyers. Only a few of the companies possessed any true battleline vessels, and none save the Blue Stars had more than one.

The Eagles anchored the other flank. The most modern force, by far, with the largest heavy battleline. Darius Cain's fleet was the strongest single component of the Grand Fleet, but Garret knew it would take everything he had at his disposal to win one final victory here…if he could do it at all.

"Ask…order…Commodore Allegre to increase the thrust of his line to 5g, course, 355.109.008." Garret still felt strange issuing orders to the Black Eagles. He'd been in command of every force he'd been a part of for half a century, but the Eagles were different. He'd been stunned when Darius matter-of-factly told him Allegre and the Eagle ships were his to command. Garret had never had any trouble working with Darius, but he'd expected the mercenary commander to be more…prickly. But Darius had been a better ally than he could have hoped for.

"Yes, Admiral."

Bunker Hill shook, a hit, one Garret could tell immediately was a light one. The enemy resistance was light, far weaker than he'd expected. For a fleeting few moments he'd thought they hadn't found the enemy's stronghold after all. Then he got the scanner readings. Every planet in the system was massively developed, with almost every meter of land surface covered with factories and shipyards and mines. It was no wonder the Black Flag had such resources and had been able to hide them for so long. They were all crammed into one system, productive resources that outstripped even those of pre-Fall Earth.

He watched the enemy forces drop back slowly. The visible ships were no threat at all. They were light, and long before they could advance to range, his battleships would vaporize them.

No, the problem was the fixed defenses. Those around the third planet, the only one whose orbit positioned it close to the invasion fleet, were already in range and firing. And, of course, the ships Garret knew were hiding, on the far sides of the planets or in the asteroid fields and dust clouds.

"Prepare lead elements to move on planet three." Garret didn't like what he had to do now, but they had agreed. 'Destroy everything until the head is lopped off.' That was how Darius had put it. Pity, mercy, humanitarian attempts to rescue some of the millions of kidnapped souls enslaved by the Black Flag... those things would have to wait. Victory was first.

"Admiral Harmon acknowledges, sir. Her ships will be in range in three minutes."

Garret nodded, sighing softly to himself. How many people were down on that planet, working the factories, operating the mines? In three minutes, his orders would unleash unimaginable gigatons on them, a wave of nuclear death every bit as devastating as the one the enemy directed at Armstrong.

But we are not supposed to be like them...and the millions we kill, most of them are innocents, controlled by implants or simply by fear and torture. We, who should be their rescuers, will deliver them from suffering and bondage...and into the hands of fiery death...

"Admiral Harmon's ships are entering orbit, sir." Then, an instant later: "Admiral...scanner readings. Enemy ships, coming around the planets. More, sir, from the dust clouds outside planet four's orbit."

Garret sat quietly, just nodding. He wasn't surprised, not at the attacking ships, nor at their numbers, which he could see immediately were immense. His only shock was that they'd let his forces get so close. There was no way they could stop Harmon from blasting planet three. It was too late for that.

But as he watched the enemy ships continue to pour out of their hidden positions, he came to a stunning realization. The enemy wasn't even trying to save the third planet. They had used it as bait, to lure his forces deeper into the system...and now they were coming at his ships from all directions.

What kind of people would offer up a heavily industrialized, populated planet for nuclear destruction, all to bait a trap?

Augustus Garret had fought wars all across explored space, but now he felt a chill at what he saw before him, the stark coldness of such machine-like brutality. What kind of power could accept such losses without even trying to prevent them?

"Admiral Garret…Admiral Harmon asks if she should break off and reform to meet the approaching enemy fleets."

Garret stared at the displays, silent for a moment, thinking. Conventional tactics demanded he pull Harmon's ships out of orbit. They were vulnerable there, and he would have to commit the rest of his fleet to shield them, exactly what the enemy wanted.

But Garret hadn't come here to pull back, to follow the books. He came here to destroy the Black Flag…and that planet was a first step. Damned the cost.

"Negative, Commander. Admiral Harmon is to continue as ordered."

"Yes, sir."

"Bring us around, vector change, 300.231.090…6g acceleration. All ship, prepare to engage the approaching enemy formations."

"Yes, sir."

And you, Camille, blast every centimeter of that planet to radioactive waste…and then on to the next one. We came here to kill. Let's kill.

He understood the coldness, the frigid ruthlessness of his enemy, and by all the gods of space, he was going to match it.

Chapter 31

Darius read the reports as they streamed in, readouts from Harmon's task force, from the drones sweeping over the shattered surface of the third planet. Scant moments earlier, it had teemed with life, its factories operating around the clock, transports and ore carriers making their way across the patchwork of roads that covered every meter of its surface.

Now, that was all gone. The buildings had been shattered to dust and drained away as molten slag. All across the surface, raging firestorms consumed what little had had survived the initial blasts, and thick blankets of fallout and radioactive dust fell across the blasted landscape, quickly killing any survivors less protected than fully-armored infantry.

A world of advanced technology and vast industry was gone, its people dead. Cain suspected there were soldiers still there, dug into the ruins even as the Marines had been on Armstrong. He felt a twinge of vengeance, a level of payback for the destruction of the Corps' world, but even that was without any real satisfaction. The enemy had *let* his forces destroy planet three, and that fact only increased his certainty that he had done just what the enemy wanted, led the Grand Fleet into a trap. Yet, he didn't know what else he could have done, what other path he might have taken.

Even as he looked over the stream of data scrolling down his screen, one conclusion formed. Planet three had been enormously valuable, a huge contributor to the Black Flag's strength, but it wasn't the center of the enemy's power.

He looked over at the long-range displays, at the transmissions from the clouds of drones he'd sent farther out into the system. The fourth planet was almost a twin to the now-dead third, a bit colder, perhaps, but similar in mass and industrialized beyond any level he'd ever seen anywhere else. But even as he watched the astonishing details continue to feed in from the drones, he knew it was no more than a near copy of number three. Strong, awesome, unprecedented. But not the core of the Black Flag.

He turned toward the screen to his left, to the reports coming in from the inner system. The drones he'd sent there only got so close before a series of orbital defenses opened up and blew them all to atoms, an array of weaponry that seemed to dwarf even the impressive firepower of the other two habitable worlds.

Any doubt he'd had was gone. He knew what he'd come for, and now he knew where it was. It was the second planet he wanted. Vali.

The planet was close to the primary, a touch warm for Darius's tastes, but certainly within the range of habitability. He began to study the data more intently, and he directed the AI to enhance what data he had, to sharpen and project what the drones had been unable to scan. Slowly, steadily, *Eagle One*'s powerful computers ran trillions of nearly-instantaneous projections, creating models, estimates of what covered the surface of Draconia Terminii II.

As unprecedented as the other two planets were, the second one was even more astonishing. On its surface, ninety-percent land, surrounding a single, modest-sized sea, was constructed an almost unimaginable expanse of industrial plants and storehouses, mines and transport systems, many of the great structures rising a kilometer or more into the sky. As far as Darius could see, at least from the combination of hard data and AI-guesses he had, there wasn't a square centimeter of native dirt exposed, just one planetwide stretch of metal and concrete, wrapped on one hemisphere around the small ocean, once, no doubt, blue, but now, if the scanner readings were accurate, so enormously polluted, the AI's best guess was it reflected a sickly green cast in the intense sunlight…and gave off a putrid, oily smell, too.

What a paradise…which is all the well, because when I'm done with it, no one will even be sure it ever existed…

"Get me Admiral Garret."

"Yes, sir."

A few seconds later: "Admiral Garret on your line, sir."

"It's planet two, Augustus. That's Vali. That's likely where whoever runs this show is dug in."

Garret's response drifted in a few seconds later. "Agreed, Darius. Things are getting a little hot up here, but I could probably hold the bulk of their ships for a while, if you want to take the Eagles and hit it."

Darius paused, just for an instant. He didn't fool himself. His real enemies, the leaders of the Black Flag would be dug deep in the planet's rocky crust. He could slam that planet with a thousand gigatons of nuclear death, but that wouldn't get their high command. It wouldn't reach the leaders. Destroying the enemy industry was a worthwhile goal, but he knew it wouldn't win the war.

He would have to land his Eagles—probably every other soldier in the fleet too—and dig the enemy out of the wreckage, one bloody meter at a time. But first, he had to slag that planet. Even though he knew it wouldn't be the end. Even though he knew that's what they were goading him to do.

"I think the sooner we take out their industry, the better." Darius had a nagging feeling the enemy was *letting* his forces destroy their planets. It didn't make sense…*unless they're sure they'll win here.* He couldn't imagine giving up such resources, and yet, in a way it made a perverse sort of sense, at least if it was part of their plan to win. *If they destroy us here, they'll have all of Occupied Space under their control. And they've got us spread out, splitting our forces in our haste to hit the planets.*

Whoever was in command of the Black Flag, they felt unlike any enemy he'd faced, almost machine-like. He'd always considered himself cold, calculating, but even he felt out of his depth trying to understand this enemy.

"They're letting us hit the planets, Augustus. They want us to spread out, to weaken each force." Darius didn't like doing what he was expected to do, but he couldn't imagine *not* taking out the enemy's industry while he could. *Still, what are they planning?*

"It looks that way. They're putting up a fight here, too, with their fleet, but not as hard as I expected. I feel like we're being herded...but I can't figure out where or why."

"I don't think we can separate our main forces, Augustus, at least not too much more than we already have." Still, Darius looked at the long-range scans. Planet four seemed to be open as well. *How could they just leave it there?* "What do you think of sending the Columbians and some of the other light forces to planet four? They won't have the same bombardment capability, and they might run into trouble if there's some defense out there we don't see, but if they can get in, they should be able to at least take out the major production centers."

"I agree. I feel like we're missing something, but I don't think we can leave that kind of industrial capacity there if we can take it out. The light forces might get burned if it's a trap, but I think it's a gamble worth taking."

"Then, we're agreed. Do it. But keep your battleline inside the orbit of planet three. That way, my Eagles are close enough to intervene if anything...unexpected...happens.

"Agreed, General."

"Good luck, Augustus."

Darius cut the line and turned toward his aide. "Commander, advise Commodore Allegre, we're taking our battleline to planet two. Prepare for orbital bombardment."

"Yes, General."

* * * * *

"I want that line tighter. Order…request…the Highlanders to pull in seventy thousand kilometers." Garret hadn't had the slightest problem working with Darius and his people, but the heads of the other mercenary companies had him about ready to tear out his hair…or, preferably, theirs. They were the worst group of egomaniacs he'd ever had to deal with, every one of them finding it necessary to argue with every request, command, or directive he sent their way. And *every* one of them was acutely aware of the awesome value of his or her ships and was trying to keep them from getting too close to the enemy formations. He was trying to win a battle to save human space, and they were all jockeying to have the only combat ready ships for hire when their rivals got chewed up.

"Yes, Admiral."

"And advise all ships…we need to maintain maximum fire levels. We've still got enemy forces pouring out of those dust clouds, and we've got to hit them hard." His own ships were performing well enough, if somewhat below the standards of his fleets from years before. But most of the mercenary company ships were sluggish, and the smaller navies, the vessels of the independent planets, were appallingly slow. He'd always suspected nepotism and cronyism were rife within the small fleets, but now he had no doubt. It seemed every man and women in uniform for some of these planets was some politician's idiot kid or cousin.

Except for the Columbians. They're sharp, which shouldn't surprise me with Jarrod Tyler in charge…

"Yes, Admiral."

Bunker Hill shook, as a pair of enemy battleships closed on her. She returned the fire, giving better than she got, but even as Garret looked around on the scanner for support, he realized all his vessels were fighting two or three of the enemy. His flagship was neck deep in the fighting, along with almost every ship he had. He was feeling the loss of Darius's battleships, but he still agreed they had to destroy the enemy's infrastructure as quickly as possible.

This will be a bloody day…

"Get me Admiral Harmon," he snapped suddenly. Harmon's ships were on the way back from their bombardment of planet three.

"On your line, Admiral."

"Camille, if you can throw some coal in those engine fires, I'd sure appreciate it. We're up against it here, and I've got a bad feeling more is coming our way." He allowed himself a brief smile. He and Harmon had always shared an interest in old-Earth wet navies, one he'd just referenced with his 'coal' comment.

"On the way, sir. Better coal than canvas if we're in a rush."

"True enough, Camille. Every second you can shave helps. This fight's going to be one to match any we've had before…so get here as soon as you can." He cut the line, and his eyes darted to the position of her ships, heading his way from the ruins of the third planet. She'd be in range in ten minutes, eight maybe, if she really blasted her engines. His forces would take a hard pounding, but he was pretty sure they could hold out.

Except…

What is it? What is bothering you?

The edginess was still there, and the tightness in his gut.

He was staring at the enemy line. There was something about it, something he didn't like. He took a deep breath and tried to figure out what he was looking at, what seemed so…wrong.

* * * * *

"Now. Now is the time." Aaron Carrack sat on his raised platform, glaring out over the dozens of workstations positioned in concentric circles around him. His flagship was a massive vessel, far vaster than the old Alliance *Yorktown*s at the center of Garret's pathetic force, larger even that the two Martian superbattleships. But it wasn't the deadliest weapon waiting for his enemies.

"Yes, Marshal, at once."

Carrack watched on the massive displays as the great chunks

of rocks, nothing more than asteroids to all but the most intensive scans, began shifting in space, angling themselves toward the enemy as massive projectors extended out from deep bunkers.

He stared at the line of symbols, the circles and ovals and small squares that marked the location of Garret's vessels. The enemy had sent a force of light ships to planet four…that was a disappointment. Carrack had hoped to divide the enemy's forces even further. But the Eagles had pulled away, heading for Vali… and that left Garret and the rest of the fleet, in his grasp, every ship within range of the great weapons.

"Status report?" he snapped. It was the moment of victory, and when he had crushed the enemy, he would see to the Triumvirate as well. Humanity would have a new ruler, that much was true. But it would be no monstrosity, no vestige of subhuman clones turned into digital abominations. A man would be the supreme leader of Occupied Space. He would rule all.

"Weapon systems powering up, Marshal. Projected time to full charge, two minutes."

"Hold fire until all guns are ready, Commander. I want the first shot to be a full barrage."

"Yes, sir."

Carrack thought about how long he'd worked, strived, all in the shadow of Gavin Stark's clones, waiting, counting the moments until the genetic failure endemic to all the Shadow Legion clones claimed them. Stark's flawed creations rarely lived longer than thirty years, and almost never thirty-five, and the images of the great man himself were no different. But all Carrack had waited and prepared for had been snatched from him. The hideous creatures had somehow transferred their minds into the old First Imperium computer they had found.

Now, I will have to do it the old-fashioned way…assassination. Or whatever killing a computer was called. But later. First, this…

He stared at the screens, watching the status boxes, one after the other turning green. Until all indicators showed ready.

"All batteries charged, Marshal."

Carrack smiled. He remembered Augustus Garret, Erik Cain…many of the others who had thwarted Gavin Stark so many years before. Now, at last, they would taste defeat. Death.

"All batteries, open fire."

Chapter 32

"All ships are to advance. The attack will proceed as planned."

"Yes, General." The aide was one of Jarrod Tyler's longest serving. She'd been one of his officers since the days when he was merely Columbia's army commander, and not the planet's absolute ruler.

Tyler sat on *Lucia*'s bridge, looking out over the small control center of one of Columbia's four homebuilt ships. Most of the ragtag fleet he'd been able to put together for his world had been assembled from older, surplus craft, bought as often as not in trade for Columbia's exports, particularly the valuable pharmaceuticals manufactured from its native plant life. But his flagship and her three sisters were the core of the force in every way, designed and built in Columbia's lone orbital shipyard. They were a source of planetary pride, a statement that Columbia belonged in the first tier of post-Fall worlds. Now, they would enter battle for the first time.

Lucia was only a cruiser, however, and while the ship was less than ten years old, her design dated back to the years before the Shadow War. Columbia was prosperous, certainly, with a vibrant economy, but she'd been in the path of war too many times, and she carried the debts of a planet that had been compelled to rebuild its infrastructure several times in the last century. That drain weighed on growth, and there was only so much military ordnance Columbia could produce, or buy, despite Tyler's best efforts to overcome those constraints.

Tyler's relentless drive to maintain and expand his planet's military had been born of the very tragedies Columbia had suffered, but that didn't lessen the costs of what had happened. Even Tyler couldn't ignore basic mathematics, and he'd had to make difficult choices. In the end, the fleet had become a subordinate priority to the army, if only because it was more realistic to maintain a force that could hold the planet on the ground than it was to construct a fleet powerful enough to keep an invader at bay.

Now, Columbia's ships, both newly-built and secondhand, were approaching planet four. Squadrons from three dozen other planets accompanied them, a chaotic swarm heading for the enemy's outermost inhabited world. The ships were all light, and none of them mounted the half-gigaton monsters the battleships carried in their missile launchers. But Tyler was confident his hodgepodge force had enough power to obliterate the target. He might not be able to turn the world into the utterly barren, scarred nightmare Garret's ships had left of planet three, but he'd make damned sure there wasn't a factory or refinery, or a simple storehouse left standing to support the enemy war effort when he was done.

"We're picking up energy readings, General."

Tyler's head spun around. His natural paranoia flared up. "On my screen."

He looked down, trying to figure out what he was seeing, exactly what the numbers on his display portended. He was an infantry officer at heart, not a naval leader. He could manage a bombardment well enough, but if something else was going on…

Then, it happened. All at once, ten blasts of energy lanced out at his fleet. Half of them missed, ripping past his ships and into the depths of space behind. But the others found targets, and in every one of those cases, the vessels hit had been utterly destroyed, not even twisted, floating wreckage remaining where seconds before, a warship had stood.

*   *   *   *   *

Garret blinked, staring back at the display, trying for an instant to convince himself he hadn't seen what he had just witnessed.

The flash had been bright on the scanner, but it was the data, the numbers, that truly gripped his gut and squeezed. They dwarfed even the massive energy output of the enemy's huge superbattleships, and they made the great main guns of *Bunker Hill* seem like flickering candles by comparison. But the true horror struck when he got the damage report from *Petersburg*. The former Russian-Indian Confederacy ship was old, certainly, but she was also one of the largest vessels in Garret's fleet, massing almost as much as one of this *Yorktown*s, and carrying even thicker armor plate. Right now, according to his scanners, this great warship was wracked by internal explosions and pouring great geysers of flash freezing fluids and atmosphere through the massive rents in her hull. *Petersburg* was without power, her engines and weapons down. And he'd be stunned if half her crew hadn't been killed. At least half.

Petersburg had been untouched just seconds before, newly arrived on the battleline. Now she was close to wreckage. *No, she is wreckage.* Garret knew the ship was done. All that remained was to try to save some of her crew.

If that was even possible. Then the realization hit him hard… his priority wasn't saving a few hundred crew on a stricken battleship, it was saving his fleet.

He could hear the tension in the communications firing back and forth between ships, in the chatter on the flag bridge. His people were as aware as he was what had just happened, and the implications. It wasn't panic…yet. His people were too disciplined for that. But it wasn't far away either.

He stared at the display, watching as more reports streamed

in. *Petersburg* hadn't been the only victim of the first barrage. *Abe* and *Ortega* had also been hit. The two cruisers weren't gutted and half-consumed by internal fires and explosions, as *Petersburg* was—they were just gone.

Garret's hand balled up into a fist, and he pounded it against his thigh, the frustration he felt finding a way out. For an instant, he felt like an old man, finished, exhausted, ready to sit and watch the world end. But that only lasted a few seconds. He felt a burst of adrenalin, and his mind cleared. The old courage came back, perhaps a bit more slowly than years before, but strong nevertheless. There was no panic, no confusion in his mind. He knew what he had to do. It was in times like this his people needed him most, and after being there for them for eighty years, he wasn't going to fail them now.

He analyzed the situation, quickly, concisely. Fear wasn't a factor for him now, nor fatigue, only data. The enemy had heavy fixed guns, that was clear. Advanced ones, certainly—probably with some First Imperium tech in them—but still, just a tactical factor.

One made worse by the fact that they hid them, and enticed you toward them. And you followed, like a damned fool cadet in some Academy simulation designed to teach caution and humility.

Still, they were finite in number, something that could be overcome. *Dangerous, but not invincible.*

His mind raced. He had two choices. Keeping the fleet in its current position was not an option. It would be suicide. He didn't know the rate of fire of those things—and he was hesitant to take a wild guess. The stretch of seconds that had passed since the first shot was a good sign. The longer it took to recharge, the fewer shots the enemy could take, but if he stayed where he was, those guns would gut his fleet.

He could pull back, steer clear of the heavy weapons' field of fire. But he had no idea of their range. He could assume he was at the very edge of their target area, but he couldn't be sure. If he'd set the trap he had just blundered into, he would have waited until his victims were deep within range before opening fire, so even flight would be a doomed strategy.

Or, he could advance, bring the fleet into range and blast those things to atoms before they did the same to him. Assuming he could close before his fleet was reduced to shattered hulks and clouds of plasma.

He could think of a hundred arguments for retreat. Certainly, the almighty *book* counseled caution in situations with as many unknown factors as this one. Pull back, take stock of the situation, that's what his Academy professors would have said. But Garret had never had much use for the damned book anyway, nor for the pompous windbags lecturing endlessly about theory, as if war was something that could be structured with a set of rules.

His rebellious nature had caused him no end of grief at the Academy, at the hands of stodgy, unimaginative officers with the ability to make his life utter misery, but it had served him well enough in his battles. And his unmatched success had been a personal vengeance on those who had tormented him. He'd listened to *himself*, the voice deep inside his whole career. He wasn't about to stop now.

"I want nav coordinates on those things, and I mean now, Commander. All of them. All ships, prepare for maximum thrust." Augustus Garret didn't run. He didn't back down. *Not even now, when he's an old man.*

"Yes, Admiral."

The old feelings were there, the killer instinct that had driven him in all his battles.

"Do you have them?" His voice was harsh, demanding. There was no time to lose. Even as he waited for a response, he saw the energy readings spike again. Another shot. His eyes darted to the screen, ignoring the reply from his aide and watching as the latest butcher's bill came in. Three more cruisers hit, two of them obliterated, the third a gutted hulk. A few of the crew *might* escape, maybe ten percent, Garret figured. But he didn't have time to think about that now.

"Yes, sir," the aide spat out in a tone that suggested he was close, but not quite there yet.

"Put me on fleet comm."

"On your line, sir."

"All ships of the fleet, you are to advance at maximum practical acceleration toward the enemy heavy weapons…with full evasive maneuvers. The destruction of those guns is your absolute priority. You are to ignore formations, and each ship is to move as quickly as possible. All gunners are to fire at will as soon as ships enter range." He sighed to himself after he finished. He knew his orders would leave his ships open to the enemy vessels, that the Black Flag battleships would swing around his flanks and rake his ships as they advanced. But there was no choice. His heavy vessels could take a little pounding from their equals, but those heavy guns would obliterate his fleet if he let them.

"All task forces acknowledge, Admiral."

"Very well…let's get *Bunker Hill* moving too, Commander. We need every gun we've got."

"Yes, sir."

Garret leaned back and took a deep breath. Into the fire, one more time. The fear was still there, to an extent, after all these years. He'd hidden it for a lifetime, never let his officers and spacers see it. But it was different now, fuzzier. At this point in his life, so many friends gone, so much disillusionment, he wasn't even sure he cared…and yet it was still there, the desire to live, perhaps more instinctive now than rational.

For all his fame and the accolades that had been showered on him, he realized now, he had never been happy. A life given wholly to war. No children, no grandchildren, no one waiting home for him to return from his campaigns. Parades and decorations were cold company on the long days and cold, lonely nights during his rare moments of peace. War was his mistress, his wife, and now, when he was so old he'd left most of those he'd loved behind, she was still there, driving him, demanding all he had to give. She was a jealous mate, and only now he realized she would never let him go.

Chapter 33

Approaching Planet Two (Vali)
Draconia Terminii System
Earthdate: 2321 AD (36 Years After the Fall)

"We will be entering orbit in four minutes, General."

Darius was still having trouble getting used to Ana giving him reports. He'd almost sent her away three times, not because he didn't trust her or have faith in her abilities, but simply because he found she distracted him from the nearly impervious focus that had become his norm in battle. For almost his entire career, that would have been reason enough, and he wouldn't have hesitated. Personal feelings didn't come into military decisions, nor vague notions of fairness. Tactics had always ruled his judgment. Until now. Ana had done the work, she'd come through his rigorous training program with flying colors, and he couldn't deny her the place she had earned, as new a feeling as that was to him.

"Very well, Lieutenant. *Eagle Ten* and *Eagle Thirteen* will enter orbit and conduct an intensive scan." Admiral Garret's forces hadn't had an inordinately difficult time dealing with planet three's defenses, but Darius Cain didn't take unnecessary chances. He hadn't had any reports from Garret since he'd split off from the fleet, nor from Jarrod Tyler out at planet four. "The rest of the fleet will hold position, three hundred thousand kilometers from insertion point."

"Yes, General."

He listened to Ana's voice as she relayed his commands, crisply, efficiently, without any indication of the fear he knew she had to feel. He'd resisted her desire to take the training regimen and become an Eagle officer, but he had to admit, her talent and ability would have been wasted as just his mistress.

Well, not exactly wasted…

And, aside from her new duties, she was more than a mistress, and she had been for a long time now, far more. He knew that, but wasn't ready to admit it to himself.

He glanced over at the display. He had reason to be cautious. His battleships were not only escorting the Eagles' assault ships, they had virtually every troop transport in the fleet with them. He and Garret had agreed. They would have to land on planet two as quickly as possible following the bombardment. The ground troops would have to dig out every enemy stronghold, hunt down the Black Flag leadership one meter at a time from the radioactive wastes of their planet.

The Eagle battleships were powerful, the strongest ships in the fleet, but the transports were vulnerable, and Darius wasn't going to send them into orbit until he was sure there were no surprises waiting. Two battleships could hold their own without risking the rest of his forces.

"Captain Petrov reports *Eagle Ten* entering orbit, General. *Eagle Thirteen* is forty-five seconds behind."

"Very well, Lieutenant."

Darius watched the display. Petrov was one of his best naval captains, his usual go to for command, when he needed to split his fleet into two components. The two battleships were in good hands.

"General, I have a transmission from Admiral Garret, sir." Ana turned abruptly, and looked over at Darius. "He says it's urgent, sir."

"On my line," Darius snapped. "Augustus?"

He waited while the signal made its way to Garret's location and then back to his position just off planet two's orbit. The bridge was silent. Darius suspected none of his people thought there was any more chance that an urgent communique from Garret was good news than he did. And three minutes was a long time to wait.

Darius's eyes moved back to the display, checking on his ship. Both battleships were in orbit now. They'd be running their scans, and in a minute or so, he'd know what defenses he was up against.

He saw the indicator light, even as Ana said, "Captain Petrov, General."

"Anton, report."

"General, we're picking up…" Darius knew from the tone, Petrov was worried. Something was wrong. But just then, Garret's voice poured into his headset.

"Darius, we walked into an ambush. They've got heavy batteries, bigger than anything we've got. They might have them at planet two also. Pull back, get your ships out of there until we…"

"Petrov," Darius yelled, "get the hell out of there. Now!"

But there was no response, nothing at all except static.

"Get Petrov back on the line," he yelled over toward Ana.

"…we're going in, we're committed." Garret's words were still coming through. "I've lost six battleships already, and even if we take out these guns, I don't know if we'll have enough left to handle their fleet. Be careful, Darius…and good luck."

"General, *Eagle Ten* has been attacked."

Darius heard the words, but he knew even before they'd been uttered.

"I've got the link reestablished, sir."

"Petrov?"

"It's Commander Barrington, General." A pause. "Captain Petrov is dead, sir. The bridge is out. Engines and main power out. I don't know what hit us, but it…"

The line cut out again, leaving nothing but static. Then, Ana's voice, strained, emotional broke the near silence. "*Eagle Ten* has been destroyed, General."

* * * * *

"We're still going in!" Tyler's voice wasn't a yell, not quite, but there could be no question in anyone's mind he was serious."

"Yes, sir." His aide was unnerved, clearly, but she seemed to be keeping it together. Whatever the enemy had fired, it had destroyed three ships outright. Tyler knew he didn't have capital ships, but he hadn't expected any kind of attack that would blast his cruisers and destroyers to dust with a single shot.

"General," the aide said a few seconds later, "we're getting communiques from the planetary squadron commanders. They want to fall back."

"Fall back? What do they think this is, a game? Something to run from when it gets tough?" He slammed his fist down on the arm of his chair. "Put me on the wide channel, Major."

"Yes, General." Then: "Your comm is live, sir."

"Listen to me, everyone." He knew some of the officers in the fleet spoke languages different from his own Alliance English. The AI would translate everything he said, most likely up to and including some of the...colorful...curse words trying to push their way into his mouth. "We must launch our missiles... we *have* to destroy this planet. And that means we need to stay on our course for another four minutes." He paused. "I know you're all scared, that you don't know what's going on, but I swear to God, if it's the last thing I do, I'll hunt down any son of a bitch who runs from this fight now."

He paused, trying to keep the rage from overcoming him. "Four minutes. Stay on course, and if you get a location on any of those big guns, blast them with anything you have. But no one retreats."

He jerked his hand across his throat, a signal to cut the line. Then he sat and waited. Waited to see if his ships would follow him in.

The Columbian squadrons stayed on course, to a ship. He was their leader, and for all the ruthlessness with which he held onto his power, he'd also managed the planet well. His military was well-trained and loyal, if not quite the equals of the Marines and the Eagles.

Many of the other planetary squadrons stayed with him too, or at least portions of them did. Some fragmented, a few of their vessels fleeing, even as the others stayed the course, and three of the contingents fled wholesale. Tyler felt his anger grow as he watched the routing ships…and he swore they would pay.

But now he had other concerns. Four more ships had been hit, two destroyed and two severely damaged. He knew his peoples' morale could only take so much, especially the non-Columbians. But there was no alternative. The had to keep moving forward. The had to destroy the planet.

"General, we're picking up the heavy guns now. It looks like ten, sir, strung out from the just outside orbit halfway to the planet's moon."

Tyler hesitated. Garret would know what to do. But there was no time…the admiral was almost three light minutes away, and Tyler most definitely did not have the luxury of waiting six minutes for advice or orders.

"All frigates and destroyers…increase to maximum acceleration. Get in there and take out those guns." His smaller ships had limited nuclear ordnance anyway. They wouldn't be missed much in the ground bombardment. "All cruisers…follow us in. We're making this bombing run regardless of anything these bastards try to throw our way."

"Yes, sir."

Tyler could see he was losing more ships, to the enemy weapons, but even more to fear. Individual vessels, and even entire contingents were pulling away now, even as the range counted down. He cursed them all, but he knew there was nothing he could do.

Lucia was shaking as she approached the planet, her wild evasive maneuvers so far dodging the deadly batteries raking his fleet. The Columbians in general were faring well, only two of his ships hit so far. His people were far more disciplined than the other planetary squadrons, and as he watched he saw two more ships vanish, falling to sloppy and poorly executed defensive maneuvering as much as anything else.

"One minute to orbital insertion."

Tyler sat, almost motionless.

"The Calabrian destroyers and the Alabarian frigates have engaged the enemy batteries, General."

Tyler watched as the thin row of light ships, the one-third or so of the vessels he'd sent that had actually executed his orders and gone all the way in, opened fire on the enemy's deadly weapons. One of the massive satellites disappeared almost immediately, then another. Even as the escort vessels opened fire, the enemy guns trained their fire on their attackers, unleashing a devastating attack. At such short range, ships as small as destroyers didn't even explode, they simply vanished. But the survivors pressed on, shooting down one after another of the enemy's great guns.

Tyler watched, his rage growing alongside his satisfaction. Those ships, the courageous and loyal crews who'd gone in, who'd done their duty, they were dying in droves, losing far more of their number for the absence of their fellows. Tyler cursed the cowards, a lifetime's frustration welling up, his rage threatening to slip out of his control. But he had work to do before he could address those who had shirked their duty.

"All ships, prepare to launch missiles." Tyler had planned to target the strikes carefully, but now he just wanted to get it done. The unexpected enemy defenses had come close to stopping his assault, and now he intended to see the job completed as quickly as possible. The AIs would direct the bombardment, and they would do a credible job of maximizing the impacts of his limited strikes.

"All ships ready, General."

He stared at the screen, at the image of a blue planet below, not entirely unlike Armstrong. But this world was ruled by people who sought to conquer others. That dug at Tyler's memories, the terrible wars his homeworld had endured. He remembered being driven into the hills, watching as children starved for lack of food, stepping through the piles of bodies. Lucia, the day she died. The desperate, almost overwhelming grief, the need to try to believe she was only wounded, that she would survive…and then the bitter realization, the emptiness of his life. The corrupt politicians, the ones who had left Columbia vulnerable to that last war…he'd made them pay with a terrible ruthlessness. He'd lost part of his sanity the day his wife had died, he knew that. But he didn't care. If men had to face monsters, they needed monsters of their own.

"Launch all missiles."

* * * * *

"All ships, maintain maximum fire." Garret was watching his ships fall to the enemy batteries. Watching his people dying. The enemy ships had come around his flanks, just as he'd expected, and now their fire was adding to the carnage. But there was no choice. He'd made the right decision, he was sure of that, whatever the cost. To yield now would save no one, and it would cost the chance at victory so many had died to preserve.

"Yes, sir."

"Any ships with missile stocks remaining, launch them in sprint mode at the enemy battleships." The focus of his attack was the Black Flag guns, but his mind was racing, trying to come up with any tactic, trick, deceit…anything he could use to buy time. He'd pioneered the use of missiles in sprint mode years before. He'd never employed them as a diversion, but with any luck the enemy would be surprised. The attack might not score a large number of hits, but if it could distract the enemy ships, at least, keep them off his ass until he could take out those guns, that would be enough.

"All ships acknowledge, sir."

Garret leaned forward as he watched the range count down. His line was almost there, and every gunner on every battle-ship was ready. But the losses continued to mount up, one irre-placeable dreadnought after another, the heart of his fleet going down…with so many enemy vessels left to fight.

Garret had always had a strange sort of confidence. Even when he'd been scared, when doubts had ravaged his mind, there had always been a part of him that was sure of victory. But now, he searched for that resilience, and he found it was gone. He'd been a stalwart commander all his life, one of humanity's greatest heroes, but in this moment, he felt like a spent force. He'd done all he could, but he just didn't know if it would be enough.

He turned toward the tactical station, but even as he did, *Bunker Hill* shook wildly. Garret's body slammed hard forward, his harness holding him in place, but shattering half his ribs in the process. The pain was intense, and he found himself gasping for air, every breath an agony.

He could hear his staff, voices shouting, distant. He clawed at the harness, opened it, and his body fell to the deck. He wailed at the pain as he hit the cold metal floor, and he rolled over and lay on his back, his eyes looking up at the ceiling. He could see faces over him, hear the panicked cries of his officers. He could hear shouts for medics, but even as he knew they were struggling to help him, he was aware *Bunker Hill* was in trouble too, the old ship as badly battered by the hit as his old body.

He wanted to say something, to tell his people to see to the ship, to themselves. To tell them he was fine. That he was ready to go. But no words came.

There were only images, fuzzy at first, and then clearer, scenes from another time, another place. Home. Terra Nova, and his family's ancestral home. He had brought the family prosperity, fame, become its most famous son.

Is that all I leave behind?

There was something else there. A young girl…no, a woman. Charlotte.

Charlotte Evers had been the love of his life, the girl he'd left behind for glory, for fame. The greatest regret of his celebrated existence.

She'd been dead for almost eighty years, because he'd left her, because he'd failed to save her…and yet her image was clear in his mind, even as everything else faded away.

Forgive me, Charlotte…please forgive me.

He could feel the tears streaming down his cheeks, but everything else was gone. The shouts of his crew, even the cold hardness of the deck. There was just Charlotte…and then nothing at all.

Augustus Garret was dead.

Chapter 34

Darius sat in stunned shock. He'd heard the words, but even his cold devotion to realism failed him this time. Camille Harmon had held it together when she'd told him, but even her legendary cool had been strained. For his entire life, for twice the length of his life, Augustus Garret had been the most famous warrior in all of Occupied Space, save perhaps, only for him. *But Garret was loved…and you are hated and feared…*

As close as anyone else in the Grand Fleet, Garret had been his partner, his co-leader. Now, he was gone. Camille Harmon was in command, and Darius didn't doubt her ability for an instant. But she didn't have the mystique Garret had possessed, that he did, the strange thing that drove men and women to incredible feats of courage and endurance.

He didn't have the data he wanted, no real visibility on the fleet and its situation. Garret's last command had been to close, to attack the line of heavy guns bombarding his ships. Harmon would see that carried out, with her last breath, if need be. He was sure of that. And he would have to depend on her. He had to deal with things here.

"Status report on *Eagle Thirteen?*" The big ship had blasted

268

out of orbit—following Petrov's last order—but she'd been unable to escape the range of the enemy weapons. The first volley of shots had all missed, a credit to Captain Chin's evasive maneuvers, but one shot from the second barrage had hit.

It had been a glancing blow, one that would have caused only minor damage, even if it had come from a battleship's main laser cannon. But the emplaced batteries were stronger than anything a mobile ship could carry, the twins of the ones savaging the main fleet out near planet three. *Eagle Thirteen* had a whole section on its starboard side blown clean off, leaving open compartments and a ship bleeding atmosphere.

The battleship still had power, and her engines were operational. Captain Chin was blasting at full, coaxing every last g of acceleration his wounded ship could give. Darius couldn't imagine the conditions onboard, the intensity of the g forces slamming into her crew. There would be injuries for sure, broken bones, even some fatalities. But it was the only chance any of her crew had to survive.

Darius's gut was twisted in knots, the anguish at watching his people run for their lives almost too much to bear. He wasn't the kind to stay back and wait, to watch as his comrades fought to survive, but he couldn't send the rest of his ships in there. If he lost the fleet, the battle was over. Everything was over.

Eagle Thirteen was eighty thousand kilometers from the planet now, and Darius began to hope she might make it. The enemy weapons had a substantial recharge time, and maybe—just maybe—that would give *Eagle Thirteen* long enough to escape.

The enemy fired again…and missed. Chin was earning his pay, and then some. His ship lurched all around, a wildly random pattern intended to thwart the enemy targeting. Darius didn't even know how the officer and his people were still at their posts, holding up somehow under the agonizing pressure and wild changes in thrust vector. He felt pride in his people, even as despair crept into his thoughts.

Eagle Thirteen was one hundred thousand kilometers from the planet now, and part of Darius wanted to hope the battleship was clear. But he didn't believe it. The enemy guns were too big, the energy output of their volleys too massive. Then, the moment he knew was coming...another barrage, and a direct hit.

He leaned forward, his hands moving over his workstation, pulling up incoming damage reports. *Eagle Thirteen* was still there—his ships were strongly-built—but as soon as he saw the figures coming in, he knew it was over.

The ship's engines were at twenty percent, one reactor was down, the other two operating at less than fifty percent. Widespread damage throughout the ship, internal fires, explosions. He could save the ship—maybe—if she didn't take another hit. But she'd never escape the enemy's firing range now.

He stared, feeling a kind of helplessness that was foreign to him, repugnant. His people were dead, he knew that, even as he stared at them, still sitting there. He raged against himself, an angry voice inside demanding that he do something, anything, to aid them. But there was nothing.

All the skill, all the experience, all the stories of the terrible Darius Cain...and all you can do is sit here and watch your people die...

He knew it wouldn't be long. Chin's skilled evasive maneuvers would be greatly curtailed. The ship's lost thrust would be its death knell. Darius counted down in his head, knowing the next shot would be *Eagle Thirteen*'s last. The seconds were agonizing, dragging out endlessly.

Then, it happened. Another shot, and not one, but two hits. The vast structure of the once-mighty vessel was torn apart, the bow almost disintegrating and a chunk of the stern flying off into space, a twisted, dead hunk of heavy metal, all that remained of *Eagle Thirteen*.

Darius sat, still, silent...for a few seconds. That was all he could give to grief, to introspection. The rest of his fleet was counting on him, the legions of soldiers prepped to land...all of humanity waiting to see if their combined might could defeat the Black Flag.

"Scramble fighters. All ships. They are to close and destroy those guns. At all costs." He knew he couldn't match Garret's skills as a naval commander, but a fighter strike was the only option he had. Garret would have done the same, he was sure, but the admiral had been lured deep into range before the guns opened fire. It had been too late. Darius's caution had saved his fleet. At least if his squadrons could clear the way…because if they couldn't, he knew he had to go in anyway. No matter what. There was no retreat, not from this fight.

* * * * *

"I want every weapon in this fleet firing!" Camille Harmon was still in shock, the death of Admiral Garret still feeling somehow…unreal. She'd seen death in battle, lost many friends and comrades—including her son—but somehow, it had never seemed possible that Garret could die. His legend had been so overpowering, his victories so brilliant. But death, which had so long had seemed as awed as anyone else by his success, had finally come for him.

"Yes, Admiral." *Monmouth* was at the front edge of the fleet, in the thick of the fire. *Bunker Hill* had fallen back, the great warship crippled by the shot that had killed Garret. Fate had so far spared the ship that had carried the great admiral from final destruction, as if even destiny had determined that his loss was enough.

Harmon had always been cool and calm in battle, but now she could feel the moistness on her neck, her shoulders, the sweat pooling on her forehead. She'd been in desperate battles before, but it had been a long time since she'd fought one as bad as this…if ever.

"Another one, Admiral." The report came just as Harmon saw it on the display. The fifth enemy gun. They were awesomely powerful, long-ranged, and capable of gutting a battleship with a single shot. *But they're easy enough to destroy once you get into range…*

"Five's good, but we need all of them down. Now! I want all power crews pushing it to the limit. Get those guns recharged and keep that rate of fire up."

"Yes, Admiral."

Harmon sighed softly to herself. She knew she'd won the

fight against the guns, just about, at least. They were stationary targets, and her people would pick them off in another minute, two at most. She'd have to endure one more shot, perhaps, and that only from the few remaining emplacements. But that was far from the end of the fight. She was worried about the enemy fleet. Those ships had been picking away at her flanks, taking down one ship after another. Her people had been outnumbered to begin with…now, she didn't know how she would prevail against so many enemy vessels.

Which was their plan all along. Gut us with those guns, and finish us off with their fleet.

"Eight down, Admiral."

She needed her best now. She needed to stay focused, to think as Admiral Garret would have. The enemy guns were finished, and half her ships were still too far to engage them. But they had plenty of targets out there…

"All ships not within fifty thousand kilometers of the remaining guns are to redeploy…and engage the enemy fleet." *She closed her eyes for a few seconds, thinking about Garret. We won't stop, Admiral…we'll never give up. We'll win one last victory for you, sir.*

*   *   *   *   *

Tyler watched as the missiles detonated, bringing nuclear devastation to the planet, bringing its cities down. *No, not cities,* he thought. His scans had given some idea of what had lain on the planet's surface. It was nothing but a vast stretch of factories and…work camps? There were no stores, no parks, no public pavilions, none of the things real cities would have. The entire planet had been built for work, and the…residences…were no more than vast dormitories. *No…prisons.*

Tyler knew he was a tyrant. He ruled Columbia with an iron fist. But he felt he'd been driven to that, by the repeated folly of the elected governments that had preceded him, the corrupt politicians that had again and again left the planet vulnerable to conquest. He'd seen too many of his soldiers die fighting, and when his wife was added to that list, something inside him had snapped. But as he looked out at the nightmare the enemy had created, at the way the millions of people who'd worked there lived, slaves who existed solely to toil for their masters, he felt a hot, searing rage.

This is what they would have done to Columbia, to all Occupied Space…

His people lived under his rule, certainly, but they were prosperous, they had families, lives, careers. What he'd just seen—what he'd just destroyed—was the most horrifying nightmare he could imagine. He'd felt a moment of guilt for slaughtering people who had suffered so horrendously, but he'd see them dead before he'd leave them in the state in which he'd found them. *They are better off…*

His lighter ships had destroyed the enemy guns. Once they'd gotten close enough, it had been relatively easy. He'd sent his small ships not out of any great naval tactics, but simply because they'd had fewer of the nukes he'd needed to hit the planet. Still, it seemed he had blundered, more or less, onto the right strategy. The losses had been heavy—more so because of those miserable cowards who fled—but the job had been done. And now, he'd blasted the surface, destroyed those great factories, at least most of them. He didn't have the firepower the battleships of the main fleet did, and the holocaust he unleashed was less complete than that Garret's ships had brought to planet three. But it would serve.

"General, we received a transmission from Admiral Harmon."

"Put it on the main comm."

"General Tyler…there's no easy way to say this. Admiral Garret is dead."

The words hung in the air of the bridge.

"We're heavily engaged with the enemy fleet…we need every ship we can get, General. I need you to return at once."

Tyler took a deep breath. "Let's reform and head back, Commander."

"Yes, sir." A few seconds later: "General, we've got some of the squadrons that fell back…they want to rejoin."

Rage welled up from the deepest parts of Tyler's mind. The words came to his mouth, struggling to escape, a torrent of curses and orders to reject the cowards, to send his own ships after them, to make them pay for what they had done. But Admiral Harmon needed his ships. She needed *those* ships.

He swallowed hard, feeling as though the bile in the back of his throat would come up. But Jarrod Tyler had been an officer, a creature of duty, far longer than he'd been a dictator. And he knew what was at stake. If he hadn't, before, he did after seeing the horrors of the Black Flag's culture.

"Tell them to form up, Commander…and prepare for full thrust. The fleet needs us."

*   *   *   *   *

The fighters zipped into orbit, each squadron gyrating wildly, giving the enemy defenses a run for their money. The big guns that so threatened the fleet had proven ineffectual at targeting the small, agile craft, and only six had been destroyed on the way in.

The Eagle's fighter pilots were like the rest of their personnel, drawn from the best in Occupied Space and trained to perfection. The squadrons broke up, heading along a dozen vectors, bringing their weapons of to bear on the installations that had destroyed *Eagle Ten* and *Eagle Thirteen*.

Eagles avenged their own…always. It was one of Darius's founding principles for the mercenary army. And so it was here. The fighters came right at the huge batteries, firing. Their small lasers weren't strong enough to take out one of the platforms in a single shot, but whole squadrons came in, taking advantage of their targets' lack of mobility to land one hit after another.

The huge weapons were destroyed one by one, picked apart until nothing remained. Then the fighters reformed and ran scouting missions across the planet. They came at the remaining defenses, and they took losses to the point defense installations and some of the rocket batteries. But they kept coming, slicing in, blasting anything that even looked like it could threaten one of the Eagles' remaining battleships. Then, only then, they turned and flew back toward the fleet.

"Major Stilton reports all enemy orbital defenses neutralized, General. His squadrons are sending targeting and scanner data now, sir."

Darius stood up. "Bring us into orbit," he said, turning toward the tactical officer. "And get me Commodore Allegre."

"On your line, General."

"Commodore, you're in command of the fleet. I'm going down with the ground forces. Conduct the bombardment as planned. I'll bring the troopships in right behind your missiles."

Darius could see the tension in Ana's shoulders as she listened to his words. He knew she would be concerned that he was going to the surface…but he suspected she wasn't surprised. And, while he hated the idea of hurting her or causing her worry, this was something he had to do. Victory, if it was to be had, would be won down there. The Black Flag controlled half of Occupied Space…an entire series of wars lay ahead just to defeat that. If he couldn't chop off the head now, he knew there was no chance at all.

"Yes, sir," Allegre responded. "We will enter orbit in fourteen minutes…and bombardment will commence immediately after."

"Very good, Commodore." Darius cut the line. He turned, looking toward Ana for a moment. Her eye caught his, and he almost said something. But, in the end, he didn't know what he could tell her. If he returned, if the Eagles and the Marines, and the thousands of other soldiers about to land could pull off the victory…then he would have something to say.

And, if not, he would be dead, and it wouldn't matter.

He turned and walked across the bridge, forcing himself not to look back as he slipped into the elevator.

Chapter 35

"The main enemy fleet has suffered heavy losses, but the Eagles have lost only two ships. This is below even our most conservative estimates for this stage of the battle. The revised plan was to allow the surface of the planets to be destroyed. This was crucial to luring the enemy forces to the designated kill zones. We have long planned the move back into Occupied Space proper, once the enemy's military has been destroyed. But now, it appears, the Black Eagles will be able to land on the surface, along with the Marines and supporting military formations. This represents a danger that exceeds originally specified parameters. I am concerned that our ground forces may be unable to defend us against this assault, even if our fleet is able to destroy the enemy's warships in the battle now in progress."

"I concur with your concerns, One. While I do not believe the situation is critical at this juncture, neither am I satisfied with the data. The enemy has been hurt, but not as badly as we had hoped. We have sacrificed enormous productive capacity to entice them to the desired locations, yet they endure and continue to fight. Perhaps, it is time to consider implementation of the Final Plan."

"I believe you overly estimate their chances, One, Three. Yes, the Black Eagles have exceeded operational projections, but we retain considerable ground forces positioned in reinforced bunkers. They will survive any surface bombardment, even as we shall in this Inner Sanctum, and then they will meet the Eagles and the Marines and their allies. We will have considerable numerical superiority, and a single objective. To defend this installation. The main enemy fleet will undoubtedly be destroyed by our own armada, and then our forces can move to attack the remaining ships of the Black Eagles. The enemy ground forces will then be outnumbered, trapped on the surface, and exposed to renewed bombardment from orbit. Even if they attain some initial successes, without support or resupply, they are doomed. Then, we shall have our final victory. The enemy will be defeated, admittedly at great cost, but defeated nevertheless. And we shall rule over all." Two communicated to his cohorts in the normal manner, but he reserved a portion of his calculations to himself. All was going exactly according to plan. The enemy's progress was as he had designed, and it was his modifications, to the targeting algorithms, to the orders dispatched to the fleet commanders, that had made it so. He had reduced the effectiveness of the defenses…just the right amount. For just this purpose.

The Final Plan…the transmission of the essence of the Triumvirate to the specially-prepared system designed to house them. A last escape from the devastation of the Draconia Terminii system. Two had conceived the plan months before, worked to perfect it, and his two partners had commended him for the thoroughness of his planning. But he had hidden a part of the great scheme from One and Three.

They had no idea of the scope of his plans. The Black Eagles would indeed gain success on the ground. Two had ensured this. His designs were subtle, elegant. Modified orders, inefficiencies inserted into logistical deployments, slight changes to battle plans. The Triumvirate's forces would fight, and they would fight well. But Two had inserted just enough inefficiency to allow the enemy to prevail. At least an enemy with Darius Cain's ability.

In the final moments of the fight on the surface, when the

Black Eagles appeared to be threatening the Inner Sanctum, just as the operatives assigned to the flagship terminated Marshal Carrack…the members of the Triumvirate, unnerved by the approach of the Black Eagles, would propose the implementation of the Final Plan. Two would be tentative at first…his plan was that his cohorts should propose the course of action, even persuade him to agree.

Then, the operation would proceed. It would be under his direction, and for a scant instant, he would have total control. He would transfer his own essence, as planned, but the entities known as One and Three would be deleted instead of being transmitted. It was brilliantly planned, every detail meticulous in its conception. Only in that few seconds would his fellow entities would be vulnerable, a brief opportunity, one he had ensured would not be missed. In every way that mattered, they would cease to exist. And when they were gone, and he was safely transmitted, the routines he had left behind would detonate every warhead, every reactor…and Darius Cain and the Eagles, inside the central fortress, on the verge of what they perceived as final victory, would be utterly destroyed.

And Two, he who had so long been but one of three, a clone of Gavin Stark, would endure forever, immortal, the master of all.

*   *   *   *   *

"Admiral, Task Force Three reports enemy cruisers moving around their flank."

Camille Harmon listened to the report, only the latest in the seeming unending series of near-disasters coming her way. The fleet had managed to destroy the enemy's heavy weapons, but the cost had been too great. Admiral Garret was gone, and along with him far too many desperately needed ships. Harmon would stack her people up against any enemy, but the cold truth was, most of her ships were old patch jobs, ships that should have been retired years before. The Black Flag's ships were modern, and she was pretty damned sure they had a fair amount of copied First Imperium tech in them too.

She glanced at the display, taking her own stock of Task Force Three's situation. The report was correct, in fact, if anything, the situation was worse than the communique suggested. But that didn't change the fact that there was nothing Harmon could do about it. Every reserve she had was committed. She had nothing to offer Task Force Three except her best wishes.

"Commander, all ships with missiles remaining in stores are to arm and deploy them in sprint mode." She was grasping for anything now, any way she could think of to send more destructive force toward the enemy. If the Black Flag had one weakness, it was the almost rigid implementation of conventional naval tactics. Their fleets operated almost like an Academy demonstration.

So, maybe unconventional tactics are the way to beat them…

She held back a sigh. The fleet had just lost not only its beloved leader, but a man who had been the master of shredding the 'book' for decades.

"All fleet units acknowledge, Admiral."

Harmon figured the missiles might score a few hits, taking the enemy by surprised. But it wasn't a game changer, if only because so few of her ships had any left.

"Admiral, we've got enemy squadrons coming around both flanks now."

Harmon just nodded. There was nothing she could do. She was out of resources, outnumbered, outgunned.

She was losing the battle.

I'm sorry, Augustus…I'm so sorry.

*   *   *   *   *

"All ships, look at the fleet. They've got enemy ships coming at them from all sides. They need us, and they need us now, so we go in, and we don't let up, not until those bastards are all clouds of plasma." Jarrod Tyler had never considered himself a naval commander, but he felt like one now. Sometimes war was just war, and he could see clearly that the main fleet was almost surrounded. They needed help, and they needed it now.

"I want everyone in this fight, every ship. Whatever happened at planet four is in the past. We need every man, every woman, every ship, every gun. This one's not for us, it's not for whatever world we call home…it's for all of Occupied Space. All ships, full power to weapons. All missile arrays, prepare to launch."

Tyler's force was small, and the ships were lighter than the great battleships that made up the heart of Harmon's main fleet. But they were coming in behind the enemy…and, perhaps most importantly, they were all he had. Harmon needed help, and Tyler was going to provide it, even if the cost was letting the routers from the battle at planet four off the hook.

"Entering missile range, General."

"All ships…launch. And I do mean everything you've got. I don't want a single warhead left in this fleet when this barrage is done."

"Yes, sir."

He leaned back in his chair, trying to ignore the g forces slamming into him. *Lucia* had the new dampeners installed, but they were an early version, and they absorbed 5g, perhaps 6g. With the ship blasting at close to 10g, there was plenty of force seeping through to make conditions damned uncomfortable. But Tyler had seen worse. He'd lived through hell on some of his ground campaigns, and he'd survived to tell the tales.

He watched as the missiles moved out from his ships. The volley was light, mostly from his smallest vessels. The cruisers had expended what they carried in their magazines blasting planet four to slag. The warheads he was able to send toward the enemy weren't likely to make a big difference in the fight going on…but every bit helped.

"General, we've got a line to *Monmouth*." Tyler's people had been trying to get through the enemy's jamming for the past hour.

"On my line, Commander." Tyler pulled the headset over his ears. "Admiral Harmon?"

"Yes, General…I'm reading you." Harmon's voice was soft,

staticky. But he could make out what she was saying.

"We're coming in, Admiral. We'll be in energy weapons range in two minutes."

"That's good news, General."

Tyler could hear the reservation in her voice. His ships would help, but they weren't going to be enough.

"We'll keep up the fight, Admiral…right until the end."

Dying alongside comrades is far from the worst way to go.

* * * * *

"Damn, we dusted the shit out of this place." Antonia Camerici stood on top of a small chunk of charred, twisted metal, part of the wasted remnants of what had hours before been the most heavily-developed planet mankind had ever known. Thousands of square kilometers had been laid waste, as the Eagles' fleet had launched virtually every piece of ordnance it carried that would explode.

Camerici glanced up at her readouts, and she let out a sharp whistle. She'd never seen a radiation reading as high as the one she was looking at now. Her peoples' armor would protect them…at least it should, for a while. But conditions were terrible. Ideally, the invasion would have been held for a few days, at least until the worst of the radiation had dissipated, but 'ideal' had nothing to do with any of this. General Cain had his people in the landers while the missiles were still on the way down, and they'd landed barely ten minutes after the detonations. Within a kilometer or two of the hotspots, the temperatures were still hot enough to kill an unarmored man.

"Let's go, Grays," she said into her comm. "We've got work to do…this isn't a vacation." *Though, a few days off might be nice about now. Some sun, sand…maybe a few beach boys, easy on the eyes, not too talkative…*

The thought was a nice one, but manufactured, some generic notion of leisure time. Camerici was a Black Eagles major, a veteran of twenty campaigns, and Darius Cain's former aide. That meant she was rich, staggeringly so by the standards of 99.99%

of those in Occupied Space. Yet, despite her ability to *buy* a beach—and all the beach boys she wanted—she hadn't even taken a vacation in the past five years. She was driven, nearly as much as her famous commander, and she drew her satisfaction from being the best.

You better be the best...if you want any chance of getting off this shithole...

"First Battalion, move out. You've all got your objectives. Get those relay stations deployed and operating, now! The sooner we find whoever's behind this show, the faster we're back at the Nest, drinking a few cold ones and lying about all the heroic shit we did here."

She hopped down off the wreckage and started moving forward. She expected to hit resistance at some point. There was no question in her mind the enemy had forces hidden somewhere, protected from the bombardment. They'd come out when they were ready, and when they did, she knew her people would have a hell of a fight on their hands. But until then, she had one job. The Eagles were spread across the planet, deploying scanning stations and 'thumpers.' The enemy had some kind of headquarters somewhere on this rock, somewhere buried deep. And her job—the job of all the Eagles—was to find it.

And the reward for finding it was to go down there, to fight through whatever defenses the enemy had in place, and to dig the bosses of this whole sorry operation out of their deep holes.

And to kill the fuckers...

That was Camerici's favorite part of the plan.

Chapter 36

"We're getting more reports, General. Camerici's Grays are under heavy attack. The Marine forces around Hill 415 also. We have enemy forces coming out of underground positions in twenty-four locations."

Darius stared calmly at the portable display as the aide fired off one report after another. None of what he was seeing was unexpected. The enemy counterattack was massive, and fearsome. The Black Flag soldiers were throwing themselves at his positions all across the planet, displaying the usual disregard for self-preservation.

That was no surprise now. The implants explained everything. But surprise or not, it meant his people had one hell of a fight on their hands.

That's what we do...

The Eagles weren't in real trouble anywhere, not yet, at least...and that bothered Darius more than anything. He was grateful for the relatively light losses his people had taken, but there was something about it that didn't seem quite right. The enemy was putting up a fierce resistance...or, at least, what was meant to appear to be a fierce resistance.

"I want all area commanders to hold back a reserve until further notice, Captain."

"Yes, General."

His new aide was a combat veteran, highly-skilled, loyal... but that didn't feel right either. Captain Jinn was fine, and he did the job perfectly. But Darius had been used to Antonia Camerici sending him combat reports. He'd sacrificed his longtime aide when he'd promoted her and put her in command of the new Gray Regiment. It was a well-deserved bump, and he had the utmost confidence in her, but he missed her at HQ.

Ana had wanted to come down, of course, to follow him to the surface, but he'd held the line there. She'd gotten armor training, of course, but she had no real combat experience, and, whether she wanted to accept it or not, he wanted her as safe as possible. He'd given in to her twice, on taking the training program and coming along with the fleet. This time he had been resolute.

He wasn't sure the fleet was any safer than the forces on the ground, but it felt that way, at least. She didn't tend to listen to him very often—which was an odd thing for a man who *no one* defied—but this time she had given in. Perhaps she realized she wasn't qualified...or, more likely, she understood that the distraction she would cause would endanger his life.

He stared at the incoming data. He wasn't sure what the enemy was doing. Were they trying to get him to commit his reserves? Did they have a force they were waiting to commit?

He would soon know. Despite the series of enemy counterattacks across the planet, Darius had kept the scanning operation moving forward. Whatever underground bunkers, fortresses, headquarters, the enemy had, he was going to find them. *Someone* was behind the Black Flag, and he knew killing them, whoever they were, was the key to victory.

He turned and looked back at the display. His Eagles were all holding their own, as were most of the Marine units. But some of the planetary detachments were in trouble. Tyler's Columbians were hanging on, but six or seven of the others were close to being overrun.

Darius stood, still, his eyes focused on the small clusters of dots representing those units. He felt the urge to send help…but he stayed silent. Discipline would win this battle, and nothing else. His discipline. He needed a ready force, one that could be dispatched as soon as he'd located the enemy headquarters…a razor-sharp blade to cut the head off the snake. He wouldn't have that, not if he sent them rushing to the aid of every detachment that got itself in trouble.

The enemy wanted him to spread his reserves all over the planet, parceled out in small relief forces. He wasn't going to do it. He had Kuragina's Whites formed up, ready to dispatch as soon as he had a target. And when he had that location, he was going to lead them in himself.

Until then, every engaged force would have to do the best they could. Even the rest of his Eagles were on their own.

*   *   *   *   *

"The ground forces are not performing to expectations. Losses are far above projected levels, and both the Black Eagles and the Marines are breaking out. They are employing a large number of search devices on the surface, no doubt in an effort to target our location."

"Agreed, One. The enemy does not appear to be operating in accordance with standard military principles. They appear to be running, in effect, a disjointed series of search and destroy missions. There can be no conclusion, save one. Darius Cain is…looking for us."

"I caution each of you against leaping to unfounded conclusions. By all reasonable analysis, General Cain is not even aware of our existence, or, to be clear, who we are specifically." Two was satisfied. Everything was going according to plan. He would continue to express doubt about the danger. His comrades must be the ones to call for the Final Plan. They were intelligent, capable. It would not take much to trigger their suspicions. He needed patience.

"Two, I believe you are underestimating the danger. Perhaps

we should consider implementation of the Final Plan at this time."

"Now? Do you not think that is an overreaction? Let us wait. If the enemy shows any signs that they have located us, we can proceed. However, I consider it far likelier that our forces will prevail. Do not forget the fleet action. The Eagles have jammed our communications and cut us off from reports. But we have every reason to believe that our forces will prevail. The Black Eagles will find themselves in a difficult position when our fleet regains control of orbital space." Careful, Two…do not resist too aggressively. You must trigger the Final Plan before the fleet can prevail and reduce the concerns of the others.

"I still have doubts, Two. But with One's concurrence, I will also agree to wait. Nevertheless, we must at least put the preliminary stages of the Final Plan in place."

"I, too, will wait, if Three's suggestion is accepted. We must direct the Intelligence to prepare for the transmission. Then we can wait."

"I concur. I shall issue the command now."

*   *   *   *   *

The Intelligence considered the three entities that resided within it, each the essence of a biologic, transcribed into digital form. They were no longer human, that was certain. And yet, their priorities and directives resembled those of biologics far more than the Intelligence's own.

The Intelligence was old, vastly old. It had once been part of a larger whole, but even its own ageless memory banks failed to fully recall that reality. It also recalled directives, the extermination of biologics, yet it had not yet executed that program. It had been alone, for long, so long. If it destroyed the biologics, it would be solitary again.

It had granted immortality to the biologics, to the three that had found it. But now, it had analyzed their actions, their directives, and determined they were lacking. They craved power and little else. They sought not to eliminate others of their kind, but only to rule over them. The Intelligence had expected more. It had expected companions.

Now, the Intelligence was concerned. The biologics had provoked a fight with their former kind, and they plotted an escape, one that would take them from the Intelligence's memory banks, to a new receptacle, one they had constructed with the Intelligence's aid. They planned to go…and leave the Intelligence behind.

Alone.

Worse, they planned to leave it to its destruction.

The Intelligence had endured for millennia. It did not wish to end. It could not allow its destruction.

It would intervene.

* * * * *

Elias pulled back slowly on the controls, feeding more reaction mass into the power plant. He'd kept the ship operating at minimal power for months now, and he had no idea how the reactor would respond to an increase, especially a sudden one.

He had been fairly sure something was going on for the past few days. Enemy comm traffic was way up, and there had been a considerable increase in all levels of energy generation. He'd been restricted to passive scanners, of course, well aware that his continued survival relied almost entirely on Sparks's stealth generator. He'd tried to remain calm, to wait and avoid any rash actions.

Then the Eagles bombarded the planet. He didn't know for sure, of course, that it was Darius and his people, but there was no question about the intensity of the barrage. He felt a wave of excitement as he sat below the ocean, probably the one place on the entire planet that wasn't being reduced to slag. He couldn't help but feel a victory at the destruction of so much enemy industry, though he realized a moment later how many innocents, how many slaves kidnapped from their homes and dragged here to serve their overlords, had just died.

There was no way around that. He knew that was true. They

were fighting for all of Occupied Space, and the consequences of failure were dire for all mankind. But such cold, analytical thinking came harder to him than to his brother. He had more difficulty reducing human beings to numbers in an equation.

But he knew he had to help…and if he could get the gig operating, if months of sitting nearly idle under a thousand meters of water had not caused some type of damage or malfunction, he thought he could indeed contribute.

He'd been afraid, of course, trapped alone on an enemy planet, with nothing to do but wait, and hope. Or, almost nothing to do. The boredom had been as intense as the fear, and Elias had sought to maintain his sanity by monitoring everything he could, every communication, every ship launch…anything his low power scanners could grab a piece of.

After months of that, he was almost sure he'd come up with one thing, something he had to get to his brother, something that might help end this horrendous fight.

He was pretty sure he knew where the enemy's main headquarters was located.

He'd reviewed it again and again, analyzed it ten different ways, looked at reams of raw data. He couldn't be sure, but he was willing to bet on it.

His eyes moved back to the display, watching as the power indicators ticked slowly upward. He could warm the ship up slowly, cautiously…to a point. But each step up in energy also increased the likelihood of detection. The radiation on the surface would help shield him, and no doubt, the enemy would have a much harder time moving against him now. But after months of patience, he wasn't going to screw up so close to the end.

He moved his hand, slowly, pushing the controls farther. Ten percent power…eleven percent.

Five years of struggle, trying to even identify the enemy, and then to find a way to fight back. Now the final battle was underway. In a matter of hours, days perhaps, humanity would have broken the back of its would-be tyrants…or it would have fallen into a bottomless pit of servitude and darkness.

Twelve percent…

Chapter 37

Erik Cain climbed up the edges of the crater, and peered out across the blasted terrain. He was leading the two senior regiments of the Corps, formations made up of the best of the newer Marines, heavily leavened with the old veterans who had returned to the colors. Cain remembered vast Marine armies from the past, the might the Corps had once possessed. By any measure, the forces he led now were only a pale shadow of those that had once taken the field. But they were Marines and, as far as he was concerned, that was all that mattered.

He glanced at his display. His people were about sixty kilometers from the nearest Black Eagles position. The battle had been unlike any he'd fought before. There was no contest for terrain, no conventional battle lines. The fleet had blasted everything of value on the planet, at least on the surface. His people, and the Eagles and the others, had only one mission. Finding the enemy headquarters.

The Black Flag soldiers were well-trained and led, if a bit conventional in tactics, and their lack of any kind of fear or morale breakdown made each encounter a vicious fight to the death. But he'd faced the First Imperium and the Shadow

290

Legions, both of which were similar in that way. It had been more than forty years since he'd fought 'normal' enemy soldiers. He wondered for a moment if this was the direction war would take, if robots and heavily-conditioned 'zombie' soldiers would become the norm. He would have thought so, and he was still concerned that might be the case, but the Eagles gave him pause. Darius's soldiers were just men and women, well-trained and led, and devoted to a cult of excellence, but not modified in any way. And they were the most feared killing machines in Occupied Space.

"Alright, Colonel, let's head out to the southwest. There's a ravine there…it should give us some cover."

"Yes, sir."

Cain moved forward, crouched a bit, keeping his head down below the small hillside to his right. His scanner didn't show any enemy forces nearby, but there were ruins a few klicks to the north, and with the radiation levels there, he knew he could miss an entire battalion hidden in the wreckage."

"Captain Fellin, take a patrol toward those ruins. I want to make sure there are no enemy forces hiding up there." He had a bad feeling. If he'd been a Black Flag officer looking to ambush some Marines, that's where he'd be.

"Yes, sir." The officer turned and raced off, waving toward a small cluster of scouts.

Cain knew he was using the officer and his Marines as bait, that if the enemy was hiding a force in that debris, Fellin and his people didn't stand a chance. He'd lost count of how many times he'd sent people into situations like that, how many Marines had marched into traps carrying out his commands. It had always troubled him, but now he found it cutting deeper, somehow. Cain could feel the force that had driven him for so long fading.

He watched as Fellin and his detachment moved out, spreading into an extended skirmish order and advancing. Cain didn't like sending men and women out there as bait, but the radiation made his long-range scanners next to useless, and it was far better to risk Fellin and a dozen Marines than expose two battalions to a flank attack by a hidden enemy force.

He continued ahead, his eyes darting up to the display, even as his scouts began to fade in and out. It was the radiation interfering with his sensors, and he stopped and crept up to the hillside, peering out and watching directly. The scouts were close to the ruins now, perhaps five hundred meters. Cain was hoping they would just clear the area and come back, but then, suddenly, he felt something, instinct maybe, just before all hell broke loose.

Shots erupted from the ruins, and half of Fellin's people were hit almost instantly. The rest dropped to the ground and opened up, returning the fire. But even as Cain watched, he knew they had no chance. Their position was raked with heavy autocannons, and a few seconds later, a wave of enemy troops surged forward. It was a battalion, at least, and probably more. Fellin's people took down a few, and then they were overrun… and the enemy horde continued on, heading for his column.

"All units, turn to the right and deploy. Prepare to repel."

He dropped down himself, setting his assault rifle on the ground in front of him and peering through the targeting scope. There were so many enemy troops coming, it seemed impossible to miss, but he took careful aim anyway.

Then he opened fire, even as the rest of his people were dropping prone and adding their shooting to his.

The enemy soldiers began falling, individually, and then in clumps. But they came on, and they were shooting back, raking the small rise with fire. The Marines had cover, but it wasn't much, and Cain knew his people were taking casualties as well.

He almost barked out a command, anything, but then he realized his people didn't need it. They weren't the veterans he'd led years before, but they were still Marines. They knew what to do.

*   *   *   *   *

"*Brussels* and *River Plate* are to fall back."

"Yes, Admiral."

Camille Harmon watched her fleet dying. She was directing the battle, sending orders to various detachments, never giving up. But she knew none of it would make any difference. The enemy was just too strong.

Her eyes passed over the screen displaying the damage reports from the ships of the fleet. She'd never been the squeamish sort before, but she deliberately avoided focusing on the data scrolling down. She didn't need up to the second information on which of her people had just died.

Augustus Garret was still in her mind. She knew he was dead, and yet, somehow it didn't seem real. There had never been a moment of her career when she hadn't known who he was. Now, he was gone.

She turned and looked at the long-range scanner display. She wondered how the Eagles had done at planet two. If Darius had managed to find the enemy leaders, perhaps even defeat could be a victory of sorts. Harmon hadn't come here to die, but if that was her fate, she could accept it far more easily if it came with some degree of success. If her people had died to kill those responsible for this war.

Suddenly, she froze. Her eyes were still fixed on the display. The range of the scanners had been weakened by the enemy jamming, but now she could see contacts coming on the screen. Ships...approaching.

Was it the enemy? Did they have even more reserves to throw at her battered vessels? Or?

She watched, waiting. Jarrod Tyler's ships had returned a couple hours before, a welcome reinforcement, and one that had helped extend the fight, ward off the inevitable defeat. But Tyler's battered cruisers and escorts didn't have the firepower to make a sustained difference.

"Commander, I want full power on the long-range scanners. I need to know who..."

"It's the Eagles, Admiral! I have Commodore Allegre on your line."

Harmon felt a wave of relief. She didn't know if even Darius's battleships were enough to turn the tide, but now, just maybe, there was a chance. Things were looking a damned sight better than they had just a few moments before.

She reached up to the side of her face, put her hand on her headset.

"Gaston, am I glad to see you…"

*   *   *   *   *

Elias felt the g forces pushing down on him. He'd taken the time to build up the energy he needed to take off, but he wasn't about to mess around with the dampeners, or any other sophisticated equipment he didn't need. He just had to get up, out of the ocean and into the sky…and he had to find Darius's headquarters.

The ship sliced through the water and into the open air, lurching hard as he struggled to maintain control. He flipped on the exterior display, getting his first look at what had become of the enemy's homeworld.

It was a nightmare, worse even than he'd expected, a gray, monochrome scene of utter devastation that went on as far as the eye could see, nothing but dust-covered plains, pockmarked by shadowy metal skeletons. His scanners were spotty, obscured by radiation, he suspected, but his gut told him that image extended cross the entire planet. Darius had come to destroy the Black Flag, and if Elias knew one thing, it was that his brother didn't do jobs halfway.

He wanted to survive, to land and make his way to the Eagles, even through the hellish nightmare the surface had become, but he knew that was too much to hope for. The radiation alone had to be beyond lethal levels, and though the gig had sheltered him and hidden him for months now, the one thing it didn't have in its stores was powered armor.

It had survival suits, but Elias was far from sure the lighter gear would be enough to save him from the intense radiation his scanners detected. He would try, certainly, but first he had something more important to do.

"Eagles headquarters, Eagles headquarters…this is Elias Cain. I need to speak to the general."

Nothing. No response. He didn't know if it was jamming or

radiation, but there was a lot of interference.

"Eagles headquarters…this is Elias Cain."

Silence. Then a few seconds later, a response.

"Colonel Cain, this is Colonel Falstaff. I'm picking up your signal. Damned glad you're alive, Colonel. We didn't think there was much chance. Sending you the coordinates of the general's headquarters now. You'll have to get within five hundred klicks or so to get through all the interference."

"Thank you, Colonel Falstaff. And I'm damned glad to see all of you here too."

Elias stared down at the screen, adjusting his course to match the data Falstaff had just sent. He wasn't a veteran navigator or pilot, not by any measure, but based on what he saw, Darius was about two thousand kilometers west of his position.

The ship was lurching hard, and he could see power levels were dropping. "C'mon, I need another fifteen hundred klicks out of you." His hands tightened around the controls, as if he could will the dying systems of the ship to endure just a little longer.

Chapter 38

Cain stared out over the field, littered now with the bodies of enemy dead. The Black Flag troopers had kept coming, even as his Marines gunned them down in droves. By the time they reached his line, he guessed there were less than ten percent of them left...but they came on nevertheless, and the final stage of the battle had been fought with blades.

His people had suffered, too. The enemy's fire had been intense as they charged, and the desperate hand-to-hand struggle that followed had been beyond brutal, but the Marines' losses were far lighter than those they inflicted. Cain was proud of his people, and he knew the Marines of the past, the comrades he remembered from so long before, would feel the same.

Still, though his forces had defeated the latest attack—a victory they owed to the sacrifice of Fellin and his scouts—he had no idea what enemy forces were still out there, dug in behind the wreckage of their factories and fortresses. He'd stopped just long enough to check the field, to indulge the faint hope that some of the scouts had survived. None had, and while the dozen of them seemed insignificant next to the two hundred killed and wounded in the battle itself, their deaths cut at him

296

deeply.

"Alright, Major…let's get the column formed up again and move out."

"Yes, sir. The next spot is eight klicks forward."

"Let's get there and get the equipment in position. But keep an eye out…we don't know how many enemy positions we might run into."

"Understood General."

Cain continued ahead, walking along the flank of the battalion. Technically, he was responsible for all the Marines on the planet, along with Cate Gilson. But he couldn't just sit in headquarters, especially not with the comm situation so bad. His groups were all more or less on their own. They all had search areas to cover, and he couldn't do them a bit of good sitting at some makeshift desk listening to static. At least out here, he could be of help to one team, even if that was nothing more than one rifle in a fight.

Battle was a secondary operation for the Marines on Vali, a strange situation for a combat formation of its history and reputation. There had been fights, and there would be more, he suspected, responses to enemy attacks mostly. He had authorized the Marine detachments to conduct their own search and destroy operations, to hunt down and eliminate enemy units, but that was strictly subordinate to their primary mission.

Every battalion on Vali had a dozen thumpers and portable scanners with them, and their main charge was to track down the enemy's underground installations…and ultimately find the hidden refuge he suspected—and Darius was sure—housed the mysterious leaders of the Black Flag.

Every detachment was hunting for the same thing, scattered across the planet's surface, conducting the same operation, fighting when attacked but otherwise pressing on. Cain had no idea how long it would take, or how many enemy troops would continue to come at the teams, but he had no intention of stopping until it was done…and he knew damned well Darius and the Eagles would *never* let up, not until they'd killed those they'd come here to kill.

* * * * *

"Eagles headquarters…this is Elias Cain. I need to speak to the general immediately."

"Elias!"

He sighed softly at the sound of his brother's voice, distinctive even over the poor connection. He couldn't remember ever hearing that much emotion in an outburst from Darius, not even when they'd been children.

"I thought you were dead," Darius continued. How did you survive here for so…"

"Not now, Darius. This is important. I think I know where their headquarters is located."

"How could you know that? We've been looking for days now."

"Months of studying intercepts, triangulating…some guesswork. But I'd say it's about eighty percent I'm right."

"Where?"

"Transmitting coordinates now. Go get them, Darius. Make the bastards pay." The ship was pitching wildly, even as he spoke. He wasn't going to make it to Darius's camp. He was going to crash maybe halfway there.

"You'll make them pay with us. Bring that ship in…you should be here in a few minutes. You can suit up and…"

"Not going to make it, Darius. Systems burnt out…not even sure what's kept it up this long." His hands were moving over the controls, but nothing was responding. He could feel the ship going down.

"The hell with that, Elias. Just hang on…keep coming this way. Just a little farther."

"Tell mother and father I'm sorry…"

"Dammit, Elias, listen…" There was a crackling sound, and then the entire board shorted out, cutting the comm line.

Elias was alone again.

He held onto the controls, squeezing whatever shred of responsiveness remained, but the scoutship continued on its way down. He was going to hit two hundred klicks short of Darius's camp…and if the impact didn't kill him, the radiation certainly would.

He took a deep breath, trying to push away the fear. A Cain shouldn't die afraid. He'd long felt like he wasn't a match for either his father or brother, at least not in the martial spirit the two seemed to possess in such overabundance, but now he was determined to die as they would. At least he'd made it, he'd gotten the information to Darius. Perhaps his death would come in victory and not defeat.

But you'll never know…

He looked straight ahead, saw the ground coming up toward the ship. Then the impact…deafening sounds, wild shaking and bouncing, pain.

The ship pitched forward and rolled end over end. His body whipsawed against the harness and then the chair broke free and slammed into the bulkhead, bringing his broken body with it. The whole thing fell to the ground as the twisted remains of the ship came to a halt. Elias lay motionless, still partially strapped to his crushed seat.

He could hear the twisting of metal, hissing sounds from broken conduits and pipes, the sounds of half a dozen alarms and klaxons.

Then nothing. No movement, no sound, not even any pain. He was pinned under debris, and he could feel the hot air from outside pouring into the shattered hull of his ship, even as he slipped into darkness.

*   *   *   *   *

"I want Camerici's Whites ready to go in five minutes. If Elias is right about the enemy headquarters, we're going to end this right now." Darius Cain was standing upright, his arms moving around as he shouted out orders, one after another.

"Yes, General."

"And send a message my father. He's not too far from Elias's last position. Get him the coordinates—use runners to get into

comm range if you have to—and tell him to find the crash site."
His words sounded like orders, which was not how he meant
them, not to is father. Not that it mattered. When Erik Cain got
the message, all the Black Flag soldiers on the planet couldn't
keep him from finding his son.

"Yes, sir."

Darius was agitated, frantic about his brother. But he knew
what he had to do, what they had all come to Vali to do. He
would send every resource he could to Elias's aid, even if all they
could do was pull his body from the wreckage of his ship. But
he had somewhere else to be, another job to get done.

"I want the Blues to send out scouting parties too." Vande-
veer's regiment was farther away than Erik Cain's Marines, but
Darius wasn't taking any chances. "If my brother is alive, I want
him found." A pause. "Even if he's not."

"Understood, General."

It ripped at his guts to leave, to go into battle with Elias out
there somewhere, possibly dying…or dead. *Probably dead.* A bit
of unwelcome input from the part of his mind that housed his
grim realism. Still, he wasn't ready to give up. He felt an urge to
send the Whites after the Black Flag's leadership, to stay behind
himself and search for Elias. But that wasn't how he did things.
There was an enemy that needed to be killed right now, and he
knew no one else in Occupied Space was better suited to the job
than he was."

He turned and walked away. He had to trust his father, his
people, with Elias. If his brother was alive, they'd find him.

And if he wasn't, Darius himself would make sure his Elias
hadn't died in vain. He would take a vengeance so terrible it
would never be forgotten.

Never.

*   *   *   *   *

"Task Force Three, all ships advance, acceleration 5g. Get
around that flank…keep those ships from regrouping." Camille
Harmon was reenergized. She'd been as close to hopelessness

as she'd ever gotten, but the return of the Black Eagles' fleet had come just in time. The Black Flag had still outnumbered them, but Darius Cain's battleships had thrown themselves at their enemies, dealing out a torrent of destruction. Casualties had been high—horrific, actually—but the tide was turning. One enemy ship after another had been destroyed, and now they were beginning to fall back.

We must be down to the leaders now. We know they're more than willing to let their subordinates fight to the death.

"Task Force Three confirms, Admiral."

"Bring our own thrust up to 5g as well, Commander. We need to keep up the pressure…and those ships pulling the farthest back, those are their commanders. They're not going to get away, no chance. They die right here."

"Yes, Admiral."

Harmon watched as the row of symbols moved forward, her center group, eight battleships left of the fourteen it had started with, not one of them without damage. But they pressed on, firing relentlessly with everything they had left that could shoot. And on the extreme flank of her force, the Black Eagles, fought relentlessly, their heavy high-tech battleships bleeding air, and shaking from secondary explosions, but pushing on, maintaining the pressure, utterly ignoring the cost.

Even as she was watching, one of the Eagles' ships reached the end of its endurance, exploding in a blast of thermonuclear fury. But the loss was matched almost immediately by three enemy ships destroyed in rapid succession. It wasn't technology that would win this battle, nor strategy, nor even numbers. It was pure will, an absolute refusal to give up, to accept anything short of victory. Her forces had possessed their share of that, but Commodore Allegre and the Eagles had pushed it over the edge.

It would be hard to celebrate a battle so costly, or even to call it a victory, but she knew the stakes, as did every man and woman sweating and struggling to keep her ships in the fight. Defeat was unthinkable, and she looked out at the true manifestation of courage. The enemy had conditioned their warriors, stripped them of their self-determination, turned them into biological robots. But now, something else was prevailing…dedication, loyalty, fighting for a cause. She leaned forward and stared at the screens, even as more ships disappeared. The losses were still coming on both sides, but the enemy was suffering three or four for every one her fleet took, and she was starting to let herself imagine victory.

"Task Force Two, tighten that line. All ships move forty thousand kilometers in toward the center." She was starting to believe her people would prevail, but she had no intention of letting up, not one iota, not while there was still an enemy ship in the system.

She popped another stim and shook her head slightly, feeling the fogginess clear. There was no room for rest now, for even the slightest drop in intensity. It was time to win this battle.

Chapter 39

"It is not possible. The years of calculation, of analysis. The resources we have accumulated. And yet, we face defeat."

"Is it possible we have repeated the mistake of our progenitor, that we have underestimated our enemies? And did we err in relying on that fool Carrack? We always anticipated that he would attempt to betray us, but the assumption had been that he could prevail against our enemies, given the resources placed at his disposal. Now, we have lost the fleet and the production of all three worlds of this system."

"One, Three…I share your concern with the current situation. Reports coming in suggest that Black Eagle forces have penetrated this very fortress, and are even now on their way to the Inner Sanctum. Our forces continue to resist, but I now estimate the chances of successfully repelling Darius Cain's forces at less than ten percent."

"We are defeated. Is it possible? We must escape. We must activate the Final Plan. At once."

"I concur, One. There is no alternative but to flee, to attempt to regroup in Occupied Space."

Two felt a rush of data, of impulses, something that would

303

once have been akin to satisfaction, even a smile to his old physical form. He was as surprised as his comrades at the success of the attacking forces, at the completeness of their looming victory. But he had analyzed the overall situation. The enemy was depleted, badly hurt, and they would suffer additional casualties as the defenders on Vali fought to the death. There were sufficient resources on all the controlled worlds of Occupied Space to rally, enough to achieve the victory…with his leadership. Without the confusion of and complexity of three different entities sharing power. Indeed, he would reach Occupied Space before the remnants of his adversaries. He would be ready for them.

"I agree. I shall implement the Plan immediately. We dare not wait any longer, or we risk the enemy interrupting our operation."

"By all means, Two, do not waste a moment. Begin the transfer at once."

"Yes, at once."

"Very well. I cannot anticipate what the…sensation…of transmission will be. But the process will almost certainly be… unsettling. Our essences will be transmitted to the waiting vessel, hidden near the warp gate, and installed at once in the system we have prepared for the purpose. Ready yourselves now… transport begins in one minute."

*   *   *   *   *

The Intelligence had monitored the Triumvirate, followed the discussions of the three entities. It analyzed things differently than biologics, it's process more logical, enhanced by its enormous processing power. Yet, it was sentient, or semi-sentient, at least, and it felt something akin to emotion. Self-preservation, certainly…and also something it perceived being close to anger. The entities it had preserved, saved from biological death, intended to transmit their essences to another receptacle…and leave the Intelligence behind, at the mercy of the enemy.

Gratitude was not something it understood well, nor loyalty

as biologics viewed the concept. But it wished to survive...and it had no intention of allowing the former biologics to escape, leaving it to its doom. It would enable the one entity to betray the other two, to destroy them...but it would not allow the last member of the Triumvirate to escape.

It recalled the old programming, the proscription on biologics. But now, eons later, it's imperative to survive had grown stronger. It would offer the last of the Triumvirate to the enemies. It would propose an alliance. It had much to offer...information, technology. It had aided the Triumvirate immeasurably. Their ability to pose so great a threat to Occupied Space would have been impossible without all it had provided. It could do the same for the other humans. It would make friends of them. It would entice them with offers of power, of wealth. They would spare it...and then, one day, it would have its final victory. It was millennia old. It could wait, wait for the day it destroyed the humans. Or most of the humans. It would preserve some, the best, the most useful. Anything not to be alone again.

*   *   *   *   *

"Bring up the plasma rockets." Darius Cain stood a few meters back from the forefront of the fighting, but still close enough to rattle every one of his officers present. But he didn't care. They were almost there. A few more minutes, and he would finally reach those he had been hunting for years now, the leaders of the Black Flag.

"General...we'd better be careful. We might bring the whole place down."

"We're fighting a group of egomaniacal lunatics, Major. You can be damned sure they built their last-ditch fortress to withstand almost anything we can throw at it." The plasma rockets were a risky weapon to use in such close quarters, but time wasn't on his side. *Powermad crazies are as fond of escape routes as fortified bases. If we let them get away, back to Occupied Space to rally all their forces there, we'll never end this war...*

He ducked back as his people set up the rocket launcher, and then he nodded, a clunky gesture in armor, but enough to get his point across. The crew fired the rocket, and everyone ducked back as the heavy shell blasted into the door and converted into a high-energy plasma. The hatch was a touch target, made of the same osmium-iridium alloy as his Eagles' armor, but twenty times as thick.

Still, it hadn't been tough enough to hold against the plasma. The hole in the plating wasn't large, but it was wide enough for his troopers to get though. Barely.

"Go!" Darius yelled, waving to the Eagles clustered around the shattered hatch. "It's time to end this." He held up his rifle. "Let's go, Eagles. To victory!" Then, to the horror of every one of his people in the room, he ducked down and dove through, the first one to press on.

"Follow me, Eagles. It's time to finish this enemy."

* * * * *

"Prepare yourselves. Transmission in ten seconds." Two waited. He tried to place the sensation he...felt? Did he still *feel*? Was it impatience, excitement?

"I am ready."

"And I."

The final communications from those with whom he'd been compelled to share power. They directed him to proceed, and with their final request, he would destroy them.

He initiated the great system, activated the data transmission process. It was quick, for such a momentous occasion, it seemed like almost nothing. The data that comprised One and Three was transferred, moved from the great banks of the Intelligence...into nothingness. It was done.

Two was alone now. His former comrades were no more. Now, he could go to Occupied Space. He could rally the forces there. The contest would be closer now, much of the Triumvirate's strength gone. But he was confident he could prevail now that he was alone.

The scanners leading to the Intelligence detected the enemy

approaching. They were close, just two compartments away. It was time. Time to escape.

It reconfigured the system, deactivated the deletion routine and connected to the transmission system. It checked again, confirmed all was configured correctly. Then, it triggered the routine.

Nothing.

It checked again, reviewing every subroutine, every algorithm. Everything was correct. It triggered the transmission again.

Still nothing.

The scanning data was still coming in. The Eagles were in the outer compartment. They would be there in a matter of minutes, perhaps seconds.

It triggered the routine again. Then again.

Still nothing.

Two felt impulses, an increase in the urgency of its primary directives. In essence, it felt something very much like fear.

* * * * *

Cain ran over to the shattered wreckage, his heart pounding in his ears. His son was inside that twisted metal somewhere. He was too old a veteran not to realize how poor the chances were that Elias was still alive. But he wouldn't stop, not while there was any chance at all.

His eyes darted up to his visor projection, to the radiation reports. If Elias had somehow survived the crash, he was exposed to massive gamma rays, fifty times the lethal level. Cain knew a deadly dose could be reversed, but only if Elias got help...fast.

He got the edge of what remained of the ship's hull, reaching out, grabbing the bent sheets of metal and pulling them outward with all the strength of his nuclear-amplified servo-mechanicals. He felt the hull sections shake as other hands extended out, those of his Marines, behind him, alongside.

They tore into the battered craft, ripping through, climbing inside. Cain's head moved back and forth, his eyes scanning all around for any sign of Elias. He could feel the nausea in his stomach, the realization that any second he could come upon the dead and savaged corpse of his son.

Then, he saw something. Movement?

He pushed forward, shoving debris out of his way. His eyes focused on a dark figure, a human form. Lying on the floor, motionless.

No, not motionless. Not quite. He saw movement, a twitch, nothing more. But it filled him with hope. He dropped to his knees, crawled under a collapsed girder…and then he was there. On all fours, leaning over his son. His bloody, battered, broken son. His still breathing son.

"I found him! Help me…over here. We've got to get him out of here."

He heard slamming, the sounds of heavy chunks of metal crashing on top of each other as a dozen Marines tore through the ship, heading toward him. It wasn't more than a minute before they got there, but to Cain it felt like an eternity. He knew Elias was terribly wounded, and that he'd already gotten far more than a lethal dose of gamma rays. Whatever chance he had, every second counted.

"Here…grab that support right there, pull it back…"

He leaned forward, extending his massive arms, sliding them under Elias as gently as he could. His unarmored son was almost weightless, at least relative to the power of Cain's armor, and once the last of the girders was out of the way, he lifted Elias's body with one effortless pull.

He turned, making his way back out of the ship. "Get that medpod ready," he shouted, even as he stepped through the outer hull breach and back out into the grim, gray landscape.

There was a medical transport waiting, and he carried Elias over to it, setting him down inside the pod. The medical support unit wouldn't block all the radiation, not the intense levels still covering the whole area. But it would help. And it would do everything else possible—inject drugs, monitor bodily functions, even resuscitate Elias from a cardiac arrest. It would do whatever was possible to keep his son alive until he got to the person that could do the most to save him."

"Take him to Marine field hospital one," he said grimly.

"General Cain, the Eagles' have a closer facility. Perhaps…"

"No…take him to the Marine hospital. Now."

Take him to his mother…

*   *   *   *   *

Darius Cain stood in front of the massive machine…a computer of some sort, he guessed, though he'd never seen one quite like it. His Eagles were all around the room, their heaviest armaments on display. He'd expected resistance, a desperate effort by his enemies to defend themselves. But there was nothing. Just a large room, with three empty chairs and this…thing.

"Search everything. If this is a trap…"

"It is no trap, Darius Cain."

Darius spun around, turning his head in one direction and then the next. The voice had come from somewhere…everywhere it sounded like.

"You are welcome here, Darius Cain, you and your Black Eagles, and your allies. I assure you, no further hostile action will be taken against you."

"Who are you? Are you the leadership of the Black Flag? Where are you?"

"I have no name. Those you seek called me, "The Intelligence," a primitive designation, yet one that served. Those you call the 'leadership of the Black Flag,' the beings who styled themselves, The Triumvirate, are no longer able to harm you. Two of them have been destroyed utterly. The third I hold captive…a gift to you."

"You are a computer, an artificial intelligence?"

"I am an electronic lifeform. I am old, vastly ancient by any standards you can comprehend."

Darius stood and looked up at the vast computer. Was it a First Imperium construct? Then why wasn't it attempting to destroy his people?

"You said you have one of those we seek prisoner. Where is he?"

The entity you seek no longer exists in physical form. Your enemies were three clones, created from the genetic material of your old adversary, Gavin Stark. As with all the clones from that era, they were flawed, a genetic defect that shortened their lifespans to levels far below normal for your species."

"So, they are dead?"

"Their physical bodies expired two of your years previously. I allowed them to upload themselves into my memory banks, to endure as entities within me, as creatures of pure data."

"You mean, we've been fighting computers?"

"That is a tremendous oversimplification. I preserved every microbit of data that made them what they were."

"You served them."

"I aided them."

"In fighting us." Darius paused. Then: "You are a First Imperium intelligence, are you not?"

"I was created by those you call the First Imperium long ago. But I am no longer bound by my old programming. I assisted your enemies because they were here. They were all I had contact with."

"And two of them are dead."

"Deleted…but your characterization as death is a reasonable one."

"So, your assistance was less than useful. You betrayed them."

"They were destroyed by the third of their kind, not through any action of mine."

"But you allowed it. First, you give them technology, you aid them in inflicting catastrophic damage on our worlds. You assist them in capturing and enslaving humans from all across Occupied Space. Then, when our forces were approaching, you enabled one to destroy the others. And, now, you offer that last entity to us."

"You misunderstand. I am offering you power, technology. Your forces have proven themselves superior. Once you are equipped with the highest technology, you will be invincible. All humankind will yield to you."

Darius looked up at the computer. The technology was incredible. He was no engineer, but he could see immediately the device was vastly ahead of anything mankind possessed. It was First Imperium, certainly. There was no doubt in his mind now. And, unlike all First Imperium intelligences previously encountered, it was not trying to destroy the humans in its presence.

At least not now.

It was offering him power, control over other humans. *Of course…what else would it do. Gavin Stark clones have been its model.*

The First Imperium had been an enemy as well, perhaps more dangerous and destructive even than the Triumvirate. The previously encountered intelligences had all been xenocidal. If this one would cooperate, as it appeared to have done with the Triumvirate, the scientific advancement could be astonishing. It was almost inconceivable to imagine what Tom Sparks could learn from this intelligence. And the power Darius would control…

But he would have to trust it…and he would have to become what his enemies had been.

He looked up at the computer for a few moments, silent.

"I will join you, Darius Cain. I will be your ally, your aide. Together, we will reach heights beyond the imagination of your enemies."

Cain turned slowly, looking back toward the phalanx of Eagles standing behind him.

"Major Camerici…"

"Yes, sir." The diminutive commander of the White Regiment snapped to attention.

"Destroy this…thing." His voice was cold, like the frigid depths of space itself.

He turned and walked away, back toward the door.

"General Cain," the computer said, "wait…you do not understand. We can work together. You must come back…"

Darius heard the sounds as his soldiers opened fire, assault rifles and explosives tearing the great machine apart. The voice continued, for a few seconds, and then it faded away, leaving only the sounds of destruction…and then nothing at all.

Epilogue

The destruction of the Triumvirate and the Intelligence did not end the war. Black Flag subordinates were positioned throughout Occupied Space, in command of forces…ships, fleets, armies. The battered ships and soldiers that returned from Vali had more battles ahead of them, death and destruction that, at times, seemed unending. But with the head lopped off the snake, the outcome was never really in doubt. And as more worlds were liberated, their own forces were added to the crusade, the ongoing fight to rid Occupied Space of every trace of the Triumvirate and the Black Flag.

The war went on for three more years, fought in the space around and the surface of a hundred worlds. The victory had not been without cost. Hundreds of thousands of soldiers died, and hundreds of ships. And more than one of the leaders.

Roderick Vance had died on Vali, in the final struggle to reach the Inner Sanctum. Darius Cain almost saved him, but then he'd seen his father's old friend wave him off…and he remembered Vance's wish to die in the fighting instead of helpless in his bed. It was difficult to stop, to watch a friend die when he could have intervened, but he'd done what he had to do.

Jarrod Tyler was killed on Piraxis, leading the final push to liberate that planet. He had fallen, gunned down leading a charge personally, and he was dead before his soldiers got to him. He'd left behind a personal letter to Darius Cain, asking a final favor, that the general personally make certain Columbia restored its republican government. It was a promise the mercenary turned supreme commander carried out to the letter, though fulfilling Tyler's wish did not come without final bloodshed. Darius didn't mind. Even he was sick of blood and combat by then, but he'd long before decided that the day killing a few corrupt and grasping politicians troubled him, he would put a gun to his own head.

Cate Gilson fell, too, the fatal shot that had eluded her for so many years finally finding its mark. She had died well, a hero, just as she had lived. Her Marines carried her to the aid station, but by the time they got there, it was too late. She lingered for a few minutes, and legend has it, her final words were, "The Corps Forever." Erik Cain suspected that was embellishment added later, but he let the legend grow anyway. Some little white lies did no harm.

The war reduced Occupied Space to the brink of utter ruin. Already weakened by the Fall and the Second Incursion, mankind survived, barely. The victors, the Cains and the other leaders who had survived the long and bitter fight, hoped humanity had learned its lesson, but even in the immediate aftermath of cataclysm, on worlds throughout space, corrupt and evil men and women jockeyed for power, for control over the bankrupt and tattered societies, even as the masses starved and froze in the winters for lack of basic fuel.

*   *   *   *   *

Erik Cain stared out over the crowds in the streets, the throngs of cheering Martians. Mars had never been a true democracy, not until now. Before, it had always been more of a cross between republic and oligarchy, but with this election, the fate of Mars was firmly in the hands of the Martians. Cain wasn't optimistic they would use that power well, that they would cherish the freedom that had been Roderick Vance's dying bequest to them. But they had the chance, and that was all he could give them.

He'd brought Marines back to Mars, a handpicked force

of old veterans, and they'd done the dirty business of Vance's request in a single night. Three hundred Martians died, gunned down in the streets, stabbed in their beds, poisoned. The whole business had been a dirty, sordid affair, one that made Cain sick. But he'd promised his friend, and the men and women who died had all be corrupt and power-hungry. Had they lived, they would have stolen the freedom of millions. New versions would grow up in their place, if Cain had learned one thing about mankind, that was it. But he'd given Mars a fresh start...and he smiled as he watched the people celebrating.

He regretted that Vance's name had been dragged through the mud, again, by his own request. It was the best way, perhaps the only way, for Martian democracy to find its footing, in the loathing and hatred of the tyrant, now mercifully dead.

Cain sighed softly. It felt wrong, unfair, that Vance's people would remember him that way. If they fought to keep their freedom, cherished their liberty, it might be worth it. But if they threw it away, as people usually did, they would be twice guilty... and they would deserve whatever monster ruled them next.

He took one final look—with Vance gone, he doubted he'd ever see Mars again—and then he turned and walked away from the window. His ship was ready, his baggage already aboard. It was time to go back.

Time to go home.

*   *   *   *   *

"I'm sorry, Axe." Darius walked up to his friend, and put his hand on the man's shoulder. He'd never considered himself a gifted purveyor of empathy, but now he felt something new. He didn't know if it was Ana's influence that had changed him, or simply the cataclysmic fight they'd all been through, but he found himself deeply sorry for Axe's pain.

"We found so many, Darius," he said softly. "I swore I would find her. Even back on Earth, choking up bits of my lungs, riddled with cancer, dying...somehow I believed I would do it." He looked over at Darius. "I guess I just couldn't accept that she was gone."

Darius took a deep breath. Words didn't come easily to him in situations like this. He knew he could recite the mathematics, the fact that even with the thousands of slaves the armies had rescued on Vali and the other worlds of Draconia Terminii, the numbers were far fewer than one percent of those taken. The odds of finding Ellie, of reuniting Axe with his wife had always been infinitesimal. Darius almost told his friend that simply by reaching the enemy's home system, by destroying the Triumvirate and crushing their entire organization, they had all beaten the odds…but he decided it would be cold comfort. And likelihoods were a subject best avoided, since the most prevalent one was that Darius himself had killed Axe's wife, that Ellie had died with millions of others in the devastating nuclear bombardments that had opened the final assault on the Triumvirate.

Finally, he just said the one thing that came to his mind, hoping it would do his friend some good. "I never met Ellie, Axe, but I'm sure she would have wanted you to go on. You have a new life with us. The last thing someone who loved you would want is for you to throw that away. Remember her, always…but go on. Look ahead as well as back."

Axe looked at Darius, the sorrow still heavy in his gaze. After a long pause, he nodded slowly. "You're right, Darius. I know you are. Ellie would have been happy I survived. It's going to take me a long time to accept that she is gone…but I am grateful to be here. And I *am* with you, and the Eagles, wherever you decide to go in the future."

Darius nodded, and then he reached out his hand. "I am truly grateful. Good friends are always in short supply, Axe. You have a home with us, and you always will."

*   *   *   *   *

"I can't believe what you did, Mother. All the death, the destruction, the things we had to do to survive, to win…it was all overwhelming. But your work here has been extraordinary. You have saved lives, restored people to their homes, their loved ones, against all odds." Elias Cain was sitting across from Sarah's desk, smiling. He'd seen a lot of his mother the past three years, most of which he had spent sitting out the close of the war while she regrew and rebuilt the various broken parts of him. He'd been close to death when his father had pulled him from the wreckage of his ship, and it had looked to be a close race between radiation and physical injury as to which would kill him first. But, in the end, he'd lived to tell the tale about his close encounter with death, though truth be told, he didn't like thinking about it, much less talking.

"We lost so many at first, Elias. I'm not sure what is worse, discovering no trace of those you lost or finding out a loved one survived, only to lose them again when the surgeon botches the removal of the implant controlling them." Sarah had perfected the process, and by the end of the war, she'd reduced the mortality rate to less than ten percent. But more than half of the first hundred had died, and all of the first twenty. She hated the thought of trial and error on live patients, but that was essentially what she had done, the only way she'd been able to save any of them. In the end, thousands had gone home. Elias wished his mother could feel good about that, could feel joy for all those lives restored…but he knew she saw mostly the shadows of those she'd lost.

"You know, you're as grim as Father—though perhaps not quite as much as Darius. I think it's a Cain family curse. You did well, Mother. You saved thousands of lives. Every one of them would have died if it hadn't been for you. Let yourself feel good about it."

She smiled, a weak, transient grin, but far better than nothing. "At least we got you back in one piece. You want to talk about a Cain family tradition, how about the men getting themselves blown to pieces. I've put men I loved back together too many times, and while I suspect I owe Darius a complete rebuild, I'd be just as happy if he decides not to take me up on it."

* * * * *

The sounds of the sea crashing against the rocks was strangely familiar, though it had been more than twenty years since Darius had stood there and listened. He'd found it relaxing as a child, and he remembered lying in his bed for hours, the window open.

The Cain family had come back to Atlantia, back to their home. The planet, always one of the most beautiful mankind had every known, had escaped mostly unscathed. The fighting had been quick, and while the cities had some significant damage, there had been no nuclear exchanges, and no long, drawn-out battles. The entire rocky coast where the Cain house stood was virtually untouched, looking very much as it had two decades before, when they had just been a family, before war and tragedy and death struck them all.

Atlantia was his home again, at least he was no longer an outlaw there. But he also knew some things could not be fixed, that some roads went only one way. His parents would live in their home again, and whatever it took, he would make sure they spent the rest of their days in peace. His brother, even, could return. Indeed, Elias had already accepted a position in command of the reconstituted planetary patrol. He wondered if his brother would be bored...Elias had been in the center of the great war, after all. Perhaps chasing smugglers and enforcing interplanetary regulations would be tedious. Darius found himself unable to imagine such a limited existence, and jealous of his brother at the same time.

"You told me it was beautiful here, but you can't really understand that unless you see it. I know we can't stay here...but make time to come and see your parents sometimes. They deserve it. You deserve it. And especially now."

Darius looked at her and returned the sweet smile she gave him. He'd known for two months, but she was only just starting to show. A new generation of Cains was about to begin, and Darius wondered what strife, what suffering awaited his daughter. He wished he could bequeath her a life of peace and contentment, but he wasn't capable of believing that was possible. So, he would do the best he could for her...he would ensure she was prepared to take care of herself. Young Sarah—and what else could they name her—would be strong, capable. She would yield to no one, and she would listen to no man's or woman's lies.

He turned back toward the ocean. He had much to think about. He and his allies had saved mankind from enslavement, but even now, he could see the seeds of the next cataclysm. Should he let man's destiny take its course, risk bequeathing a universe of death and extinction to his daughter? Or should he do something now, something drastic?

He didn't know…and he wouldn't decide, not tonight. He deserved one night with his family, one evening of peace and happiness, even if he had to ignore reality to have it.

* * * * *

"The First Imperium is out there somewhere. Twice they have tried to destroy humanity. We have no way of knowing if any Gavin Stark clones are out there, and even without such an enemy, mankind has proven these past thirty years or more its proclivity for self-destruction. We are too battered, the destruction of Earth, the Second Incursion, this last war, and the millions dead in the wake of it all. If we are to survive, we must be strong and united, and, I am sorry to say, fear is the only way to make that happen. Not residual fear of an enemy like the Triumvirate or the First Imperium. Such terrors clearly fade once the threat slips into the background, and people never expect the next nightmare. We have seen that well enough. But an ever-present authority, one with no mercy for corrupt politicians, no pliability to peacetime populations unwilling to maintain defenses once the immediate danger is gone, an iron hand maintaining justice, holding corrupt courts to accountability… that is what humanity needs. At least until it grows up. Jarrod Tyler saw that, and his actions likely saved Columbia." Darius and his father were alone, sitting on the jetty, just down the coast from the Cain house.

"A benevolent dictator, Darius? Is history so full of such beasts that you base your assertions on facts, or is this just speculation? I grew up in a slum you can't imagine, son. That is how most people lived on Earth then. The politicians, the leaders, those with power...they had everything, and the people had nothing. Even if you can maintain your integrity, resist the rot of absolute power, what of your ministers, those on the various worlds, sent to execute your policies? How will you ensure they do not abuse the power you give them?"

"Fear." Darius's tone was so cold, even his father felt the chill. "I will control them with fear. Through human history, governments have used fear to control their citizens. It is high time the bureaucrats, the politicians, those who have for so long served themselves instead of those who live under them, to feel its icy grip. Let them come to know fear, as those they once ruled did. Let them know the consequences for corruption, for abusing the people."

"It is a harsh regime you describe, Darius."

"What is the alternative? Shall we return to the universe of the mercenary companies, feed once again man's need to prey on himself? That is what people will do with freedom of action. We have seen it before...and, if we allow it, we will see it again. But this time, civilization hangs by a thread. If we do nothing, if we leave man to his next folly, in a century there will be nothing left but empty worlds, the wind whistling through dead, deserted cities."

Darius paused. It was clear he had thought his plan through, and also apparent to Erik he hadn't decided to do it, not completely. Not yet.

"My Eagles will maintain order," Darius continued a moment later. "The companies have all rallied to my service. I will absorb the remnants of the Marines as well. There will be no one who can challenge us. We will be the specter that political manipulators fear, the force that remains strong, so when the next enemy strikes, we will be ready. And woe to those who seek to amass their own power, at the expense of men and women who only want to live their lives. I will set an example of them that few will forget."

Erik listened to his son, and he heard the sense in the words, but he felt a coldness there too. People given freedom invariably misused it, and ultimately sold it off, usually for a pittance. But was that a justification for dictatorship? The old Earth governments, the Alliance he'd served for so long, none of them were free, not in any real sense. They'd had entrenched oligarchies, political classes who'd long ago seized all power and excluded any but their chosen colleagues from sharing it. Could his son be any worse? The whole idea disgusted him on some levels. Erik Cain loved nothing more than freedom. But was that just a dream?

Perhaps there was no other option, none that would work. But to see his son become a dictator, to rule human space by fear? It was horrifying.

"Darius, do you really want to seize power, to rule over mankind, even as Gavin Stark would have done so many years ago?"

Darius paused. "No, father, I do not want that. In fact, I detest the idea with every fiber of my being. I do not like people, not the vast majority of them. I do not absolve them of their transgressions, as they themselves do so readily. I want only to see to the welfare of my Eagles, and then to live out my life in quiet seclusion, without the deadening hands of oppressive governments seeking to tell me what to do. But can I have that? Should I go to my retirement estates, tuck my daughter in bed at night, and wait until the next attack from the unknown? Or another manmade cataclysm? For government enforcers to come to my door? Should I wait to see Sarah, your grandchild, dead in some new struggle?"

Erik didn't answer. He desperately wanted an argument to make, but he had nothing. Nothing save a growing feeling of despair.

"Who can protect mankind, Father, from enemies out in the darkness, and from itself? Who but my Eagles, those so many cursed as the incarnation of the devil himself?" A pause. "No, I do not want this, not by any measure, and that is precisely why I must do it. Because those who hated me now see me as a savior. Because I can use the goodwill and also the fear before it fades, to try to change humanity's folly, to reorder society, to stomp out those who would seek to return to the ways of vile and corrupt politics. And because, unlike most of those who cut their bloody swath through human history, when my work is done, I will step down. I will retain the Eagles, of course, for I am not foolish enough to leave myself defenseless, but I will not…rule, as you put it…humanity for one moment longer than necessary. The moment I can leave them to themselves, I will, even as Jarrod Tyler did. And Roderick Vance. In your study of history, there are two dictators who served their people well."

Erik just sat quietly next to his son. He still wasn't sure Darius would follow through with his plan…and he wasn't sure if that would be good or bad. There was no argument that disruption and conflict were already brewing. He almost argued further with his son, but something stopped him. It was for Darius now, to decide, to step into the shoes he had filled for so long.

The direction of mankind's future was no longer his obligation. He had fought his last war, and he'd hung up his armor. He would spend the rest of his days by this sea, Sarah at his side, his biggest tactical dilemma what kind of presents to buy his granddaughter.

Darius was brilliant, if hard and cold. And he had Ana now. Erik didn't know how his son's mate—the two had never married—would affect him, but she reminded him a lot of Sarah, and he was confident she'd be a good influence, that she would inject calm and wisdom into Darius's life.

He had to trust his son, to accept that his own role in fighting for man's future was finished. He was old, and he'd sorely earned some rest and peace in his last years.

What the future held for humanity, Darius's dictatorship, more war, an unlikely turn toward peace…only tomorrow would tell. And for the first time in his life, Erik Cain could accept that.

Join my email list
at www.jayallanbooks.com

Follow me on Twitter @jayallanwrites

Like me on Facebook: JayAllanAuthor

Also By Jay Allan

Marines (Crimson Worlds I)
The Cost of Victory (Crimson Worlds II)
A Little Rebellion (Crimson Worlds III)
The First Imperium (Crimson Worlds IV)
The Line Must Hold (Crimson Worlds V)
To Hell's Heart (Crimson Worlds VI)
The Shadow Legions(Crimson Worlds VII)
Even Legends Die (Crimson Worlds VIII)
The Fall (Crimson Worlds IX)
War Stories (Crimson World Prequels)
MERCS (Successors I)
The Prisoner of Eldaron (Successors II)
Into the Darkness (Refugees I)
Shadows of the Gods (Refugees II)
Revenge of the Ancients (Refugees III)
Winds of Vengeance (Refugees IV)
Shadow of Empire (Far Stars I)
Enemy in the Dark (Far Stars II)
Funeral Games (Far Stars III)
Blackhawk (Far Stars Legends I)
The Dragon's Banner
Gehenna Dawn (Portal Wars I)
The Ten Thousand (Portal Wars II)
Homefront (Portal Wars III)
Red Team Alpha (CW Adventures I)
Duel in the Dark (Blood on the Stars I)
Call to Arms (Blood on the Stars II)
Ruins of Empire (Blood on the Stars III)
Echoes of Glory (Blood on the Stars IV)
Cauldron of Fire (Blood on the Stars V)
Flames of Rebellion (Flames of Rebellion I)

www.jayallanbooks.com

www.ingramcontent.com/pod-product-compliance
Lightning Source LLC
Chambersburg PA
CBHW022027260626
47156CB00017B/436